ISAAC ASIMOV, one of ... has by now written ... other writer in history ... such a wide variety of subjects, which range from science fiction and murder novels to books on history, the physical sciences, and Shakespeare. Born in the Soviet Union and raised in Brooklyn, he lives in New York City with his wife, electric typewriter, and word processor.

MARTIN H. GREENBERG, who has been called 'the king of anthologists', now has some 130 to his credit. Greenberg is professor of regional analysis and political science at the University of Wisconsin, Green Bay, USA, where he also teaches a course in the history of science fiction.

CHARLES G. WAUGH, a professor of psychology and mass communications at the University of Maine at Augusta, USA. He is a leading authority on science fiction and fantasy who has collaborated on more than 80 anthologies and single-author collections with Isaac Asimov, Martin H. Greenberg, and assorted colleagues.

Also available in
ISAAC ASIMOV'S MAGICAL WORLD OF FANTASY

Devils
Mythic Beasts
Spells

Also edited by Isaac Asimov,
Martin H. Greenberg and Charles G. Waugh

The Mammoth Book of
Short Fantasy Novels

The Mammoth Book of
Short Science Fiction Novels

The Mammoth Book of
Classic Science Fiction –
Short Novels of the 1930s

The Mammoth Book of
Golden Age Science Fiction –
Short Novels of the 1940s

Intergalactic Empires

Monsters

Supermen

Isaac Asimov's Magical World of Fantasy

GHOSTS

Edited by Isaac Asimov,
Martin H. Greenberg
and Charles G. Waugh

Robinson Publishing
London

Robinson Publishing
11 Shepherd House
5 Shepherd Street
London W1Y 7LD

First published in the UK by Robinson Publishing in 1989

Collection copyright © Nightfall Inc.,
Martin H. Greenberg and
Charles G. Waugh, 1988

Cover illustration copyright © Solar Wind Ltd.

This book is sold subject to the condition that it shall not, by way of trade or otherwise, be lent, re-sold, hired out or otherwise circulated without the publisher's prior consent in any form of binding or cover other than that in which it is published and without a similar condition including this condition being imposed on the subsequent purchaser.

ISBN 1 85487 036 X

Printed by Wm. Collins & Sons Ltd., Glasgow

10　9　8　7　6　5　4　3　2　1

ACKNOWLEDGEMENTS

Grateful acknowledgement for permission to reprint material is hereby given to the following:

"Ringing the Changes" by Robert Aickman. Copyright © 1971 by Mercury Press, Inc. From *The Magazine of Fantasy & Science Fiction*. Reprinted by permission of Kirby McCauley, Ltd.

"Author! Author!" by Isaac Asimov. Copyright © 1964 by Isaac Asimov. Reprinted by permission of the author.

"Touring" by Gardner Dozois, Jack, and Michael Swanwick. Copyright © 1981 by Penthouse International Ltd. Reprinted by permission of the authors and their agent, Virginia Kidd.

"Come Dance with Me on My Pony's Grave" by Charles L. Grant. Copyright © 1973 by Mercury Press, Inc. From *The Magazine of Fantasy & Science Fiction*.

"The Fire When It Comes" by Parke Godwin. Copyright © 1981 by Mercury Press, Inc., from *The Magazine of Fantasy & Science Fiction*. Reprinted by permission of the author.

"The Invasion of the Church of the Holy Ghost" by Russell Kirk. Copyright © 1987 by Russell Kirk. Reprinted by permission of Kirby McCauley, Ltd.

"Elle Est Trois (La Mort)" by Tanith Lee. Copyright © 1983 by Tanith Lee. Reprinted by permission of the author.

"A Passion for History" by Stephen Minot. Copyright © 1976 by Stephen Minot. First published in *The Sewanne Review*. Reprinted by permission of the author.

"Daemon" By C. L. Moore. Copyright © 1946 by All Fiction Field, Inc., renewed 1974 by Catherine Reggie. Reprinted by permission of Don Congdon Associates, Inc.

"King of Thieves" by Jack Vance. Copyright © 1949 by Standard Publications, Inc; renewed © 1977 by Jack Vance. Reprinted by permission of Kirby McCauley, Ltd.

CONTENTS

Introduction: *Ghosts*
by Isaac Asimov 7

Ringing the Changes
by Robert Aickman 11

Author! Author!
by Isaac Asimov 39

Touring
by Gardner Dozois, Jack Dann, and Michael Swanwick 67

The Wind in the Rose Bush
by Mary Wilkins Freeman 85

Come Dance with Me on My Pony's Grave
by Charles L. Grant 102

The Fire When It Comes
by Parke Godwin 115

The Toll-House
by W. W. Jacobs 159

The Invasion of the Church of the Holy Ghost
by Russell Kirk 169

A Terrible Vengeance
by Mrs. J. H. Riddell 213

Elle Est Trois, (La Mort)
by Tanith Lee 254

A Passion for History
    by Stephen Minot 275

Daemon
    by C. L. Moore 286

The Lady's Maid's Bell
    by Edith Wharton 309

King of Thieves
    by Jack Vance 329

INTRODUCTION: GHOSTS

Belief in ghosts is almost universal. Primitive peoples build complex religions centered about ghosts, and even advanced societies retain them in some form. What we call ancestor worship is a kind of ghost belief.

Such beliefs extend far back, and are certainly to be found in prehistoric times. Indeed, some feel that Neanderthal man must have had such beliefs, too, a hundred thousand years ago and more. After all, they seem to have buried their dead and to have placed flowers with the corpse. That would make us think they may have believed in a kind of afterlife, and surely this is one of the necessary prerequisites for believing in ghosts.

But how did such beliefs start? Obviously, no one can possibly *know,* but we can guess. I have my own thoughts on the matter, and I would like to advance them now.

Death is universal among all organisms other than the very simplest, but there are few organisms who can possibly be aware of it. Among the most advanced animals other than human beings, there may be some who will not ignore dead individuals of their species. There is the case of the chimpanzee that died of what can only be called heartbreak when his mother died. Other animals might also show signs of distress at another's death.

It is hard to believe, however, that any animal other than the human being has the capacity for forethought. Much as they may be aware of death *when it happens,* can they possibly know that death is inevitable and *must* someday happen? In particular, can an animal be aware that this inevitability is universal and that it itself must die someday? Certainly no animal has ever been observed to behave in such a way as to give us the impression that it realizes it must someday die.

This may also have been true of the early hominids, our ancestors of a million years ago or so. But at some stage, human beings or their recent ancestors must have discovered death, must have come to realize they themselves would surely die. I suspect this happened only with the development of homo sapiens (and the Neanderthals were, like ourselves, members of this species.)

It must have been a frightening, and even paralyzing, discovery, and it placed homo sapiens into a position of unique despair that no other organism needed to endure. It must have threatened to poison human life, to place a pall on all pleasure, to deprive one of all hope. Surely, this was a penalty that destroyed all the benefits one might otherwise expect of advanced intelligence.

That is, provided human beings *accepted* this realization of the inevitability of death. It is clear that they did not, and that they still do not. Faced with a certainty of death, human beings said, "No. It isn't true."

Even if the body dies, human beings decided stubbornly, that body was simply a temporary outer shell that housed the essential "I." Within each body there must be something immaterial that represents one's personality and that does *not* die, but is immortal. We call that immaterial something a soul, which is a word of unknown origin; or a spirit, which originally meant "air" or "breath." (You find the stem of the word in "respiration," for instance.)

An old Teutonic word for spirit is *gaisto,* which appears as *Geist* in modern German, *geest* in Dutch, *gast* in Anglo-Saxon, and so on. In modern English the word has become "ghost."

The basic meaning of ghost, then, is "soul" or "spirit," the immortal entity that dwells within the body and that will not die. Thus the Bible speaks of "the Spirit of God" (Genesis 1:2), in which God is pictured as an immaterial and immortal entity. However, a synonym for Spirit of God is the Holy Ghost (see, for instance, Matthew 3:11), which is usually considered one of the components of the Christian trinity.

In a more mundane application, when a human being (or rather, the body that houses the human being) dies, the immortal component simply leaves, just as you would leave your house if it caught fire. For that reason, a now rather old-fashioned euphemism for "to die" is "to give up the ghost" (Job 14:10).

INTRODUCTION: GHOSTS

Nowadays, however, the word "soul" is usually used for the immortal component within the body, and the word "ghost" for the immortal component once it has left the body. A ghost is a disembodied spirit.

One might easily suppose that a ghost having left the body might quit the Earth, and go to some totally other abode—to Heaven or to Hell, for instance. This would indeed seem to be the view in the more formal, "advanced" religions of today.

In more primitive religions and among the more unsophisticated followers of advanced religions, this is not at all the view. The ghosts are viewed as having a tendency to hang about the earthly realm they had dwelt in for years and decades. (A particularly effective, and grisly, literary description of this tendency is to be found in Charles Dickens's *A Christmas Carol.*)

But what could possibly have given prehistoric people the feeling that ghosts remained in the vicinity and bothered themselves with those who were still alive? To me, it is always insufficient to suppose that people merely make things up or that something is just superstition. People with intelligence and understanding, however lacking in education and experience they might be, require some sort of evidence. It seems to me the evidence lay in dreams.

People have always taken dreams very seriously. In the Bible, dreams are considered divine messages giving the dreamer instruction, or foretelling the future. As Joseph said, when Pharaoh told him his dream, "God hath shewed Pharaoh what he is about to do." (Genesis 41:25). Most people still believe this.

What's more, unsophisticated people are likely to confuse dreams with reality. It is not at all uncommon to dream of a dead relative or friend, who seems to be alive. How easy it is to suppose that it is the spirit of the individual, the ghost, who had returned to visit you, so that he might give you a friendly warning, or a threat.

As time went on, it became easy to suppose a person who has died by violence may cling to the place where it happened (to haunt it) in order to seek revenge. Or a dead malefactor may haunt the place of his misdeed to find a way to make restitution.

Ghosts, since they are immaterial, immortal, and not bound by earthly limitations, are naturally supposed to have powers human beings do not have. These might be used beneficently (as in the case of the ghosts in *A Christmas Carol*) or malevolently. Somehow, human beings, being what they are, expect malevolence so that, in general, they become afraid of ghosts. In fact, the word is traced back to old Indo-European roots meaning "to rage" and "to terrify." The ghosts are angry and those haunted by them are "terrified."

And that brings us to the stories in this book; a collection of tales in which disembodied spirits of one form or another—some good, some evil, some neutral—are important components. People have always enjoyed ghost stories, and here you have a group of varied ones united only in this—that they are sophisticated and intelligent.

—Isaac Asimov

RINGING THE CHANGES

By Robert Aickman

He had never been among those many who deeply dislike church bells, but the ringing that evening at Holihaven changed his view. Bells could certainly get on one's nerves he felt, although he had only just arrived in the town.

He had been too well aware of the perils attendant upon marrying a girl twenty-four years younger than himself to add to them by a conventional honeymoon. The strange force of Phrynne's love had borne both of them away from their previous selves: in him a formerly haphazard and easygoing approach to life had been replaced by much deep planning to wall in happiness; and she, though once thought cold and choosy, would now agree to anything as long as she was with him. He had said that if they were to marry in June, it would be at the cost of not being able to honeymoon until October. Had they been courting longer, he had explained, gravely smiling, special arrangement could have been made; but, as it was, business claimed him. This, indeed, was true because his business position was less influential than he had led Phrynne to believe. Finally, it would have been impossible for them to have courted longer because they had courted from the day they met, which was less than six weeks before the day they married.

" 'A village,' " he had quoted as they entered the branch line train at the junction (itself sufficiently remote), " 'from which (it was said) persons of sufficient longevity might hope to reach Liverpool Street.' " By now he was able to make jokes about age, although perhaps he did so rather too often.

"Who said that?"
"Bertrand Russell."
She had looked at him with her big eyes in her tiny face.

"Really." He had smiled confirmation.

"I'm not arguing." She had still been looking at him. The romantic gaslight in the charming period compartment had left him uncertain whether she was smiling back or not. He had given himself the benefit of the doubt and kissed her.

The guard had blown his whistle and they had rumbled out into the darkness. The branch line swung so sharply away from the main line that Phrynne had been almost toppled from her seat.

"Why do we go so slowly when it's so flat?"

"Because the engineer laid the line up and down the hills and valleys such as they are, instead of cutting through and embanking over them." He liked being able to inform her.

"How do you know? Gerald! You said you hadn't been to Holihaven before."

"It applies to most of the railways in East Anglia."

"So that even though it's flatter, it's slower?"

"Time matters less."

"I should have hated going to a place where time mattered or that you'd been to before. You'd have had noting to remember me by."

He hadn't been quite sure that her words exactly expressed her thought, but the thought had lightened his heart.

Holihaven station could hardly have been built in the days of the town's magnificence, for they were in the Middle Ages; but it still implied grander functions than came its way now. The platforms were long enough for visiting London expresses, which had since gone elsewhere; and the architecture of the waiting rooms would have been not insufficient for occasional use by foreign royalty. Oil lamps on perches like those occupied by macaws lighted the uniformed staff, who numbered two and, together with every native of Holihaven, looked like storm-habituated mariners.

The stationmaster and porter, as Gerald took them to be, watched him approach down the platform with a heavy suitcase in each hand and Phrynne walking deliciously by his side. He saw one of them address a remark to the other, but neither offered to help. Gerald had to put down the cases in order to give up their tickets. The other passengers had already disappeared.

"Where's the Bell?"

Gerald had found the hotel in a reference book. It was the only one allotted to Holihaven. But as Gerald spoke, and before the ticket collector could answer, the sudden deep note of an actual bell rang through the darkness. Phrynne caught hold of Gerald's sleeve.

Ignoring Gerald, the stationmaster, if such he was, turned to his colleague. "They're starting early."

"Every reason to be in good time," said the other man.

The stationmaster nodded and put Gerald's tickets indifferently in his jacket pocket.

"Can you please tell me how I get to the Bell Hotel?"

The stationmaster's attention returned to him. "Have you a room booked?"

"Certainly."

"Tonight?" The stationmaster looked inappropriately suspicious.

"Of course."

Again the stationmaster looked at the other man.

"It's them Pascoes."

"Yes," said Gerald. "That's the name. Pascoe."

"We don't use the Bell," explained the stationmaster. "But you'll find it in Wrack Street." He gesticulated vaguely and unhelpfully. "Straight ahead. Down Station Road. Then down Wrack Street. You can't miss it."

"Thank you."

As soon as they entered the town, the big bell began to boom regularly.

"What narrow streets!" said Phrynne.

"They follow the lines of the medieval city. Before the river silted up, Holihaven was one of the most important seaports in Great Britain."

"Where's everybody got to?"

Although it was only six o'clock the place certainly seemed deserted.

"Where's the hotel got to?" rejoined Gerald.

"Poor Gerald! Let me help." She laid her hand beside his on the handle of the suitcase nearest to her, but as she was about fifteen inches shorter than he, she could be of little assistance. They must already have gone more than a quarter of a mile. "Do you think we're in the right street?"

"Most unlikely, I should say. But there's no one to ask."

"Must be early closing day."

The single deep notes of the bell were now coming more frequently.

"Why are they ringing that bell? Is it a funeral?"

"Bit late for a funeral."

She looked at him a little anxiously.

"Anyway it's not cold."

"Considering we're on the east coast it's quite astonishingly warm."

"Not that I care."

"I hope that bell isn't going to ring all night."

She pulled on the suitcase. His arms were in any case almost parting from his body. "Look! We've passed it."

They stopped and he looked back. "How could we have done that?"

"Well, we have."

She was right. He would see a big ornamental bell hanging from a bracket attached to a house about a hundred yards behind them.

They retraced their steps and entered the hotel. A woman dressed in a navy blue coat and skirt, with a good figure but dyed red hair and a face ridged with makeup, advanced upon them.

"Mr. and Mrs. Banstead? I'm Hilda Pascoe. Don, my husband, isn't very well."

Gerald felt full of doubts. His arrangements were not going as they should. Never rely on guidebook recommendations. The trouble lay partly in Phrynne's insistence that they go somewhere he did not know. "I'm sorry to hear that," he said.

"You know what men are like when they're ill?" Mrs. Pascoe spoke understandingly to Phrynne.

"Impossible," said Phrynne. "Or very difficult."

"Talk about 'Women in our hours of ease.' "

"Yes," said Phrynne. "What's the trouble?"

"It's always been the same trouble with Don," said Mrs. Pascoe, then checked herself. "It's his stomach," she said. "Ever since he was a kid, Don's had trouble with the lining of his stomach."

Gerald interrupted. "I wonder if we could see our rooms?"

"So sorry," said Mrs. Pascoe. "Will you register first?" She produced a battered volume bound in peeling imitation leather. "Just the name and address." She spoke as if Gerald might contribute a résumé of his life.

It was the first time he and Phrynne had ever registered in a hotel, but his confidence in the place was not increased by the long period which had passed since the registration above.

"We're always quiet in October," remarked Mrs. Pascoe,

her eyes upon him. Gerald noticed that her eyes were slightly bloodshot. "Except sometimes for the bars, of course."

"We wanted to come out of the season," said Phrynne soothingly.

"Quite," said Mrs. Pascoe.

"Are we alone in the house?" inquired Gerald. After all the woman was probably doing her best.

"Except for Commandant Shotcroft. You won't mind him, will you? He's a regular."

"I'm sure we shan't," said Phrynne.

"People say the house wouldn't be the same without Commandant Shotcroft."

"I see."

"What's that bell?" asked Gerald. Apart from anything else, it really was much too near.

Mrs. Pascoe looked away. He thought she looked shifty under her entrenched makeup. But she only said "Practice."

"Do you mean there will be more of them later?"

She nodded. "But never mind," she said encouragingly. "Let me show you to your room. Sorry there's no porter."

Before they had reached the bedroom, the whole peal had commenced.

"Is this the quietest room you have?" inquired Gerald. "What about the other side of the house?"

"This *is* the other side of the house. Saint Guthlac's is over there." She pointed out through the bedroom door.

"Darling," said Phrynne, her hand on Gerald's arm, "they'll soon stop. They're only practicing."

Mrs. Pasco said nothing. Her expression indicated that she was one of those people whose friendliness has a precise and never exceeded limit.

"If *you* don't mind," said Gerald to Phrynne, hesitating.

"They have ways of their own in Holihaven," said Mrs. Pascoe. her undertone of militancy implied, among other things, that if Gerald, and Phrynne chose to leave, they were at liberty to do so. Gerald did not care for that either: her attitude would have been different, he felt, had there been anywhere else for them to go. The bells were making him touchy and irritable.

"It's a very pretty room," said Phrynne. "I adore four-posters."

"Thank you," said Gerald to Mrs. Pascoe. "What time's dinner?"

"Seven-thirty. You've time for a drink in the bar first."

She went.

"We certainly have," said Gerald when the door was shut. "it's only just six."

"Actually," said Phrynne, who was standing by the window looking down into the street, "I *like* church bells."

"All very well," said Gerald, "but on one's honeymoon they distract the attention."

"Not mine," said Phrynne simply. Then she added, "There's still no one about."

"I expect they're all in the bar."

"I don't want a drink. I want to explore the town."

"As you wish. But hadn't you better unpack?"

"I ought to, but I'm not going to. Not until after I've seen the sea." Such small shows of independence in her enchanted Gerald.

Mrs. Pascoe was not about when they passed through the lounge, nor was there any sound of activity in the establishment.

Outside, the bells seemed to be booming and bounding immediately over their heads.

"It's like warriors fighting in the sky," shouted Phrynne. "Do you think the sea's down there?" She indicated the direction from which they had previously retraced their steps.

"I imagine so. The street seems to end in nothing. That would be the sea."

"Come on. Let's run." She was off before he could even think about it. Then there was nothing to do but run after her. He hoped there were not eyes behind blinds.

She stopped and held wide her arms to catch him. The top of her head hardly came up to his chin. He knew she was silently indicating that his failure to keep up with her was not a matter for self-consciousness.

"Isn't it beautiful?"

"The sea?" There was no moon, and little was discernible beyond the end of the street.

"Not only."

"Everything but the sea. The sea's invisible."

"You can smell it."

"I certainly can't hear it."

She slackened her embrace and cocked her head away from him.

"The bells echo so much, it's as if there were two churches."

"I'm sure there are more than that. There always are in old towns like this." Suddenly he was struck by the significance of his words in relation to what she had said. He shrank into himself, tautly listening.

"Yes," cried Phrynne delightedly. "It is another church."

"Impossible," said Gerald. "Two churches wouldn't have practice ringing on the same night."

"I'm quite sure. I can hear one lot of bells with my left ear, and another lot with my right."

They had still seen no one. The sparse gaslights fell on the furnishings of a stone quay, small but plainly in regular use.

"The whole population must be ringing the bells. His own remark discomfited Gerald.

"Good for them," she took his hand. "Let's go down on the beach and look for the sea."

They descended a flight of stone steps at which the sea had sucked and bitten. The beach was as stony as the steps, but lumpier.

"We'll just go straight on," said Phrynne. "Until we find it."

Left to himself, Gerald would have been less keen. The stones were very large and very slippery, and his eyes did not seem to be becoming accustomed to the dark.

"You're right, Phrynne, about the smell."

"Honest sea smell."

"Just as you say." He took it rather to be the smell of dense rotting weed across which he supposed they must be slithering. It was not a smell he had previously encountered in such strength.

Energy could hardly be spared for thinking, and advancing hand in hand was impossible.

After various random remarks on both sides, and the lapse of what seemed a very long time, Phrynne spoke again. "Gerald, where is it? What sort of seaport is it that has no sea?"

She continued onwards, but Gerald stopped and looked back. He had thought the distance they had gone overlong but was startled to see how great it was. The darkness was doubtless deceitful, but the few lights on the quay appeared as on a distant horizon.

The far glimmering specks still in his eye, he turned and looked after Phrynne. He could barely see her. Perhaps she was progressing faster without him.

"Phrynne! Darling!"

Unexpectedly she gave a sharp cry.

"Phrynne!"

She did not answer.

"Phrynne!"

Then she spoke more or less calmly. "Panic over. Sorry, darling. I stood on something."

He realized that a panic it had indeed been, at least in him.

"You're all right?"

"Think so."

He struggled up to her. "The smell's worse than ever." It was overpowering.

"I think it's coming from what I stepped on. My foot went right in and then there was the smell."

"I've never known anything like it."

"Sorry, darling," she said, gently mocking him. "Let's go away."

"Let's go back. Don't you think?"

"Yes," said Phrynne. "But I must warn you I'm very disappointed. I think that seaside attractions should include the sea."

He noticed that as they retreated, she was scraping the sides of one shoe against the stones, as if trying to clean it.

"I think the whole place is a disappointment," he said. "I really must apologize. We'll go somewhere else."

"I like the bells," she replied, making a careful reservation.

Gerald said nothing.

"I don't want to go somewhere where you've been before."

The bells rang out over the desolate unattractive beach. Now the sound seemed to be coming from every point along the shore.

"I suppose all the churches practice on the same night in order to get it over with," said Gerald.

"They do it in order to see which can ring the loudest," said Phrynne.

"Take care you don't twist your ankle."

The din as they reached the rough little quay was such as to suggest that Phrynne's idea was literally true.

The coffee room was so low that Gerald had to dip beneath a sequence of thick beams.

"Why 'Coffee Room'?" asked Phrynne, looking at the words on the door. "I saw a notice that coffee will only be served in the lounge."

"It's the *lucus a non lucendo* principle."

"That explains everything. I wonder where we sit." A single electric lantern, mass-produced in an antique pattern, had been turned on. The bulb was of that limited wattage which is peculiar to hotels. It did little to penetrate the shadows.

"The *lucus a non lucendo* principle is the principle of calling white black."

"Not at all," said a voice from the darkness. "On the contrary. The word *black* comes from an ancient root which means 'to bleach.'"

They had thought themselves alone but now saw a small man seated by himself at an unlighted corner table. In the darkness he looked like a monkey.

"I stand corrected," said Gerald.

They sat at the table under the lantern.

The man in the corner spoke again. "Why are you here at all?"

Phrynne looked frightened, but Gerald replied quietly. "We're on holiday. We prefer it out of the season. I presume you are Commandant Shotcroft?"

"No need to presume." Unexpectedly the commandant switched on the antique lantern which was nearest to him. His table was littered with a finished meal. It struck Gerald that he must have switched off the light when he heard them approach the coffee room. "I'm going anyway."

"Are we late?" asked Phrynne, always the assuager of situations.

"No, you're not late," called the commandant in a deep moody voice. "My meals are prepared half an hour before the time the rest come in. I don't like eating in company." He had risen to his feet. "So perhaps you'll excuse me."

Without troubling about an answer, he stepped quickly out of the coffee room. He had cropped white hair; tragic, heavy-lidded eyes; and a round face which was yellow and lined.

A second later his head reappeared round the door.

"Ring," he said and again withdrew.

"Too many other people ringing," said Gerald. "But I don't see what else we can do."

The coffee room bell, however, made a noise like a fire alarm.

Mrs. Pascoe appeared. She looked considerably the worse for drink.

"Didn't see you in the bar."

"Must have missed us in the crowd," said Gerald amiably.

"Crowd?" inquired Mrs. Pascoe drunkenly. Then, after a difficult pause, she offered them a handwritten menu.

They ordered, and Mrs. Pascoe served them throughout. Gerald was apprehensive lest her indisposition increase during the course of the meal, but her insobriety, like her affability, seemed to have an exact and definite limit.

"All things considered, the food might be worse," remarked Gerald toward the end. It was a relief that something was going reasonably well. "Not much of it, but at least the dishes are hot."

When Phrynne translated this into a compliment to the cook, Mrs. Pascoe said, "I cooked it all myself, although I shouldn't be the one to say so."

Gerald felt really surprised that she was in a condition to have accomplished this. Possibly, he reflected with alarm, she had had much practice under similar conditions.

"Coffee is served in the lounge," said Mrs. Pascoe.

They withdrew. In a corner of the lounge was a screen decorated with winning Elizabethan ladies in ruffs and hoops. From behind it projected a pair of small black boots. Phrynne nudged Gerald and pointed to them. Gerald nodded. They felt themselves constrained to talk about things which bored them.

The hotel was old and its walls thick. In the empty lounge the noise of the bells would not prevent conversation being overheard, but still came from all around, as if the hotel were fortress beleaguered by surrounding artillery.

After their second cups of coffee, Gerald suddenly said he couldn't stand it.

"Darling, it's not doing us any harm. I think it's rather cozy." Phrynne subsided in the wooden chair with its sloping back and long mud-colored mock-velvet cushions and opened her pretty legs to the fire.

"Every church in the town must be ringing its bells. It's been going on for two and a half hours, and they never seem to take the usual breathers."

"We wouldn't hear. Because of all the other bells ringing. I think it's nice of them to ring the bells for us."

Nothing further was said for several minutes. Gerald was beginning to realize that they had yet to evolve a holiday routine.

"I'll get you a drink. What shall it be?"

"Anything you like. Whatever *you* have." Phrynne was

immersed in female enjoyment of the fire's radiance on her body.

Gerald missed this and said, "I don't quite see why they have to keep the place like a hothouse. When I come back, we'll sit somewhere else."

"Men wear too many clothes, darling," said Phrynne drowsily.

Contrary to his assumption, Gerald found the lounge bar as empty as everywhere else in the hotel and the town. There was not even a person to dispense.

Somewhat irritably Gerald struck a brass bell which stood on the counter. It rang out sharply as a pistol shot.

Mrs. Pascoe appeared at a door among the shelves. She had taken off her jacket, and her make up had begun to run.

"A cognac, please. Double. And a Kummel."

Mrs. Pascoe's hands were shaking so much that she could not get the cork out of the brandy bottle.

"Allow me." Gerald stretched his arm across the bar.

Mrs. Pascoe stared at him blearily. "O.K. But I must pour it."

Gerald extracted the cork and returned the bottle. Mrs. Pascoe slopped a far from precise dose into a balloon.

Castastrophe followed. Unable to return the bottle to the high shelf where it resided, Mrs. Pascoe placed it on a waist-level ledge. Reaching for the alembic of Kummel, she swept the three-quarters-full brandy bottle onto the tiled floor. The stuffy air became fogged with the fumes of brandy from behind the bar.

At the door from which Mrs. Pascoe had emerged appeared a man from the inner room. Though still youngish, he was puce and puffy, and in his braces, with no collar. Streaks of sandy hair laced his vast red scalp. Liquor oozed all over him, as if from a perished gourd. Gerald took it that this was Don.

The man was too drunk to articulate. He stood in the doorway, clinging with each red hand to the ledge, and savagely struggling to flay his wife with imprecations.

"How much?" said Gerald to Mrs. Pascoe. It seemed useless to try for the Kummel. The hotel must have another bar.

"Three and six," said Mrs. Pascoe, quite lucidly; but Gerald saw that she was about to weep.

He had the exact sum. She turned her back on him and

flicked the cash register. As she returned from it, he heard the fragmentation of glass as she stepped on a piece of the broken bottle. Gerald looked at her husband out of the corner of his eye. The sagging, loose-mouthed figure made him shudder. Something moved him.

"I'm sorry about the accident," he said to Mrs. Pascoe. He held the balloon in one hand and was just going.

Mrs. Pascoe looked at him. The slow tears of desperation were edging down her face, but she now seemed quite sober. "Mr. Banstead," she said in a flat, hurried voice. "May I come and sit with you and your wife in the lounge? Just for a few minutes."

"Of course." It was certainly not what he wanted, and he wondered what would become of the bar, but he felt unexpectedly sorry for her, and it was impossible to say no.

To reach the flap of the bar, she had to pass her husband. Gerald saw her hesitate for a second; then she advanced resolutely and steadily, and looking straight before her. If the man had let go with his hands, he would have fallen; but as she passed him, he released a great gob of spit. He was far too incapable to aim, and it fell on the side of his own trousers. Gerald lifted the flap for Mrs. Pascoe and stood back to let her precede him from the bar. As he followed her, he heard her husband maundering off into unintelligible inward searchings.

"The Kummel!" said Mrs. Pascoe, remembering in the doorway.

"Never mind," said Gerald. "Perhaps I could try one of the other bars?"

"Not tonight. They're shut. I'd better go back."

"No. We'll think of something else." It was not yet nine o'clock, and Gerald wondered about the licensing justices.

But in the lounge was another unexpected scene. Mrs. Pascoe stopped as soon as they entered, and Gerald, caught between two imitation leather armchairs, looked over her shoulder.

Phrynne had fallen asleep. Her head was slightly on one side, but her mouth was shut, and her body no more than gracefully relaxed, so that she looked most beautiful and, Gerald thought, a trifle unearthly, like a dead girl in an early picture by Millais.

The quality of her beauty seemed also to have impressed Commandant Shotcroft; for he was standing silently behind her and looking down at her, his sad face transfigured.

Gerald noticed that a leaf of the pseudo-Elizabethan screen had been folded back, revealing a small cretonne-covered chair, with an open tome face downward in its seat.

"Won't you join us?" said Gerald boldly. There was that in the commandant's face which boded no hurt. "Can I get you a drink?"

The commandant did not turn his head and for a moment seemed unable to speak. Then in a low voice he said, "For a moment only."

"Good," said Gerald. "Sit down. And you, Mrs. Pascoe." Mrs. Pascoe was dabbing at her face. Gerald addressed the commandant. "What shall it be?"

"Nothing to drink," said the commandant in the same low mutter. It occurred to Gerald that if Phrynne awoke, the commandant would go.

"What about you?" Gerald looked at Mrs. Pascoe, earnestly hoping she would decline.

"No thanks." She was glancing at the commandant. Clearly she had not expected him to be there.

Phrynne being asleep, Gerald sat down too. He sipped his brandy. It was impossible to romanticize the action with a toast.

The events in the bar had made him forget about the bells. Now, as they sat silently round the sleeping Phrynne, the tide of sound swept over him once more.

"You mustn't think," said Mrs. Pascoe, "that he's always like that." They all spoke in hushed voices. All of them seemed to have reason to do so. The commandant was again gazing somberly at Phrynne's beauty.

"Of course not." But it was hard to believe.

"The licensed business puts temptations in a man's way."

"It must be very difficult."

"We ought never to have come here. We were happy in South Norwood."

"You must do good business during the season."

"Two months," said Mrs. Pascoe bitterly, but still softly. "Two and a half at the very most. The people who come during the season have no idea what goes on out of it."

"What made you leave South Norwood?"

"Don's stomach. The doctor said the air would do him good.

"Speaking of that, doesn't the sea go too far out? We went down on the beach before dinner but couldn't see it anywhere."

On the other side of the fire, the commandant turned his eyes from Phrynne and looked at Gerald.

"I wouldn't know," said Mrs. Pascoe. "I never have time to look from one year's end to the other." It was a customary enough answer, but Gerald felt that it did not disclose the whole truth. He noticed that Mrs. Pascoe glanced uneasily at the commandant, who by now was staring neither at Phrynne nor at Gerald but at the toppling citadels in the fire.

"And now I must get on with my work," continued Mrs. Pascoe, "I only came in for a minute." She looked Gerald in the face. "Thank you," she said, and rose.

"Please stay a little longer," said Gerald. "Wait till my wife wakes up." As he spoke, Phrynne slightly shifted.

"Can't be done," said Mrs. Pascoe, her lips smiling. Gerald noticed that all the time she was watching the commandant from under her lids and knew that were he not there, she would have stayed.

As it was, she went. "I'll probably see you later to say good-night. Sorry the water's not very hot. It's having no porter."

The bells showed no sign of flagging.

When Mrs. Pascoe had closed the door, the commandant spoke.

"He was a fine man once. Don't think otherwise."

"You mean Pascoe?"

The commandant nodded seriously.

"Not my type," said Gerald.

"D.S.O. and bar. D.F.C. and bar."

"And now bar only. Why?"

"You heard what she said. It was a lie. They didn't leave South Norwood for the sea air."

"So I supposed."

"He got into trouble. He was fixed. He wasn't the kind of man to know about human nature and all its rottenness."

"A pity," said Gerald. "But perhaps, even so, this isn't the best place for him?"

"It's the worst," said the commandant, a dark flame in his eyes. "For him or anyone else."

Again Phrynne shifted in her sleep: this time more convulsively, so that she nearly woke. For some reason the two men remained speechless and motionless until she was again breathing steadily. Against the silence within, the bells sounded louder than ever. It was as if the tumult were tearing holes in the roof.

"It's certainly a very noisy place," said Gerald, still in an undertone.

"Why did you have to come tonight of all nights?" The commandant spoke in the same undertone, but his vehemence was extreme.

"This doesn't happen often?"

"Once every year."

"They should have told us."

"They don't usually accept bookings. They've no right to accept them. When Pascoe was in charge, they never did."

"I expect that Mrs. Pascoe felt they were in no position to turn away business."

"It's not a matter that should be left to a woman."

"Not much alternative surely?"

"At heart, women are creatures of darkness all the time." The commandant's seriousness and bitterness left Gerald without a reply.

"My wife doesn't mind the bells," he said after a moment. "In fact she rather likes them." The commandant really was converting a nuisance, though an acute one, into a melodrama.

The commandant turned and gazed at him. It struck Gerald that what he had just said in some way, for the commandant, placed Phrynne also in a category of the lost.

"Take her away, man," said the commandant, with scornful ferocity.

"In a day or two perhaps," said Gerald, patiently polite. "I admit that we are disappointed with Holihaven."

"Now. While there's still time. This *instant*."

There was an intensity of conviction about the commandant which was alarming.

Gerald considered. Even the empty lounge, with its dreary decorations and commonplace furniture, seemed inimical. "They can hardly go on practicing all night," he said. But now it was fear that hushed his voice.

"Practicing!" The commandant's scorn flickered coldly through the overheated room.

"What else?"

"They're ringing to wake the dead."

A tremor of wind in the flue momentarily drew on the already roaring fire. Gerald had turned very pale.

"That's a figure of speech," he said, hardly to be heard.

"Not in Holihaven." The commandant's gaze had returned to the fire.

Gerald looked at Phrynne. She was breathing less heavily. His voice dropped to a whisper. "What happens?"

The commandant also was nearly whispering. "No one can tell how long they have to go on ringing. It varies from year to year. I don't know why. You should be all right up to midnight. Probably for some while after. In the end the dead awake. First one or two, then all of them. Tonight even the sea draws back. You have seen that for yourself. In a place like this there are always several drowned each year. This year there've been more than several. But even so that's only a few. Most of them come not from that water but from the earth. It is not a pretty sight."

"Where do they go?"

"I've never followed them to see. I'm not stark staring mad." The red of the fire reflected in the commandant's eyes. There was a long pause.

"I don't believe in the resurrection of the body," said Gerald. As the hour grew later, the bells grew louder. "Not of the body."

"What other kind of resurrection is possible? Everything else is only theory. You can't even imagine it. No one can."

Gerald had not argued such a thing for twenty years. "So," he said, "you advise me to go. Where?"

"Where doesn't matter."

"I have no car."

"Then you'd better walk."

"With her?" He indicated Phrynne only with his eyes.

"She's young and strong." A forlorn tenderness lay within the commandant's words. "She's twenty years younger than you and therefore twenty years more important."

"Yes," said Gerald. "I agree . . . What about you? What will you do?"

"I've lived here some time now. I know what to do."

"And the Pascoes?"

"He's drunk. There is nothing in the world to fear if you're thoroughly drunk. D.S.O. and bar. D.F.C. and bar."

"But you're not drinking yourself?"

"Not since I came to Holihaven. I lost the knack."

Suddenly Phrynne sat up. "Hallo," she said to the commandant, not yet fully awake. Then she said, "What fun! The bells are still ringing."

The commandant rose, his eyes averted. "I don't think

there's anything more to say," he remarked, addressing Gerald. "You've still got time." He nodded slightly to Phrynne and walked out of the lounge.

"What have you still got time for?" asked Phrynne, stretching. "Was he trying to convert you? I'm sure he's an Anabaptist."

"Something like that," said Gerald, trying to think.

"Shall we go to bed? Sorry, I'm so sleepy."

"Nothing to be sorry about."

"Or shall we go for another walk? That would wake me up. Besides, the tide might have come in."

Gerald, although he half-despised himself for it, found it impossible to explain to her that they should leave at once; without transport or a destination; walk all night if necessary. He said to himself that probably he would not go even were he alone.

"If you're sleepy, it's probably a *good* thing."

"Darling!"

"I mean with these bells. God knows when they will stop." Instantly he felt a new pang of fear at what he had said.

Mrs. Pascoe had appeared at the door leading to the bar and opposite to that from which the commandant had departed. She bore two steaming glasses on a tray. She looked about, possibly to confirm that the commandant had really gone.

"I thought you might both like a nightcap. Ovaltine, with something in it."

"Thank you," said Phrynne. "I can't think of anything nicer."

Gerald set the glasses on a wicker table, and quickly finished his cognac.

Mrs. Pascoe began to move chairs and slap cushions. She looked very haggard.

"Is the commandant an Anabaptist?" asked Phrynne over her shoulder. She was proud of her ability to outdistance Gerald in beginning to consume a hot drink.

Mrs. Pascoe stopped slapping for a moment. "I don't know what that is," she said.

"He's left his book," said Phrynne, on a new tack.

"I wonder what he's reading," continued Phrynne. "Foxe's *The Book of Martyrs,* I expect." A small unusual devil seemed to have entered into her.

But Mrs. Pascoe knew the answer. "It's always the same,"

she said contemptuously. "He only reads one. It's called *Fifteen Decisive Battles of the World*. He's been reading it ever since he came here. When he gets to the end, he starts again."

"Should I take it up to him?" asked Gerald. It was neither courtesy nor inclination, but rather a fear lest the commandant return to the lounge: a desire, after those few minutes of reflection, to cross-examine.

"Thanks very much," said Mrs. Pascoe, as if relieved of a similar apprehension. "Room One. Next to the suit of Japanese armor." She went on tipping and banging. To Gerald's inflamed nerves, her behavior seemed too consciously normal.

He collected the book and made his way upstairs. The volume was bound in real leather, and the top of its pages were gilded: apparently a presentation copy. Outside the lounge, Gerald looked at the fly-leaf: in a very large hand was written "To my dear Son, Raglan, on his being honored by the Queen. From his proud Father, B. Shotcroft, Major-General." Beneath the inscription a very ugly military crest had been appended by a stamper of primitive type.

The suit of Japanese armor lurked in a dark corner as the commandant himself had done when Gerald had first encountered him. The wide brim of the helmet concealed the black eyeholes in the headpiece; the moustache bristled realistically. It was exactly as if the figure stood guard over the door behind it. On this door was no number, but, there being no other in sight, Gerald took it to be the door of Number One. A short way down the dim empty passage was a window, the ancient sashes of which shook in the din and blast of the bells. Gerald knocked sharply.

If there was a reply, the bells drowned it; and he knocked again. When to the third knocking there was still no answer, he gently opened the door. He really had to know whether all would, or could, be well if Phrynne, and doubtless he also, were at all costs to remain in their room until it was dawn. He looked into the room and caught his breath.

There was no artificial light, but the curtains, if there were any, had been drawn back from the single window, and the bottom sash forced up as far as it would go. On the floor by the dusky void, a maelstrom of sound, knelt the commandant, his cropped white hair faintly catching the moonless glimmer as his head lay on the sill, like that of a man about to be guillotined. His face was in his hands, but slightly sideways, so that Gerald received a shadowy distorted idea of his expression. Some might have called it ecstatic, but Gerald found it agonized. It frightened him more than anything which had yet happened. Inside the room the bells were like plunging roaring lions.

He stood for some considerable time quite unable to move. He could not determine whether or not the commandant knew he was there. The commandant gave no direct sign of it, but more than once he writhed and shuddered in Gerald's direction, like an unquiet sleeper made more unquiet by an interloper. It was a matter of doubt whether Gerald should leave the book; and he decided to do so mainly because the thought of further contact with it displeased him. He crept into the room and softly laid it on a hardly visible wooden trunk at the foot of the plain metal bedstead. There seemed no other furniture in the room. Outside the door, the hanging mailed fingers of the Japanese figure touched his wrist.

He had not been away from the lounge for long, but it was long enough for Mrs. Pascoe to have begun to drink again. She had left the tidying up half-completed, or rather the room half-disarranged, and was leaning against the overmantel, drawing heavily on a dark tumbler of whisky. Phrynne had not yet finished her Ovaltine.

"How long before the bells stop?" asked Gerald as soon as he opened the lounge door. Now he was resolved that, come what might, they must go. The impossibility of sleep should serve as an excuse.

"I don't expect Mrs. Pascoe can know any more than we can," said Phrynne.

"You should have told us about this—this annual event before accepting our booking."

Mrs Pascoe drank some more whisky. Gerald suspected that it was neat. "It's not always the same night," she said throatily, looking at the floor.

"We're not staying," said Gerald wildly.

"Darling." Phrynne caught him by the arm.

"Leave this to me, Phrynne." He addressed Mrs. Pascoe. "We'll pay for the room, of course. Please order me a car."

Mrs. Pascoe was now regarding him stonily. When he asked for a car, she gave a very short laugh. Then her face changed, she made an effort, and she said, "You mustn't take the commandant so seriously, you know."

Phrynne glanced quickly at her husband.

The whisky was finished. Mrs. Pascoe placed the empty glass on the plastic overmantel with too much of a thud. "No one takes Commandant Shotcroft seriously," she said. "Not even his nearest and dearest."

"Has he any?" asked Phrynne. "He seemed so lonely and pathetic."

"He's Don and I's mascot," she said, the drink interfering with her grammar. But not even the drink could leave any doubt about her rancor.

"I thought he had personality," said Phrynne.

"That and a lot more no doubt," said Mrs. Pascoe. "But they pushed him out, all the same."

"Out of what?"

"Cashiered, court-martialled, badges of rank stripped off, sword broken in half, muffled drums, the works."

"Poor old man. I'm sure it was a miscarriage of justice."

"That's because you don't know him."

Mrs. Pascoe looked as if she were waiting for Gerald to offer her another whisky.

"It's a thing he could never live down," said Phrynne, brooding to herself and tucking her legs beneath her. "No wonder he's so queer if all the time it was a mistake."

"I just told you it was not a mistake," said Mrs. Pascoe insolently.

"How can we possibly know?"

"*You* can't. *I* can. No one better." She was at once aggressive and tearful.

"If you want to be paid," cried Gerald, forcing himself in, "make out your bill. Phrynne, come upstairs and pack." If only he hadn't made her unpack between their walk and dinner.

Slowly Phrynne uncoiled and rose to her feet. She had no intention of either packing or departing but nor was she going to argue. "I shall need your help," she said softly. "if I'm going to pack."

In Mrs. Pascoe there was another change. Now she looked terrified. "Don't go. Please don't go. Not now. It's too late."

Gerald confronted her. "Too late for what?" he asked harshly.

Mrs. Pascoe looked paler than ever. "You said you wanted a car," she faltered. "You're too late." Her voice trailed away.

Gerald took Phrynne by the arm. "Come on up."

Before they reached the door, Mrs. Pascoe made a further attempt. "You'll be all right if you stay. Really you will." Her voice, normally somewhat strident, was so feeble that the bells obliterated it. Gerald observed that from somewhere she had produced the whisky bottle and was refilling her tumbler.

With Phrynne on his arm he went first to the stout front door. To his surprise it was neither locked nor bolted, but opened at a half turn of the handle. Outside the building the whole sky was full of bells, the air an inferno of ringing.

He thought that for the first time Phrynne's face also seemed strained and crestfallen. "They've been ringing too long," she said, drawing close to him. "I wish they'd stop."

"We're packing and going. I needed to know whether we could get out this way. We must shut the door quietly."

It creaked a bit on its hinges, and he hesitated with it half-shut, uncertain whether to rush the creak or to ease it. Suddenly, something dark and shapeless, with its arm seeming to hold a black vesture over its head, flitted, all sharp angles, like a bat, down the narrow ill-lighted street, the sound of its passage audible to none. It was the first being that either of them had seen in the streets of Holihaven; and Gerald was acutely relieved that he alone had set eyes upon it. With his hand trembling, he shut the door much too sharply.

But no one could possibly have heard, although he stopped for a second outside the lounge. He could hear Mrs. Pascoe now weeping hysterically and again was glad that Phrynne was a step or two ahead of him. Upstairs the commandant's door lay straight before them: they had to pass close beside the Japanese figure in order to take the passage to the left of it.

But soon they were in their room, with the key turned in the big rim lock.

"Oh God," cried Gerald, sinking on the double bed. "It's pandemonium." Not for the first time that evening he was instantly more frightened than ever by the unintended appositeness of his own words.

"It's pandemonium all right," said Phrynne, almost calmly. "And we're not going out in it."

He was at a loss to divine how much she knew, guessed, or imagined; and any word of enlightenment from him might be inconceivably dangerous. But he was conscious of the strength of her resistance and lacked the reserves to battle with it.

She was looking out of the window into the main street. "We might *will* them to stop," she suggested wearily.

Gerald was now far less frightened of the bells continuing than of their ceasing. But that they should go on ringing until day broke seemed hopelessly impossible.

Then one peal stopped. There could be no other explanation for the obvious diminution in sound.

"You see!" said Phrynne.

Gerald sat up straight on the side of the bed.

Almost at once further sections of sound subsided, quickly one after the other, until only a single peal was left, that which had begun the ringing. Then the single peal tapered off into a single bell. The single bell tolled on its own, disjointedly, five or six or seven times. Then it stopped, and there was nothing.

Gerald's head was a cave of echoes, mountingly muffled by the noisy current of his blood.

"Oh goodness," said Phrynne, turning from the window and stretching her arms above her head. "Let's go somewhere else tomorrow." She began to take off her dress.

Sooner than usual they were in bed and in one another's arms. Gerald had carefully not looked out of the window, and neither of them suggested that it should be opened, as they usually did.

"As it's a four-poster, shouldn't we draw the curtains?" asked Phrynne. "And be really snug? After those damned bells?"

"We should suffocate."

"They only drew the curtains when people were likely to pass through the room."

"Darling, you're shivering. I think we *should* draw them."

"Lie still instead and love me."

But all his nerves were straining out into the silence. There was no sound of any kind beyond the hotel or within it; not a creaking floorboard or a prowling cat or a distant owl. He had been afraid to look at his watch when the bells stopped, or since: the number of the dark hours before they could leave Holihaven weighed on him. The vision of the commandant kneeling in the dark window was clear before his eyes, as if the intervening paneled walls were made of stage gauze; and the thing he had seen in the street darted on its angular way back and forth through memory.

Then passion began to open its petals within him, layer upon slow layer; like an illusionist's red flower which, without soil or sun or sap, grows as it is watched. The languor of tenderness began to fill the musty room with its texture and perfume. The transparent walls became again opaque, the old man's vaticinations mere obsession. The street must have been empty, as it was now; the eye deceived.

But perhaps rather it was the boundless sequacity of love that deceived, and most of all in the matter of the time which had passed since the bells stopped ringing; for suddenly Phrynne drew very close to him, and he heard steps in the thoroughfare outside a voice calling. These were loud steps, audible from afar even through the shut window; and the voice had the possessed stridency of the street evangelist.

"The dead are awake!"

Not even the thick bucolic accent, the guttural vibrato of emotion, could twist or mask the meaning. At first Gerald lay listening with all his body and concentrating the more as the noise grew; then he sprang from the bed and ran to the window.

A burly, long-limbed man in a seaman's jersey was running down the street, coming clearly into view for a second at each lamp and between them lapsing into a swaying lumpy wraith. As he shouted his joyous message he crossed from side to side and waved his arms like a Negro. By flashes, Gerald could see that his weatherworn face was transfigured.

"The dead are awake!"

Already, behind him, people were coming out of their houses and descending from the rooms above shops. There were men, women, and children. Most of them were fully dressed and must have been waiting in silence and darkness for the call; but a few were disheveled in night attire or the first garments which had come to hand. Some formed themselves into groups and advanced arm in arm, as if toward the conclusion of a Blackpool beano. More came singly, ecstatic and waving their arms above their heads, as the first man had done. All cried out, again and again, with no cohesion or harmony. "The dead are awake! The dead are awake!"

Gerald became aware that Phrynne was standing behind him.

"The commandant warned me," he said brokenly. "We should have gone."

Phrynne shook her head and took his arm. "Nowhere to go," she said. But her voice was soft with fear and her eyes blank. "I don't expect they'll trouble *us*."

Swiftly Gerald drew the thick plush curtains, leaving them in complete darkness. "We'll sit it out," he said, slightly histrionic in his fear. "No matter what happens."

He scrambled across to the switch. But when he pressed it, light did not come. "The current's gone. We must get back into bed."

"Gerald! Come and help me." He remembered that she was curiously vulnerable in the dark. He found his way to her and guided her to the bed.

"No more love," she said ruefully and affectionately, her teeth chattering.

He kissed her lips with what gentleness the total night made possible.

"They were going toward the sea," she said timidly.

"We must think of something else."

But the noise was still growing. The whole community seemed to be passing down the street, yelling the same dreadful words again and again.

"Do you think we can?"

"Yes," said Gerald. "It's only until tomorrow."

"They can't be actually dangerous," said Phrynne. "Or it would be stopped."

"Yes, of course."

By now, as always happens, the crowd has amalgamated their utterances and were beginning to shout in unison. They were like agitators bawling a slogan, or massed troublemakers at a football match. But at the same time the noise was beginning to draw away. Gerald suspected that the entire population of the place was on the march.

Soon it was apparent that a processional route was being followed. The tumult could be heard winding about from quarter to quarter, sometimes drawing near, so that Gerald and Phrynne were once more seized by the first chill of panic, then again almost fading away. It was possibly this great variability in the volume of the sound which led Gerald to believe that there were distinct pauses in the massed shouting, periods when it was superseded by far, disorderly cheering. Certainly it began also to seem that the thing shouted had changed; but he could not make out the new cry, although unwillingly he strained to do so.

"It's extraordinary how frightened one can be," said

Phrynne, "even when one is not directly menaced. It must prove that we all belong to one another, or whatever it is, after all."

In many similar remarks they discussed the thing at one remove. Experience showed that this was better than not discussing it at all.

In the end there could be no doubt that the shouting had stopped and that now the crowd was singing. It was no song that Gerald had ever heard, but something about the way it was sung convinced him that it was a hymn or psalm set to an out-of-date popular tune. Once more the crowd was approaching, this time steadily, but with strange, interminable slowness.

"What the hell are they doing now?" asked Gerald of the blackness, his nerves wound so tight that the foolish question was forced out of them.

Palpably the crowd had completed its peregrination and was returning up the main street from the sea. The singers seemed to gasp and fluctuate, as if worn out with gay exercise, like children at a party. There was a steady undertow of scraping and scuffing. Time passed and more time.

Phrynne spoke. "I believe they're *dancing*."

She moved slightly as if she thought of going to see.

"No, no," said Gerald and clutched her fiercely.

There was a tremendous concussion on the ground floor below them. The front door had been violently thrown back. They could hear the hotel filling with a stamping, singing mob.

Doors banged everywhere, and furniture was overturned, as the beatic throng surged and stumbled through the involved darkness of the old building. Glasses went and china and Birmingham brass warming pans. In a moment, Gerald heard the Japanese armor crash to be boards. Phrynne screamed. Then a mighty shoulder, made strong by the sea's assault, rammed at the paneling and their door was down.

The living and the dead dance together.
Now's the time. Now's the place. Now's the weather.

At last Gerald could make out the words.

The stresses in the song were heavily beaten down by much repetition.

Hand in hand, through the dim gray gap of the doorway,

the dancers lumbered and shambled in, singing frenziedly and brokenly, ecstatic but exhausted. Through the stuffy blackness they swayed and shambled, more and more of them, until the room must have been packed tight with them.

Phrynne screamed again. "The smell. Oh, God, the smell."

It was the smell they had encountered on the beach; in the congested room, no longer merely offensive, but obscene, unspeakable.

Phrynne was hysterical. All self-control gone, she was scratching and tearing and screaming again and again. Gerald tried to hold her, but one of the dancers struck him so hard in the darkness that she was jolted out of his arms. Instantly it seemed that she was no longer there at all.

The dancers were thronging everywhere, their limbs whirling, their lungs bursting with the rhythm of the song. It was difficult for Gerald even to call out. He tried to struggle after Phrynne, but immediately a blow from a massive elbow knocked him to the floor, an abyss of invisible, tramping feet.

But soon the dancers were going again: not only from the room but, it seemed, from the building also. Crushed and tormented though he was, Gerald could hear the song being resumed in the street, as the various frenzied groups debouched and reunited. Within, before long there was nothing but the chaos, the darkness, and the putrescent odor. Gerald felt so sick that he had to battle with unconsciousness. He could not think or move, despite the desperate need.

Then he struggled into a sitting position and sank his head on the torn sheets of the bed. For an uncertain period he was insensible to everything, but in the end he heard steps approaching down the dark passage. His door was pushed back, and the commandant entered gripping a lighted candle. He seemed to disregard the flow of hot wax which had already congealed on much of his knotted hand.

"She's safe. Small thanks to you."

The commandant stared icily at Gerald's undignified figure. Gerald tried to stand. He was terribly bruised, and so giddy that he wondered if this could be concussion. But relief rallied him.

"Is it thanks to *you*?"

"She was caught up in it. Dancing with the rest." The commandant's eyes glowed in the candlelight. The singing and the dancing had almost died away.

Still Gerald could do no more than sit upon the bed. His voice was low and indistinct, as if coming from outside his body. "Were they . . . were some of them . . ."

The commandant replied, more scornful than ever of his weakness. "She was between two of them. Each had one of her hands."

Gerald could not look at him. "What did you do?" he asked in the same remote voice.

"I did what had to be done. I hope I was in time." After the slightest possible pause he continued. "You'll find her downstairs."

"I'm grateful. Such a silly thing to say, but what else is there?"

"Can you walk?"

"I think so."

"I'll light you down." The commandant's tone was as uncompromising as always.

There were two more candles in the lounge, and Phrynne, wearing a woman's belted overcoat which was not hers, sat between them, drinking. Mrs. Pascoe, fully dressed but with eyes averted, pottered about the wreckage. It seemed hardly more than as if she were completing the task which earlier she had left unfinished.

"Darling, look at you!" Phrynne's words were still hysterical, but her voice was as gentle as it usually was.

Gerald, bruises and thoughts of concussion forgotten, dragged her into his arms. They embraced silently for a long time; then he looked into her eyes.

"Here I am," she said and looked away. "Not to worry."

Silently and unnoticed, the commandant had already retreated.

Without returning his gaze, Phrynne finished her drink as she stood there. Gerald supposed that it was one of Mrs. Pascoe's concoctions.

It was so dark where Mrs. Pascoe was working that her labors could have been achieving little; but she said nothing to her visitors, nor they to her. At the door Phrynne unexpectedly stripped off the overcoat and threw it on a chair. Her nightdress was so torn that she stood almost naked. Dark though it was, Gerald saw Mrs. Pascoe regarding Phrynne's pretty body with a stare of animosity.

"May we take one of the candles?" he said, normal standards reasserting themselves in him.

But Mrs. Pascoe continued to stand silently staring; and

they lighted themselves through the wilderness of broken furniture to the ruins of their bedroom. The Japanese figure was still prostrate, and the commandant's door shut. And the smell had almost gone.

Even by seven o'clock the next morning surprisingly much had been done to restore order. But no one seemed to be about, and Gerald and Phrynne departed without a word.

In Wrack Street a milkman was delivering, but Gerald noticed that his cart bore the name of another town. A minute boy whom they encountered later on an obscure purposeful errand might, however, have been indigenous; and when they reached Station Road, they saw a small plot of land on which already men were silently at work with spades in their hands. They were as thick as flies on a wound, and as black. In the darkness of the previous evening, Gerald and Phrynne had missed the place. A board named it the New Municipal Cemetery.

In the mild light of an autumn morning the sight of the black and silent toilers was horrible; but Phrynne did not seem to find it so. On the contrary, her cheeks reddened and her soft mouth became fleetingly more voluptuous still.

She seemed to have forgotten Gerald, so that he was able to examine her closely for a moment. It was the first time he had done so since the night before. Then, once more, she became herself. In those previous seconds Gerald had become aware of something dividing them which neither of them would ever mention or ever forget.

AUTHOR! AUTHOR!

Isaac Asimov

It occurred to Graham Dorn, and not for the first time, either, that there was one serious disadvantage in swearing you'll go through fire and water for a girl, however beloved. Sometimes she takes you at your miserable word.

This is one way of saying that he had been waylaid, shanghaied and dragooned by his fiancée into speaking at her maiden aunt's Literary Society. Don't laugh! It's not funny from the speaker's rostrum. Some of the faces you have to look at!

To race through the details, Graham Dorn had been jerked onto a platform and forced upright. He had read a speech on. "The Place of the Mystery Novel in American Literature" in an appalled tone. Not even the fact that his own eternally precious June had written it (part of the bribe to get him to speak in the first place) could mask that fact that it was essentially tripe.

And then when he was weltering, figuratively speaking, in his own mental gore, the harpies closed in, for lo, it was time for the informal discussion and assorted feminine gush.

—Oh, Mr. Dorn, do you work from inspiration? I mean, do you just sit down and then an idea strikes you—all at once? And you must sit up all night and drink black coffee to keep you awake till you get it down?"

—Oh, yes. Certainly. (His working hours were two to four in the afternoon every other day, and he drank milk.)

—Oh, Mr. Dorn, you must do the most awful research to get all those bizarre murders. About how much must you do before you can write a story?

—About six months, usually. (The only reference books he ever used were a six-volume encyclopedia and year-before-last's World Almanac.)

—Oh, Mr. Dorn, did you make up your Reginald de

Meister from a real character? You must have. He's oh, so convincing in his every detail.

—He's modeled after a very dear boyhood chum of mine. (Dorn had never known *anyone* like de Meister. He lived in continual fear of meeting someone like him. He had even a cunningly fashioned ring containing a subtle Oriental poison for use just in case he did. So much for de Meister.)

Somewhere past the knot of women, June Billings sat in her seat and smiled with sickening and proprietary pride.

Graham passed a finger over his throat and went through the pantomime of choking to death as unobtrusively as possible. June smiled, nodded, threw him a delicate kiss, and did nothing.

Graham decided to pass a stern, lonely, woman-less life and to have nothing but villainesses in his stories forever after.

He was answering in monosyllables, alternating yesses and noes. Yes, he did take cocaine on occasion. He found it helped the creative urge. No, he didn't think he could allow Hollywood to take over de Meister. He thought movies weren't true expressions of real Art. Besides, they were just a passing fad. Yes, he would read Miss Crum's manuscripts if she brought them. Only too glad to. Reading amateur manuscripts was such fun, and editors are really such brutes.

And then refreshments were announced, and there was a sudden vacuum. It took a split-second for Graham's head to clear. The mass of femininity had coalesced into a single specimen. She was four feet ten and about eighty-five pounds in weight. Graham was six-two and two hundred ten worth of brawn. He could probably have handled her without difficulty, especially since both her arms were occupied with a pachyderm of a purse. Still, he felt a little delicate, to say nothing of queasy, about knocking her down. It didn't seem quite the thing to do.

She was advancing, with admiration and fervor disgustingly clear in her eyes, and Graham felt the wall behind him. There was no doorway within arm reach on either side.

"Oh, Mr. de Meister—do, do please let me call you Mr. de Meister. Your creation is so real to me, that I can't think of you as simply Graham Dorn. You don't mind, do you?"

"No, no, of course not," gargled Graham, as well as he could through thirty-two teeth simultaneously set on edge.

"I often think of myself as Reginald in my more frivolous moments."

"Thank you. You can have no idea, *dear* Mr. De Meister, how I have looked *forward* to meeting you. I have read *all* your works, and I think they are wonderful."

"I'm glad you think so." He went automatically into the modesty routine. "Really nothing, you know. Ha, ha, ha! Like to please the readers, but lots of room for improvement. Ha, ha, ha!"

"But you really are, you know." This was said with intense earnestness. "I mean good, *really* good. I think it is wonderful to be an author like you. It must be almost like being God."

Graham stared blankly. "Not to editors, sister."

Sister didn't get the whisper. She continued, "To be able to create living characters out of nothing; to unfold souls to all the world; to put thoughts into words; to build pictures and create worlds. I have often thought that an author was the most gloriously gifted person in creation. Better an inspired author starving in a garret than a king upon his throne. Don't you think so?"

"Definitely," lied Graham.

"What are the crass material goods of the world to the wonders of weaving emotions and deeds into a little world of its own?"

"What, indeed?"

"And posterity, think of posterity!"

"Yes, yes. I often do."

She seized his hand. "There's only one little request. You might," she blushed faintly, "you might give poor Reginald—if you will allow me to call him that just once—a chance to marry Letitia Reynolds. You make her just a little too cruel to him. I'm sure I weep over it for hours together sometimes. But then he is too, too real to me."

And from somewhere, a lacy frill of handkerchief made its appearance, and went to her eyes. She removed it, smiled bravely, and scurried away. Graham Dorn inhaled, closed his eyes, and gently collapsed into June's arms.

His eyes opened with a jerk. "You may consider," he said severely "our engagement frazzled to the breaking point. Only my consideration for your poor, aged parents prevents your being known henceforward as the ex-fiancée of Graham Dorn."

"Darling, you are so noble." She massaged his sleeve

with her cheek. "Come, I'll take you home and bathe your poor wounds."

"All right, but you'll have to carry me. Has your precious, loveable aunt got an axe?"

"But why?"

"For one thing, she had the gall to introduce me as the brain-father, God help me, of the famous Reginald de Meister."

"And aren't you?"

"Let's get out of this creep-joint. And get this. I'm no relative by brain or otherwise, of that character. I disown him. I cast him into the darkness. I spit upon him. I declare him an illegitimate son, a foul degenerate, and the offspring of a hound, and I'll be damned if he ever pokes his lousy patrician nose into my typewriter again."

They were in the taxi, and June straightened his tie. "All right, Sonny, let's see the letter."

"What letter?"

She held out her hand. "The one from the publishers."

Graham snarled and flipped it out of his jacket pocket. "I've thought of inviting myself to his house for tea, the damned flintheart. He's got a rendezvous with a pinch of strychnine."

"You may rave later. What does he say? Hmm—uh-huh— 'doesn't quite come up to what is expected—feel that de Meister isn't in his usual form—a little revision perhaps towards—feel sure the novel can be adjusted—are returning under separate cover—' "

She tossed it aside. "I told you you shouldn't have killed off Sancha Rodriguez. She was what you needed. You're getting skimpy on the love interest."

"*You* write it! I'm through with de Meister. It's getting so club-women call me Mr. de Meister, and my picture is printed in newspapers with the caption Mr. de Meister. I have no individuality. No one ever head of Graham Dorn. I'm always: Dorn, Dorn, you know, the guy who writes the de Meister stuff, *you* know."

June squealed, "Silly! You're jealous of your own detective."

"I am not jealous of my own character. Listen! I hate detective stories. I never read them after I got into the two-syllable words. I wrote the first as a clever, trenchant, biting satire. It was to blast the entire false school of mystery writers. That's why I invented this de Meister. He was the detective to end all detectives. The Compleat Ass, by Graham Dorn.

"So the public, along with snakes, vipers, and ungrateful children takes this filth to its bosom. I wrote mystery after mystery trying to convert the public—"

Graham Dorn drooped a little at the futility of it all.

"Oh, well." He smiled wanly, and the great soul rose above adversity. "Don't you see? I've got to write other things. I can't waste my life. But who's going to read a serious novel by Graham Dorn, now that I'm so thoroughly identified with de Meister?"

"You can use a pseudonym."

"I will not use a pseudonym. I'm proud of my name."

"But you can't drop de Meister. Be sensible, dear."

"A normal fiancée," Graham said bitterly, "would want her future husband to write something really worthwhile and become a great name in literature."

"Well, I do want you to, Graham. But just a little de Meister once in a while to pay the bills that accumulate."

"Ha!" Graham knocked his hat over his eyes to hide the sufferings of a strong spirit in agony. "Now you say that I can't reach prominence unless I prostitute my art to that unmentionable. Here's your place. Get out. I'm going home and write a good scorching letter on asbestos to our senile Mr. MacDunlap."

"Do exactly as you want to, cookie," soothed June. "And tomorrow when you feel better, you'll come and cry on my shoulder, and we'll plan a revision of *Death of the Third Deck* together, shall we?"

"The engagement," said Graham, loftily, "is broken."

"Yes, dear. I'll be home tomorrow at eight."

"That is of no possible interest to me. Good-bye!"

Publishers and editors are untouchables, of course. Theirs is a heritage of the outstretched hand and the well-toothed smile; the nod of the head and the slap of the back.

But perhaps somewhere, in the privacy of the holes to which authors scurry when the night falls, a private revenge is taken. There, phrases may be uttered where no one can overhear, and letters may be written that need not be mailed, and perhaps a picture of an editor, smiling pensively, is enshrined above the typewriter to act the part of bulls-eye in an occasional game of darts.

Such a picture of MacDunlap, so used, enlightened Graham Dorn's room. And Graham Dorn himself, in his usual writing costume (street-clothes and typewriter), scowled at the fifth sheet of paper in his typewriter. The other four were draped over the edge of the wastebasket, condemned for their milk-and-watery mildness.

He began:

"Dear Sir—" and added slowly and viciously, "or Madam, as the case may be."

He typed furiously as the inspiration caught him, disregarding the faint wisp of smoke curling upward from the overheated keys:

"You say you don't think much of de Meister in this story. Well, I don't think much of De Meister, period. You can handcuff your slimy carcass to his and jump off the Brooklyn Bridge. And I hope they drain the East River just before you jump.

"From now on, my works will be aimed higher than your scurvy press. And the day will come when I can look back on this period of my career with the loathing that is its just—"

Someone had been tapping Graham on the shoulder during the last paragraph. Graham twitched it angrily and ineffectively at intervals.

Now he stopped, turned around, and addressed the stranger in his room courteously: "Who the devilish damnation are you? And you can leave without bothering to answer. I won't think you rude."

The newcomer smiled graciously. His nod wafted the delicate aroma of some unobtrusive hair-oil toward Graham. His lean, hard-bitten jaw stood out keenly, and he said in a well-modulated voice:

"De Meister is the name. Reginald de Meister."

Graham rocked to his mental foundations and heard them creak.

"Glub," he said.

"Pardon?"

Graham recovered. "I said, 'glub', a little code word meaning *which* de Meister."

"*The* de Meister," explained de Meister, kindly.

"My character? My detective?"

De Meister helped himself to a seat, and his finely-chiseled features assumed that air of well-bred boredom so admired in the best circles. He lit a Turkish cigarette, which Graham at once recognized as his detective's favorite brand, tapping it slowly and carefully against the back of his hand first, a mannerism equally characteristic.

"Really, old man," said de Meister. "This is really excruciatin'ly funny. I suppose I am your character, y'know, but lets not work on that basis. It would be so devastatin'ly awkward."

"Glub," said Graham again, by way of rejoinder.

His mind was feverishly setting up alternatives. He didn't drink, more, at the moment, was the pity, so he wasn't drunk. He had a chrome-steel digestion and he wasn't overheated, so it wasn't a hallucination. He never dreamed, and his imagination—as befitted a paying commodity—was under strict control. And since, like all authors, he was widely considered more than half a screwball, insanity was out of the question.

Which left de Meister simply an impossibility, and Graham felt relieved. It's a very poor author indeed who hasn't learned the fine art of ignoring impossibilities in writing a book.

He said smoothly, "I have here a volume of my latest work. Do you mind naming your page and crawling back into it. I'm a busy man and God knows I have enough of you in the tripe I write."

"But I'm here on business, old chap. I've got to come to a friendly arrangement with you first. Things are deucedly uncomfortable as they are."

"Look, do you know you're bothering me? I'm not in the habit of talking to mythical characters. As a general thing, I don't pal around with them. Besides which, it's time your mother told you that you really don't exist."

"My dear fellow, I always existed. Existence is such a subjective thing. What a mind thinks exists, *does* exist. I existed in your mind, for instance, ever since you first thought of me."

Graham shuddered. "But the question is, what are you doing *out* of my mind? Getting a little narrow for you? Want elbow room?"

"Not at all. Rather satisfact'ry mind in its way, but I achieved a more concrete existence only this afternoon, and so I seize the opportunity to engage you face to face in the aforementioned business conversation. You see, that thin, sentimental lady of your society—"

"What society?" questioned Graham hollowly. It was all awfully clear to him now.

"The one at which you made a speech—" de Meister shuddered in his turn—" on the detective novel. She believed in my existence, so naturally, I exist."

He finished his cigarette and flicked it out with a negligent twist of the wrist.

"The logic," declared Graham, "is inescapable. Now, what do you want and the answer is no."

"Do you realize, old man, that if you stop writing de Meister stories my existence will become that dull, wraithlike one of all superannuated fictional detectives. I'd have to gibber through the gray mists of Limbo with Holmes, Lecocq, and Dupin."

"A very fascinating thought, I think. A very fitting fate."

Reginald de Meister's eyes turned icy, and Graham suddenly remembered the passage on page 123 of *The Case of the Broken Ashtray:*

> *His eyes, hitherto lazy and unattentive, hardened into twin pools of blue ice and transfixed the butler, who staggered back, a stifled cry on his lips.*

Evidently, de Meister lost none of his characteristics out of the novels he adorned.

Graham staggered back, a stifled cry on his lip.

De Meister said menacingly, "It would be better for you if the de Meister mysteries continue. Do you understand?"

Graham recovered and summoned a feeble indignation. "Now, wait a while. You're getting out of hand. Remember: in a way, I'm your father. That's right. Your mental father. You can't hand me ultimatums or make threats. It isn't filial. It's lacking in the proper respect and love."

"And another thing," said de Meister, unmoved. "We've got to straighten out this business of Letitia Reynolds. It's gettin' deucedly borin', y'know."

"Now you're getting silly. My love scenes have been widely heralded as miracles of tenderness and sentiment not found in one murder mystery out of a thousand. —Wait, I'll get you a few reviews. I don't mind your attempts to dictate my actions so much, but I'm damned if you'll criticize my writing."

"Forget the reviews. Tenderness and all that rot is what I don't want. I've been driftin' after the fair lady for five volumes now, and behavin' the most insufferable ass. This has got to stop."

"In what way?"

"I've got to marry her in your present story. Either that, or make her a good, respectable mistress. And you'll have to stop making me so damned Victorian and gentlemanly toward ladies. I'm only human, old man."

"Impossible!" said Graham, "and that includes your last remark."

De Meister grew severe. "Really, old chap, for an author, you display the most appallin' lack of concern for the well-bein' of a character who has supported you for a good many years."

Graham choked eloquently. "Supported me? In other words, you think I couldn't sell real novels, hey? Well, I'll show you. I wouldn't write another de Meister story for a million dollars. Not even for a fifty percent royalty and all television rights. How's that?"

De Meister frowned and uttered those words that had been the sound of doom to so many criminals: "We shall see, but you are not yet done with me."

With firmly jutting jaw, he vanished.

Graham's twisted face straightened out, and slowly—very slowly—he brought his hands up to his cranium and felt carefully.

For the first time in a long and reasonably ribald mental life, he felt that his enemies were right and that a good dry cleaning would not hurt his mind at all.

The *things* that existed in it!

Graham Dorn shoved the doorbell with his elbow a second time. He distinctly remembered her saying she would be home at eight.

The peep-hole shoved open. "Hello!"

"Hello!"

Silence!

Graham said plaintively, "It's raining outside. Can't I come in to dry?"

"I don't know. Are we engaged, Mr. Dorn?"

"If I'm not," was the stiff reply. "then I've been turning down the frenzied advances of a hundred passion-stricken girls—beautiful ones, all of them—for no apparent reason."

"Yesterday, you said—"

"Ah, but who listens to what I say? I'm just quaint that way. Look, I brought you posies." He flourished roses before the peep-hole.

June opened the door, "Roses! How plebeian. Come in, cookie and sully the sofa. Whoa, whoa, before you move a step, what have you got under the other arm? Not the manuscript of *Death on the Third Deck*?"

"Correct. Not that excrescence of a manuscript. This is something different."

June's too chilled. "That isn't your precious novel, is it?"

Graham flung his head up, "How did you now about it?"

"You slobbered the plot all over me at MacDunlap's silver anniversary party."

"I did not. I couldn't unless I were drunk."

"Oh, but you were. Stinking is the term. And on two cocktails too."

"Well, if I was drunk, I couldn't have told you the right plot."

"Is the setting a coal-mine district?"

"—Uh—yes."

"And are the people concerned real, earthy, unartificial, down-to-earth characters, speaking and thinking just like you and me? Is it a story of basic economic forces? Are the human characters lifted up and thrown down and whirled around, all at the mercy of the coal mine and mechanized industry of today?"

"—Uh—yes."

She nodded head retrospectively. "I remember distinctly. First, you got drunk and were sick. Then you got better, and told me the first few chapters. Then I got sick."

She approached the glowering author. "Graham." She leant her golden head upon his shoulder and cooed softly. "Why don't you continue with the de Meister stories? You get such pretty checks out of them."

Graham writhed out of her grasp. "You are a mercenary wretch, incapable of understanding an author's soul. You may consider our engagement broken."

He sat down hard on the sofa, and folded his arms. "Unless you will consent to read the script of my novel and give me the usual story analysis."

"May I give you my analysis of *Death on the Third Deck* first?"

"No."

"Good! In the first place, your love interest is becoming sickening."

"It is not." Graham pointed his finger indignantly. "It breathes a sweet and sentimental fragrance, as of an older day. I've got the review here that says it." He fumbled in his wallet.

"Oh, bullfeathers. Are you going to start quoting that guy in the Pillsboro (Okla.) Clarion? He's probably your second cousin. You know that your last two novels were completely below par in royalties. And *Third Deck* isn't even being sold."

"So much the better—Ow!" He rubbed his head violently. "What did you do that for?"

"Because the only place I could hit as hard as I wanted to, without disabling you, was your head. Listen! The public is tired of your corny Letitia Reynolds. Why don't you let her soak her 'gleaming golden crown of hair' in kerosene and get familiar with a match?"

"But June, that character is drawn from life. From you!"

"Graham Dorn! I am not here to listen to insults. The mystery market today is swinging towards action and hot, honest love and you're still in the sweet, sentimental stickiness of five years ago."

"But that's Reginald de Meister's character."

"Well, change his character. Listen! You introduce Sancha Rodriguez. That's fine. I approve of her. She's Mexican, flaming, passionate, sultry, and in love with him. So what do you do? First he behaves the impeccable gentleman, and then you kill her off in the middle of the story."

"Hmm, I see— You really think it would improve things to have de Meister forget himself. A kiss or so—"

June clenched her lovely teeth and her lovely fists. "Oh, darling, how glad I am love is blind! If it ever peeked one tiny little bit, I couldn't stand it. Look, you squirrel's blue plate special, you're going to have de Meister and Rodriguez fall in love. They're going to have an affair through the entire book and you can put your horrible Letitia into a nunnery. She probably be happier there from the way you make her sound."

"That's all *you* know about it, my sweet. It so happens that Reginald de Meister is in love with Letitia Reynolds and wants *her*, not this Roderiguez person."

"And what makes you think that?"

"He told me so."

"Who told you so?"

"Reginald de Meister."

"What Reginald de Meister?"

"My Reginald de Meister."

"What do you mean, your Reginald de Meister?"

"My *character*, Reginald de Meister."

June got up, indulged in some deep-breathing and then said in a very calm voice, "Let's start all over."

She disappeared for a moment and returned with an aspirin. "Your Reginald de Meister, from your books, told you, in person, he was in love with Letitia Reynolds?"

"That's right."

June swallowed the aspirin.

"Well, I'll explain, June, the way he explained it to me. All characters really exist—at least, in the minds of the authors. But when people really begin to believe in them, they begin to exist in reality, because what people believe in, is, so far as they're concerned, and what is existence anyway?"

June's lips trembled. "Oh, Gramie, please don't. Mother will never let me marry you if they put you in an asylum."

"Don't call me Gramie, June, for God's sake. I tell you he was there, trying to tell me what to write and how to write it. He was almost as bad as you. Aw, come on, Baby, don't cry."

"I can't help it. I always thought you were crazy, but I never thought you were *crazy*!"

"All right, what's the difference? Let's not talk about it, any more. I'm never going to write another mystery novel. After all—" (he indulged in a bit of indignation) —"when it gets so that my own character—my *own* character—tries to tell me what to do, it's going too far."

June looked over her handkerchief. "How do you know it was really de Meister?"

"Oh, golly. As soon as he tapped his Turkish cigarette on the back of his hand and started dropping g's like snowflakes in a blizzard, I knew the worst had come."

The telephone rang. June leaped up. "Don't answer, Graham. It's probably from the asylum. I'll tell them you're not here. Hello. Hello. Oh, Mr. MacDunlap." She heaved a sigh of relief, then covered the mouthpiece and whispered hoarsely, "It might be a trap."

"Hello, Mr. MacDunlap! . . . No, he's not here. . . . Yes, I think I can get in touch with him . . . At Martin's tomorrow, noon . . . I'll tell him . . . With who? . . . With who???" She hung up suddenly.

"Graham, you're to lunch with MacDunlap tomorrow."

"At his expense! Only at his expense!"

Her great blue eyes got greater and bluer, "And Reginald de Meister is to dine with you."

"What Reginald de Meister?"

"Your Reginald de Meister."

"*My* Reg—"

"Oh, Gramie, *don't*. Her eyes misted, "Don't you see, Gramie, now they'll put us both in an insane asylum—and Mr. MacDunlap, too. And they'll probably put us all in the same padded cell. Oh, Gramie, three is such a dreadful crowd."

And her face crumpled into tears.

Grew S. MacDunlap (that the S. stands for "Some" is a vile untruth spread by his enemies) was alone at the table when Graham Dorn entered. Out of this fact, Graham extracted a few fleeting drops of pleasure.

It was not so much, you understand, the presence of MacDunlap that did it, as the absence of de Meister.

MacDunlap looked at him over his spectacles and swallowed a live pill, his favorite sweetmeat.

"Aha. You're here. What is this corny joke you're putting over on me? You had no right to mix me up with a person like de Meister without warning me he was real. I might have taken precautions. I could have hired a bodyguard. I could have bought a revolver."

"He's *not* real. God damn it! Half of him was *your* idea.

"That, returned MacDunlap with heat, "is libel. And what do you mean, he's not real? When he introduced himself, I took three liver pills at once and he didn't disappear. Do you know what three pills are? Three pills, the kind I've got (the doctor should only drop dead), could make an elephant disappear—if he weren't real. I *know*."

Graham said wearily, "Just the same, he exists only in my mind,"

"In your mind, I know he exists. Your mind should be investigated by the Pure Food and Drugs Act."

The several polite rejoinders that occurred simultaneously to Graham were dismissed almost immediately as containing too great a proportion of pithy Anglo-Saxon expletives. After all—ha, ha—a publisher is a publisher however Anglo-Saxony he may be.

Graham said, "The question arises, then, how we're to get rid of de Meister."

"Get rid of de Meister?" MacDunlap jerked the glasses

off his nose in his sudden start, and caught them in one hand. His voice thickened with emotion. "Who wants to get rid of him?"

"Do you want him around?"

"God forbid," MacDunlap said between shudders. "Next to him, my brother-in-law is an angel."

"He has no business outside my books."

"For my part, he has no business inside them. Since I started reading your manuscripts, my doctor added kidney pills and cough syrups to my medicines." He looked at his watch, and took a kidney pill. "My worst enemy should be a book publisher only a year."

"Then why," asked Graham patiently, "don't you want to get rid of de Meister?"

"Because he is publicity."

Graham stared blankly.

"Look! What other writer has a real detective? All the others are fictional. Everyone know that. But yours—*yours* is real. We can let him solve cases and have big newspaper writeups. He'll make the Police Department look silly. He'll make—"

"That," interrupted Graham, categorically, "is by all odds the most obscene proposal I have ever had my ears manured with."

"It will make money."

"Money isn't everything."

"Name one thing it isn't . . . Shh!" He kicked a near-fracture into Graham's left ankle and rose to his feet with a convulsive smile, "Mr. de Meister!"

"Sorry, old dear," came a lethargic voice. "Couldn't quite make it, you know. Loads of engagements. Must have been most borin' for you."

Graham Dorn's ears quivered spasmodically. He looked over his shoulder and reeled backward as far as a person could reel while in a sitting position. Reginald de Meister had sprouted a monocle since his last visitation, and his monocular glance was calculated to freeze blood.

De Meister's greeting was casual. "My dear Watson! So glad to meet you. Overjoyed deucedly."

"Why don't you go to hell?" Graham asked curiously.

"My dear fellow. Oh, my dear fellow."

MacDunlap cackled, "That's what I like. Jokes! Fun! Makes everything pleasant to start with. Now shall we get down to business?"

"Certainly. The dinner is on the way, I trust? Then I'll just order a bottle of wine. The usual, Henry." The waiter ceased hovering, flew away, and skimmed back with a bottle that opened and gurgled into a glass.

De Meister sipped delicately, "So nice of you, old chap, to make me a habitué of this place in your stories. It holds true even now, and it is most convenient. The waiters all know me. Mr. MacDunlap, I take it you have convinced Mr. Dorn of the necessity of continuing the de Meister stories."

"Yes," said MacDunlap.

"No," said Graham.

"Don't mind him," said MacDunlap. "He's temperamental. You know these authors."

"Don't mind him," said Graham. "He's microcephalic. You know these publishers."

"Look, old chappie. I take it MacDunlap hasn't pointed out to you the unpleasanter side of acting stubborn."

"For instance what, old stinkie?" asked Graham, courteously.

"Well, have you ever been haunted?"

"Like coming behind me and saying, Boo!"

"My dear fellow, I say. I'm much more subtle than that. I can really haunt one in modern, up-to-date methods. For instance, have you ever had your individuality submerged?"

He snickered.

There was something familiar about that snicker. Graham suddenly remembered. It was on page 103 of *Murder Rides the Range:*

> *His lazy eyelids flicked down and up. He laughed lightly and melodiously, and though he said not a word, Hank Marslowe cowered. There was hidden menace and hidden power in that light laugh, and somehow the burly rancher did not dare reach for his guns.*

To Graham it still sounded like a nasty snicker, but he cowered, and did not dare reach for his guns.

MacDunlap plunged through the hole the momentary silence had created.

"You see, Graham. Why play around with ghosts? Ghosts aren't reasonable things. They're not *human!* If it's more royalties, you want—"

Graham fired up. "Will you refrain from speaking of

money? From now on, I write only great novels of tearing human emotions."

MacDunlap's flushed face changed suddenly.

"No," he said.

"In fact, to change the subject just a moment—" and Graham's tone became surpassingly sweet, as the words got all sticky with maple syrup—"I have a manuscript here for you to look at."

He grasped the perspiring MacDunlap by the lapel firmly. "It is a novel that is the work of five years. A novel that will grip you with its intensity. A novel that will shake you to the core of your being. A novel that will open a new world. A novel that will—"

"No," said MacDunlap.

"A novel that will blast the falseness of this world. A novel that pierces to the truth. A novel—"

MacDunlap, being able to stretch his hand no higher, took the manuscript.

"No," he said.

"Why the bloody hell don't you read it?" inquired Graham.

"Now?"

"Well, start it."

"Look, supposing I read it tomorrow, or even the next day. I have to take my cough syrup now."

"You haven't coughed once since I got here."

"I'll let you know immediately—"

"This," said Graham, "is the first page. Why don't you begin it? It will grip you instantly."

"MacDunlap read two paragraphs and said, "Is this laid in a coal-mining town?"

"Yes."

"Then I can't read it. I'm allergic to coal dust."

"But it's not real coal dust, MacIdiot."

"That," pointed out MacDunlap, "is what you said about de Meister."

Reginald de Meister tapped a cigarette carefully on the back of his hand in a subtle manner which Graham immediately recognized as betokening a sudden decision.

"That is all devastatin'ly borin', you know. Not quite gettin' to the point, you might say. Go ahead, MacDunlap, this is no time for half measures."

MacDunlap girded his spiritual loins and said, "All right Mister Dorn, with you it's no use being nice. Instead of de Meister, I'm getting coal dust. Instead of the best publicity in fifty years, I'm getting social significance. All right, Mister Smartaleck Dorn, if in one week you don't come to terms with me, *good* terms, you will be blacklisted in every reputable publishing firm in the United States and foreign parts." He shook his finger and added in a shout, "Including Scandinavian."

Graham Dorn laughed lightly, "Pish," he said, "tush. I happen to be an officer of the Author's Union, and if you try to push me around I'll have *you* blacklisted. How do you like that?"

"I like it fine. Because supposing I can prove you're a plagiarist."

"Me," gasped Graham, recovering narrowly from merry suffocation. "Me, the most original writer of the decade."

"Is that so? And maybe you don't remember that in each case you write up, you casually mention de Meister's notebooks on previous cases."

"So what?"

"So he has them. Reginald, my boy, show Mister Dorn your notebook of your last case. —You see that. That's *Mystery of the Milestones* and it has, in detail, every incident in your book—and dated the year before the book was published. Very authentic."

"Again so what?"

"Have you maybe got the right to copy his notebook and call it an original murder mystery?"

"Why, you case of mental poliomyelitis, that notebook is my invention."

"Who says so? It's in de Meister's handwriting, as any expert can prove. And maybe you have a piece of paper, some little contract or agreement, you know, that gives you the right to use his notebooks?"

"How can I have an agreement with a mythical personage?"

"What mythical personage?"

"You and I know de Meister doesn't exist."

"Ah, but does the jury know? When I testify that I took three strong liver pills and he didn't disappear, what twelve men will say he doesn't exist?"

"This is blackmail."

"Certainly. I'll give you a week. Or in other words, seven days."

Graham Dorn turned desperately to de Meister. "You're in on this, too. In my books I give you the keenest sense of honor. Is this honorable?"

De Meister shrugged. "My dear fellow. All this—and haunting, too."

Graham rose.

"Where are you going?"

"Home to write you a letter." Graham's brows beetled defiantly. "And this time I'll mail it. I'm not giving in. I'll fight to the last ditch. And, de Meister, you let loose with one single little haunt and I'll rip your head out of its socket and spurt the blood all over MacDunlap's new suit."

He stalked out, and as he disappeared through the door, de Meister disappeared through nothing at all.

MacDunlap let out a soft yelp and then took a liver pill, a kidney pill, and a tablespoon of cough syrup in rapid succession.

Graham Dorn sat in June's front parlor, and having long since consumed his fingernails, was starting on the first knuckles.

June, at the moment, was not present, and this, Graham felt, was just as well. A dear girl; in fact, a dear, sweet girl. But his mind was not on her.

It was concerned instead with a miasmic series of flashbacks over the preceding six days:

—Say, Graham, I met your side-kick at the club yesterday. You know, de Meister. Got an awful shock. I always had the idea he was a sort of Sherlock Holmes that didn't exist. That's one on me, boy. Didn't know—Hey, where are you going?"

—Hey, Dorn, I hear your boss de Meister is back in town. Ought to have material for more stories soon. You're lucky you've got someone to grind out your plots ready-made— Huh? Well, good-bye."

—Why, Graham, darling, wherever were you last night? Ann's affair didn't get *anywhere* without you; or at least, it wouldn't have, if it hadn't been for Reggie de Meister. He asked after you; but then, I guess he felt lost without his Watson. It must feel wonderful to Watson for such—*Mister* Dorn! And the same to you, sir!

—You put one over on me. I thought you made up those wild things. Well, truth is stranger than fiction, ha, ha!

—Police officials deny that the famous amateur criminologist Reginald de Meister had interested himself in this case. Mr. de Meister himself could not be reached by our reporters for comment. Mr. de Meister is best known to the public for his brilliant solutions to over a dozen crimes, as chronicled in fiction form by his so-called "Watson," Mr. Grayle Doone.

Graham quivered and his arms trembled in an awful desire for blood. De Meister was haunting him—but good. He was losing his individuality, exactly as had been threatened.

It gradually dawned upon Graham that the monotonous ringing noise he heard was not in his head, but, on the contrary, from the front door.

Such seemed likewise the opinion of Miss June Billings, whose piercing call shot down the stairs and biffed Graham a sharp uppercut to the ear-drums.

"Hey, dope, see who's at the front door, before the vibration tears the house down. I'll be down in half an hour."

"Yes, dear!"

Graham shuffled his way to the front door and opened it.

"Ah, there, Greetin's," said de Meister, and brushed past.

Graham's dull eyes stared, and then fired high, as an animal snarl burst from his lips. He took up that gorilla posture, so comforting to red-blooded American males at moments like this, and circled the slightly-confused detective.

"My dear fellow, are you ill?"

"I," explained Graham, "am not ill, but you will soon be past all interest in that, for I am going to bathe my hands in your heart's reddest blood."

"But I say, you'll only have to wash them afterwards. It would be such an obvious clue, wouldn't it?"

"Enough of this gay banter. Have you any last words?"

"Not particularly."

"It's just as well. I'm not interested in your last words."

He thundered into action, bearing down upon the unfortunate de Meister like a bull elephant. De Meister faded to the left, shot out an arm and a foot, and Graham described a parabolic arc that ended in the total destruction of an end table, a case of flowers, a fish-bowl, and a five-foot section of wall.

Graham blinked, and brushed away a curious goldfish from his left eyebrow.

"My dear fellow," murmured de Meister, "oh, my dear fellow."

Too late, Graham remembered that passage in *Pistol Parade:*

De Meister's arms were whipcord lightning, as with sure, rapid thrusts, he rendered the two thugs helpless. Not by brute force, but by his expert knowledge of judo, he defeated them easily without hastening his breath. The thugs groaned in pain.

Graham groaned in pain.

He lifted his right thigh an inch or so to let his femur slip back into place.

"Hadn't you better get up, old chap?"

"I will stay here," said Graham with dignity, "and contemplate the floor in profile view, until such time as it suits me or until such time as I find myself capable of moving a muscle. I don't care which. And now, before I proceed to take further measures with you, what the hell do you want?"

Reginald de Meister adjusted his monocle to a nicety. "You know, I suppose, that MacDunlap's ultimatum expires tomorrow?"

"And you and he with it, I trust."

"You will not reconsider."

"Ha!"

"Really," de Meister sighed, "this is borin' no end. You have made things comfortable for me in this world. After all, in your books you've made me well-known in all the clubs and better restaurants, the bosom friend, y'know, of the mayor and commissioner of police, the owner of a Park Avenue penthouse and a magnificent art collection. And it all lingers over, old chap. Really quite affectin'."

"It is remarkable," mused Graham, "the intensity with which I am not listening and the distinctness with which I do not hear a word you say."

"Still," said de Meister, "there is no denyin' my book world suits me better. It is somehow more fascinatin', freer from dull logic, more apart from the necessities of the world. In short, I must go back, and to active participation. You have till tomorrow!"

Graham hummed a gay little tune with flat little notes.

"Is this a new threat, de Meister?"

"It is the old threat intensified. I'm going to rob you of every vestige of your personality. And eventually public opinion will force you to write as, to paraphrase you, de Meister's Compleat Stooge. Did you see the name the newspaper chappies pinned on you today, old man?"

"Yes, Mr. Filthy de Meister, and did you read a half-column item on page ten in the same paper. I'll read it *for* you: 'Noted Criminologist in 1-A. Will be inducted shortly draft board says.' "

For a moment, de Meister said and did nothing. And then one, after another, he did the following things: removed his monocle slowly, sat down heavily, rubbed his chin abstractedly, and lit a cigarette after long and careful tamping. Each of these, Graham Dorn's trained authorial eye recognized as singly representing perturbation and distress on the part of his character.

And never, in any of his books, did Graham remember a time when de Meister had gone through all four consecutively.

Finally, de Meister spoke, "Why you had to bring up draft registrations in your last book, I really don't know. This urge to be topical; this fiendish desire to be up to the minute with the news is the curse of the mystery novel. A true mystery is timeless; should have no relation to current events; should—"

"There is one way," said Graham, "to escape induction—"

"You might at least have mentioned a deferred classification on some vital ground."

"There is one way," said Graham, "to escape induction—"

"Criminal negligence," said de Meister.

"Look! Go back to the books and you'll never be filled with lead."

"Write them and I'll do it."

"Think of the war."

"Think of your ego."

Two strong men stood face to face (or would have, if Graham weren't still horizontal) and neither flinched.

Impasse!

And the sweet, feminine voice of June Billings interrupted and snapped the tension:

"May I ask, Graham Dorn, what you are doing on the floor. It's been swept today and you're not complimenting me by attempting to improve the job."

"I am not sweeping the floor. If you looked carefully," replied Graham gently, "you would see that your own adored fiancé is lying here a mass of bruises and a hotbed of pains and aches."

"You've ruined my end table!"

"I've broken my leg."

"And my best lamp."

"And two ribs."

"And my fishbowl."

"And my Adam's apple."

"And you haven't introduced your friend."

"And my cervical verte—What friend?"

"This friend."

"Friend! Ha!" And a mist came over his eyes. She was so young, so fragile to come into contact with hard, brutal facts of life. "This," he muttered brokenly, "is Reginald de Meister."

De Meister at this point broke a cigarette sharply in two, a gesture pregnant with the deepest emotion.

June said slowly, "Why—why, you're different from what I had thought."

"How had you expected me to look?" asked de Meister, in soft, thrilling tones.

"I don't know. Differently than you do,—from the stories I heard."

"You remind me, somehow, Miss Billings, of Letitia Reynolds."

"I think so. Graham said he drew her from me."

"A very poor imitation, Miss Billings, Devastatin'ly poor."

They were six inches apart now, eyes fixed with a mutual glue, and Graham yelled sharply. He sprang upright as memory smote him a nasty smite on the forehead.

A passage from *Case of the Muddy Overshoe* occurred to him. Likewise one from *The Primrose Murders*. Also one from *The Tragedy of Hartley Manor*, *Death of a Hunter*, *White Scorpion* and, to put it in a small nutshell, from every one of the others.

The passage read:

There was a certain fascination about de Meister that appealed irresistibly to women.

And June Billings was—as it had often, in Graham's idler moments, occurred to him—a woman.

And fascination simple gooed out of her ears and coated the floor six inches deep.

"Get out of this room, June," he ordered.

"I will not."

"There is something I must discuss with Mr. de Meister, man to man. I demand that you leave this room."

"Please go, Miss Billings," said de Meister.

June hesitated, and in a very small voice said, "Very well."

"Hold on," shouted Graham. "Don't let him order you about. I demand that you stay."

She closed the door very gently behind her.

The two men faced each other. There was that in either pair of eyes that indicated a strong man brought to bay. There was stubborn, undying antagonism; no quarter; no compromise. It was exactly the sort of situation Graham Dorn always presented his readers with, when two strong men fought for one hand, one heart, one girl.

The two said simultaneously, "Let's make a deal!"

Graham said, "You have convinced me, Reggie. Our public needs us. Tomorrow I shall begin another de Meister story. Let us shake hands and forget the past."

De Meister struggled with his emotion. He laid his hand on Graham's lapel, "My dear fellow, it is I who have been convinced by your logic. I can't allow you to sacrifice yourself for me. There are great things in you that must be brought out. Write your coal-mining novels. They count, not I."

"I couldn't, old chap. Not after all you've done for me, and all you've meant to me. Tomorrow we start anew."

"Graham, my—my spiritual father, I couldn't allow it. Do you think I have no feelings, *filial* feelings—in a spiritual sort of way."

"But the war, think of the war. Mangled limbs. Blood. All that."

"I must stay. My country needs me."

"But if I stop writing, eventually you will stop existing. I can't allow that."

"Oh, that!" De Meister laughed with a careless elegance. "Things have changed since. So many people believe in my existence now that my grip upon actual existence has become too firm to be broken. I don't have to worry about Limbo any more."

"Oh." Graham clenched his teeth and spoke in searing sibilants: "So that's your scheme, you snake. Do you suppose I don't see you're stuck on June?"

"Look here, old chap," said de Meister haughtily. "I can't permit you to speak slightingly of a true and honest love. I love June and she love me—I know it. And if you're going to be stuffy and Victorian about it, you can swallow some nitro-glycerine and tap yourself with a hammer."

"I'll nitro-glycerine you! Because I'm going home tonight and beginning another de Meister story. You'll be part of it and you'll get back into it, and what do you think of that?"

"Nothing, because you can't write another de Meister story. I'm too real now, and you can't control me just like *that*. And what do you think of that?"

It took Graham Dorn a week to make up his mind what to think of that, and then his thoughts were completely and startlingly unprintable.

In fact, it was impossible to write.

That is, startling ideas occurred to him for great novels, emotional dramas, epic poems, brilliant essays—but he couldn't write anything about Reginald de Meister.

The typewriter was simply fresh out of Capital R's.

Graham wept, cursed, tore his hair, and anointed his finger tips with liniment. He tried typewriter, pen, pencil, crayon, charcoal, and blood.

He could not write.

The doorbell rang, and Graham threw it open.

MacDunlap stumbled in, falling over the first drifts of town paper directly into Graham's arms.

Graham let him drop. "Hah!" he said, with frozen dignity.

"My heart!" said MacDunlap, and fumbled for his liver pills.

"Don't die there," suggested Graham, courteously. "The management won't permit me to drop human flesh into the incinerator."

"Graham, my boy," MacDunlap said, emotionally, "no more ultimatums! No more threats! I come now to appeal to your finer feelings, Graham—" he went through a slight choking interlude— "I love you like a son. This skunk de Meister must disappear. You must write more de Meister stories for my sake. Graham—I will tell you something in private. My wife is in love with this detective. She tells me I am not romantic. I! Not romantic! Can you understand it?"

"I can," was the tragic response. "He fascinates all women."

"With that face? With that monocle?"

"It says so in all my books."

MacDunlap stiffened. "Ah ha. You again. Dope! If only you ever stopped long enough to let your mind know what your typewriter was saying."

"You insisted. Feminine trade." Graham didn't care any more. Women! He snickered bitterly. Nothing wrong with any of them that a block-buster wouldn't fix.

MacDunlap hemmed. "Well, feminine trade. Very necessary. —But Graham, what shall I do? It's not only my wife. She owns fifty shares in MacDunlap, Inc. in her own name. If she leaves me, I lose control. Think of it, Graham. The catastrophe to the publishing world."

"Grew, old chap," Graham sighed a sigh so deep, his toenails quivered sympathetically. "I might as well tell you. June, my fiancée, you know, loves this worm. And he loves her because she is the prototype of Letitia Reynolds."

"The what of Letitia?" asked MacDunlap, vaguely suspecting an insult.

"Never mind. My life is ruined." He smiled bravely and choked back the unmanly tears, after the first two had dripped off the end of his nose.

"My poor boy!" The two gripped hands convulsively.

"Caught in a vise by this foul monster," said Graham.

"Trapped like a German in Russia," said MacDunlap.

"Victim of an inhuman fiend," said Graham.

"Exactly," said MacDunlap. He wrung Graham's hand as if he were milking a cow. "You've got to write de Meister stories and get him back where, next to Hell, he most belongs. Right?"

"Right! but there's one little catch."

"What?"

"I can't write. He's so real now, I *can't* put him into a book."

MacDunlap caught the significance of the massed drifts of used paper on the floor. He held his head and groaned, "My corporation! My wife!"

"There's always the Army," said Graham.

MacDunlap looked up. "What about *Death on the Third Deck,* the novel I rejected three weeks ago?"

"That doesn't count. It's past history. It's already affected him."

"Without being published?"

"Sure. That's the story I mentioned his draft board in. The one that put him in 1-A."

"I could think of better places to put him."

"MacDunlap!" Graham Dorn jumped up, and grappled MacDunlap's lapel. "Maybe it can be revised."

MacDunlap coughed hackingly, and stifled out a dim grunt.

"We can put anything we want into it."

MacDunlap choked a bit.

"We can fix things up."

MacDunlap turned blue in the face.

Graham shook the lapel and everything thereto attached, "Say something, won't you?"

MacDunlap wrenched away and took a tablespoon of cough syrup. He held his hand over his heart and patted it a bit. He shook his head and gestured with his eyebrows.

Graham shrugged. "Well, if you just want to be sullen, go ahead. I'll revise it without you."

He located the manuscript and tried his fingers gingerly on the typewriter. They went smoothly with practically no creaking at the joints. He put on speed, more speed, and then went into his usual race, with the portable jouncing along merrily under the accustomed head of steam.

"It's working," he shouted. "I can't write new stories, but I can revise old, unpublished ones."

MacDunlap watched over his shoulder. He breathed only at odd moments.

"Faster," said MacDunlap, "faster!"

"Faster than thirty-five?" said Graham, sternly. "OPA forbid! Five more minutes."

"Will he be there?"

"He's always there. He's been at her house every evening this week." He spat out the fine ivory dust into which he had ground the last inch of his incisors. "But God help you if your secretary falls down on the job."

"My boy, on my secretary you can depend."

"She's got to read that revision by nine."

"If she doesn't drop dead."

"With my luck, she will. Will she believe it?"

"Every word. She's seen de Meister. She *knows* he exists."

Brakes screeched, and Graham's soul cringed in sympathy with every molecule of rubber frictioned off the tires.

He bounded up the stairs, MacDunlap hobbling after.

He rang the bell and burst in at the door. Reginald de Meister standing directly inside received the full impact of a pointing finger, and only a rapid backward movement of the head kept him from becoming a one-eyed mythical character.

June Billings stood aside, silent and uncomfortable.

"Reginald de Meister," growled Graham, in sinister tones, "prepare to meet your doom."

"Oh, boy," said MacDunlap, "are you going to get it."

"And to what," asked de Meister, "am I indebted for

your dramatic but unilluminatin' statement? Confusin', don't you know." He lit a cigarette with a fine gesture and smiled.

"Hello, Gramie," said June, tearfully.

"Scram, vile woman."

June sniffed. She felt like a heroine out of a book, torn by her own emotions. Naturally, she was having the time of her life.

So she let the tears dribble and looked forlorn.

"To return to the subject, what is this all about?" asked de Meister, wearily.

"I have rewritten *Death on the Third Deck*."

"Well?"

"The revision," continued Graham, "is at present in the hands of MacDunlap's secretary, a girl on the style of Miss Billings, my fiancée that was. That is, she is a girl who aspires to the status of a moron, but has not yet quite attained it. She'll believe every word."

"Well?"

Graham's voice grew ominous, "You remember, perhaps, Sancha Rodriguez?"

For the first time, Reginald de Meister shuddered. He caught his cigarette as it dropped. "She was killed by Sam Blake in the sixth chapter. She was in love with me. Really, old fellow, what messes you get me into."

"Not half the mess you're in now, old chap. Sancha Rodriguez did *not* die in the revision."

"Die!" came a sharp, but clear female voice, "I'll show him if I died. And where have *you* been this last month, you two-crosser?"

De Meister did not catch his cigarette this time. He didn't even try. He recognized the apparition. To an unprejudiced observer, it might have been merely a svelte Latin girl equipped with dark, flashing eyes, and long, glittering fingernails, but to de Meister, it was Sancha Rodriguez—*undead!*

MacDunlap's secretary had read and believed.

"Miss Rodriguez," throbbed de Meister, charmingly, "how fascinatin' to see you."

"*Mrs.* de Meister to you, you double-timer, you two-crosser, you scum of the ground, you scorpion of the grass. And who is this woman?"

June retreated with dignity behind the nearest chair.

Mrs. de Meister," said Reginald pleadingly, and turned helplessly to Graham Dorn.

"Oh, you have forgotten, have you, you smooth talker,

you low dog. I'll show you what it means to deceive a weak woman. I'll make you mince-meat with my fingernails."

De Meister back-pedaled furiously. "But darling—"

"Don't you make sweet talk. What are you doing with this woman?"

"But, darling—"

"Don't give me any explanation. What are you doing with this woman?"

"But darling—"

"Shut up! What are you doing with this woman?"

Reginald de Meister was up in a corner, and Mrs. de Meister shook her fists at him. "Answer me!"

De Meister disappeared.

Mrs. de Meister disappeared right after him.

June Billings collapsed into real tears.

Graham Dorn folded his arms and looked sternly at her.

MacDunlap rubbed his hands and took a kidney pill.

"It wasn't my fault, Gramie," said June. "You said in your books he fascinated all women, so I couldn't help it. Deep inside, I hated him all along. You believe me, don't you?"

"A likely story!" said Graham, sitting down next to her on the sofa. "A likely story. But I forgive you, maybe."

MacDunlap said tremulously, "My boy, you have saved my stocks. Also, my wife, of course. And remember—you promised me one de Meister story each year."

Graham gritted, "Just one, and I'll henpeck him to death, and keep one unpublished story forever on hand, just in case. And you're publishing my novel, aren't you, Grew, old boy?"

"Glug," said MacDunlap.

"Aren't you?"

"Yes, Graham. Of course, Graham, Definitely, Graham. Positively, Graham."

"Then leave us now. There are matters of importance I must discuss with my fiancée."

MacDunlap smiled and tiptoed out the door.

Ah, love, love, he mused, as he took a liver pill and followed it up by a cough-syrup chaser.

TOURING

Gardner Dozois, Jack Dann, and Michael Swanwick

The four-seater Beechwood Bonanza dropped from a gray sky to the cheerless winter runways of Fargo Airport. Tires touched pavement, screeched, and the single-engine plane taxied to a halt. It was seven o'clock in the morning, February 3, 1959.

Buddy Holly duckwalked down the wing and hopped to the ground. It had been a long and grueling flight; his bones ached, his eyes were gritty behind the large, plastic-framed glasses, and he felt stale and curiously depressed. Overnight bag in one hand, laundry sack in the other, he stood beside Ritchie Valens for a moment, looking for their contact. White steam curled from their nostrils. Brown grass poked out of an old layer of snow beside the runway. Somewhere a dog barked, flat and far away.

Behind the hurricane fence edging the field, a stocky man waved both hands overhead. Valens nodded, and Holly hefted his bags. Behind them, J.P. Richardson grunted as he leaped down from the plane.

They walked toward the man across the tarmac, their feet crunching over patches of dirty ice.

"Jack Blemings," the man rasped as he came up to meet them. "I manage the dance hall and the hotel in Moorhead." Thin mustache, thin lips, cheeks going to jowl—Holly had met this man a thousand times before: the stogie in his mouth was inevitable; the sporty plaid hat nearly so. Blemings stuck out a hand, and Holly shuffled his bags awkwardly, trying to free his own hand. "Real pleased to meet you, Buddy," Blemings said. His hand was soggy and boneless. "Real pleased to meet a real artist."

He gestured them into a showroom-new '59 Cadillac. It dipped on its springs as Richardson gingerly collapsed into the backseat. Starting the engine, Blemings leaned over the seat for more introductions. Richardson was blowing his nose but hastily transferred the silk handkerchief into his other hand so that they could shake. His delighted-to-meet-you expression lasted as long as the handshake, then the animation went out of him, and his face slumped back into lines of dull fatigue.

The Cadillac jerked into motion with an ostentatious squeal of rubber. Once across the Red River, which still ran steaming with gunmetal predawn mist, they were out of North Dakota and into Moorhead, Minnesota. The streets of Moorhead were empty—not so much as a garbage truck out yet. "Sleepy little burg," Valens commented. No one responded. They pulled up to an undistinguished six-story brick hotel in the heart of town.

The hotel lobby was cavernous and gloomy, inhabited only by a few tired-looking potted rubber plants. As they walked past a grouping of battered armchairs and sagging sofas toward the shadowy information desk in the back, dust puffed at their feet from the faded gray carpet. An unmoving ceiling fan cast thin-armed shadows across the room, and everything smelled of old cigar butts and dead flies and trapped sunshine.

The front desk was as deserted as the rest of the lobby. Blemings slammed the bell angrily until a balding bored-looking man appeared from the back, moving as though he were swimming through syrup. As the desk clerk doled out room keys, still moving like a somnambulist, Blemings took the cigar out of his mouth and said, "I spoke with your road manager, must've been right after you guys left the Surf Ballroom. Needed his okay for two acts I'm adding to the show." He paused. "S'awright with you, hey?"

Holly shrugged. "It's your show," he said.

Holly unlaced one shoe, letting it drop heavily to the floor. His back ached, and the long, sleepless flight had made his suit rumpled and sour smelling. One last chore and he could sleep: he picked up the bedside telephone and dialed the hotel operator for an outside line so that he could call his wife, Maria, in New York and tell her that he had arrived safely.

The phone was dead; the switchboard must be closed down. He sighed and bent over to pick up his shoe again.

Eight or nine men were standing around the lobby when Holly stepped out of the elevator, husky fellows, southern boys by the look of them. Two were at the front desk, making demands of the clerk, who responded by spreading his arms wide and rolling his eyes upward.

Waiting his turn for service, Holly leaned back against the counter, glancing about. He froze in disbelief. Against all logic, all possibility, Elvis Presley himself was standing not six yards away on the gray carpet. For an instant Holly struggled with amazement. Then a second glance told him the truth.

Last year Elvis had been drafted into the army, depriving his fans of his presence and creating a ready market for those who could imitate him. A legion of Presley impersonators had crowded into the welcoming spotlights of stages across the country, trying vainly to fill the gap left by the King of Rock and Roll.

This man, though, he stood out. At first glance he *was* Elvis. An instant later you saw that he was twenty years too old and as much as forty pounds overweight. There were dissolute lines under his eyes and a weary, dissipated expression on his face. The rigors of being on the road had undone his ducktail so that his hair was an untidy mess, hanging down over his forehead and curling over his ears. He wore a sequined shirt, now wrinkled and sweaty, and a suede jacket.

Holly went over to introduce himself. "Hi," he said, "I guess you're playing tonight's show."

The man ignored his outthrust hand. Dark, haunted eyes bored into Holly's. "I don't know what kind of game you're playing, son," he said. A soft Tennessee accent underlay his words. "But I'm packing a piece, and I know how to use it." His hand darted inside his jacket and emerged holding an ugly-looking .38.

Involuntarily Holly sucked in his breath. He slowly raised his hands shoulder-high and backed away. "Hey, it's, okay," he said. "I was just trying to be friendly." The man's eyes followed his retreat suspiciously, and he didn't reholster the gun until Holly was back at the front desk.

The desk clerk was free now. Holly slid three bills across the counter, saying, "Change please." From the corner of his eyes, he saw the imitation Elvis getting into the elevator, surrounded by his entourage. They were solicitious, almost subservient. One patted the man's back as she shakily recounted his close call. *Poor old man,* Holly thought pityingly. The man was really cracking under the pressures of the road. He'd be lucky to last out the tour.

In the wooden booth across the lobby, Holly dumped his change on the ledge below the phone. He dialed the operator for long distance. The earpiece buzzed, made clicking noises. Then if filled with harsh, actinic static, and the clicking grew faster and louder. Holly jiggled the receiver, racked the phone angrily.

Another flood of musicians and crew coursed through the lobby. Stepping from the booth, ruefully glancing back at the phone, he collided with a small woman in a full-length mink. "Oof," she said and then reached out and gave him a squeeze to show there were no hard feelings. A mobile, hoydenish face grinned up at him.

"Hey, sport," she said brightly. "I *love* that bow tie. And those glasses—! Jesus, you look just like Buddy Holly!"

"I know," he said wryly. But she was gone. He trudged back to the elevators. Then something caught his eye, and he swung about, openly staring. Was that a *man* she was talking to? My God, he had hair down to his shoulders!

Trying not to stare at this amazing apparition, he stepped into the elevator. Back in his room, he stopped only long enough to pick up his bag of laundry before heading out again. He was going to have to go outside the hotel to find a working phone anyway; he might as well fight down his weariness, hunt up a Laundromat, and get his laundry done.

The lobby was empty when he returned through it, and he couldn't even find the desk clerk to ask where the nearest Laundromat was. Muttering under his breath, Holly trudged out of the hotel.

Outside, the sun was shining brilliantly but without warmth from out of a hard, high blue sky. There was still no traffic, no one about on the street, and Holly walked along through an early-morning silence broken only by the squeaking of his sneakers, past closed-up shops and shuttered brownstone houses. He found a Laundromat after a few more blocks, and although it was open, there was no one in there either, not even the inevitable elderly Negro attendant. The rows of unused washing machines glinted dully in the dim light cast by a flyspecked bulb. Shrugging, he dumped his clothes into a machine. The change machine didn't work, of course, but you got used to dealing with things like that on the road, and he'd brought a handkerchief full of change with him.

He got the machine going and then went out to look for a phone.

The streets were still empty, and after a few more blocks it began to get on his nerves. He'd been in hick towns before—had grown up in one—but this was the sleepiest, *deadest* damn town he'd ever seen. There was still no traffic, although there were plenty of cars parked by the curbs, and he hadn't seen another person since leaving the hotel. There weren't even any *pigeons,* for goodness sake!

There was a five-and-dime on the corner, its doors standing open. Holly poked his head inside. The lights were on, but there were no customers, no floorwalkers, no salesgirls behind the counters. True, small-town people weren't as suspicious as folk from the bigger cities—but still, this *was* a business, and it looked as if anyone could just walk in here and walk off with any of the unguarded merchandise. It was gloomy and close in the empty store, and the air was filled with dust. Holly backed out of the doorway, somehow not wanting to explore the depth of the store for the sales personnel who *must* be in there somewhere.

A slight wind had come up now, and it flicked grit against his face and blew bits of scrap paper down the empty street.

He found a phone on the next corner, hunted through his handkerchief for a dime while the wind snatched at the edges of the fabric. The phone buzzed and clicked at him again, and this time there was the faint, high wailing of wind in the wires, an eerie, desolate sound that always made him think of ghosts wandering alone through the darkness. The next phone he found was also dead, and the next.

Uneasily, he picked up his laundry and headed back to the hotel.

The desk clerk was spreading his hands wide in a gesture of helpless abnegation of responsibility when the fat southerner in the sequined shirt leaned forward, poked a hard finger into the clerk's chest, and said softly, "You know who I am, son?"

"Why, of course I do, Mr. Presley," the clerk said nervously. "Yessir, of course I do, sir."

"You say you know who I am, son," Elvis said in a cottony voice that slowly mounted in volume. "If you know who I am, then you *know* why I don't have to stay in a goddamned flophouse like this! Isn't that right? Would you give your mother a room like that? You know goddamned well you wouldn't. Just what are you people thinking of? I'm *Elvis Presley,* and you'd give me a room like that!"

Elvis was bellowing now, his face grown red and mottled, his features assuming that look of sulky, sneering meanness that had thrilled millions. His eyes were hard and bright as glass. As the frightened clerk shrank back, his hands held up now as much in terror as in supplication, Elvis suddenly began to change. He looked at the clerk sadly, as if pitying him, and said, "Son, do you know who I am?"

"Yessir," whispered the clerk.

"Then can't you see it?" asked Elvis.

"See what, sir?"

"That I'm *chosen!* Are you an atheist? Are you a goddamned atheist?" Elvis pounded on the desk and barked, "I'm the star, I've been given that, and you can't soil it, you atheist bastard! You *sonovabitch!"* Now that was the worst thing he could call anyone, and he never, almost never used it, for his mother, may she rest in peace, was holy. *She* had believed in him, had told him that the Lord had chosen *him,* that as long as he sang and believed, the Lord would take care of him. Like this? Is this the way He was going to take care of me?

"I'm the star, and I could *buy* this hotel out of my spare change! Buy it, you hear that?" And even as he spoke, the incongruity of the whole situation hit him, really hit him hard for the first time. It was as though his mind had suddenly cleared after a long, foggy daze, as if the scales had fallen from his eyes.

Elvis stopped shouting and stumbled back from the desk, frightened now, fears and suspicions flooding in on him like the sea. What was he doing *here?* Dammit, he was the King! He's made his comeback, and he'd played to capacity crowds at the biggest concert halls in the country. And now he couldn't even remember how he'd gotten here—he'd been at Graceland, and then everything had gotten all foggy and confused, and the next thing he knew he was climbing out of the bus in front of this hotel with the roadies and the rest of the band. Even if he'd agreed to play this one-horse town, it would have to have been for charity. That's it; it had to be for charity. But then where were the reporters, the TV crews? His coming here would be the biggest damn thing that had ever happened in Moorhead, Minnesota. Why weren't there any screaming crowds being held back by police?

"What in hell's going on here?" Elvis shouted. He snatched out his revolver and gestured to his two bodyguards to close up on either side of him. His gaze darted wildly about the lobby as he tried to look into every corner at once. "Keep your eyes open! There's something funny—"

At that moment Jack Blemings stepped out of his office, shut the door smoothly behind him, and sauntered across the musty old carpet toward them. "Something wrong here, Mr. Presley?"

"Damn *right* there is," Elvis raged, taking a couple of steps toward Blemings and brandishing his gun. "You know how many *years* it's been since I played a tank town like this. I don't know what in hell the Colonel was thinking of to send me down here. I—"

Smiling blandly and ignoring the gun, Blemings reached out and touched Elvis on the chest.

Elvis shuddered and took a lurching step backward, his eyes glazing over. He shook his head, looked foggily around the lobby, glanced down at the gun in his hand as though noticing it for the first time, then holstered it absentmindedly. "Time's the show tonight?" he mumbled.

"About eight, Mr. Presley," Blemings answered, smiling. "You've got plenty of time to relax before then."

Elvis looked around the lobby again, running a hand through his greased-back hair. "Anything to do around here?" he asked, a hint of the old sneer returning .

"We got a real nice bar right over there the other side of the lobby," Blemings said.

"I don't drink," Elvis said sullenly.

"Well, then," Blemings added brightly, "we got some real nice pinball machines in that bar, too."

Shaking his head, Elvis turned and moved away across the lobby, taking his entourage with him.

Blemings went back to his office.

J. P. Richardson had unpacked the Scotch and was going for ice when he saw the whore. There was no mistaking what she was. She was dressed in garish gypsy clothes with ungodly amounts of jewelry about her neck and wrists. Beneath a light blouse her breasts swayed freely—she wasn't even wearing a bra. Richardson didn't have to be told how she had earned the mink coat that was draped over one arm.

"Hey, little sister," Richardson said softly. He was still wearing the white suit that was his onstage trademark, his "Big Bopper" outfit. He looked good in it and knew it. "Are you available?"

"You talking to me, honey?" She spoke defiantly, almost jeeringly, but something in her stance, her bold stare, told him she was ready for almost anything. He discreetly slid a twenty from a jacket pocket, smiled and nodded.

"I'd like to make an appointment," he said, slipping the folded bill into her hand. "That is, if you *are* available now."

She stared from him to the bill and back, a look of utter disbelief on her face. Then, suddenly, she grinned. "Why, 'course I'm available, sugar. What's your room number? Gimme ten minutes to stash my coat, and I'll be right there."

"It's room four-eleven." Richardson watched her flounce down the hall, and, despite some embarrassment, was pleased. There was a certain tawdry charm to her. Probably ruts like a mink, he told himself. He went back to his room to wait.

The woman went straight to the hotel bar, slapping the bill down, and shouted, "Hey, kids, pony up! The drinks are on Janis!"

There was a vague stirring, and three lackluster men eddied toward the bar.

Janis looked about, saw that the place was almost empty. A single drunk sat walleyed at a table, holding onto its edges with clenched hands to keep from falling over. To the rear, almost lost in gloom, a big stud was playing pinball. Two unfriendly types, who looked like bodyguards, stood nearby protecting him from the empty tables. Otherwise— nothing. "Shoulda taken the fat dude up on his offer," she grumbled. "There's nothing happening, *here*." Then, to the bartender, "Make mine a whiskey sour."

She took a gulp of her drink, feeling sorry for herself. The clatter of pinball bells ceased briefly as the stud lost his ball. He slammed the side of the machine viciously with one hand. She swiveled on her stool to look at him.

"Damn," she said to the bartender. "You know, from this angle that dude looks just like *Elvis*."

Buddy Holly finished adjusting his bow tie, reached for a comb, then stopped in midmotion. He stared about the tiny dressing room with its cracked mirror and bare light bulbs, and asked himself, *How did I get here?*

It was no idle, existential question. He really did not know. The last thing he remembered was entering his hotel room and collapsing on the bed. Then—here. There was nothing in between.

A rap at the door. Blemings stuck his head in, the stench of his cigar permeating the room. "Everything okay in here, Mr. Holly?"

"Well," Holly began. But he went no further. What could he say? "How long before I go on?"

"Plenty of time. You might want to catch the opener, though—good act. On in ten."

"Thanks."

Blemings left, not quite shutting the door behind him. Holly studied his face in the mirror. It looked haggard and unresponsive. He flashed a toothy smile but did not feel it. God, he was tired. Being on the road was going to kill him. There had to be a way off the treadmill.

The woman from the hotel leaned into his room. "Hey Ace—you see that Blemings motherfucker anywhere?"

Holly's jaw dropped. To hear that kind of language from a woman—from a *white* woman. "He just went by," he said weakly.

"Shit!" She was gone.

Her footsteps echoed in the hallway, were swallowed up by silence. And that was *wrong*. There should be the murmur and nervous bustle of acts preparing to go on, last-minute errands being run, equipment being tested. Holly peered into the corridor—empty.

To one side, the hall dead-ended into a metal door with a red EXIT sign overhead. Holly went the other way, toward the stage. Just as he reached the wings, the audience burst into prolonged, almost frenzied applause. The Elvis impersonator was striding onstage. It was a great crowd.

But the wings were empty. No stagehands or go-fers, no idlers, nobody preparing for the next set.

"Elvis," spread his legs wide and crouched low, his thick lips curling in a sensual sneer. He was wearing a gold lamé jumpsuit, white scarf about his neck. He moved his guitar loosely, adjusting the strap, then gave his band the downbeat.

*Well it's one for the money
Two for the show
Three to get ready
Now go, cat, go!*

And he was off and running into a brilliant rendition of "Blue Suede Shoes." Not an easy song to do, because the lyrics were laughable. It relied entirely on the music, and it took a real entertainer to make it work.

This guy had it all, though. The jumps, gyrations, and forward thrusts of the groin were stock stuff—but somehow he made them look right. He played the audience, too, and his control was perfect. Holly could see shadowy shapes beyond the glare of the footlights, moving in a more than sexual frenzy, was astonished by their rapturous screams. All this in the first minutes of the set.

He's good, Holly marveled. Why was he wasting that kind of talent on a novelty act? There was a tug at his arm, and he shrugged it off.

The tug came again. "Hey, man," somebody said, and he turned to find himself again facing the woman. Their eyes met, and her expression changed oddly, becoming a mixture of bewilderment and outright fear. "Jesus God," she said in awe. "You are Buddy Holly!"

"You've already told me that," he said, irritated. He wanted to watch the man on stage—who *was* he, any way?—not be distracted by the foul-mouthed and probably not very clean woman.

"No, I mean it—you're *really* Buddy Holly. And that dude on stage"—she pointed—"he's Elvis Presley."

"It's a good act," Holly admitted, "But it wouldn't fool my grandmother. That good ol' boy's forty if he's a day."

"Look," she said. "I'm Janis Joplin. I guess that don't mean nothing to *you,* but—hey, lemme show ya something." She tried to tug him away from the stage.

"I want to see the man's act," he said mildly.

"It won't take a minute, man. And it's important. I swear it. It's—you just gotta see it, is all."

There was no denying her. She led him away, down the corridor to the metal door with its red EXIT sign, and threw it open. "Look!"

He squinted into a dull winter evening. Across a still, car-choked parking lot was a row of faded brick buildings. A featureless gray sky overhung all. "There used ta be a lot more out here," Janis babbled. "All the rest of the town. It all went away. Can you dig it, man? It just all—went away."

Holly shivered. This woman was crazy! "Look, Miss Joplin," he began. Then the buildings winked out of existence.

He blinked. The buildings had not faded away—they had simply ceased to be. As crisply and sharply as if somebody had flipped a switch. He opened his mouth, shut it again.

Janis was talking quietly, fervently. "I don't know what it is, man, but something *very weird* is going down here." Everything beyond the parking lot was a smooth, even gray. Janis started to speak again, stopped, moistened her lips. She looked suddenly hesitant and oddly embarrassed. "I mean, like, I don't know how to break this to ya, Buddy, but you're *dead*. You bought it in a plane crash way back in 'fifty-nine."

"This *is* 'fifty-nine," Holly said absently, looking out across the parking lot, still dazed, her words not really sinking in. As he watched, the cars snapped out of existence row by row, starting with the farthest row, working inward to the nearest. Only the asphalt lot itself remained, and a few bits of litter lying between the painted slots. Holly's groin tightened, and as fear broke through astonishment, he registered Janis's words and felt rage grow alongside fear.

"No, honey," Janis was saying, "I hate to tell ya, but this is 1970." She paused, looking uncertain. "Or maybe not. Ol' Elvis looks a deal older than I remember him being. We must be in the future or something, huh? Some kinda sci-fi trip like that, like on 'Star Trek'? You think we—"

But Holly had swung around ferociously, cutting her off. *"Stop it!"* he said. "I don't know what's going on, what kind of trick you people are trying to play on me, or how you're doing all these things, but I'm not going to put up with any more of—"

Janis put her hand on Holly's shoulder; it felt hot and small and firm, like a child's hand. "Hey, listen," Janis said quietly, cutting him off. "I know this is hard for you to accept, and it is pretty heavy stuff . . . but, Buddy, you're *dead*. I mean, really you are . . . It was about ten years ago, you were on tour, right? And our plane *crashed*, spread you *all* over some farmer's field. It was in all the goddamn papers, you and Ritchie Valens and . . ." She paused, startled and then grinned. "And that fat dude at the hotel, that must've been the *Big Bopper*. Wow! Man, if I'd known *that* I might've taken him up on it. You were all on your way to some diddlyshit hick town like . . ." She stopped, and when she started to speak again, she had gone pale. ". . . like Moorhead, Minnesota. Oh, Christ, I think it *was* Moorhead. Oh, boy, is that spooky . . ."

Holly sighed. His anger had suddenly collapsed, leaving him feeling hollow and confused and tired. He blinked away a memory that wasn't a memory of torn-up black ground and twisted shards of metal. "I don't *feel* dead," he said. His stomach hurt.

"You don't *look* dead, either," Janis reassured him. "But, honey, I mean, you really *were*."

They stood staring out across the now vacant parking lot, a cold, cinder-smelling wind tugging at their clothes and hair. At last, Janis said, her brassy voice gone curiously shy, "You got real famous, ya know, after . . . afterwards. You even influenced, like, the *Beatles* . . . Shit, I forgot—I guess you don't even know who they *are*, do you?" She paused uncomfortably, then said, "Anyway, honey, you got real famous."

"That's nice," Holly said dully.

The parking lot disappeared. Holly gasped and flinched back. Everything was gone. Three concrete steps with an iron pipe railing led down from the door into a vast, unmoving nothingness.

"What a trip," Janis muttered. "What a trip . . ."

They stared at the oozing gray nothingness until it seemed to Holly that it was creeping closer, and then, shuddering, he slammed the door shut.

Holly found himself walking down the corridor, going no place in particular, his flesh still crawling. Janis tagged along after him, talking anxiously. "Ya, know, I can't even really remember how I got to this burg. I was in L.A. the last I remember, but then everything gets all foggy. I thought it was the booze, but now I dunno."

"Maybe you're dead, too," Holly said almost absentmindedly.

Janis paled, but a strange kind of excitement shot through her face, under the fear, and she began to talk faster and faster. "Yeah, honey, maybe I am. I thought of that, too, man, once I saw you. Maybe whoever's behind all this are *magicians,* man, black magicians, and they conjured us all *up.*" She laughed a slightly hysterical laugh. "And you wanna know another weird thing? I can't find any of my sidemen here or roadies or *anybody*, ya know? Valens and the Bopper don't seem to be here either. All of 'em were at the hotel, but backstage here it's just you and me and Elvis and that motherfucker Blemings. It's like *they're* not really interested in the rest of them, right? They were just window dressing, man, but now they don't need 'em anymore, and so they sent them *back*. We're the headline acts, sweetie. Everybody else *they* vanished, just like they vanished the fucking parking lot, right? Right?"

"I don't know," Holly said. He needed time to think. Time alone.

"Or, hey—how about this? Maybe you're *not* dead. Maybe we got nabbed by flying saucers, and these aliens faked our death, right? Snatched you out of your plane, maybe. And they put us together here—wherever here is—not because they dig rock. Shit, they probably can't even *understand* it—but to study us and all that kinda shit. Or maybe it is 1959; maybe we got kidnapped by some time-traveler who's a big rock freak. Or maybe it's a million years in the future, and they've got us all *taped*, see? And they want to hear us; so they put on the tape, and we *think* we're here, only we're not. It's all a recording. Hey?"

"I don't *know*."

Blemings came walking down the corridor, cigar trailing a thin plume of smoke behind him. "Janis, honey! I been beating the bushes for you, sweetie pie. You're on in two."

"Listen, motherfuck," Janis said angrily. "I want a few answers from you!" Blemings reached out and touched her hand. Her eyes went blank, and she meekly allowed him to lead her away.

"A real trouper, hey?" Blemings said cheerfully.

"Hey!" Holly said. But they were already gone.

Elvis laid down his guitar, whipped the scarf from his neck, and mopped his brow with it. He kissed the scarf and threw it into the crowd. The screams reached crescendo pitch as the little girls fought over its possession. With a jaunty wave of one hand, he walked offstage.

In the wings, he doubled over, breathing heavily. Sweat ran out of every pore in his body. He reached out a hand, and no one put a towel in it. He looked up angrily.

The wings were empty, save for a kid in big glasses. Elvis gestured weakly toward a nearby piece of terry cloth. "Towel," he gasped, and the kid fetched it.

Toweling off his face, Elvis threw back his head, began to

catch his breath. He let the cloth slip to his shoulders and for the first time got a good look at the kid standing before him. "You're Buddy Holly," he said. He was proud of how calmly it came out.

"A lot of people have told me that today," Holly said.

The crowd roared, breaking off their conversation. They turned to look. Janis was dancing onstage from the opposite side. Shadowy musicians to the rear were laying down a hot, bluesy beat. She grabbed the microphone, laughed into it.

"Well! Ain't this a kick in the ass? Yeah. Real nice, real nice." There were anxious lines about her eyes, but most of the audience wouldn't be able to see that. "Ya know, I been thinking a lot about life lately. 'Deed I have. And I been thinkin' how it's like one a dem ole-time blues songs. Ya know? I mean, it *hurts* so bad, and it feels so *good!*" The crowd screamed approval. The band kept on laying down the rhythm. "So I got a song here that kind of proves my point."

She swung an arm up and then down, giving the band the beat, and launched into "Heart and Soul."

"Well?" Elvis said. "Give me the message."

Holly was staring at the woman onstage. "I never heard anyone sing like that before," he murmured. Then, "I'm sorry—I don't know what you mean, Mr. Presley."

"Call me Elvis," he said automatically. He felt disappointed. There had been odd signs and omens, and now the spirits of departed rock stars were appearing before him—there really ought to be a message. But it was clear the kid was telling the truth; he looked scared and confused.

Elvis turned on a winning smile and impulsively plucked a ring from one of his fingers. It was a good ring; lots of diamonds and rubies. He thrust it into Holly's hands. "Here, take this. I don't want the goddamned thing anymore, anyway."

Holly squinted at the ring quizzically. "Well, put it on," Elvis snapped. When Holly had complied, he said, "Maybe you'd better tell me what you *do* know."

Holly told his story. "I understand now," Elvis said. "We're caught in a snare and delusion of Satan."

"You think so?" Holly looked doubtful.

"Squat down." Elvis hunkered down on the floor, and after an instant's hesitation, Holly followed suit. "I've got powers," Elvis explained. "The power to heal—stuff like that. Now me and my momma, we were always close. Real close. So she'll be able to help us, if we ask her."

"Your mother?"

"She's in Heaven," Elvis said matter-of-factly.

"Oh," Holly said weakly.

"Now join hands and concentrate real *hard*."

Holly felt embarrassed and uncomfortable. Since he was a good Baptist, which he certainly tried to be, the idea of a backstage seance seemed blasphemous. But Elvis, whether he was real item or not, scared him. Elvis's eyes were screwed shut, and he was saying, "Momma. Can you hear me, Momma?" over and over in a fanatic drone.

The seance seemed to go on for hours. Holly suffering through it in mute misery, listening as well as he could to Janis, as she sung her way through number after amazing number. And finally she was taking her last bows, crowing "Thank you, thank you" at the crowd.

There was a cough at his shoulder and a familiar stench of tobacco. Holly looked up. "You're on," Blemings said. He touched Holly's shoulder.

Without transition, Holly found himself onstage. The audience was noisy and enthusiastic, a good bunch. A glance to the rear, and he saw that the backup musicians were not his regular sidemen. They stood in shadow, and he could not see their faces.

But the applause was long and loud, and it crept up under his skin and into his veins, and he knew he had to play *something*. "Peggy Sue," he called to the musicians, hoping they knew the number. When he started playing his guitar, they were right with him. Tight. It was a helluva good backup band; their playing had bone and sinew to it. The audience was on its feet now, bouncing to the beat.

He gave them "Rave On," "Maybe Baby," "Words of Love," and "That'll be the Day," and the audience yelped and howled like wild beasts, but when he calld out "Not Fade Away" to the musicians, the crowd quieted, and he felt special, higher tension come into the hall. The band did a good, strong, intro, and he began singing.

I wanna tell you how it's gonna be
You're gonna give your love to me

He had never felt the music take hold of him this immediately, this strongly, and he felt a surge of exhilaration that seemed to instantly communicate itself to the audience and be reflected back at him redoubled, bringing them all up to a deliriously high level of intensity. Never had he performed better. He glanced offstage, saw that Janis was swaying to the beat, slapping a hand against her thigh. Even Elvis was following the music, caught up in it, grinning broadly and clapping his ring-studded hands.

For love is love and not fade away.

Somewhere to the rear, one of the ghostly backup musicians was blowing blues harmonica, as good as any he'd ever heard.

There was a flash of scarlet, and Janis had run onstage. She grabbed a free mike, and joined him in the chorus. When they reached the second verse, they turned to face each other and began trading off lines. Janis sang:

My love's bigger than a Cadillac

and he responded. His voice was flat next to hers. He couldn't give the words the emotional twist she could, but their voices synched, they meshed, they work together perfectly.

When the musical break came, somebody threw Janis a tambourine so she could stay onstage, and she nabbed it out of the air. Somebody else kicked a bottle of Southern Comfort across the stage and she stopped it with her foot, lifted it, downed a big slug. Holly was leaping into the air, doing splits using every trick of an old rocker's repertoire, and miraculously he felt he could keep on doing so forever, could stretch the break out to infinity if he tried.

Janis beckoned widely toward the wings. "Come on out," she cried into the microphone, "Come on."

To a rolling avalanche of applause, Elvis strode onstage. He grabbed a guitar and strapped it on, taking a stance behind Holly. "You don't mind?" he mumbled.

Holly grinned.

They went into the third verse in unison. Standing between the other two, Holly felt alive and holy and—better than either alive or holy—*right*. They were his brother and sister. They were in tune; he could not have sworn which body was his.

Well, love is love and not fade away

Elvis was wearing another scarf. He whipped it off, mopped his brow, and went to the footlights to dangle it into the crowd. Then he retreated as fast as if he'd been bitten by a snake.

Holly saw Elvis talking to Janis, frantically waving an arms at the crowd beyond the footlights. She ignored him, shrugging off his words. Holly squinted, could not make out a thing in the gloom.

Curious, he duckwalked to the edge of the stage, peered beyond.

Half the audience was gone. As he watched, the twenty people farthest from the stage snapped out of existence. Then another twenty. And another.

The crowd noise continued undiminished, the clapping and whopping and whistling, but the audience was *gone* now—except for Blemings, who sat alone in the exact center of the empty theater. He was smiling faintly at them, a smile that could have meant anything, and as Holly watched, he began softly, politely, to applaud.

Holly retreated backstage, pale, still playing automatically. Only Janis was singing now.

Not fade away

Holly glanced back at the musicians, saw first one, then another, cease to exist. Unreality was closing in on them. He stared into Elvis's face, and for an instant saw mirrored there the fear he felt.

Then Elvis threw back his head and laughed and was singing into his mike again. Holly gawked at him in disbelief.

But the *music* was right, and the *music* was good, and while all the rest—audience, applause, someplace to go when the show was over—was nice, it wasn't necessary. Holly glanced both ways and saw that he was not the only one to understand this. He rejoined the chorus.

Janis was squeezing the microphone tight, singing, when the last sideman blinked out. The only backup now came from Holly's guitar—Elvis had discarded his. She knew it was only a matter of minutes before the nothingness reached them, but it didn't really matter. *The music's all that matters*, she thought. *It's all that made any of it tolerable, anyway. She sang.*

Not fade away

Elvis snapped out. She and Holly kept on singing.

If anyone out there is listening, she thought. *If you can read my mind or some futuristic bullshit like that—I just want you to know that I'd do this again anytime. You want me, you got me.*

Holly disappeared. Janis realized that she had only seconds to go herself, and she put everything she had into the last repetition of the line. She wailed out her soul and a little bit more. *Let it echo after I'm gone,* she thought. *Let it hang on thin air.* And as the last fractional breath of music left her mouth, she felt something seize her, prepare to turn her off.

Not fade away

It had been a good session.

THE WIND IN THE ROSE-BUSH

by Mary Wilkins Freeman

Ford Village has no railroad station, being on the other side of the river from Porter's Falls, and accessible only by the ford which gives it its name, and a ferry line.

The ferry-boat was waiting when Rebecca Flint got off the train with her bag and lunch basket. When she and her small trunk were safely embarked she sat stiff and straight and calm in the ferry-boat as it shot swiftly and smoothly across stream. There was a horse attached to a light country wagon on board, and he pawed the deck uneasily. His owner stood near, with a wary eye upon him, although he was chewing, with as dully reflective an expression as a cow. Beside Rebecca sat a woman of about her own age, who kept looking at her with furtive curiosity; her husband, short and stout and saturnine, stood near her. Rebecca paid no attention to either of them. She was tall and spare and pale, the type of a spinster, yet with rudimentary lines and expressions of matronhood. She all unconsciously held her shawl, rolled up in a canvas bag, on her left hip, as if it had been a child. She wore a settled frown of dissent at life, but it was the frown of a mother who regarded life as a froward child, rather than as an overwhelming fate.

The other woman continued staring at her; she was mildly stupid, except for an over-developed curiosity which made her at times sharp beyond belief. Her eyes glittered, red spots came on her flaccid cheeks; she kept opening her mouth to speak, making little abortive motions. Finally she could endure it no longer; she nudged Rebecca boldly.

"A pleasant day," said she.

Rebecca looked at her and nodded coldly.

"Yes, very," she assented.

"Have you come far?"

"I have come from Michigan."

"Oh!" said the woman, with awe. "It's a long way," she remarked presently.

"Yes, it is," replied Rebecca, conclusively.

Still the other woman was not daunted; there was something which she determined to know, possibly roused thereto by a vague sense of incongruity in the other's appearance. "It's a long ways to come and leave a family," she remarked with painful slyness.

"I ain't got any family to leave," returned Rebecca shortly.

"Then you ain't——"

"No, I ain't."

"Oh!" said the woman.

Rebecca looked straight ahead at the race of the river.

It was a long ferry. Finally Rebecca herself waxed unexpectedly loquacious. She turned to the other woman and inquired if she knew John Dent's widow who lived in Ford Village. "Her husband died about three years ago," sad she, by way of detail.

The woman started violently. She turned pale, then she flushed; she cast a strange glance at her husband, who was regarding both women with a sort of stolid keenness.

"Yes, I guess I do," faltered the woman finally.

"Well, his first wife was my sister," said Rebecca with the air of one imparting important intelligence.

"Was she?" responded the other woman feebly. She glanced at her husband with an expression of doubt and terror, and he shook his head forbiddingly.

"I'm going to see her, and take my niece Agnes home with me," said Rebecca.

Then the woman gave such a violent start that she noticed it.

"What is the matter?" she asked.

"Nothin', I guess," replied the woman, with eyes on her husband, who was slowly shaking his head, like a Chinese toy.

"Is my niece sick?" asked Rebecca with quick suspicion.

"No, she ain't sick," replied the woman with alacrity, then she caught her breath with a gasp.

"When did you see her?"

"Let me see; I ain't seen her for some little time," replied the woman. Then she caught her breath again.

"She ought to have grown up real pretty, if she takes after my sister. She was a real pretty woman," Rebecca said wistfully.

THE WIND IN THE ROSE-BUSH 87

"Yes, I guess she did grow up pretty," replied the woman in a trembling voice.

"What kind of a woman is the second wife?"

The woman glanced at her husband's warning face. She continued to gaze at him while she replied in a choking voice to Rebecca:

"I—guess she's a nice woman," she replied. "I—don't know, I—guess so. I—don't see much of her."

"I felt kind of hurt that John married again so quick," said Rebecca; "but I suppose he wanted his house kept, and Agnes wanted care. I wasn't so situated that I could take her when her mother died. I had my own mother to care for, and I was school-teaching. Now mother has gone, and my uncle died six months ago and left me quite a little property, and I've given up my school, and I've come for Agnes. I guess she'll be glad to go with me, though I suppose her stepmother is a good woman, and has always done for her."

The man's warning shake at his wife was fairly portentous.

"I guess so," said she.

"John always wrote that she was a beautiful woman," said Rebecca.

Then the ferry-boat grated on the shore.

John Dent's widow had sent a horse and wagon to meet her sister-in-law. When the woman and her husband went down the road, on which Rebecca in the wagon with her trunk soon passed them, she said reproachfully:

"Seems as if I'd ought to have told her, Thomas."

"Let her find it out herself," replied the man. "Don't you go to burnin' your fingers in other folks' puddin', Maria."

"Do you s'pose she'll see anything?" asked the woman with a spasmodic shudder and a terrified roll of her eyes.

"See!" returned her husband with stolid scorn. "Better be sure there's anything to see."

"Oh, Thomas, they say—"

"Lord, ain't you found out that what they say is mostly lies?"

"But if it should be true, and she's a nervous woman, she might be scared enough to lose her wits," said his wife, staring uneasily after Rebecca's erect figure in the wagon disappearing over the crest of the hilly road.

"Wits that so easy upset ain't worth much," declared the man. "You keep out of it, Maria."

Rebecca in the meantime rode on in the wagon, beside a

flaxen-headed, boy, who looked, to her understanding, not very bright. She asked him a question, and he paid no attention. She repeated it, and he responded with a bewildered and incoherent grunt. Then she let him alone, after making sure that he knew how to drive straight.

They had traveled about half a mile, passed the village square, and gone a short distance beyond, when the boy drew up with a sudden Whoa! before a very prosperous-looking house. It had been one of the aboriginal cottages of the vicinity, small and white, with a roof extending on one side over a piazza, and a tiny "L" jutting out in the rear, on the right hand. Now the cottage was transformed by dormer windows, a bay window on the piazzaless side, a carved railing down the front steps, and a modern hard-wood door.

"Is this John Dent's house?" asked Rebecca.

The boy was as sparing of speech as a philosopher. His only response was in flinging the reins over the horse's back, stretching out one foot to the shaft, and leaping out of the wagon, then going around to the rear for the trunk. Rebecca got out and went toward the house. Its white paint had a new gloss; its blinds were an immaculate apple green; the lawn was trimmed as smooth as velvet, and it was dotted with scrupulous groups of hydrangeas and cannas.

"I always understood that John Dent was well-to-do," Rebecca reflected comfortably. "I guess Agnes will have considerable. I've got enough, but it will come in handy for her schooling. She can have advantages."

The boy dragged the trunk up the fine gravel-walk, but before he reached the steps leading up to the piazza, for the house stood on a terrace, the front door opened and a fair, frizzled head of a very large and handsome woman appeared. She held up her black silk skirt, disclosing voluminous ruffles of starched embroidery, and waited for Rebecca. She smiled placidly, her pink, double-chinned face widened and dimpled, but her blue eyes were wary and calculating. She extending her hand as Rebecca climbed the steps.

"This is Miss Flint, I suppose," said she.

"Yes, ma'am," replied Rebecca, noticing with bewilderment a curious expression compounded of fear and defiance on the other's face.

"Your letter only arrived this morning," said Mrs. Dent, in a steady voice. Her great face was a uniform pink, and her china-blue eyes were at once aggressive and veiled with secrecy.

"Yes, I hardly thought you'd get my letter," replied Rebecca. "I felt as if I could not wait to hear from you before I came. I supposed you would be so situated that you could have me a little while without putting you out too much, from what John used to write me about his circumstances, and when I had that money so unexpected I felt as if I must come for Agnes. I suppose you will be willing to give her up. You know she's my own blood, and of course she's no relation to you, though you must have got attached to her. I know from her picture what a sweet girl she must be, and John always said she looked like her own mother, and Grace was a beautiful woman, if she was my sister."

Rebecca stopped and stared at the other woman in amazement and alarm. The great handsome blonde creature stood speechless, livid, gasping, with her hand to her heart, her lips parted in a horrible caricature of a smile.

"Are you sick!" cried Rebecca, drawing near. "Don't you want me to get you some water!"

Then Mrs. Dent recovered herself with a great effort. "It is nothing," she said. "I am subject to—spells. I am over it now. Won't you come in, Miss Flint?"

As she spoke, the beautiful deep-rose colour suffused her face, her blue eyes met her visitor's with the opaqueness of turquoise—with a revelation of blue, but a concealment of all behind.

Rebecca followed her hostess in, and the boy, who had waited quiescently, climbed the steps with the trunk. But before they entered the door a strange thing happened. On the upper terrace, close to the piazza-post, grew a great rose-bush, and on it, late in the season though it was, one small red, perfect rose.

Rebecca looked at it, and the other woman extended her hand with a quick gesture. "Don't you pick that rose!" she brusquely cried.

Rebecca drew herself up with stiff dignity.

"I ain't in the habit of picking other folks' rose without leave," said she.

As Rebecca spoke she started violently, and lost sight of her resentment, for something singular happened. Suddenly the rose-bush was agitated violently as if by a gust of wind, yet it was a remarkably still day. Not a leaf of the hydrangea standing on the terrace close to the rose trembled.

"What on earth—" began Rebecca, then she stopped with a gasp at the sight of the other woman's face. Although a face, it gave somehow the impression of a desperately clutched hand of secrecy.

"Come in!" said she in a harsh voice, which seemed to come forth from her chest with no intervention of the organs of speech. "Come into the house. I'm getting cold out here."

"What makes that rose-bush blow so when there isn't any wind?" asked Rebecca, trembling with vague horror, yet resolute.

"I don't see as it is blowing," returned the woman calmly. And as she spoke, indeed, the bush was quiet.

"It was blowing," declared Rebecca.

"It isn't now," said Mrs. Dent. "I can't try to account for everything that blows out-of-doors. I have too much to do."

She spoke scornfully and confidently, with defiant, unflinching eyes, first on the bush, then on Rebecca, and led the way into the house.

"It looked queer," persisted Rebecca, but she followed, and also the boy with the trunk.

Rebecca entered an interior, prosperous, even elegant, according to her simple ideas. There were Brussels carpets, lace curtains, and plenty of brilliant upholstery and polished wood.

"You're real nicely situated," remarked Rebecca, after she had become a little accustomed to her new surroundings and the two women were seated at the tea-table.

Mrs. Dent stared with a hard complacency from behind her silver-plated service. "Yes, I be," said she.

"You got all the things new?" said Rebecca hesitatingly, with a jealous memory of her dead sister's bridal furnishings.

"Yes," said Mrs. Dent; "I was never one to want dead folks' things, and I had money enough of my own, so I wasn't beholden to John. I had the old duds put up at auction. They didn't bring much."

"I suppose you saved some for Agnes. She'll want some of her poor mother's things when she is grown up," said Rebecca with some indignation.

The defiant stare of Mrs. Dent's blue eyes waxed more intense. "There's a few things up garret," said she.

"She'll be likely to value them," remarked Rebecca. As she spoke she glanced at the window. "Isn't it most time for her to be coming home?" she asked.

"Most time," answered Mrs. Dent carelessly; "but when

she gets over to Addie Slocum's she never knows when to come home."

"Is Addie Slocum her intimate friend?"

"Intimate as any."

"Maybe we can have her come out to see Agnes when she's living with me," said Rebecca wistfully. "I suppose she'll be likely to be homesick at first."

"Most likely," answered Mrs. Dent.

"Does she call you mother?" Rebecca asked.

"No, she calls me Aunt Emeline," replied the other woman shortly. "When did you say you were going home?"

"In about a week, I thought, if she can be ready to go so soon," answered Rebecca with a surprised look.

She reflected that she would not remain a day longer than she could help after such an inhospitable look and question.

"Oh, as far as that goes," said Mrs. Dent, "it wouldn't make any difference about her being ready. You could go home whenever you felt that you must, and she could come afterward."

"Alone?"

"Why not? She's a big girl now, and you don't have to change cars."

"My niece will go home when I do, and not travel alone; and if I can't wait here for her, in the house that used to be her mother's and my sister's home, I'll go and board somewhere," returned Rebecca with warmth.

"Oh, you can stay here as long as you want to. You're welcome," said Mrs. Dent.

Then Rebecca started. "There she is!" she declared in a trembling, exultant voice. Nobody knew how she longed to see the girl.

"She isn't as late as I thought she'd be," said Mrs. Dent, and again that curious, subtle change passed over her face, and again it settled into that stony impassiveness.

Rebecca stared at the door, waiting for it to open. "Where is she?" she asked presently.

"I guess she's stopped to take off her hat in the entry," suggested Mrs. Dent.

Rebecca waited. "Why don't she come? It can't take her all this time to take off her hat."

"For answer Mrs. Dent rose with a stiff jerk and threw open the door.

"Agnes!" she called. "Agnes." Then she turned and eyed Rebecca. "She ain't there."

"I saw her pass the window," said Rebecca in bewilderment.

"You must have been mistaken."

"I know I did," persisted Rebecca.

"You couldn't have."

"I did. I saw first a shadow go over the ceiling, then I saw her in the glass there," —she pointed to a mirror over the sideboard opposite—"and then the shadow passed the window."

"How did she look in the glass?"

"Little and light-haired, with the light hair kind of tossing over her forehead."

"You couldn't have seen her."

"Was that like Agnes?"

"Like enough; but of course you didn't see her. You've been thinking so much about her that you thought you did."

"You thought *you* did."

"I thought I saw a shadow pass the window, but I must have been mistaken. She didn't come in, or we would have seen her before now. I knew it was too early for her to get home from Addie Slocum's, anyhow."

When Rebecca went to bed Agnes had not returned. Rebecca had resolved that she would not retire until the girl came, but she was very tired, and she reasoned with herself that she was foolish. Besides, Mrs. Dent suggested that Agnes might go to the church social with Addie Slocum. When Rebecca suggested that she be sent for and told that her aunt had come, Mrs. Dent laughed meaningly.

"I guess you'll find out that a young girl ain't so ready to leave a sociable, where there's boys, to see her aunt," said she.

"She's too young," said Rebecca incredulously and indignantly.

"She's sixteen," replied Mrs. Dent; "and she's always been great for the boys."

"She's going to school four years after I get her before she thinks of boys," declared Rebecca.

"We'll see," laughed the other woman.

After Rebecca went to bed, she lay awake a long time listening for the sound of girlish laughter and a boy's voice under her window; then she fell asleep.

The next morning she was down early. Mrs. Dent, who kept no servants, was busily preparing breakfast.

"Don't Agnes help you about breakfast?" asked Rebecca.

"No, I let her lay," replied Mrs. Dent shortly.
"What time did she get home last night?"
"She didn't get home."
"What?"
"She didn't get home. She stayed with Addie. She often does."
"Without sending you word?"
"Oh, she knew I wouldn't worry."
"When will she be home?"
"Oh, I guess she'll be along pretty soon."

Rebecca was uneasy, but she tried to conceal it, for she knew of no good reason for uneasiness. What was there to occasion alarm in the fact of one young girl staying overnight with another? She could not eat much breakfast. Afterward she went out on the little piazza, although her hostess strove furtively to stop her.

"Why don't you go out back of the house? It's real pretty—a view over the river," she said.

"I guess I'll go out here," replied Rebecca. She had a purpose: to watch for the absent girl.

Presently Rebecca came hustling into the house through the sitting-room, into the kitchen where Mrs. Dent was cooking.

"That rose-bush!" she gasped.

Mrs. Dent turned and faced her.

"What of it?"

"It's a-blowing."

"What of it?"

"There isn't a mite of wind this morning."

Mrs. Dent turned with an inimitable toss of her fair head. "If you think I can spend my time puzzling over such nonsense as—" she began, but Rebecca interrupted her with a cry and a rush to the door.

"There she is now!" she cried.

She flung the door wide open, and curiously enough a breeze came in and her own gray hair tossed, and a paper blew off the table to the floor with a loud rustle, but there was nobody in sight.

"There's nobody here," Rebecca said.

She looked blankly at the other woman, who brought her rolling-pin down on a slab of pie-crust with a thud.

"I didn't hear anybody," she said calmly.

"I saw somebody pass that window!"

"You were mistaken again."

"I *known* I saw somebody."

"You couldn't have. Please shut that door."

Rebecca shut the door. She sat down beside the window and looked out on the autumnal yard, with its little curve of footpath to the kitchen door.

"What smells so strong of roses in this room?" she said presently. She sniffed hard.

"I don't smell anything but these nutmegs."

"It is not nutmeg."

"I don't smell anything else."

"Where do you suppose Agnes is?"

"Oh, perhaps she has gone over the ferry to Porter's Falls with Addie. She often does. Addie's got an aunt over there, and Addie's got a cousin, a real pretty boy."

"You suppose she's gone over there?"

"Mebbe. I shouldn't wonder."

"When should she be home?"

"Oh, not before afternoon."

Rebecca waited with all the patience she could muster. She kept reassuring herself, telling herself that it was all natural, that the other woman could not help it, but she made up her mind that if Agnes did not return that afternoon she should be sent for.

When it was four o'clock she started up with resolution. She had been furtively watching the onyx clock on the sitting-room mantel; she had timed herself. She had said that if Agnes was not home by that time she should demand that she be sent for. She rose and stood before Mrs. Dent, who looked up coolly from her embroidery.

"I've waited just as long as I'm going to," she said. "I've come 'way from Michigan to see my own sister's daughter and take her home with me. I've been here ever since yesterday—twenty-four hours—and I haven't seen her. Now I'm going to. I want her sent for."

Mrs. Dent folded her embroidery and rose.

"Well, I don't blame you," she said. "It is high time she came home. I'll go right over and get her myself."

Rebecca heaved a sigh of relief. She hardly knew what she had suspected or feared, but she knew that her position had been one of antagonism if not accusation, and she was sensible of relief.

"I wish you would," she said gratefully, and went back to her chair, while Mrs. Dent got her shawl and her little white head-tie. "I wouldn't trouble you, but I do feel as if I couldn't wait any longer to see her," she remarked apologetically.

"Oh, it ain't any trouble at all," said Mrs. Dent as she went out. "I don't blame you; you have waited long enough."

Rebecca sat at the window watching breathlessly until Mrs. Dent came stepping through the yard alone. She ran to the door and saw, hardly noticing it this time, that the rose-bush was again violently agitated, yet with no wind evident elsewhere.

"Where is she?" she cried.

Mrs. Dent laughed with stiff lips as she came up the steps over the terrace. "Girls will be girls," said she. "She's gone with Addie to Lincoln. Addie's got an uncle who's conductor on the train, and lives there, and he got 'em passes, and they're goin' to stay to Addie's Aunt Margaret's a few days. Mrs. Slocum said Agnes didn't have time to come over and ask me before the train went, but she took it on herself to say it would be all right, and—"

"Why hadn't she been over to tell you?" Rebecca was angry, though not suspicious. She even saw no reason for her anger.

"Oh, she was putting up grapes. She was coming over just as soon as she got the black off her hands. She heard I had company, and her hands were a sight. She was holding them over sulphur matches."

"You say she's going to stay a few days?" repeated Rebecca dazedly.

"Yes; till Thursday, Mrs. Slocum said."

"How far is Lincoln from here?"

"About fifty miles. It'll be a real treat to her. Mrs. Slocum's sister is a real nice woman."

"It is goin' to make it pretty late about my goin' home."

"If you don't feel as if you could wait, I'll get her ready and send her on just as soon as I can," Mrs. Dent said sweetly.

"I'm going to wait," said Rebecca grimly.

The two women sat down again, and Mrs. Dent took up her embroidery.

"Is there any sewing I can do for her?" Rebecca asked finally in a desperate way. "If I can get her sewing along some—"

Mrs. Dent arose with alacrity and fetched a mass of white from the closet. "Here," she said, "if you want to sew the lace on this nightgown. I was going to put her to it, but she'll be glad enough to get rid of it. She ought to have this and one more before she goes. I don't like to send her away without some good underclothing."

Rebecca snatched at the little white garment and sewed feverishly.

That night she wakened from a deep sleep a little after midnight and lay a minute trying to collect her faculties and explain to herself what she was listening to. At last she discovered that it was the then popular strains of "The Maiden's Prayer" floating up through the floor from the piano in the sitting-room below. She jumped up, threw a shawl over her nightgown, and hurried downstairs trembling. There was nobody in the sitting-room; the piano was silent. She ran to Mrs. Dent's bedroom and called hysterically:

"Emeline! Emeline!"

"What is it?" asked Mrs. Dent's voice from the bed. The voice was stern but had a note of consciousness in it.

"Who—who was that playing. 'The Maiden's Prayer' in the sitting-room, on the piano?"

"I didn't hear anybody."

"There was some one."

"I didn't hear anything."

"I tell you there was some one. But—*there ain't anybody there.*"

"I didn't hear anything."

"I did—somebody playing 'The Maiden's Prayer' on the piano. Has Agnes got home? I *want to know.*"

"Of course Agnes hasn't got home," answered Mrs. Dent with rising inflection. "Be you gone crazy over that girl? The last boat from Porter's Falls was in before we went to bed. Of course she ain't come."

"I heard—"

"You were dreaming."

"I wasn't; I was broad awake."

Rebecca went back to her chamber and kept her lamp burning all night.

The next morning her eyes upon Mrs. Dent were wary and blazing with suppressed excitement. She kept opening her mouth as if to speak, then frowning, and setting her lips hard. After breakfast she went upstairs, and came down presently with her coat and bonnet.

"Now, Emeline," she said, "I want to know where the Slocums live."

Mrs. Dent gave a strange, long, half-lidded glance at her. She was finishing her coffee.

"Why?" she asked.

"I'm going over there and find out if they have heard anything from her daughter and Agnes since they went away. I don't like what I heard last night."

"You must have been dreaming."

"It don't make any odds whether I was or not. Does she play 'The Maiden's Prayer' on the piano? I want to know."

"What if she does? She plays it a little, I believe. I don't know. She don't half play it, anyhow; she ain't got an ear."

"That wasn't half played last night. I don't like such things happening. I ain't superstitious, but I don't like it. I'm going. Where do the Slocum's live?"

"You go down the road over the bridge past the old grist mill, then you turn to the left; it's the only house for half a mile. You can't miss it. It has a barn with a ship in full sail on the cupola."

"Well, I'm going. I don't feel easy."

About two hours later Rebecca returned. There were red spots on her cheeks. She looked wild. "I've been there," she said, "and there isn't a soul at home. Something *has* happened."

"What has happened?"

"I don't know. Something. I had a warning last night. There wasn't a soul there. They've been sent for to Lincoln."

"Did you see anybody to ask?" asked Mrs. Dent with thinly concealed anxiety.

"I asked the woman that lives on the turn of the road. She's stone deaf. I suppose you know. She listened while I screamed at her to know where the Slocums were, and then she said, 'Mrs. Smith don't live here.' I didn't see anybody on the road, and that's the only house. What do you suppose it means?"

"I don't suppose it means much of anything," replied Mrs. Dent coolly. "Mr. Slocum is conductor on the railroad, and he'd be away anyway, and Mrs. Slocum often goes early when he does, to spend the day with her sister in Porter's Falls. She'd be more likely to go away than Addie."

"And you don't think anything has happened?" Rebecca asked with diminishing distrust before the reasonableness of it.

"Land, no!"

Rebecca went upstairs to lay aside her coat and bonnet. But she came hurrying back with them still on.

"Who's been in my room?" she gasped. Her face was pale as ashes.

Mrs. Dent also paled as she regarded her.

"What do you mean?" she asked slowly.

"I found when I went upstairs that—little nightgown of—Agnes's on—the bed, laid out. It was—*laid out*. The sleeves were folded across the bosom and there was that little red rose between them. Emeline what is it? Emeline, what's the matter? Oh!"

Mrs. Dent was struggling for breath in great, choking gasps. She clung to the back of a chair. Rebecca, trembling herself so she could scarcely keep on her feet, got her some water.

As soon as she recovered herself Mrs. Dent regarded her with eyes full of the strangest mixture of fear and horror and hostility.

"What do you mean talking so?" she said in a hard voice.

"It *is there*."

"Nonsense. You threw it down and it fell that way."

"It was folded in my bureau drawer."

"It couldn't have been."

"Who picked that red rose?"

"Look on the bush," Mrs. Dent replied shortly.

Rebecca looked at her; her mouth gaped. She hurried out of the room. When she came back her eyes seemed to protrude. (She had in the meantime hastened upstairs, and come down with tottering steps, clinging to the banisters.)

"Now I want to know what all this means?" she demanded.

"What what means?"

"The rose is on the bush, and it's gone from the bed in my room! Is this house haunted, or what?"

"I don't know anything about a house being haunted. I don't believe in such things. Be you crazy?" Mrs. Dent spoke with gathering force. The color flashed back to her cheeks.

"No," said Rebecca shortly. "I ain't crazy yet, but I shall be if this keeps on much longer. I'm going to find out where that girl is before night."

Mrs. Dent eyed her.

"What be you going to do?"

"I'm going to Lincoln."

A faint triumphant smile overspread Mrs. Dent's large face.

"You can't," said she; "there ain't any train."

"No train?"

"No; there ain't any afternoon train from the Falls to Lincoln."

"Then I'm going over to the Slocums' again to-night."

However, Rebecca did not go; such a rain came up as deterred even her resolution, and she had only her best dresses with her. Then in the evening came the letter from the Michigan village which she had left nearly a week ago. It was from her cousin, a single woman, who had come to keep her house while she was away. It was a pleasant unexciting letter enough, all the first of it, and related mostly how she missed Rebecca; how she hoped she was having pleasant weather and kept her health; and how her friends, Mrs. Greenaway, had come to stay with her since she had felt lonesome the first night in the house; how she hoped Rebecca would have no objections to this, although nothing had been said about it, since she had not realized that she might be nervous alone. The cousin was painfully conscientious, hence the letter. Rebecca smiled in spite of her disturbed mind as she read it, then her eye caught the postscript. That was in a different hand, purporting to be written by the friend, Mrs. Hannah Greenaway, informing her that the cousin had fallen down the cellar stairs and broken her hip, and was in a dangerous condition, and begging Rebecca to return at once, as she herself was rheumatic and unable to nurse her properly, and no one else could be obtained.

Rebecca looked at Mrs. Dent, who had come to her room with the letter quite late; it was half-past nine, and she had gone upstairs for the night.

"Where did this come from?" she asked.

"Mr. Amblecrom brought it," she replied.

"Who's he?"

"The postmaster. He often brings the letters that come on the late mail. He knows I ain't anybody to send. He brought yours about your coming. He said he and his wife came over on the ferry-boat with you."

"I remember him," Rebecca replied shortly. "There's bad news in this letter."

Mrs. Dent's face took on an expression of serious inquiry.

"Yes, my Cousin Harriet has fallen down the cellar stairs—

they were always dangerous—and she'd broken her hip, and I've got to take the first train home to-morrow."

"You don't say so. I'm dreadfully sorry."

"No, you ain't sorry!" said Rebecca, with a look as if she leaped. "You're glad. I don't know why, but you're glad. You've wanted to get rid of me for some reason ever since I came. I don't know why. You're a strange woman. Now you've got your way, and I hope you're satisfied."

"How you talk."

Mrs. Dent spoke in a faintly injured voice, but there was a light in her eyes.

"I talk the way it is. Well, I'm going to-morrow morning, and I want you, just as soon as Agnes Dent comes home, to send her out to me. Don't you wait for anything. You pack what clothes she'd got, and don't wait even to mend them, and you buy her ticket. I'll leave the money, and you send her along. She don't have to change cars. You start her off, when she gets home, on the next train!"

"Very well," replied the other woman. She had an expression of covert amusement.

"Mind you do it."

"Very well, Rebecca."

Rebecca started on her journey the next morning. When she arrived, two days later, she found her cousin in perfect health. She found, moreover, that the friend had not written the postscript in the cousin's letter. Rebecca would have returned to Ford Village the next morning, but the fatigue and nervous strain had been too much for her. She was not able to move from her bed. She had a species of low fever induced by anxiety and fatigue. But she could write, and she did, to the Slocums, and she received no answer. She also wrote to Mrs. Dent; she even sent numerous telegrams, with no response. Finally she wrote to the postmaster, and an answer arrived by the first possible mail. The letter was short, curt and to the purpose. Mr. Amblecrom, the postmaster, was a man of few words, and especially wary as to his expressions in a letter.

"Dear madam," he wrote, "your favour rec'ed. No Slocums in Ford's Village. All dead. Addie ten years ago, her mother two years later her father five. House vacant. Mrs. John Dent said to have neglected stepdaughter. Girl was sick. Medicine not given. Talk of taking action. Not enough evidence. House said to be haunted. Strange sights and sounds. Your niece, Agnes Dent, died a year ago, about this time.

"Yours truly,
"THOMAS AMBLECROM."

COME DANCE WITH ME ON MY PONY'S GRAVE

by Charles L. Grant

November, and an aged slate sky; a wind snapping across the fields like a bullwhip and cracking around a golden brown house that squatted warmly on the grey landscape.

Aaron, huddled in a winter-worn and crimson jacket, was slumped, seemingly relaxed, against the jamb of the open front door, his hands flat in his pockets. His eyes were narrowed against the wind, and they shifted quickly along the partially wooded horizon, blurring the Dakota spruce and pine to a green-and-grey smear of almost preternatural fear. Behind him the house was empty, and silent. There was only the wind and an occasional wooden creak.

He shivered.

Suddenly an explosive gust caught him unprepared and shoved him off balance; a magazine was blown to the floor in the living room, and a shade snapped against glass. Reluctantly he closed the door and cut off the warmth from his back. His lips twisted into a half smile. A good thing Miriam's not here, he thought as his mind mimicked her laughing scold: Aaron Jackoson, what do you think we are—Eskimos? Just look at my curtains blown all over, and the cold, Aaron, the cold . . . He grinned, shook his head and closed his eyes briefly to allow her face to flash before him reassuringly. The wind gusted again, and his smile faded. Come home, Miriam, he thought (nearly prayed), come home soon—the boy frightens me yet.

Then he resettled himself to wait, arms folded and pressed tightly against his chest. He squinted into the cold, his eyes moving, moving as they had once been trained to do, watching and waiting . . .

. . . under a multigreen canopy of broad leaves, twisted vines and knee-high, waist-high brush beside the paths he and his men rarely used as they climbed for hours through the bugs

sweat heat dirt world. A ragged clearing ahead where the village so often visited was hidden, and the smoke-skinned, half-naked Montagnards who gave them the news that the enemy had long since fled—all save one who, this time, belonged to them, not the soldiers. Water, then with iodine tablets to kill the bacteria, and orange flavoring to kill the taste. While he watched the jungle and his men relaxed, finally. And the boy—eight, perhaps nine—stood by a black patch of earth where several men were racing the sun, digging what looked to be a grave. A shout . . .

. . . and Aaron blinked and watch a slight figure break from the trees and zigzag swiftly across the field, arms waving wildly in greeting. He grinned and, pushing himself away from the house, limped heavily toward the fence as grass crackled sharply beneath his feet. He shivered and wondered how the boy had managed to adapt so rapidly to the four seasons so radically different from the hot and not-so-hot of the mountain jungles.

At last the boy reached the yard and with a melodramatic gasp draped himself over the faded white rail, his face darker, but not red, from exertion.

"Hey, dad."

"Hey, yourself."

"Boy, am I . . . bushed?"

Aaron nodded. "Bushed, pooped, beat, tired . . . in fact, you look like all of them rolled into one." He was tempted to ask where his adopted son had been, and thought better of it. "Come on inside, David and get yourself warm. Your mother'll kill me if she finds I let you catch cold the minute she decides to go visiting."

The boy was thirteen and still quite short (would never be much taller), and as he dashed back to the house ahead of his father, his long straight black hair whipped his shoulders and the air, while Aaron watched carefully for hints of the past until he realized what he was doing and scolded himself silently for behaving like a damned fool. The boy, he insisted to his shadow, was an American now. But he could not help the growing feeling that, without Miriam, David thought of him only as the lieutenant who took him away. He glanced back at the trees and shut the door.

"Sit down, dad," David called from the kitchen. "I'll make you some hot tea. Did mother call today?"

"Yes, I'm afraid she already has," he answered. "About ten, ten thirty. You were out with Pinto, I think."

"Nuts."

Aaron laughed and, after shucking his coat, stretched out on the sofa, letting the room draw the cold from his skin to die in the dark glow of the beams and paneled walls. And everywhere, the scent of Miriam.

Then he heard a cup shatter and he sighed when David, none too quietly, began muttering to himself. "Hey, in there," he shouted. "We speak English in this house, remember?"

The boy poked his head out of the kitchen and grinned broadly. "Sorry, dad, but that's all I remember any more."

"The swearing?"

"But, dad, they're the best kind, don't you know? I heard the GIs use them all the time."

There was a sharp silence before David finally giggled and thrust out an open hand. "Look, dad, I was only counting. I don't remember any more than that, honest." He waited a moment, staring, then frowned and disappeared.

Now that's got to be a crime, Aaron thought, recalling all the tedious, impatient hours he had spent scraping together enough of the tribe's language to make himself, and his mission, understood; there were still a few isolated words and phrases that returned to him when he pressed, yet the boy had forgotten a lifetime. So he said. Once, when Aaron had been feeling particularly moody over his crippled leg, he had asked David if he minded being away from his old home, toppled through a sargasso of red tape and interviews into a country and life style as alien to the boy as the jungle was to Aaron. David had smiled, a little softly, and shook his head. But the black eyes were expressionless; they always had been since the death of his father.

"Hey, dad! Quit daydreaming, please? This stuff is hot."

Aaron smiled and took the steaming cup from the offered tray. David sat cross-legged on the rug, watching intently as Aaron tasted the tea and nodded his approval. "Your mother," he said, "will be jealous."

David finally returned the smile, then turned his head toward the bay window as if he were plotting the darkening sky, listening for the invisible wind. He squirmed. Coughed. Aaron amused himself with the boy's impatience as long as he could; then, softly, "Pinto must be starving. Is he on a diet or something?"

And the boy was gone. To a pony named Pinto, horse enough for a youngster who would never be tall, not even average. They had both arrived on the same day and five years later they were inseparable. Wild, Aaron thought. Both of them.

The telephone shrilled. Aaron grunted away a cramp that knifed his mine-shattered leg as he headed into the hallway and picked up the receiver.

"Jackoson, that you?"

Aaron winced. "Yes, Mr. Sorrentino, it's me."

"Damned good thing. Want to tell you those wolves are back again. Went after two of my rams this morning. Saw them. Big as horses they were. Chased them into the woods, I did." Right to my place, Aaron thought bitterly, thanks a lot. "I got a shot at them."

"You what?"

"Said I got a shot at them."

"Damn it, Sorrentino, my boy was playing there today. You know he always—"

"Did I hit him?" The voice was singularly unconcerned.

"Christ, no! If you had, do you think I'd be—"

"Then don't worry about it, Jackoson. I'm a perfect shot. I hit what I aim at. That kid—"

"My son."

"—won't get hurt, don't you worry about that. But one thing, Jackoson . . . I, uh, don't want to make any trouble, you understand, but I wish you would straighten out your kid about where your property ends. Him and that damn pony scare hell out of my sheep."

"If I didn't know you better, Mr. Sorrentino, I'd be tempted to think that you were somehow trying to threaten me."

A raucous laugh and a harsh gasping for breath. Aaron wanted to spit at the phone. "Just wanted you to know, Jackoson, don't get so worked up. You soldier boys get excited too easy."

"I just don't like the tone of your voice, Sorrentino."

"So sue me," Sorrentino said, and hung up.

Aaron breathed deeply and grabbed the edge of the hall table. "I could kill you so easily, Mr. Franklin Sorrentino," he said to the wall. "So goddamned easily."

"Dad?"

Aaron spun around to face the boy standing in the hall . . .

. . . standing by the gash of a grave while the jungle severed the sun's scattered light and a pit fire substituted shadows for trees. Lt. Jackoson shifted uneasily on the ground

and lighted a cigarette as the boy stared at him. There was no recognition in the black bullet eyes though the man and the boy had often played together whenever the squad came to stay and use the friendly village as a base. Now Jackoson saw only a new, weary emptiness, and deeper: a purpose. The grave was for the boy's father, the shaman of the tribe. . . .

. . . the boy's voice was quiet. "I don't like him, dad." The words spun high, and Aaron shivered a remembrance while he stood in the tunnel-dark hall. David moved as silently as he spoke. Even on the Shetland he was noiseless—in the early days, when the boy was still learning, Miriam had said: He's like a ghost, Aaron, and he frightens me. In the early days. There were still remnants of the mountain in him, but Miriam no long saw them. "He's greedy, dad, and doesn't . . . feel for things."

Aaron nodded, just barely stopping himself from patting the boy on the head. He had learned early that "sin" was too weak a word for such a gesture. Instead, he grabbed his shoulders. "Go watch some TV, son. Forget it. It's not worth worrying yourself."

They walked, the son just behind, into the living room and dimmed the lights. Before Aaron switched on the set, David curled into a corner chair where the age in his voice belied his thin body. "Why doesn't he like me, dad?"

Aaron knew this was not a time to smile away a question. Five years before, his greatest fear had been what the other youngsters would think of his adopted son, but the smoke-grey skin and the hint of Polynesia in his features had given him instant acceptance, especially with the girls; David, however, was only always superficially friendly. "I don't know, son. Perhaps he's lonely with no children of his own, and that wife of his is enough for any man.'"

"He thinks I'm different." The tone said: he knows I'm different, and you're afraid that maybe he's right.

"Perhaps."

"I don't like him."

"David, he's not going to be the only one in your life to think you're . . . well, not the same as others. You're quite a unique young man."

"He hates Pinto. He say, last week when he run me away, it was a silly name for a horse. Pinto doesn't like him either. He try to kick his stomach once."

"Oh." Aaron, forgetting to correct the boy's English, thought he was beginning to understand Sorrentino's surliness.

"He missed."

In spite of himself, Aaron said, "Too bad."

The boy laughed quietly.

"Listen, David, Mr. Sorrentino doesn't really understand how you can . . . can *be* with animals. Most boys . . . do you know what rapport means?"

"No, dad, but I think I can make guesses."

"Well, good. Rapport, you see, isn't always explainable. Sometimes it's something that just happens or belongs to a way of life that people just can't grasp. Like . . ." and he stopped, thought and decided not to mention the shaman. "And, if you don't mind me asking," he said instead, falsely lighter, "why did you name him Pinto?"

David laughed again. "It suits him."

"How? He's all brown?"

"It feels right, dad. It suits him. He runs and leaps and . . . he's like me in many ways. His name is right."

"Well, Sorrentino can't understand that, son."

"I know. He doesn't . . . feel. I don't like him."

Aaron frowned in concentration, seeking the speeches that would stifle the hatred he knew the boy was feeling. It was wrong to allow this to fester, wrong not to show the boy that some men must be tolerated, that, as the saying goes, it takes all kinds. He tried, but he took too long.

"I'm going to bed, dad. Good night." David uncurled from the chair, stayed out of the light until his bedroom door closed behind him. Always closed. Sanctum.

Aaron hesitated in following, then sat again. For the first time since they had been together, David had lied to him. So blatantly, in fact, that its very obviousness pained more than the deceit itself. The language. He knew David had not forgotten all but the numbers. Once in a while, from behind the door, a muttering filtered through the house and filled him with dreams. Songs chanted on horseback across the fields and through the half-light in the pines; the whispering to the animals. Black hair and black eyes and a strength in slender arms that contradicted their frailty. Montagnard. Mountain dweller. Outcast.

Christ! he thought and chided himself for allowing his mind to become so morbid. The weather, his leg and Miriam's absence were getting to be too much. He decided to call her first thing in the morning and ask her to cut her visit short. Her mother wasn't that lonely and, he needed her laughter.

He dozed fitfully until the telephone twisted him stiffly from the couch. His watch had stopped. He stood, scratching his head vigorously, then stretched his arms over his head. "All right," he mumbled, "All right, all right, for god's sake." *Daylight*, he thought in amazement. That little dope didn't even wake me so I could sleep in a bed; how the hell did I oversleep? Glancing at the front window, he noticed streaks on the glass and the shimmer of ice on the walk. Rain, freezing rain was the last thing he needed with David pouting and his wife gone. For a moment he was ready to let the phone ring and crawl into bed to hide. The house and that damned phone were making him nervous.

Still rubbing the sleep from his face, he leaned awkwardly against the wall and snatched up the receiver. "Yeah, yeah Jackoson here."

"Aaron, this here is Will."

He stiffened. "Yes, sheriff, what can I do for you?" There were excited noises in the background; a man was bellowing angrily.

"I'm over at the Sorrentino place. You'd better get over here.".

"David?"

"No, nothing's happened to the boy. But Sorrentino accidentally shot the pony. He's dead."

"I'll be right there," No thought, then, only an endless stream of cursing accusations: half in relief for his son's safety, half in anger at the rancher's murder of the boy's pet. His coat, first jamming on its hanger, refused to slide on easily. The pickup stalled twice. He shook uncontrollably, and his leg throbbed.

The truck skidded on the icy road, but Aaron, barely aware that he was driving at all, ignored the warning. Twice in two days he had wanted to kill, and twice he was unashamed for it.

There were two town patrol cars parked on the shoulder of the road when he arrived, and he nearly ran up the back of one as he slid to a halt and scrambled out. There were a small crowd hunched coldly in the vast, well-tended yard: police, several neighbors looking ill-at-ease, Sorrentino himself pounding his arms against the air by the sheriff, and David standing quietly to one side . . .

. . . *while the oldest men carefully lowered the body of the shaman into the oversized grave. They scuttled away, then, and the boy stepped up to drop in the trappings of his father's profession, a lock of his own hair, a brown seed, a young branch freshly cut. They buried the war-murdered man beneath black earth and passed the remainder of the night mourning. Lt. Jackoson continued to watch the boy—a onetime, now distant friend. He watched the boy sitting calmly on the grave, staring at the prisoner, a scarred man in a tattered blue uniform. Jackoson had warned his men to mind their own business this time, and they did, gratefully; but few slept and all were uneasy. And still the little boy stared. . .*

. . . at the ground until Aaron placed an arm lightly around his shoulders and he looked up. No greeting. A look was all. Sheriff Jenkins, a scowl and sympathy fighting in his face, walked hurriedly over with Sorrentino directly behind him. Aaron glared at them. barely able to contain the rage he felt for his son. "How?" he demanded without preliminaries. Sorrentino tried to bull forward, but Jenkins held up a hand to stop him.

"Frank here called me about forty-five minutes ago, Aaron. Said he was afraid he'd shot your son."

"I was just inside the wood, Jackoson," Sorrentino said, his voice oddly harsh. "I was chasing them wolves. I heard this noise right where I spotted them last, so I let go—"

"Without being sure?" Momentarily, Aaron was too appalled at the big man's stupidity to be angry. "You know kids are playing in there all the time. My God, Frank, you're a good enough shot to have waited a. . ." He stopped, seeing the retreat in the other man's eyes. "You . . . no, you couldn't have. Not even you. "

"Now wait a damn minute, Jackoson."

"Shut up a minute, Frank."

"But, sheriff, that man just accused me of deliberately killing that kid's animal!"

"He didn't say that, did he?"

Sorrentino sputtered, then wheeled and stalked away, muttering. Jenkins didn't watch him leave; Aaron did. "Listen, Aaron, I couldn't find any evidence that it happened any other way than he said. I know how you two feel about each other, but as far as I'm concerned, his story holds up. I'm sorry, Aaron, but it was an accident."

Aaron nodded, though he was just as sure the sheriff was wrong.

"Look, if you want, the boys and I will take the—"

"No," David said.

Aaron saw the look on Jenkins' face and knew it was the first thing David had said that morning. Against his better judgement he agreed. "We'll take him. Will. But thanks anyway. I'd appreciate it if some of your men would help me put him in the truck."

The sheriff started to say, something, but the boy walked between them, past the neighbors to the truck where he let down the gate and stood by, waiting.

"The boy wasn't on the pony," Will said. "It must have wandered off while David was playing."

Aaron nodded. And what, he thought, was David playing?

Pinto's head had been hastily wrapped in a blanket now matted with blood. David sat stroking the animal's rigid flank. Through the rear-view mirror, Aaron could see the hand moving smoothly over the cooling flesh. In his own eyes were the stirrings of tears. For once he thought he knew how the boy felt, to lose a friend much more than a pet. He drove slowly, turning off the road just before his own land began. There was a rutted path leading into the wood to a clearing where the boys of the surrounding farms had erected forts and castles, trenches and space ships. At it western end was a slight rise, and it was there that they sweated in the cold noon of the grey slate day and buried Pinto. The wind was listless, the rain stopped. When the grave was filled, Aaron walked painfully back to the truck to wait for David, and an hour passed before they were headed for home, and all the way Aaron tried vainly to joke the boy back into a fair humor, even promising him a new pet as soon as they could get into town. David, however, only stared at the road, one hand unconsciously working at his throat.

Immediately they arrived at the house, the telephone rang and Aaron grabbed for it, hoping it was Miriam. It was Sorrentino, apologizing and sounding unsettlingly desperate; and Aaron, eager to talk, eager to turn from his son's depression, profusely acknowledged the other's story, and damned himself as he spoke. Sorrentino kept on. And on, He was babbling, Aaron realized, very often incoherent, and in his puzzlement at the rancher's behavior, he responded in kind, knowing he sounded like an idiot, trying not to admit that he was somehow, inexplicably afraid of his own son.

When Sorrentino at last rang off, Aaron felt rather than saw the boy's bedroom door open. He would not turn. He was not going to watch grief harden the young face. "It'll be all right, son," he said weakly. "In time. In time. You . . . you have to give it time."

The boy was a shadow. "He could see, dad."

"We can't prove that, son."

"He could see everything. The brush isn't that high."

"David, we cannot prove it. Things are different here, you know that. We have to prove things first."

And still he did not turn.

"He did it on purpose. You now that, and you won't do anything. You know it and . . ."

Turn around you old fool. He's only a boy. He's only a boy, for God's sake . . .

. . . for God's sake, the lieutenant thought as he watched the boy sitting on the grave, how long is he going to stay there? His eyes, burning from the darkness and the fire's acrid smoke, shifted to the prisoner. The man was staring at the shaman's son, entranced, it seemed, and unmoving. He was unbound, but none of the tribesmen seemed to care. They were confident with knowledge that Jackoson didn't have, and Jackoson didn't like it. He tried instead to think of home and a place where people behaved the way they were supposed to . . .

. . . behave yourself, stupid, he thought, and send the boy to bed. He'll feel better in the morning.

"You'd better lie down, now, dad," the shadow said. "Your leg must be hurting after all that digging."

Aaron closed his eyes and nodded, feeling for the first time since leaving the house eons ago the painful strain that nearly buckled him. A moment later he felt the boy's arm around his waist, guiding him firmly to the bedroom. In the dim curtained light, he watched David prepare the bed, then stand aside while he eased himself between the cold sheets. David smiled at him.

"Well . . . we'll see the sheriff again in a few days, son. We'll talk to him."

"Sure, dad."

"And David, don't . . . I mean, you know, don't try to do anything on your own, you know what I mean? I mean, don't go off chasing his sheep into the next county or smashing windows. Okay?'

The boy paused in the doorway. "Sure, dad. You want your medicine?"

"No, thanks. I'll be all right in a little while. Just call me for dinner."

"Okay. I'm going to read or something. You need anything, please call."

Aaron smiled. "Go on, son." And after the door closed, he wondered, not for the first time, if he had been right in taking the boy away. Neither, in half a decade, seemed closer to understanding the other than when they had started out on the plane from Saigon. They spoke the same language, shared the same house, but the rapport David has with the animals, with Pinto, was missing between father and son. The war was no longer a threat, its use as a bond had dissolved.

I don't know my own son, he thought.

A part of his mind told him to stop feeling sorry for himself: the problem wasn't a new one.

I'm not feeling sorry for myself.

You sound like one of Miriam's soap operas.

I don't.

He's an ordinary boy who needs time. He's seen war.

He's had five years, and so, by the way, have I.

And when he slept, he dreamt of a slight mound in a path supposedly clear and the sound he felt and heard before waking screaming in a hospital in Japan with a leg raw, twisted. He had refused amputation. He needed the leg.

When he opened his eyes, it was dark. He tried to fall asleep again, but a rising wind nudged him back to wakefulness. Finally he swung out of bed and dressed quietly. He was hungry and thirsty. Cautiously, he crept into the kitchen to fix a snack and unaccountably remembered a rancher he knew in passing who had a string of Shetlands he rented to pony rides during the summer fairs. Maybe, he thought, he could persuade this man to part with one of his animals on credit. It would be easy enough to explain what had happened to Pinto. The man would have to help him. Slowly the idea grew, hurrying his actions, making him grin at himself. Without stopping to drink the coffee he had poured, he hastened down the hall to David's room.

It was empty. His boots were gone, and his jacket. There was a hint of panic before Aaron realized that David, still mourning, had probably gone out to the barn to Pinto's stall. Snatching his coat from the closet, he rushed outside, gasping once at the cold air and the strong wind that slid across the now-frozen ground. A digging pain in his thigh caused him to slow up, but long before he'd fling open he barn door, he knew the building would be empty. He stood in the barnyard, aimlessly turning, seeking a direction to travel until he saw the faint orange glow over the trees. He stared, hands limp at his sides, squinting, thinking, denying all the fears that founded his nightmares. He knew his century and still refused to believe what he had seen on the jungled mountain, dreaded what he might see if he followed the light.

It was just before dawn . . .

. . . *and Lt. Jackoson was the only squad member still awake, the others sleeping in luxurious safety for the first time in days. Night noises. Night wind. He was drowsy and rubbed the blur from his eyes. Curiosity prodded him; he rubbed his eyes again. The fire burned sullenly at the side of the grave. The boy was naked, now, and standing* . . .

. . . running over the ice-crusted ground, Aaron was pushed from behind by the wind. He ignored his leg as long as he could, concentrating on the wavering line of trees ahead. Then, just inside the tiny wood, his foot pushed through a hidden burrow and he slammed to the ground. Palms, knees, forehead stung. When he tried to stand, his leg wrenched out from under him, and he cried out. Before him, trunks and branches, brush and grass twisted slowly in the light of the fire, weaving darkness within darkness. Aaron pushed himself to one leg, his teeth clamped to his lips and, using the trees for support, hobbled toward the clearing. His left leg went numb, the pain felt only from the hip, and finally he collapsed.

Not now, he begged, not now!

He crawled, forearms and one foot, seeing his breath puff in front of his face, seeing his hands turn a dry red from the cold. Then there was a break in the pine, and he saw the boy. . . .

. . . *on his father's grave, shuffling slowly from side to side, humming to himself as he stared at the mound beneath his feet. The tribe had reassembled, squatting in the shadows silent. The pit fire cracked* . . .

. . . on the rise, and the smell of burning pine pierced the brittle air. And between himself and his son, Aaron saw . . .

. . . *the prisoner seemingly rooted in place, turned so his face was hidden. The boy, not looking up, not acknowledging the world's existence muttered something and the man shuddered.* . . .

. . . beneath his heavy furtrimmed hunting jacket. There was a rifle, useless now, dangling from one hand. Aaron tried to push himself up, to stand, but the agony was too great, and at the moment all he wanted was the heat from the fire that silhouetted the boy . . .

. . . shuffling faster, mumbling in rapid bursts while the prisoner swayed, slipped back, then lurched forward. Slowly, toward the grave, in the light of the fire. Jackoson thought he was dreaming . . .

. . . but the cold was too real, and he wondered how the boy, so lately his son, could stand the wind that whipped the flames from side to side and drew . . .

. . .the prisoner toward them, stiff-jointed like a grotesque marionette. The jungle . . .

. . . the clearing was quiet, and Aaron could hear the boy, chanting now, urging, taunting the big man forward. Aaron tried shouting, but his throat was too dry, his mind unable to break loose his tongue. All he could see was the rifle glinting. Sorrentino moved. Lumbered. Silent.

Prisoner/rancher reached the grave.

The boy, still chanting, reached out, palms up, waiting until the other grasped them (the rifle dropping soundlessly). A pair now, circling in slow motion. Dirt shifted beneath their feet. Aaron watched . . .

. . . more drowsy still from the fire's heat and the boy's monotonic voice, still undecided whether or not he was dreaming . . .

. . . numb from the cold and drawing blood from his lips as he fought the pain enshrouding his thoughts. He lay flat on the ground, his head barely raised, his eyes glazed.

The boy abruptly dropped his hands and stepped down from the grave.

The prisoner waited, standing, and made no attempt to resist when the shaman's hand/pony's teeth reached through the earth and took hold.

Jackoson slept, though he was dreaming.

Aaron fainted, thought he was screaming.

David, smiling, picked up a shovel.

THE FIRE WHEN IT COMES

by Parke Godwin

Got to wake up soon.

I've been sick a long time, I mean really sick. Hard to remember why or how long, but it feels like that time I had hundred-and-three fever for a week. Sleep wasn't rest but endless, meaningless movement, and I'd wake up to change my sweaty nightdress for a clean one which would be soaked by sunup.

But this boring, weary dream has gone on for ages. I'm walking up and down the apartment trying to find the door. The furniture isn't mine. People come and go, replaced by others with even tackier sofas in colors loud enough to keep them awake, and I flutter around and past them on my own silly route as if I'd lost an earring and had to find it before I could get on with life. None of it's very real, murky as *cinema-verité* shot in a broom closet. I have to strain to recognize the apartment, and the sound track just mumbles. No feeling at all.

Just that it's gone on so long.

All right, enough of this. Lying around sick and fragile is romantic as hell, but I have to get it together, drop the needle on the world again and let it play. I'm—

Hell, I am out of it, can't even remember my name, but there's a twinge of pain in trying. Never mind, start with simple things. Move your hand, spider your fingers out from under the covers. Rub your face, open your eyes.

That hasn't worked the last thousand times. I can't wake up, and in a minute the stupid dream will start again with a new cast and no script, and I'll be loping up and down after that earring or the lost door. Hell, yes. Here it comes. Again.

No. It's different this time. I'd almost swear I was awake, standing near the balcony door with the whole long view of my apartment stretching out before me: living room, pullman kitchen, the bedroom, bathroom like an afterthought in the rear. It's clear daylight, and the apartment is bare. Sounds are painfully sharp. The door screams open and shut like thunder.

A boy and a girl.

She's twenty-two at the outside, he's not much older. He looks sweet, happy and maybe a little scared. Nice face, the kind of sensitive expression you look at twice. The girl's mouth is firmer. Small and blonde and compact. I know that expression, tentative only for a moment before she begins to measure my apartment for possibilities, making it hers.

"Really a lot of room," she says. "I could do things with this place if we had the money."

My God, they're so *loud*. The boy drifts toward me while she bangs cupboard doors, checks out the bathroom, flushes the toilet.

"The john works. No plumbing problems."

"Al, come here. Look, a balcony."

"Wow, Lowen, is that for real?"

Of course it's real, love. Open the door, take a look and then get the hell out of my dreams.

"Let's look, Al." He invites the girl with one hand and opens the balcony door. He's in love with her and doesn't quite know how to handle it all yet. They wander out onto my tiny balcony and look down at 77th Street and out over the river where a garbage scow is gliding upstream. It's a lovely day. Jesus, how long since I've seen the sun? Kids are romping in the playground across Riverside Drive. Lowen and Al stand close together. When he pulls her to him, her hand slips up over his shoulder. The gold ring looks new.

"Can we afford it, Lowen?"

"We can if you want it."

"If? I never wanted anything so much in my life."

They hold each other and talk money as if it were a novelty, mentioning a rent way over what I pay. The frigging landlord would love to hang that price tag on this place. Lowen points to the drainpipe collar bedded in a patch of cement, monument stone to my epic battle with that bastard to clear the drain and anchor it so every rain didn't turn my balcony into a small lake. Lowen's pointing to letters scratched in the cement.

"GAYLA."

That's right, that's me. I remember now.

They look through the apartment again, excited now that they think they want it. Yes, if they're careful with their budget, if they get that cash wedding present from Aunt Somebody, they can work it. I feel very odd; something is funny here. They're too real. The dream is about them now.

Hey, wait a minute, you two.

The door bangs shut after them.

Hey, wait!

I run out onto the balcony and call to them in the street, and for the first time in this fever dream, I'm conscious of arms and legs that I still can't feel, and a fear growing out of a clearing memory.

Hey, hello. It's me, Gayla Damon.

Lowen turns and tilts his head as if he heard me, or perhaps for one more look at where he's going to live with Al-short-for-Alice. I can't tell from his smile, but I lean to it like a fire in winter, out over the low stone parapet—and then, oh Christ, I remember. For one terrible, sufficient flash, the memory flicks a light switch.

If I could cry or be sick, I'd do that. If I screamed loud enough to crack the asphalt on West End Avenue, nobody would hear. But I let it out anyway, and my scream fills the world as Lowen and Al stroll away toward Riverside Drive.

As if they could actually see me hunched over the balcony edge, head shaking back and forth in despair. They could will their real bodies to stop, real eyes lift again to a real, vacant balcony.

Because they're real. I'm not. Not sick or dreaming, just not.

You died, Gayla baby. You're dead.

The last couple of days have been bad. Panic, running back and forth, scared to death or life, I don't know which, trying to find a way out without knowing where to go or why. I know I died, God, am I sure of that, but not how or how to get out.

There's no frigging door! Lowen and Al sail in and out unloading their junk, but when I try to find the door, it's Not, like me. I'm stuck here. I guess that's what frightens all of us because you can't imagine Not. I never bought the MGM version of heaven. For me, being dead was simply not being, zero, zilch, something you can't imagine. The closest you can come is when a dentist knocks you out with pentothol or how you felt two years before you were born.

No. I don't end, you say. Not me, not the center of the universe. And yet it's happened and I'm stuck with it, no way out, trying to hack the whole thing at once, skittering back and forth from the bedroom to the living room, through the kitchen with its new cream paint, crawling like cigarette smoke in the drapes, beating my nothing-fists against the wall sometimes, collapsing out of habit and exhaustion into a chair or bed I can't feel under me, wearing myself out with the only sensation left, exhaustion and terror.

I'm not dead. I can't be dead, because if I am, why am I still here. Let me out!

To go where, honey?

There's a kind of time again. Al's pinned up a Japanese art calendar in the kitchen, very posh. This month it's a samurai warrior drawing his sword; either that or playing with himself. I can't see it that well, but the date is much too clear. 1981. No wonder the rent's gone up. Seven years since I—

No, that word is a downer. Exited is better. Just how is still a big fat blank wrapped in confusion. All I remember is my name and a few silly details about the apartment. No past, no memory to splice the little snippets of film that flash by too swiftly to catch. Not that it matters, but where's my body? Was I buried or burned, scattered or canned in memoriam in some mausoleum? Was there a husband, a lover? What kind life did I have?

When I think hard, there's the phantom pain of someone gone, someone who hurt me. That memory is vaguely connected with another of crying into the phone, very drunk. I can't quite remember, just how it made me feel. Got to organize and think, I've worn myself out running scared, and still no answers. The only clear thought is an odd little thing; there must have been a lot of life in me to be kept so close to it.

Don't ask me about death. The rules are all new. I might be the first of the breed. It's still me, but unable to breathe or sleep or get hungry. Just energy that can still run down from overuse, and when that happens, Lowen and Al grow faint. That's all there is to me now, energy, and not much of that. I have to conserve, just float here by Al's painfully correct window drapes and think.

Does anyone know I'm here. I mean, Anyone?

*   *   *

A few more days. Al and Lowen are all moved in. Al's decor works very hard at being House Beautiful, an almost militant graciousness. Style with clenched teeth. And all her china matches—hell, yes, it would. But let's face it: whatever's happening to me is because of them. When they're close, I get a hint of solid objects around me, as if I could reach out and touch tables and chairs or Lowen, but touching life costs me energy. The degree of nearness determines how much of my pitiful little charge is spent. Like being alive in a way. Living costs. I learned that somewhere.

Just got the hell scared out of me. Al has a mirror in the bedroom, a big antique affair. Sometimes when she brushes her hair, I stand behind her, aching out of habit to get that brush into my own mop. Tonight as I watched, I saw myself behind her.

I actually jumped with fright, but Al just went on pumping away with the brush while I peered over her head at Gayla Damon. Thirty-three—I remember that now—and beginning to look it. Thank God that won't bother me any more. Yes, I was tall. Brownish-black hair not too well cut. Thin face, strong jaw, eyes large and expressive. They were my best feature, they broadcast every feeling I ever had. Lines starting around my mouth. Not a hard mouth but beginning to turn down around the edges, a little tired. Hardness would have helped, I guess. Some of Natalie Bond's brass balls.

Nattie Bond: a name, another memory.

No, it's gone, but there was a kind of pain with it. I stared at the mirror. Cruddy old black sweater and jeans: was I wearing them? You'd think I could check out in something better. Hey, brown eyes, how did they do you for the curtain call? Touch of pancake, I hope. You always looked dead without it. Oh, shit . . .

A little crying helps. Even dry it's something.

I watch Lowen more and more, turning to him as a flower follows the sun, beginning to learn why I respond to him. Lowen's a listener and a watcher. He can be animated when he's feeling good or way down if he's not. Tired, depressed or angry, his brown eyes go almost black. Not terribly aggressive, but he does sense and respond to the life going on around him.

He likes the apartment and being quiet in it. He smokes, too, not much but enough to bother Al. They've worked out a compromise: anywhere but the bedroom. So, sometimes, I get a surprise visit in the living room when Lowen wakes up and wants a smoke. He sits for a few minutes in the dark, cigarette a bright arc from his mouth to the ashtray. I can't tell, but sometimes it seems he's listening to pure silence. He turns his head this way and that—toward me sometimes—and I feel weird; like he was sifting the molecules of silence, sensing a weight in them. Sometimes in the evening when he and Al are fixing dinner, Lowen will raise his head in that listening way.

It's a long-shot hope, but I wonder if he can feel *me*.

Why has he brought me back to time and space and caring? All these years there's been only blurred shadows and voices faint as a radio in the next room. Real light and sound and thought came only when he walked in. When Lowen's near, I perk up and glow; when he leaves, I fade to drift, disinterested, by the balcony door.

Lowen Sheppard: twenty-four at most, gentle, unconsciously graceful, awkward only when he tries to be more mature than he is. Don't work at it, lover, it'll come. Soft, straight brown hair that he forgets to cut until Al reminds him, which is often. She's great on detail, lives by it. Faces this apartment like a cage of lions to be tamed. Perhaps it's the best she ever had.

Lowen seems used to this much or maybe better. Mister nice guy, not my type at all, and yet I'm bound to him by a kind of fascination, bound without being able to touch his hair or speak to him. And it's no use wondering why, I'm learning that, too. Like that old Bergman flick where Death comes to collect Max Von Sydow. Max says, "Tell me what eternity is like." And Death says, "Who knows? I just work here."

Don't call us. We'll call you."

Well, damnit, *someone* is gong to know I'm here. If I can think, I can do, and I'm not going to sit here forever just around the corner from life. Lowen and Al are my world now, the only script left to work with. I'm a part of their lives like a wart on the thigh, somewhere between God and a voyeur.

Wait, a memory just . . . no. Gone too quick again.

If I could touch Lowen somehow. Let him know.

Lowen and Al are settled in, place for everything and everything in its place, and Al daring it to get out of line. Lowen works full time, and Al must do some part-time gig.

She goes out in the early afternoon. The lights dim then. Just as well; I don't like what she's done with my apartment. Everything shrieks its price at you, but somehow Al's not comfortable with it. Maybe she never will be. That mouth is awful tight. She wanted to keep plastic covers over the sofa and chairs, the kind that go *crunkle* when you sit on them and make you feel like you're living in a commercial. But Lowen put his foot down on that.

"But, Al, they're to use, not just to look at."

"I know, but they're so nice and new."

"Look, I wear a rubber when we make love. I don't need them on the furniture."

She actually blushed. "Really, Lowen."

Son of a—she makes him—? Do guys still wear those things? Whatever happened to the sexual revolution?

It's indicative of their upbringing the way each eats, too. Al sits erect at the table and does the full choreography with her knife and fork, as if disapproving mama was watching her all the time. Cut the meat, lay the knife down, cross the fork to her right hand, spear, chew, swallow, and the whole thing over again. Left hand demurely in her lap.

Lowen leans slightly into his plate, what-the-hell elbows on the table. More often than not, he uses the fork in his left hand, placing things on it with his knife. The way he handles them both, he's definitely lived in England or Europe. Not born there, though. The fall of his speech has a hint of softness and mid-South nasal. Virginia or Maryland. Baltimore, maybe.

Perhaps it's just plain jealousy that puts me off Alice. She's alive. She can reach out and touch, hold, kiss what I can only look at. She's the strength in this marriage, the one who'll make it work. Lowen's softer, easier, with that careless assurance that comes from never having to worry about the rent or good clothes. He's been given to; Al's had to grab and fight. Now he's got a job and trying to cut it on his own for the first time. That's scary, but Al helps. She does a pretty fair job of supporting Lowen without letting him notice it too much.

She has her problems, but Lowen comes first. She gets home just before him, zips out to get fresh flowers for the table. A quick shower and a spritz of perfume, another swift agony at the mirror. And then Lowen is home and sitting down to dinner, telling her about the day. And Al listens, not so much to the words but the easy, charming sound, the quality she loves in him, as if she could learn it for herself. She's from New York, probably the Bronx. I remember the accent somehow. Petite and pretty, but she doesn't believe it no matter how much attention Lowen gives her. Spends a lot of time at the mirror when he's gone, not admiring but wondering. What does she really look like. What type is she, what kind of an image does she, should she, project; and can she do it? Lipstick: this shade or that? So she fiddles and narrows her eyes, scrutinizing the goods, hopes for the advertised magic of Maybelline and ends up pretty much the same: more attractive then she thinks, not liking what she sees.

Except she doesn't see. She's carried it around all her life, too busy, too nervous and insecure to know what she's got. Striped down for a bath, Al looks like she never had a pimple or a pound of fat in her life, but I swear she'll find something wrong, something not to like.

Don't slop that goo on your face, girl. You're great already. God, I only wish I had your skin. The crap I had to put on and take off every night, playing parts like—

Parts like . . .

My God, I remember!

I was an actress. That's what I remember in quick flashes of hard light. The pictures whiz by like fast cars, but they're slowing down: stage sets, snatches of dialogue, dim faces in the front rows. Bill Wrenn gives me a piece of business to work out. Fragments of me like a painting on shattered glass. I grope for the pieces, fitting them together one by one.

Bill Wrenn: there's a warm feeling when I think of him, a trusting. Where did I meet him? Yes, it's coming back.

Bill directed that first season at Lexington Rep. Gentle and patient with a weariness that no longer expected any goodies from life, he always reminded me of a harried sheepdog with too many sheep to hustle. Forty years old, two marriages and struck out both times, not about to fall hard again.

But he did for me. I made it easy for him. We were out of the same mold, Bill and I. He sensed my insecurity as a woman and found ways to make it work for me onstage, found parts in me I'd never dream of playing. With most men, my whole thing began in bed and usually ended there. Bill and I didn't hurry; there was a love first. We enjoyed and respected each other's work, and theater was a church for us. We'd rehash each performance, sometimes staying up all night to put an extra smidge of polish on business or timing, to get a better laugh, to make something good just a hair better. We started with a love of something beyond us that grew toward each other, so that bed, when it came, was natural and easy as it was gorgeous.

I made him love me, my one genuine conquest. We even talked about getting married—carefully skirting around a lot of it's. I seem to remember him asking me one night in Lexington. I *think* he asked then; there's a thick haze of vodka and grass over that night. Did I say yes? Not likely; by that time the old habits were setting in.

It was too good with Bill. That's not funny. Perfection, happiness, these are frightening things. Very few of us can live with them. After a while, I began to resent Bill. I mean, who the hell was he to take up so much of my life? I began to pick at him, finding things not to like, irritating habits like the nervous way he cleared his throat or dug in his ear when he was thinking out some stage problem; the way he picked his feet in bed and usually left the bathroom a mess. Just bitchiness. I even over reacted when he gave me notes after a performance. All bullshit and panic; just looking for a way out. How dare you love me, Bill Wrenn? Who asked you? Where did I get that way, where did it begin?

When Nick Charreau came into the company, he was tailor-made for me.

He was alone onstage the first time I saw him, a new cast replacement going through his blocking with the stage manager. Everything his predecessor did, Nick adjusted to show himself in a better light. He wasn't a better actor, but so completely, insolently sure of himself that he could pull off anything and make it look good, even a bad choice. Totally self-centered: if there were critics in the house, Nick lit up like a sign, otherwise it was just another working night in the sticks.

Nick was a lot better looking than Bill and eighteen years younger. Even-featured with a sharp, cool, detached expression. Eyes that looked right through you. He could tell me things wrong with myself that would earn Bill Wrenn a reaming out, but I took it from Nick. He didn't get close or involved all the way down. Perhaps that's why I chose him, out of cowardice. He wouldn't ever ask me to be a person.

When he finished the blocking session, I came down to lean on the stage apron. "You play that far back, you'll upstage everyone else in the scene."

"It's my scene. I'm beautifully lit up there." Nick's smile was friendly with just the right soupçon of cockiness. A little above us all, just enough to tickle my own self-doubt and make me want to take him on. I can handle you, mister. You're not so tough.

But he was. There was always part of Nick I couldn't reach or satisfy. I started out challenged, piqued, to cut him down to size in bed and ended up happy if he'd just smile at me.

Looking over Al's shoulder in the mirror, I know it's not what we're born but what we're made into. The game is called Hurt me, I haven't suffered enough. I needed a son of a bitch like Nick. You don't think I'd go around deserving someone like Bill, do you?

Call that weird, Alice? You're the same song, different verse. You have that wary, born-owing-money look yourself. You handle it better than I did—you knew a good man when you saw one—but you still feel like a loser.

The fights with Bill grew large, bitter and frequent. He knew what was happening and it hurt him. And one night we split.

"When will you grow up, Gayla?"

"Bill, don't make it harder than it has to be. Just wish me luck."

Dogged, tired, plopping fresh icecubes into his drink. "I care about you. About you, Gayla. That makes it hard. Nick's twenty-two and about an inch deep. He'll split in six months and you'll be out in the cold. When will you learn, Gay? It's not a game, it's not a great big candy store. It's people."

"I'm sorry, Bill."

"Honey," he sighed, "you sure are."

I still hovered, somehow needing his blessing. "Please? Wish me luck?"

Bill raised his glass, not looking up. "Sure, Gay. With Nick you'll need it."

"What's that mean?"

"Nothing, forget it."

"No, you don't just say things like that."

"Sorry, I'm all out of graciousness."

"What did you mean I'll need it."

Bill paused to take a swallow of his drink. "Come on, Gay. You're not blind."

"Other women? So what."

"Other anybody."

"Oh boy, you're—"

"Nick swings both ways."

"That's a lie!"

"He'd screw a light socket if it helped him to a part."

That was the nastiest thing Bill ever said about anyone. I felt angry and at the same time gratified that he made it easier to walk out mad. "Good-bye, Bill."

And then he looked up at me, showing what was hidden before. Bill Wrenn was crying. Crying for me, the only person in this fucking world who ever did. All the pain, anger, loss, welling up in those sad sheepdog eyes. I could have put my arms around him, and stayed . . . no, wait, the picture's changing. I'm here in the apartment. *Get out of here, Nick—*

No, it goes to fast or I will it to go. I can't, won't remember that yet because it hurts too much, and like a child I reach, cry out for one thing I could always trust.

Bill-l-l—

Not a scream, just the memory of sound.

Lowen looks up from his book, puzzled. "Al? You call me?"

No answer. It's late, she's asleep.

Once more Lowen seems to listen, feeling the air and the silence, separating its texture with his senses. Searching. Then he goes back to his book, but doesn't really try to read.

He heard me. He heard *me*. I can reach him.

Sooner or later, he'll know I'm here. Bust my hump or break my heart, I'll do it. Somehow. I've got to live, baby. Even dead, it's all I know how to do.

I've hit a new low, watched Lowen and Al make love. At first I avoided it, but gradually the prospect drew me as hunger draws you to a kitchen; hunger no longer a poignant memory but sharp need that grows with my strength.

I've never watched love-making before. Porn, yes, but that's for laughs, a nowhere fantasy. One of the character men in Lexington had a library of films we used to dig sometimes after a show, hooting at their ineptness. They could make you laugh or even horny now and then, but none of them ever dealt with reality. Porn removes you from the act, puts it at a safe distance.

Real sex is awkward, banal and somehow very touching

to watch. It's all the things we are and want: involvement, commitment, warmth, passion, clumsiness, generosity or selfishness. Giving and receiving or holding back, all stained with the colors of openness or fear, lovely—and very vulnerable. All that, and yet the words are inadequate; you can't get any of that from watching. Like the man said, you had to be there.

Rogers and Astaire these two are not. It's all pretty straight missionary and more of an express than a local. Lowen does certain things and Al tries a few herself, sort of at arm's length and without much freedom. I don't think Lowen's had much experience, and Al, though she needs sex, probably learned somewhere that she oughtn't like it all that much. She's the new generation; she's heard it's her right and prerogative, but the no-no was bred in early. So she compromises by not enjoying it, by making it uphill for both of them. She inhibits Lowen without meaning to. He has to wait so long for her to relax and then work so hard to get her going. And of course at the best moment, like an insurance commercial in the middle of a cavalry charge, he has to stop and put on that stupid rubber. I wonder if Al's Catholic, she never heard of a diaphragm? Or maybe it's money. That's not so far out. Maybe she's uptight about getting pregnant because she remembers how it was to grow up poor. Maybe it's a lot of things adding up to tense ambivalence, wondering why the bells don't ring and the earth shake like she read in *Cosmopolitan*. I seem to remember that trip.

She doesn't give herself much time to relish it afterward, either. Kiss-kiss-bang-bang, then zip with the kleenex and pit-pat into the shower as if someone might catch them. Maybe that's the way it was before they married, a habit that set before either of them realized it.

But I've touched Lowen. God, yes, for one galvanized split-second I felt his body against me. I paid for it, but it had to be.

It was after they made love and Al did her sprint from bed through the shower and into her nightie-cocoon. Lowen went into the bathroom then. I heard the shower running and drifted in after him.

His body looked marvelous; smooth light olive against Al's blue flower-patterned bath curtains, the soap lather standing out sharp white against the last of his summer tan.

Not too muscular; supple like Nick. It'll be a while before he has to worry about weight.

Lowen soaped and rinsed, and I enjoyed the shape of his chest and shoulders when he raised his arms over his head.

You're beautiful, Mr. Sheppard.

I had to do it then. I moved in and kissed him, *felt* his chest, stomach, his hardness against the memory of my pelvis. Only a second, a moment when I had to hold him.

The sensation that shivered through me was like a sudden electric shock. I pulled back, frightened and hurt, hovering in the shower curtain. Lowen jerked, grabbing for the towel rack, taut, scared as myself. Then, slowly, the fear faded and I saw that listening, probing attitude in the lift of his head before the instinctive fear returned. Lowen snapped the water off, stumbled out of the tub and just sat down on the john, dripping and shaking. He sat there for minutes, watching the water drying on his skin, runneling down the sides of the tub. Once he put a hand to his lips. They moved, forming a word I couldn't hear.

You felt me, damn you. You know I'm here. If I could just talk to you.

But the exhaustion and pain ebbed me. We slumped at opposite ends of the small bathroom, Lowen staring through me, not hearing the sob, the agony of the pictures that flashed into life. Touching him, I remember. After the shock of life comes the memory, filling me out by one more jagged fragment, measuring me in pain.

Al, Al, frowning at your mirror, wondering what magic you lack—I should have your problem. The guys probably lined up around the block when you were in school. Not for Gayla Damon; hell, that wasn't even my real name, not for a long, hard time. First there was big, fat Gail Danowski from the Bronx like you, and at seventeen what your men prayed for and likely never got, I couldn't give away.

Why do I have to remember that? Please, I tried so hard to get away from it. My father who worked for the city as a sandhog, my dumpy mother with her permanent look of washed-out disgust, both of them fresh off the boat in 1938. My sister Sasha who got married at seventeen to get away from them. Big change: all Zosh did after that was have kids for that beer-drinking slob husband of hers. Jesus, Charlie disgusted me. Sunday afternoons he'd come over and watch football with my father, swill beer and stuff potato chips. Every once in a while he'd let out a huge belch, then sigh and pat his pot gut like he was so goddamn pleased with himself. For years, while Zosh's teeth went and her skin faded to chalk delivering five kids.

And me growing up in the middle of it, waiting for the big event of the day in the south Bronx, the Good Humor truck out on the street.

"Mommy, Mommy, the goojoomer's here! C'n I have a dime for the goojommer?"

"Y'fadda din leave me no money."

Urgent jingling from the Good Humor, ready to leave and take excitement with it. "Mommy!"

"Geddouda here. I ain't got no dime, now shaddup."

I used to think about that a lot: a lousy dime. So little and so much to a kid. Go to hell, Momma. Not for the dime, but for a whole beauty you never had and never missed. You weren't going to keep me from it.

It wasn't much better in high school. I was embarrassed to undress for gym because of the holes in my underwear. And the stains sometimes because I had to use Momma's kotex and she didn't care if she ran out. I could have used tampax; virgin or not, I was a big, healthy ox like her and Zosh. I could have conceived an army. When Momma found the tampax I bought, she slapped me halfway across the room.

"What's this, hah? *Hah?* I ain't got enough trouble, you started already? You sneakin around, you little bitch?"

No such luck, Momma. They didn't want me. The closest I got to boys was talking about them. Sitting in a coffee shop over the debris of my cheap, starch lunch, the table a garbage dump of bread crusts, spilled sugar and straw wrappers, shredding food bits and paper ends like our envious gossip dissected the girls we knew and the boys we wanted to know.

I never had any sense about men or myself. That happens when you're five foot seven in high school and still growing. A sequoia in a daisy bed, lumpy and lumbering, addicted to food, my refuge when I lost the courage for school dances. I fled home to the ice box and stayed there, eating myself out of my clothes, smearing my acne with Vis-o-Hex, or huddled for hours in a movie, seeing it twice over to pretend I was Hepburn or Bacall, slim, brittle and clever. Or Judith Anderson, tearing hell out of *Medea*. I read the play and practiced the lines at my mirror with stiff approximations of her gestures.

But it was *A Streetcar Named Desire* that changed my life.

I hardly spoke for days after seeing it. The play stabbed me deep and sparked something that was going to be. I bought more plays and devoured them. Fewer trips to the movies now and more downtown to Broadway and the Village. Live theater, not unreeling on a spool, but happening the moment I saw it.

I was still a lump, still a hundred and fifty pounds of un-lusted-after virgin bohunk, and nobody was going to star Gail Danowski in anything but lunch. I walked alone with my dreams while the hungers grew.

You can go a little mad with loneliness, past caring. Virginity? I couldn't give it away, Momma; so I threw it away. No big Zanuck production, just a boy and a party I can't picture too clearly. We were drinking and wrestling, and I thought: all right, why not? Just once I'm gonna grab a little happiness even if it's just getting laid, what am I saving it for? But I had to get drunk before he fumbled at me. If there was pain or pleasure, I barely felt them, only knew that at last I tasted life where it sprang from the fountain. A meager cup, the cut version, the boy pulling at his clothes afterward, distant, disgusted.

"Shit, whyn't you tell me, Gail?"

Tell you what, lover? That I was a virgin, that by accident you were first? Is that a guilt trip? Whatever I lost, don't mourn it. Cry for the other things we lose in parked cars and motel beds because we're too drunk or there's too much guilt or fear for beauty. It was the beauty I missed. Be first any time, score up a hundred stiff, clumsy girls, say the silly words, break a hundred promises, brag about it afterwards. But leave something of yourself, something of beauty. Only that, and you part with a blessing.

He didn't.

The next morning, hung over and miserable, I looked at that frazzled thing in the mirror, had clean through and down to rock bottom, and knew from here on out I'd have to be me or just another Zosh. That day I started to build Gayla Damon.

I graduated an inch taller and thirty pounds lighter, did hard one-week stock as an apprentice. Seventeen hours a day of walk-ons, painting scenery, fencing and dance classes. Diction: practicing for hours with a cork between my teeth—

"Baby, the word is dance. DAAnce, hear the A? Not de-e-ance. Open your mouth and *use* it when you speak."

—Letting my hair grow and moving down to Manhattan,

always running away from that lump in the mirror. I never outran her. She was always there, worrying out of my eyes at a thousand auditions, patting my stomach and thighs, searching a hundred dressing room mirrors, plastering pancake on imagined blemishes, grabbing any man's hand because it was there. The years just went, hurrying by like strangers on a street, trailing bits of memory like broken china from a dusty box: buses, planes, snatches of rehearsal, stock, repertory, old reviews.

Miss Damon's talent is raw but unmistakable. When she's right, she *is* theater, vivid, filled with primordial energy that can burn or chill. If she can learn to control . . . she was superbly cast as. . . .

—A self-driven horse record-time sprinting from nowhere to no place. Life? I lived it from eight to eleven o'clock every night and two matinees a week. For three hours each night, I loved, hated, sang, sorrowed enough for three lifetimes. Good houses, bad houses, they all got the best of me because my work had a love behind it. The rest was only fill, and who cared? Season after season of repertory, a dozen cities, a dozen summer towns barely glimpsed from opening night to closing, a blur of men and a lot of beds, flush or broke, it didn't matter.

Zosh caught a show once when I was playing in Westchester. Poor Zosh: pasty and fat as Momma by then, busting out of her dresses and her teeth shot. She came hesitantly into my dressing room, wondering if someone might throw her out. The first stage play she ever saw. She didn't know what to make of it.

"Oh, it was great and all. You look good, Gail. God, you really got some figure now, what size you wear? I never knew about plays. You know me'n school, I always got my girlfriend to write my reports."

She barely sipped the scotch I poured her. "Charlie never buys nothin' but beer." I wanted to take her out for a good dinner, but, no, she had a sitter at home and it was expensive, and Charlie would yell if she came home too late when he was out bowling.

"Let the dumb ox yell. You're entitled once in a while."

"Hey, you really gettin'a mouth on you, Gail."

"Speaking of that, doesn't Charlie ever look at yours? Doesn't he know you need a dentist?"

"Well, you know how it is. The kids take it out of you."

I gave Zosh a hundred dollars to get her teeth fixed. She

wrote that she spent it on the house and kids. *There was the gas bill and Christmas. You can't complain theres nobody on the other end of the phone. Ha-ha. My friends all want to know when your on TV.*

Are you still around, Zosh? Not that it matters. They buried you years ago. No one was going to do that to me.

And then suddenly I was thirty, that big, scary number. Working harder, running harder without knowing where, doing the where-did-it-all-go bit now and then (while the lights caught her best, most expensive angle). Where are you now, Bill? You must be pushing fifty. Did you find someone like me or just the opposite. I wouldn't blame you.

And how about you, Nick?

He'll split in six months. You'll be out in the cold.

When Bill said that, I remember thinking: hell, he's right. I'm thirty-two and after that comes thirty-three. Fourteen years, seven dollars in the bank, and where the hell am I?

But I was hung up on Nick's body and trying to please him. Perhaps there were other, unspoken things that have nothing to do with loving or sex. You get used very early to not liking yourself. You know you're a fraud, someday they'll all know. The Lump hiding inside your dieted figure and with-it clothes knows you haven't changed, no matter what. The Lump doesn't want to like you. How can she tolerate anyone who does? No, she'll sniff out someone who'll keep her in her lowly place.

Crimes and insanities. Hurting Bill was a very countable sin, but I knew what I needed. So it was Nick, not Bill, who moved in here with me.

And where are you this dark night, Nick? Did you make the big time? I hope so. You're almost thirty now. That's getting on for what you had to sell. Your kind of act has a short run.

My mind wanders like that when Lowen's not around.

Energy builds again, the lights dim up. I drift out onto the balcony, feeling that weight of depression it always brings. My sense of color is dimmed because the kids are asleep. 77th Street is a still shot in black and white. Not a soul, not even a late cab whispering up Riverside Drive.

Hey, look: there's a meteor, a falling star. Make a wish: be happy, Bill Wrenn.

And listen! A clock tower. Even with Lowen asleep, I can hear it. Two-three-four o'clock. Definitely, I'm getting stronger. More and more I can feel and sometimes see my legs when I walk, less like floating in a current. I move back through the apartment to hover over Lowen as he sleeps. Wanting. Wondering.

After all this time, why should it be Lowen who wakes me? Nothing's clear but that I can touch life again with him. If that's wrong, I didn't write the script. Name any form of life you want. A cold germ is just a bug trying to make a living in the only way it knows, in a place it doesn't understand, and it only takes a little out of the place trying. That's me, that's all of us. I'll take what I need to live. If there's air to breathe, don't tell me I can't. That's academic.

Al sleeps tiny and still beside Lowen, hardly a bump under the covers. It must be wonderful to sleep like that. I could never stay out more than two hours at a time. No, wait: here she comes up out of it with a sigh and turnover that barely whispers the covers. She slides out of bed and pit-pats to the bathroom. Bladder the size of an acorn, up three times a night like I was.

When the john flushes, Lowen stirs and mumbles, flops over and sinks again. The bathroom door creaks, Al slips back in beside him. She doesn't settle down yet, but rests on one elbow, a momentary vigil over Lowen, a secret protecting. I'll bet he doesn't know she watches him like that. Then she slides under the covers very close, one arm over him, fingers spread lightly on his skin.

To lie beside Lowen like that, to touch him simply by willing it. If that were my hand resting on his skin. What wouldn't I give for that?

The idea is sudden and frightening. Why not?

If I could get inside Al, stretch out my arm inside hers, wear it like a glove; just for a moment move one real finger over Lowen's skin. It couldn't hurt her, and I need it so.

I wait for Al to fall asleep, scared of the whole notion. It could hurt. It hurt to touch Lowen before. Maybe it's against some natural law. They're flesh, I'm memory. Lots of maybe's, but I have to try. Slow and scared, I drift down over Al and will what shape there is to me into the attitude of her body. There's no shock when I touch her, but a definite sensation like dipping into swift-running water. So weird, I pull away and have to build up my nerve to try again, settling like a sinking ship as the current of Al's healthy young life surges and tingles around me, and her chest rises and falls like a warm blanket over cozy sleep. My breasts nestle into hers, my arm stretching slowly to fill out the slim contour of her shoulder, elbow, wrist. It's hard and slow, like half-frozen syrup oozing through a hose. My fingers struggle one by one into hers.

So tired. Got to rest.

But I feel life, I *feel* it, humming and bubbling all around me. Jesus, I must have sounded like a steel mill inside, the way I drove myself. The power, such a wonder. Why did I waste so much time feeling miserable?

The electric clock glows at 5:03. More minutes pass while each finger tests itself in Al's, and then I try to move one on Lowen's skin.

The shock curdles me. I cringe away from it, shriveling back up Al's arm, all of me a shaky little ball in her middle. Just as in the shower, I felt skin against skin, even the tiny moisture of pores, but it drains me as if I've run five miles.

Rest and try again. Slow, so slow, so hard, but my fingers creep forward into Al's again. Same thing: the instant I let myself feel with Al's flesh, there's a bright shock and energy drains. If that's not enough, those delicate fingers weigh ten pounds each. I push, poop out, rest, try again, the hardest battle of my life, let alone death, and all in dogged silence broken only by their breathing and the muted *whir* of the clock.

6:32. The dark bedroom grays up to morning. I can see Lowen's face clearly now: very young, crumpled with sleep. He can't hear my soundless, exhausted panting like the heartbeat of a hummingbird.

6:48. Twelve minutes before the clock beeps the beginning of their day, one finger, one slender thread binding me to Lowen . . . moves. Again. I go dizzy with the sensation but hang on, pouring the last strength into one huge effort. The small hand flexes all five fingers like a crab, sliding over the sparse hair on Lowen's chest. A flash-frame of Bill, of Nick, and a thrill of victory.

Hi, baby. I made it.

Then Al stirs, moves *don't, please, wait!* and flips over on her other side, unconcerned as a pancake. I let go, used up, drifting out to nowhere again, barely conscious of space or objects, too burned out even to feel frustrated after all that work.

But I did it. I know the way now. I'll be back.

* * *

Night after night I kept at it, fitting to Al's body, learning how to move her fingers without burning myself out. Stronger and surer, until I could move the whole hand and then the arm, and even if Lowen pressed the hand to his mouth or nestled his cheek against it, I could hold on.

And then I blew it, the story of my life. Klutz-woman strikes again. I tried to get in when they were making love.

I said before they're not too dexterous in the bedroom. Al gets uptight from the start, and I can see her lying there, eyes tight shut over Lowen's shoulder, hoping he'll come soon and get it over with. Not always; sometimes she wants it as much as him, but the old hangups are always there. She holds back, so he holds back. It's usually one-sided and finished soon.

But that evening everything seemed perfect. They had a light supper, several drinks rather than the usual one, and Lowen didn't spare the vodka. They just naturally segued to the bedroom, not rushed or nervous, undressing each other slowly, enjoyably, melting into each other's arms. Al brought in a candle from the supper table. Nice touch: Nick and I used to do that. They lie there caressing each other, murmuring drowsily. Lowen looks gorgeous in the soft glow, Al like a little Dresden doll. And me—poor, pathetic afterthought—watching it all and yearning.

Jesus, Al, act like you're alive. That's a man. Take hold of him.

Damn, it was too much. The hell with consequences. I draped myself over Al with the ease of practice, stretched my arms and legs along hers. Foolhardy, yes, but at last *my* arms went around Lowen, smoothing, then clawing down his back.

Love me, baby. Love all of me.

My mouth opened hungrily under his, licking his lips and then nipping at them. I writhed Al's slim body under his, pushed her hands to explore him from shoulders to thighs. I never had much trouble in bed. If the guy had anything going and didn't run through it like a fire drill, I could come half a dozen times, little ones and big ones, before he got there.

With Lowen it was like all the best orgasms I ever had. The moment before you start to go, you want to hold back, prolong it, but you can't. I was dependent on Al's chemistry now. Her body was strangely stiff as I hauled her over on top of Lowen. Something new for her. She went taut, resisting it.

"Lowen, wait."

He can't wait, though I'm the only one who sees the irony and the lie. Lowen is coming, I certainly want to, but Al is out of it. I want to *scream* at her, though I should have guessed it long before this. She always times her cries with his, as if they came together.

But it's a lie. She's faking it. She's learned that much.

My God, you're alive, the greatest gift anyone ever got. Does a past tense like me have to show you how?

With a strength like life itself, I churned her up and down on Lowen, hard, burning myself out to tear Al's careful controls from her emotions. She moaned, fighting me, afraid.

"Lowen, stop. Please stop."

You don't fake tonight, kid.

"Stop!"

No way. Go . . . *go!*

Lowen gripped her spasmodically, and I felt his hips tremble under mine/hers. He couldn't hold back any longer. With that last ounce of my will, I bent Al's body down over his, mouth to mouth.

"Now, Lowen. Now!"

Not Al's voice but mine, the first time I've heard it in seven years. Deeper, throatier than Al's. In the middle of coming, an alien bewilderment flooded Lowen's expression. Al stiffened like she was shot. With a cry of bleak terror, she tore herself loose and leaped clear off the bed, clawing for the lamp switch, big-eyed and terrified in the hard light.

"Oh, God. Oh, Jesus, what's happening?"

Confused, a little out of it himself now, Lowen sat up to stare back at her. "Al, what's the matter?"

She shuddered. "It's not me."

"What?"

"It's not *me*." She snatched up her bathrobe like the last haven in the world. Lowen reached for her instinctively, comforting.

"It's all right, honey, it's—"

"No. It's like something hot inside me."

He went on soothing her, but he knew. I could see that in his eyes as he pulled Al down beside him. He knew: the last thing I saw, because the lights were going down for me, their last spill playing over memory-fragments before fading. A confused montage: Nick putting on his jacket, me fumbling for the phone, then pulling at the balcony door, and the darkness and the silence then were like dying again.

I've had some hangovers in my time, mornings of agony after a messy, screaming drunk. Coming back to queasy consciousness while the night's party repeats in your mind like a stupid film loop, and you wonder, in a foggy way, if you really spilled that drink on somebody, and—oh, no—you couldn't have said *that* to him, and if you're going to be sick right then or later.

Then the smog clears and you remember. Yeah. You spilled it and did it and you sure as hell said it, and the five best bloody mary's in the world won't help.

I blew it good this time, a real production number. Now they both know I'm here.

December 23. I know the date because Al's carefully crossed the days off her calendar where she never bothered before. I've been turned off for days. Almost Christmas, but you'd never know it around here. No holly, no tree, just a few cards opened and dropped on the little teakwood desk where they keep their bills. When Lowen brushes one aside, I can see a thin line of dust. Al hasn't been cleaning.

The kitchen is cluttered. The morning dishes are still in the sink. Three cardboard boxes stand on the floor, each half full of wrapped dishes and utensils.

So that's it. They're moving. A moment of panic: where do I go from here, then? All right, it was my fault, but . . . don't go, Lowen. I'm not wild about this script myself, but don't ask me to turn out the lights and die gain. Because I won't.

There's a miasma of oppression and apprehension all through the apartment. Al's mouth is tighter, her eyes frightened. Lowen comes out into the living room, reluctant and dutiful. Furtively, he tests the air as if to feel me in it. He sits down in his usual chair; 3:13 by the miniature grandfather clock on the book case. The lights and sound come up slowly with Lowen's nearness. He's home early this afternoon.

Al brings out the Waterford sherry set and puts it on the coffee table. She sits down, waiting with Lowen. The whole scene reminds me of actors taking places before the curtain rises; Al poised tensely on the sofa, revolving her sherry glass in white fingers; Lowen distant, into his own thoughts. The sound is still lousy.

"... feel silly," Lowen ventures. "... all this way ... time off from ... just to ..."

"No! ... live here like this, not with ..." Al is really shook; takes a cigarette from Lowen's pack on the coffee table and smokes it in quick, inexpert puffs. "You say you can feel her?"

Lowen nods, unhappy. He doesn't like any of this. "I loved this place from the first day."

"Lowen, answer me. Please."

"Yes."

"Where?"

"Somewhere close. Always to me."

Al stubs out the cigarette. "And we sure know it's *she*, don't we?"

"Al—"

"Oh, hell! I loved this place too, but this is crazy. I'm *scared*, Lowen. How long have you known?"

"Almost from the start."

"And you never told me."

"Why?" Lowen looks up at her. "I'm not a medium; nothing like this ever happened before. It was weird at first, but then I began to feel that she was just *here*—"

"What!"

"—and part of things ... like the walls. I didn't even know it was a woman at first."

"Until that time in the shower," Al finishes for him. "Bitch."

Thanks a lot, kid. At least I know what to do with him.

"Look, Al, I can't tell you how I know, but I don't think she means any harm."

Al gulps down her sherry and fills the glass. "The—hell—she—doesn't. I'm not into church anymore. Even if I were, I wouldn't go running for the holy water every time a floor creaked, but don't tell me she doesn't mean anything, Lowen. You know what I'm talking about." Her hands dry-wash each other jerkily. "I mean that night, the way we made love. I—always wanted to make love to you like that. That ... free."

The best you ever had, love.

Al gets up and paces, nervous. "All right, I've got these goddamned problems. You get taught certain things are wrong. If it's not for babies, it's wrong. It's wrong to use contraceptives, but we can't afford a baby, and—I don't know, Lowen. The world is crazy. But that night, it wasn't me. Not even my voice."

"No, it wasn't."

Lowen must be way down, depressed, because my energy is wavering with his, and sound fades in and out. There's a muffled knock at the door. Lowen opens it to a bald little man like a wizened guru in a heavy, fur-collared overcoat.

Wait, I know this guy. It's that little weasel, Hirajian, from Riverside Realty. He rented me this place. Hirajian settles himself in a chair, briefcase on his knee, declining the sherry Al offers. He doesn't look too happy about being here, but the self-satisfied little bastard doesn't miss Al's legs, which make mine look bush league in retrospect.

I can't catch everything, but Hirajian's puzzled by something Al's saying. No problem about the lease, he allows, apartments rent in two days now, but she's apparently thrown him a curve.

Al now: ". . . not exactly our wish, but . . ."

"Unusual request . . . never anything . . ."

Now Al is flat and clear: "Did you find out?"

Hirajian opens his briefcase and brings out a sheet of paper while I strain at his through-the-wall mumble.

"Don't know why . . . however . . . before you . . ." He runs through a string of names until I make the connection. The tenants who came after me, all those damned extras who wandered through my dreams before Lowen.

Lowen stops him suddenly. He's not as depressed as Al; there's an eagerness in the question. "Did anyone die here?"

"Die?"

"It's very important." Al says.

Hirajian looks like an undertaker's assistant now, all professional solemnity and reluctance. "As a matter of fact, yes. I was getting to that. In 1974, a Miss Danowski."

Lowen's head snaps up. "First name?"

"Gail."

"Anyone named Gayla? Someone cut the name Gayla in the cement on the balcony."

"That was the Danowski woman. Gayla Damon was her stage name. She was an actress. I remember because she put that name on the lease and had to do it again with her legal signature."

"Gayla."

"You knew her, Mr. Sheppard?"

"Gayla Damon. I should, it's awfully familiar, but—"

"Single?" Al asks. "What sort of person was she?"

Hirajian cracks his prim little smile like a housewife leaning over a back fence to gossip. "Yes and no, you know show people. Her boyfriend moved in with her. I know it's the fashion nowadays, but *we*," evidently Riverside and God, "don't approve of it."

There's enough energy to laugh, and I wish you could hear me, you little second-string satyr. You made a pass when you showed me this place. I remember: I was wearing that new tan suit from Bergdorf's, and I couldn't split fast enough. But it was the best place yet for the money, so I took it.

Damn it, how did I die? What happened. Don't fade out, weasel. Project, let me hear you.

Al sets down her sherry glass. "We just can't stay here. It's impossible."

Don't go, Lowen. You're all I have, all there is. I won't touch Al, I promise never again. But don't go.

Of course there were promises, Nick. There's always a promise. No one has to spell it out.

I said that once. I'm starting to remember.

While Hirajian patters on, Lowen's lost in some thought. There's something in his eyes I've never seen before. A concern, a caring.

"You mean he didn't come back even when he heard Gayla was dead?"

I love the way he says my name. Like a song, new strength.

"No end of legal trouble," Hirajian clucks. "We couldn't locate him or any family at first. A Mister . . . yes, a Mister Wrenn came and made all the arrangements. An old boyfriend, I suppose."

You did that for me, Bill? You came back and helped me out. Boy, what I had and threw away. Sand through my fingers.

"Gayla. Gayla Damon." I grow stronger as Lowen repeats my name, stronger yet as he rises and takes a step toward the balcony door. I could touch him, but I don't dare now. "Yes. Just the name I forgot. It's hard to believe, Al, but it's the only thing I can believe."

Such a queer, tender look. Al reads it too. "What, Lowen?"

He strides quickly away to the bedroom, and the lights dim a little. Then he's back with a folded paper, so lost in some thought that Al just stares at him and Hirajian is completely lost.

"The things we learn about life," Lowen says. "An English professor of mine said once that life is too coincidental for art; that's why art is structured. Mr. Hirajian, you said no one else ever complained of disturbances in this apartment. I'm not a medium, can't even predict the weather. But I'm, beginning to understand a little of this."

Will you tell me, for Christ's sake?

He hands the paper to Al. It looks like an old theater program. "You see, Mister Hirajian, she's still here."

He has to say it again, delicately as possible. Hirajian pooh-poohs the whole notion. "Oh really, now, you can't be sure of something like that."

"We know," Al says in a hard voice. "We haven't told you everything. She, it, something's here, and it's destructive."

"No, I don't think so." Lowen nods to the program. I can't see it too well. "Eagle Lake Playhouse, 1974. I saw her work."

You couldn't have. You were only—"

"She played Gwendolyn in *Becket*. That's her autograph by her name."

Where the hell is Eagle Lake? Wait a minute. Wait—a—minute. I'm remembering.

"My father was taking me back to school. I spent my whole life in boarding schools all the way through college. Dad thought for our last night together, he'd take me to an uplifting play and save himself making conversation. My parents were very efficient that way.

"Gayla only had one scene, but she was so open, so completely translucent that I couldn't take my eyes off her."

I did play Eagle Lake, and there's a faint memory of some double-breasted country-club type coming back for an autograph for his kid.

"I still remember, she had a line that went: 'My lord cares for nothing in this world, does he?' She turned to Becket then, and you could see a *line* in that turn, a power that reached the other actor and came out to the audience. The other actors were good, but Gayla lit up the stage with something—unbearably human."

Damn right, love. I was gangbusters in that role. And you saw me? I could almost believe in God now, though He hasn't called lately.

"I was sixteen, and I thought I was the only one in the

world who could be so lonely. She showed me we're all alike in that. All our feelings touch. Next day I hitchhiked all the way back to the theater from school...." Lowen trails off, looking at Al and the apartment. "And this was her place. She wasn't very old. How did she die?"

"Depressing," Hirajian admits. "Very ugly and depressing, but then suicide always is."

What!

"But as regards your moving out just because—"

The hell I did, no *way*, mister. No. No. NO! I won't listen to any more. Don't believe him, Lowen.

Lowen's on his feet, head tilted in that listening attitude. Al puts down her glass, pale and tense. "What is it?"

"She's here now. She's angry."

"How do you know?"

"Don't ask me how, damn it. I know. She's here."

No, Lowen. On the worst, weakest day of my life, I couldn't do that. Listen. Hear me. Please.

Then Al's up, frightened and desperate. "Go away, whoever you are. For the love of God, go away."

I barely hear her, flinging myself away from them out onto the balcony, silent mouth screaming at the frustration and stupid injustice of it. A lie, a lie, and Lowen is leaving, sending me back to nothing and darkness. But the strength is growing, born of rage and terror. Lowen. Lowen. Lowen. Hear me. I didn't. *Hear me*.

"Lowen, don't!"

I hear Al's voice, then the sudden, sharp sound of the balcony door wrenching open. And as I turn to Lowen, the whole, uncut film starts to roll. And, oh Jesus, I remember.

Eagle Lake. That's where it ended, Lowen. Not here, no matter what they tell you. That's where all the years, parts, buses, beds, the whole game came to an end. When I found that, no matter what, none of it worked any more. Maybe I was growing up a little at last, looking for the *me* in all of it.

Funny: I wasn't even going to audition for stock that summer, Bill called me to do a couple of roles at Eagle Lake, and Nick urged me to go. It was a good season, closing with *A Streetcar Named Desire*. The owner, Ermise Stour, jobbed in Natalie Bond for Blanche DuBois, and I was to her understudy. Nattie's name wasn't smash movie box office any more, but still big enough for stock and star-package houses. She'd be Erm's insurance to make up whatever they lost on the rest of the season.

Erm, you tough old bag. You were going to sell that broken-down theater after every season. I'll bet you're still there, chain-smoking over a bottle of Chivas and babying that ratty poodle.

Ermise lived in a rambling ex-hotel with a huge fireplace in the lounge. We had all our opening-night parties there with a big blaze going because Eagle Lake never warmed up or dried out even in August.

At the opening party for *Becket*, all of us were too keyed up to get drunk, running on adrenalin from the show, slopping drinks and stuffing sandwiches, fending off the local reviewers, horny boy scouts with a course in journalism.

Dinner? No thanks. I've got a horrible week coming up, and it's all I can do to shower and fall into bed. Bill, let's get *out* of here. Thanks, you're a jewel, I needed a refill. Gimme your sweater. Jesus, doesn't it ever get warm in this place? You could age beef in our dressing room.

Nick was down for a few days the week before. Bill rather pointedly made himself scarce. He was still in love with me. That must have hurt, working with me day after day, keeping it inside, and I didn't help matters by dragging Nick everywhere like a prize bull: hey, look what I got! Smart girl, Gayla. With a year's study, you could be an idiot.

But Nick was gone, and we'd managed to get *Becket* open despite falling energy, colds, frayed nerves and lousy weather. It was good just to stand with Bill against the porch railing, watching moths bat themselves silly against the overhead light. Bill was always guarded when we were alone now. I kept it light and friendly, asked about his preparations for *Streetcar*. He sighed with an Old Testament flavor of doom.

"Don't ask. Erm had to cut the set budget, first read-through is tomorrow morning, and Nattie's plane won't get in until one. I'm going to be up all night and I'll still only be about five pages ahead of you people on blocking."

"Why's she late?"

"Who the hell knows? Business with her agent or something. You'll have to read in for her."

Good. One more precious rehearsal on my Blanche, one more time to read those beautiful words and perhaps find one more color in them before Natalie Bond froze it all in star glitter. That was all I had to look forward to now. The fatigue, the wet summer, lousy houses, all of it accumulated to a desolation I couldn't shrug off. I had a small part in *Streetcar*, but understudying Natalie Bond meant watching her do my role, never to touch the magic myself. Maybe her plane could crash—just a little—but even then, what? Somehow even the thought of Nick depressed me. Back in New York he'd get in to see the right agents where I couldn't, landing commercials, lining up this, grabbing that, always smarter at business than me.

That night before the party, I sat on my bed, staring glumly at the yellow-green wallpaper and my battered Samsonite luggage, and thought: *I'm tired of you. Something's gone. There's gotta be more than this.* And I curled up in my old gray bathrobe, wallowing in self-pity. Nick, you want to get married? Bring me the towel and wash my back? Baby me a little when I feel rotten, like now? There's a big empty place in me wants to be pregnant with more than a part. Tired, negative, I knew Nick would never marry me; I was kidding myself.

So it was good to have Bill there on the porch for a minute. I leaned against him and he put an arm around me. We should have gone to bed and let it be beautiful one more time. It would have been the last.

"Tired, Gay?"

"I want to go home."

Except I never in my whole life found where it was.

Natalie Bond came and conquered. She knew her lines pretty well going in and crammed the rest with me in her room or the restaurant down our street. No one recognized her at first with her hair done just the right shade of fading dishwater blonde for Blanche, most of her thin face hidden behind a huge pair of prescription sunglasses.

She was near-sighted to blindness; some of her intensity on film must have come from trying to feel out the blocking by Braille. But a pro she was. She soaked up Bill's direction, drove herself and us, and I saw the ruthless energy that made Nattie a star.

I saw other things, too. Nattie hadn't been on a live stage for a lot years. She missed values left and right in Blanche and didn't have time to pick them up on a two-week stock schedule. Film is a director's medium. He can put your attention where he wants with the camera. Stage work takes a whole different set of muscles, and hers were flabby, unused to sustaining an action or mood for two and a half hours.

But for the first time that season, we were nearly sold out at the box office. Erm was impressed. Bill wasn't.

"They're coming to see a star. She could fart her way through Blanche and they'll still say she's wonderful." Maybe but life wasn't all skittles for Nattie. She had two children in expensive schools and got endless phone calls from her manager in California about taxes.

"I gotta work, honey," she told me over black coffee and dry toast. "The wolf's got my ass in his chops already."

She meant it. Another phone call, and that same afternoon between lunch and rehearsal call, Nattie Bond was gone, and I was sitting in Ermise's living room again while Erm swore back and forth across the worn carpet, waving her drink like a weapon, and Bill tried to look bereaved. He always wanted me for Blanche. He had me now.

"Screwed me from the word go." Ermise sprayed ashes over the rug and her poodle. "She knew this when she signed and never said a goddamn word."

The fact filtered through my rosy haze. Natalie's agent had a picture deal on the coast so close to signing that it was worth it to let Ermise sue. They'd just buy up her contract—if she could be in Los Angeles tomorrow.

Ermise hurled her cigarette into the trash-filled fireplace, gulped the last of her drink and turned a mental page. Nattie was one problem, the show another. "You ready to go, Gayla?"

"In my sleep, love."

I was already readjusting the role to the Blanche in my ear and not as sorry for the box office as Erm. Screw 'em all, they were going to see ten times the Blanche Nattie Bond could give them on the best day she ever worked.

"Bill wants me to give you a raise," Ermise said. "Wish I could, Gay, but things are tight."

I pulled the worn script out of my jeans, grinning like a fool back at Bill, who couldn't hide his glee any more. "Just pay on time, Erm. Keep out of my hair and don't clutter up my stage. Bill, let's go to work."

From my first rehearsal, the play convulsed and became a different animal. The whole cast had to shift gears for me, but no longer suffused by Nattie's hard light they began to find themselves and glimmer with life. I ate and slept with the script while Blanche came sure and clear. Hell, I'd been rehearsing her for fourteen years. It wasn't hard to identify: the hunger for love half appeased in bed-hopping and sexual junk food, and what that does to a woman. The blurred, darkening picture of a girl waiting in her best dress to go to the dance of life with someone who never came.

Then, just as it seemed to be coming together, it went flat, deader than I am now. But out of that death came a beautiful, risky answer.

Blanche DuBois is a bitch of a role and demands a powerhouse actress. That's the problem. Like the aura that surrounds Hamlet, the role accumulates a lot of star-shtick, and something very subtle can get lost. I determined to strip away the layers of gloss and find what was there to begin with.

"The part's a trap, Bill. All those fluttery, curlicued lines reach out and beg you to *act* them. And you wind up with dazzle again, a concert performance."

"Cadenzas," he agreed with me. "The old Williams poetry."

"Right! Cadenzas, scales. No, by God. I've played the Deep South. There's a smothered quality to those women that gets lost that way. The script describes her as a moth. Moths don't dazzle. They don't glitter.

"Remember that night on the porch," Bill said thoughtfully. "They don't glitter, but they do need the light."

And that was it. Blanche aspired to the things she painted with foolish words. A dream of glitter seen by a nearsighted person by a failing candle. The lines are ornate, but just possibly, Blanche is not quite as intelligent as she's been played.

A long artistic chance, but they're the only ones worth taking. If you don't have the guts to be wrong, take up accounting.

So my Blanche emerged a very pathetic woman, a little grotesque as such women are, not only desperate for love but logical in her hopes for Mitch. For all Belle Reeve and the inbred magnolias, she's not that far above him. Bill gave me my head, knowing that by finding my own Blanche, even being wrong for a while, I'd find the play's as well. On my terms and with my own reality.

I had three lovely labor-pained days of seeing her come alive. On the third day, I was sitting in a corner of the stage with coffee and a sandwich, digging at the script while the others lunched. When Sally Kent walked in, I snapped at her.

"Where's the rest. It's two o'clock. Let's go."

"They want you over at the office, Gay."

"What the hell for? I don't have time. Where's Bill?"

"At the office," Sally admitted reluctantly. "Natalie Bond is here. She's back in the show."

The kiss of death. Even as I shook my head, no, Erm wouldn't do this to me, I knew she would.

Ermise hunched in a chair by the fireplace, bitter with what she had to do, trying not to antagonize Bill any further. He poised on the sofa, seething like a malevolent cat.

"Nattie will do the show after all," Ermise said. "I have to put her back in, Gay."

I couldn't speak at first; sick, quivering on my feet with that horrible end-of-the-rope hollowness in my stomach. No place to go from here. No place...

"When we pulled her name off the advertising, we lost more than a third of our reservations." Erm snorted. "I don't like it. I don't like her right now, but she's the only thing'll keep my theater open."

Bill's comment cut with the hard edge of disgust. "You know what this does to the cast, don't you? They've readjusted once. Now they have to do it again and open in two days. They were an ensemble with Gayla. Now they're the tail of a star vehicle."

Bill knew it was already lost, but he was doing this for me.

Ermise shook her head. "Gay, honey, I can't afford it, but I'm gonna raise you retroactive to the first week of your contract." Her hands fluttered in an uncharacteristically helpless gesture. "I owe you that. And you'll go back in as Eunice. But next season—"

I found my voice. It was strange, old. "Don't do this to me. This role, it's mine, I earned it. She'll ruin it."

"Don't look at me," Bill snapped to Ermise. "She's right."

Ermise went defensive. "I don't care who's right. You're all for Gay. Fine, but I can't run a theater that way. Lucky to break even as it is. Nattie's back, she plays, and that's the end of it. Gay's contract reads 'as cast.' She's Eunice. What else can I say?"

I showed her what else. I ripped the *Streetcar* script in four parts and threw them in the fireplace. "You can say good-bye Ermise. Then you can take your raise and shove it." I was already lurching toward the door, voice breaking. "Then you can put someone in my roles, because I'm leaving."

I meant it. Without Blanche, there was no reason to stay another minute. Finished. Done.

Except for Natalie Bond. I found her in her hotel room, already dressed for rehearsal and running over the script.

"Come on in, Gayla. Drink?"

"No."

She read my tension as I crouched with my back against the door. "All right, hon. Get it off your chest."

"I will."

I told the bitch what I felt and what I thought and didn't leave anything out. It was quite a speech for no rehearsal, beginning with my teens when I first knew I had to play Blanche, and the years and hard work that made me worthy of it. There wasn't a rep company in the east I hadn't worked, or a major role from Rosalind to Saint Joan I hadn't played. To walk out on the show like she did was pure shit. To crawl back was worse.

"Right," said Nattie. She faced me all through it, let me get it all out. I was crying when I finished. I sank down on a chair, grabbing for one of her kleenex.

"Now do you want a drink?"

"Yes, what the hell."

She wasn't all rat, Nattie. She could have put me down with the star routine, but she fixed me a stiff gin and soda without a word. I remember her fixing that drink: thick glasses and no make up, gristly thin. She had endless trouble with her uterus, infection after painful infection and a work schedule that never allowed her to heal properly. A hysterectomy ended the whole thing. Nattie's face was thinner than mine, all the softness gone, mouth and cheeks drawn tight. No matter how sincere, the smile couldn't unclench.

And this, I thought, is what I want to be? Help me, Nick. Take me home. There's gotta be a home somewhere, a little rest.

"Know what we're like?" Nattie mused. "A little fish swimming away from a big, hungry fish who's just about to be eaten by a bigger fish. That's us, honey. And that's me in the middle."

She screwed Ermise, but someone shafted her too. The picture deal was a big fat fake. The producer wanted someone a little bigger and hustled Nattie very plausibly to scare the lady into reaching for a pen.

"I'm broke, Gayla. I owe forty thousand in back taxes,

my house is on a second mortgage, and my kids' tuition is overdue. Those kids are all I have. I don't know where the hell to go from here, but Ermise needs me and I sure as hell need the job."

While I huddled over my drink, unable to speak, Nattie scribbled something on a memo pad.

"You're too good to waste, you're not commercial, and you'll probably die broke. But I saw your rehearsal this morning."

I looked up at her in a weepy surprise. The smile wasn't quite so hard just then.

"If I can do it half that well, Gay. Half."

She shoved the paper into my hand. "That's my agent in New York. He's with William Morris. If he can't get you work, no one can. I'll call him myself." She glanced at her dressing table clock. "Time, gotta run."

Nattie divined the finality in my shoulders as I sagged toward the door. "You going to play Eunice?"

"No. I'm leaving."

Pinning her hair, she shot me a swift, unsmiling appraisal through the mirror. "Good for you. You got a man in New York?"

"Yeah."

"Get married," she mumbled through a mouthful of pins. "It's not worth it." As the door closed, she raised her voice. "But call my agent."

My bags were packed, but I hadn't bothered to change clothes. That's why my permanent costume, I suppose. Who knew then I'd get very tired of black. Bill insisted on driving me to the airport. When he came for me, I must have looked pathetic, curled up on the bed in one more temporary, damp summer room just waiting to eject me. No love lost; I got damned sick of yellow-green wallpaper.

Bill sat on the edge of the bed. "Ready, love?"

I didn't move or answer. Done, finished. Bill put aside the old hurt and lay down beside me, bringing me into his arms. I guess something in him had to open in spite of his defenses. He opened my heart gently as a baby's hand clutched around something that might harm it, letting me cry the last of it out against his shoulder. The light faded in the room while we lay together.

We kissed good-by like lovers at the departure gate. Bill

was too much a part of me for anything else. Maybe he knew better than I how little was waiting for me.

"Be good, Gay."

"You too." I fiddled with his collar. "Don't forget to take your vitamins, you need them. Call me when you get back."

He hugged me one last time. "Why don't you marry me sometime?"

For a lot of reasons, Bill. Because I was a fool and something of a coward. The stunting begins in the seed when we learn not to like ourselves. The sad thing about life is that we usually get what we really want. Let it be.

Funny, though: that was my first and last proposal, and I kissed him goodby, walked out of his life, and four hours later I was dead.

There was time on the plane to get some of it together. Natalie was a star, at the top where I wanted to be, and look at her: most of the woman cut out of her, flogged to work not by ambition but need. Driven and used. She reminded me of a legless circus freak propelling herself on huge, overdeveloped arms, the rest of her a pitiful afterthought cared for by an expensive gynecologist. I thought: at least when I get home there'll be Nick. Don't call him from the airport; let it be a surprise. We'll get some coffee and coldcuts, make love and talk half the night. I needed to talk, to see us plain.

Get married, Nattie said. It isn't worth it.

Maybe not the way I chased it for fourteen years. I'd call her agent, keep working, but more New York jobs with time left over to be with Nick, to sit on my balcony and just breathe or read. To make a few friends outside of theater. To see a doctor and find out how tough I really am, and if everything in the baby box is working right, so that maybe—

Like she said, so maybe get married and have kids while I can. A little commitment, Nick, a little tomorrow. If the words sound strange, I just learned it. Give me this, Nick. I need it.

The light was on in our living room as I hauled my suitcase out of the cab and started up. Hell, I won't even buzz, just turn the key in the lock and reach for him.

I did that.

There was—yes, I remember—one blessed moment of breathing the good, safe air of my own living room as I set down the luggage. I heard a faint stirring from the bedroom.

Good, I've surprised him. If Nick was just waking from a nap, we'd have that much more time to touch each other.

"It's me, baby."

I crossed to the bedroom door, groping inside for the light switch. "I'm home."

I didn't need the switch. There was enough light to see them frozen on the torn-up bed. The other one was older, a little flabby. He muttered something to Nick. I stood there, absurd myself, and choked: "Excuse me."

Then, as if someone punched me in the stomach, I stumbled to the bathroom, pushed the door shut and fell back against it.

"Get him out of here, Nick!"

The last word strangled off as I doubled over the john and vomited all the horrible day out of me, with two hours left to live, retching and sobbing, not wanting to hear whatever was said beyond the door. After a short time, the front door closed. I washed my face, dried it with the stiff, clumsy movements of exhaustion, and got out to the living room somehow, past the bed where Nick was smoking a cigarette, the sheet pulled up over his lean thighs.

I remember pouring a drink. That was foolish on an empty stomach, the worst thing anyone could have done. I sat on the sofa, waiting.

"Nick." The silence from the bedroom was the only thing I could feel in my shock. "Nick, please come out. I want to talk to you."

I heard him rustle into his clothes. In a moment Nick came out, bleak and sullen.

"Why are you back so early?"

"No, they—" My reactions were still disjointed, coming out of shock, but the anger was building. "They put Nattie Bond back in the show. I walked out."

That seemed to concern him more than anything else. "You just walked out? They'll get Equity on you."

"Never mind about Equity, what are *we* gonna do?"

"What do you mean?" he asked calmly.

"Oh, man, are you for real?" I pointed at the door. "What was that?"

"That may be a Broadway job." He turned away into the kitchen. "Now get off my back."

"The hell I—"

"Hey look, Gayla. I haven't made any promises to you.

You wanted me to move in. Okay, I moved in. We've had it good."

I began to shake. "Promises? Of course there were promises. There's always a promise, nobody has to spell it out. I could have gone to bed with Bill Wrenn plenty of times this summer, but I didn't."

He only shrugged. "So whose fault is that? Not mine."

"You bastard!" I threw my glass at him. He ducked, the thing went a mile wide, then Nick was sopping up whisky and bits of glass while I shook myself apart on the couch, teeth chattering so hard I had to clamp my mouth tight shut. It was all hitting me at once, and I couldn't handle half of it. Nick finished cleaning up without a word, but I could see even then the tight line of his mouth and the angry droop of his eyelids. He had guts of a kind, Nick. He could face anything because it didn't matter. All the important things were outside, to be reached for. Inside I think he was dead.

"The meanest thing Bill ever said to me," I stuttered. "When I left him for you, h-he said you played both sides of the fence. And I c-called him a goddamn liar. I couldn't believe he'd be small enough to—Nick, I'm falling apart. They took my show, and I came home to you because I don't know what to do."

Nick came over, sat down and held me in his arms. "I'm not, Gayla."

"Not what?"

"What Bill said."

"Then w-what was this?"

He didn't answer, just kissed me. I clung to Nick like a lost child.

Why do we always try to rewrite what happened? Even now I see myself pointing to the door and kissing him off with a real Bette Davis sizzler for a curtain. Bullshit. I needed Nick. The accounting department was already, toting up the cost of what I wanted and saying: *I'll change him. It's worth it.*

I only cried wearily in his arms while Nick soothed and stroked me. "I'm not that," he said again. "Just that so many guys are hung up on role-playing and all that shit. Oh, it's been said about me."

I twisted in his lap to look at him. "Nick, why did you come to me?"

The question gave him more trouble than it should. "I like you. You're the greatest girl I ever met."

Something didn't add up. Nothing ever bugged Nick before; he could always handle it, but he was finding this hard.

"That's not enough," I persisted. "Not tonight."

Nick disengaged himself with a bored sigh. "Look, I have to go out."

"Go out? Now?" I couldn't believe he'd leave me like this. "Why?"

He walked away toward the bedroom. I felt the anger grow cold with something I'd never faced before, answers to questions that gnawed at the back of my mind from our first night. "Why, Nick? Is it him? Did that fat queer tell you to come over after you ditched the hag?"

Nick turned on me, lowering. "I don't like that word."

"Queer."

"I said—"

"Queer."

"All right." He kicked viciously at the bedroom door with all the force he wanted to spend stopping my mouth. "It's a fact in this business. That's why I get in places you don't. It's a business, cut and dried, not an *aht fawm* like you're always preaching."

"Come off it, Nick." I stood up, ready for him and wanting the fight. "That casting couch bit went out with Harlow. Is that how you get jobs? That, and the cheap, scene-stealing tricks you use when you know and I know I played you against the wall in Lexington, you hypocritical son of a bitch."

Nick threw up a warning hand. "Hey, wait just one damn minute, Bernhardt. I never said I was or ever could be as good as you. But I'll tell you one thing." Nick opened the closet and snaked his jacket off a hanger. "I'll be around and working when nobody remembers you, because I know the business. You've been around fourteen years and still don't know the score. You won't make rounds, you don't want to be bothered waiting for an agent to see you. You're a goddamn *ahtist*. You won't wait in New York for something to develop, hell no. You'll take any show going out to Noplaceville, and who the hell ever sees you but some jerkoff writing for a newspaper no one reads. Integrity? Bullshit, lady. You are *afraid* of New York, afraid to take a chance on it."

Nick subsided a little. "That guy who was here, he produces. He's got a big voice where it counts." Again he looked away with that odd, inconsistent embarrassment.

"He didn't want to sleep with me, really. He's basically straight."

That was too absurd for anger. "Basically?"

"He only wanted a little affection."

"And you, Nick. Which way do you go basically. I mean was it his idea or yours?"

That was the first totally vulnerable moment I ever saw in Nick. He turned way, leaning against the sink. I could barely hear him. "I don't know. It's never made much difference. So what's the harm? I don't lose anything, and I may gain."

He started for the door, but I stopped him. "Nick, I need you. What's happened to me today, I'm almost sick. Please don't do this to me."

"Do what? Look." He held me a moment without warmth or conviction. "I'll only be gone a little while. We'll talk tomorrow, okay?"

"Don't go, Nick."

He straightened his collar carefully with a sidelong glance at the mirror. "We can't talk when you're like this. There's no point."

I dogged him desperately, needing something to hang onto. "Please don't go. I'm sorry for what I said. Nick, we can work it out, but don't leave me alone."

"I have to." His hand was already on the door, cutting me off like a thread hanging from his sleeve.

"Why!" It ripped up out of the bottom, out of the hate without which we never love or possess anything. "Because that fat faggot with his job means more than I do, right? How low do you crawl to make a buck in this business? Or is it all business? Jesus, you make me sick."

Nick couldn't be insulted. Even at the end, he didn't have that to spare me. Just a look from those cool blue eyes I tried so hard to please, telling me he was a winner in a game he knew, and I just didn't make it.

"It's your apartment. I'll move."

"Nick, don't go."

The door closed.

What did I do then? I should remember, they were the last minutes of my life. The door closed. I heard Nick thumping down the carpeted stairs, and thank God for cold comfort I didn't run after him. I poured a straight shot and finished it in one pull.

A hollow, eye-of-the-storm calm settled on me and then a

depression so heavy it was a physical pain. I wandered through the apartment drinking too much and too fast, talking to Nick, to Bill, to Nattie, until I collapsed, clumsy, hiccuping drunk on the floor with half an hour to live:

Another drink. Get blind, drunk enough to reach ... something, to blot out the Lump. Yeah, she's still with you, the goddamn little loser. Don't you ever learn, loser? No, she won't ever learn. Yesterday did this day's madness prepare. What play was that and who cares?

I tried to think but nothing came together. My life was a scattered tinkertoy, all joints and pieces without meaning or order. A sum of apples and oranges: parts played, meals eaten, clothes worn, he said and I said, old tickets, old programs, newspaper reviews yellowed and fragile as Blanche's love letters. Apples and oranges. Where did I leave anything of myself, who did I love, what did I have? No one. Nothing.

Only Bill Wrenn.

"Christ, Bill, help me!"

I clawed for the phone with the room spinning and managed to call the theater. One of the girl apprentices answered. I struggled to make myself understood with a thickening tongue. "Yeah, Bill Wrenn, 'simportant. Gayla Damon. Yeah, hi, honey. He's not? Goddamnit, he's gotta be. I *need* him. When'll he be back? Yeah ... yeah. Tell'm call Gayla, please. Please. Yeah, trouble. Real trouble. I need him."

That's how it happened. I dropped the phone in the general vicinity of the hook and staggered to the pitching sink to make one more huge, suicidal drink, crying and laughing, part drunk, part hysteria. But Bill was going to bail me out like he always had, and, boy, ol' Gay had learned her lesson. I was a fool to leave him. He loved me. Bill loved me and I was afraid of that. Afraid to be loved. How dumb can you get?

"How dumb?" I raged mushily at the Lump in the mirror. "You with the great, soulful eyes. You never knew shit, baby."

I was sweating. The wool sweater oppressed my clammy skin. Some sober molecule said take it off, but no. It's cooler out on my balcony. I will go out on my beautiful, nighted balcony and present my case to the yet unknowing world.

I half fell through the door. The balcony had a low

railing, lower than I judged as I stumbled and heaved my drunken weight behind the hand flung out to steady myself and—

Fell. No more time.

That's it, finished. Now I've remembered. It was that sudden, painless, meaningless. No fade out, no end title music resolving the conflict themes, only torn film fluttering past the projector light, leaving a white screen.

There's a few answers anyway. I could get a lump in my throat, if I had one, thinking how Bill came and checked me out. God, let's hope they kept me covered. I must have looked awful. Poor Bill; maybe I gave you such a rotten time because I knew you could take it and still hang in. That's one of the faces of love, Mister Wrenn.

But I'd never have guessed about Lowen. Just imagine: he saw me that long ago and remembered all these years because I showed him he wasn't alone. I still can't add it up. Apples and oranges.

Unless, just maybe. . . .

"Lowen!"

The sound track again, the needle dropped on time. The balcony door thunders open and slams shut. Al calls again, but Lowen ignores her, leaning against the door, holding it closed.

"Gayla?"

His eyes move searchingly over the balcony in the darkening winter afternoon. From my name etched in the cement, around the railing. Lowen's whole concentrated being probes the gray light and air, full of purpose and need.

"Gayla, I know you're here."

As he says my name, sound and vision and my own strength treble. I turn to him, wondering if through the sheer power of his need he can see me yet.

Lowen, can you hear me?

"I think I know what this means."

I stretch out my hand, open up, let it touch his face, and as I tingle and hurt with it, Lowen turns his cheek into the caress.

"Yes, I feel you close."

Talk to me, love.

"Isn't it strange, Gayla?"

Not strange at all, not us.

"When I saw you that night, I wanted to reach out and

touch you, but I was just too shy. Couldn't even ask for my own autograph."

Why not? I could have used a little touching.

"But I hitched all the way from school next day just to catch a glimpse of you. Hid in the back of the theater and watched you rehearse."

That was Blanche. You saw that?

"It was the same thing all over again. You had something that reached out and showed me how we're all alike. I never saw a lonelier person than you on that stage. Or more beautiful. I cried."

You saw Blanche. She did have a beauty.

"Oh, Gayla, the letters I wrote you and never sent. Forgive me. I forgot the name but not the lesson. If you hear me: you were the first woman I ever loved, and you taught me right. It's a giving."

I can hear Al's urgent knock on the other side of the door. "Lowen, what is it? Are you all right?"

He turns his head and smiles. God, he's beautiful. "Fine, Al. She loves this place, Gayla. Don't drive her away."

I won't, but don't go. Now when I'm beginning to understand so much.

He shakes his head. "This is our first house. We're new, all kinds of problems. Parents, religion, everything."

Can you *hear* me?

"We were never loved by anyone before, either of us. That's new, too. You pray for it—"

Like a fire:

"—like a fire to warm yourself."

You do hear me.

"But it's scary. What do you do with the fire when it comes?" Lowen's hands reach out, pleading. "Don't take this away from her. Don't hurt my Al. You're stronger than us. You can manage."

I stretch my hand to touch his. With all my will, I press the answer through the contact.

Promise, Lowen.

"Don't make me shut you out, I don't know if I could. Go away and keep our secret? Take a big piece of love with you?"

Yes. Just that I was reaching for something, like you, and I had it all the time. So do you, Lowen. You're a—

I feel again as I did when the star fell across the sky, joyful and new and big as all creation without needing a reason, as Lowen's real fingers close around the memory of mine.

You're a *mensche,* love. Like me.

Lowen murmurs: "I feel your hand. I don't care what anyone says. Your kind of woman doesn't kill herself. I'll never believe it."

Bet on it. And thank you.

So it was a hell of a lot more than apples and oranges. It was a giving, a love. Hear that, Bill? Nattie? What I called life was just the love, the giving, like kisses on the wind, thrown to the audience, to my work, to the casual men, to whom it may concern. I was a giver, and if the little takers like Nick couldn't dig that, tough. That's the way it went down. All the miserable, self-cheating years, something heard music and went on singing. If Nattie could do it half as well. If she was half as alive as me, she meant. I loved all my life, because they're the same thing. Man, I was beautiful.

That's the part of you that woke me, Lowen. You're green, but you won't go through life like a tourist. You're going to get hurt and do some hurting yourself, but maybe someday. . . .

That's it, Lowen. that's the plot. You said it: we all touch, and the touching continues us. All those nights, throwing all of myself at life, and who's to say I did it alone?

So when you're full up with life, maybe you'll wake like me to spill it over into some poor, scared guy or girl. Your full of life like me, Lowen. It's a beautiful, rare gift.

It's dark enough now to see stars and the fingernail sliver of moon. A lovely moment for Lowen and me, like a night with Bill a moment before we made love for the first time. Lowen and I holding hands in the evening. Understanding. His eyes move slowly from my hand up, up toward my face.

"Gayla, I can see you."

Can you, honest?"

"Very clear. You're wearing a sweater and jeans. And you're smiling."

Am I ever!

"And very beautiful."

Bet your ass, love. I feel great, like I finally got it together.

One last painful, lovely current of life as Lowen squeezes my hand. "Good-bye, Gayla."

So long, love.

Lowen yanks open the door. "Al, Mister Hirajian? Come on out. It's a lovely evening."

Alice peeks out to see Lowen leaning over the railing, enjoying the river and the early stars. His chest swells; he's laughing and he looks marvelous, inviting Al into his arms the way he did on their first day here. She comes unsurely to nestle in beside him, one arm around his waist. "Who were you talking to?"

"She's gone, Al. You've got nothing to be afraid of. Except being afraid."

"Lowen, I'm not going to—"

"This is our house, and nobody's going to take it away from us." He turns Al to him and kisses her. "Nobody wants to, that's a promise. So don't run away from it or yourself."

She shivers a little, still uncertain. "Do you really think we can stay. I can't—"

"Hey, love." Lowen leans into her, cocky and charming, but meaning it. "Don't tell a *mensche* what you can't. Hey, Hirajian."

When the little prune pokes his head out the door, Lowen sweeps his arm out over the river and the whole lit-up West Side. "Sorry for all the trouble, but we've changed our minds. I mean, look at it! Who could give up a balcony with a view like this?"

He's the last thing I see before the lights change: Lowen holding Al and grinning out at the world. I thought the lights were dimming, but it's something else, another cue coming up. The lights cross-fade up, up, more pink and amber, until—my God, it's gorgeous!

I'm not dead, not gone. I feel more alive than ever. I'm Gail and Gayla and Lowen and Bill and Al and all of them magnified, heightened, fully realized, flowing together like bright, silver streams into—

Will you look at that *set*. Fantastic. Who's on the lights?

So that's what You look like. Ri-i-ght. I'm with it now, and I love You too. Give me a follow-spot, Baby.

I'm on.

THE TOLL-HOUSE

by W. W. Jacobs

"It's all nonsense," said Jack Barnes. "Of course people have died in the house; people die in every house. As for the noises—wind in the chimney and rats in the wainscot are very convincing to a nervous man. Give me another cup of tea, Meagle."

"Lester and White are first," said Meagle, who was presiding at the tea-table of the Three Feathers Inn. "You've had two."

Lester and White finished their cups with irritating slowness, pausing between sips to sniff the aroma, and to discover the sex and dates of arrival of the "strangers" which floated in some numbers in the beverage. Mr. Meagle served them to the brim, and then, turning to the grimly expectant Mr. Barnes, blandly requested him to ring for hot water.

"We'll try and keep your nerves in their present healthy condition," he remarked. "For my part I have a sort of half-and-half belief in the supernatural."

"All sensible people have," said Lester. "An aunt of mine saw a ghost once."

White nodded.

"I had an uncle that saw one," he said.

"It always is somebody else that sees them," said Barnes.

"Well, there is a house," said Meagle, "a large house at an absurdly low rent, and nobody will take it. It has taken toll of at least one life of every family that has lived there—however short the time—and since it has stood empty caretaker after caretaker has died there. The last caretaker died fifteen years ago."

"Exactly," said Barnes. "Long enough ago for legends to accumulate."

"I'll bet you a sovereign you won't spend the night there alone, for all your talk," said White, suddenly.

"And I," said Lester.

"No," said Barnes slowly. "I don't believe in ghosts nor in any supernatural things whatever; all the same I admit that I should not care to pass a night there alone."

"But why not?" inquired White.

"Wind in the chimney," said Meagle with a grin.

"Rats in the wainscot," chimed in Lester.

"As you like," said Barnes coloring.

"Suppose we all go," said Meagle. "Start after supper, and get there about eleven. We have been walking for ten days now without an adventure—except Barnes's discovery that ditchwater smells longest. It will be a novelty, at any rate, and, if we break the spell by all surviving, the grateful owner ought to come down handsome."

"Let's see what the landlord has to say about it first," said Lester. "There is no fun in passing a night in an ordinary empty house. Let us make sure that it is haunted."

He rang the bell, and, sending for the landlord, appealed to him in the name of our common humanity not to let them waste a night watching in a house in which spectres and hobgoblins had no part. The reply was more than reassuring, and the landlord, after describing with considerable art the exact appearance of a head which had been seen hanging out of a window in the moonlight, wound up with a polite but urgent request that they would settle his bill before they went.

"It's all very well for you young gentlemen to have your fun," he said indulgently; "but supposing as how you are all found dead in the morning, what about me? It ain't called the Toll-House for nothing, you know."

"Who died there last?" inquired Barnes, with an air of polite derision.

"A tramp," was the reply. "He went there for the sake of half a crown, and they found him next morning hanging from the balusters, dead."

"Suicide," said Barnes. "Unsound mind."

The landlord nodded. "That's what the jury brought it in," he said slowly; "but his mind was sound enough when he went in there. I'd known him, off and on, for years. I'm a poor man, but I wouldn't spend the night in that house for a hundred pounds."

He repeated this remark as they started on their expedition a few hours later. They left as the inn was closing for the night; bolts shot noisily behind them, and, as the regular customers trudged slowly homewards, they set off at a brisk pace in the direction of the house. Most of the cottages were already in darkness, and lights in others went out as they passed.

"It seems rather hard that we have got to lose a night's rest in order to convince Barnes of the existence of ghosts," said White.

"It's in a good cause," said Meagle. "A most worthy object; and something seems to tell me that we shall succeed. You didn't forget the candles, Lester?"

"I have brought two," was the reply; "all the old man could spare."

There was but little moon, and the night was cloudy. The road between high hedges was dark, and in one place, where it ran through a wood, so black that they twice stumbled in the uneven ground at the side of it.

"Fancy leaving our comfortable beds for this!" said White again. "Let me see; this desirable residential sepulchre lies to the right, doesn't it?"

"Farther on," said Meagle.

They walked on for some time in silence, broken only by White's tribute to the softness, the cleanliness, and the comfort of the bed which was receding farther and farther into the distance. Under Meagle's guidance they turned off at last to the right, and, after a walk of a quarter of a mile, saw the gates of the house before them.

The lodge was almost hidden by overgrown shrubs and the drive was choked with rank growths. Meagle leading, they pushed through it until the dark pile of the house loomed above them.

"There is a window at the back where we can get in, so the landlord says," said Lester, as they stood before the hall door.

"Window?" said Meagle. "Nonsense. Let's do the thing properly. Where's the knocker?"

He felt for it in the darkness and gave a thundering rat-tat-tat at the door.

"Don't play the fool," said Barnes crossly.

"Ghostly servants are all asleep," said Meagle gravely, "but *I'll* wake them up before I've done with them. It's scandalous keeping us out here in the dark."

He plied the knocker again, and the noise volleyed in he emptiness beyond. Then with a sudden exclamation he put out his hands and stumbled forward.

"Why, it was open all the time," he said, with an odd catch in his voice. "Come on."

"I don't believe it was open," said Lester, hanging back. "Somebody is playing us a trick."

"Nonsense," said Meagle sharply. "Give me a candle. Thanks. Who's got a match?"

Barnes produced a box and struck one, and Meagle, shielding the candle with his hand, led the way forward to the foot of the stairs. "Shut the door, somebody," he said, "there's too much draught."

"It is shut," said White, glancing behind him.

Meagle fingered his chin. "Who shut it?" he inquired, looking from one to the other. "Who came in last?"

"I did," said Lester, "but I don't remember shutting it—perhaps I did, though."

Meagle, about to speak, thought better of it, and, still carefully guarding the flame, began to explore the house, with the others close behind. Shadows danced on the walls and lurked in the corners as they proceeded. At the end of the passage they found a second staircase, and ascending it slowly gained the first floor.

"Careful!" said Meagle, as they gained the landing.

He held the candle forward and showed where the balusters had broken away. Then he peered curiously into the void beneath.

"This is where the tramp hanged himself, I suppose," he said thoughtfully.

"You've got an unwholesome mind," said White, as they walked on. "This place is quite creepy enough without your remembering that. Now let's find a comfortable room and have a little nip of whiskey apiece and a pipe. How will this do?"

He opened a door at the end of the passage and revealed a small square room. Meagle led the way with the candle, and, first melting a drop or two of tallow, stuck it on the mantelpiece. The others seated themselves on the floor and watched pleasantly as White drew from his pocket a small bottle of whiskey and a tin cup.

"H'm! I've forgotten the water," he exclaimed.

"I'll soon get some," said Meagle.

He tugged violently at the bell-handle, and the rusty jangling of a bell sounded from a distant kitchen. He rang again.

"Don't play the fool," said Barnes roughly.

Meagle laughed. "I only wanted to convince you," he said kindly. "There ought to be, at any rate, one ghost in the servants' hall."

Barnes held up his hand for silence.

"Yes?" said Meagle with a grin at the other two. "Is anybody coming?"

"Suppose we drop this game and go back," said Barnes suddenly. "I don't believe in spirits, but nerves are outside anybody's command. You may laugh as you like, but it really seemed to me that I heard a door open below and steps on the stairs."

His voice was drowned in a roar of laughter.

"He is coming round," said Meagle with a smirk. "By the time I have done with him he will be a confirmed believer. Well, who will go and get some water? Will you, Barnes?"

"No," was the reply.

"If there is any it might not be safe to drink after all these years," said Lester. "We must do without it."

Meagle nodded, and taking a seat on the floor held out his hand for the cup. Pipes were lit and the clean, wholesome smell of tobacco filled the room. White produced a pack of cards; talk and laughter rang through the room and died away reluctantly in distant corridors.

"Empty rooms always delude me into the belief that I possess a deep voice," said Meagle. "Tomorrow I—"

He started up with a smothered exclamation as the light went out suddenly and something struck him on the head. The others sprang to their feet. Then Meagle laughed.

"It's the candle," he exclaimed. "I didn't stick it enough."

Barnes struck a match and relighting the candle stuck it on the mantelpiece, and sitting down took up his cards again.

"What was I going to say?" said Meagle. "Oh, I know; to-morrow I—"

"Listen!" said White, laying his hand on the other's sleeve. "Upon my word I really thought I heard a laugh."

"Look here!" said Barnes. "What do you say to going back? I've had enough of this. I keep fancying that I hear things too; sounds of something moving about in the passage outside. I know it's only fancy, but it's uncomfortable."

"You go if you want to," said Meagle, "and we will play dummy. Or you might ask the tramp to take your hand for you, as you go downstairs."

Barnes shivered and exclaimed angrily. He got up and, walking to the half-closed door, listened.

"Go outside," said Meagle, winking at the other two. "I'll dare you to go down to the hall door and back by yourself."

Barnes came back and, bending forward, lit his pipe at the candle.

"I am nervous but rational," he said, blowing out a thin cloud of smoke. "My nerves tell me that there is something prowling up and down the long passage outside; my reason tells me that it is all nonsense. Where are my cards?"

He sat down again, and taking up his hand, looked through it carefully and led.

"Your play, White," he said after a pause.

White made no sign.

"Why, he is asleep," said Meagle. "Wake up, old man. Wake up and play."

Lester, who was sitting next to him, took the sleeping man by the arm and shook him, gently at first and then with some roughness; but White, with his back against the wall and his head bowed, made no sign. Meagle bawled in his ear and then turned a puzzled face to the others.

"He sleeps like the dead," he said, grimacing. "Well, there are still three of us to keep each other company."

"Yes," said Lester, nodding. "Unless— Good Lord! suppose—"

He broke off and eyed them trembling.

"Suppose what?" inquired Meagle.

"Nothing," stammered Lester. "Let's wake him. Try him again. *White! White!*"

"It's no good," said Meagle seriously; "there's something wrong about that sleep."

"That's what I meant," said Lester; "and if *he* goes to sleep like that, why shouldn't—"

Meagle sprang to his feet. "Nonsense," he said roughly. "He's tired out; that's all. Still, let's take him up and clear out. You take his legs and Barnes will lead the way with the candle. *Yes? Who's that?*"

He looked up quickly towards the door. "Thought I heard somebody tap," he said with a shamefaced laugh. "Now, Lester, up with him. One, two—Lester! Lester!"

He sprang forward too late; Lester, with his face buried in his arms, had rolled over on the floor fast asleep, and his utmost efforts failed to awaken him.

"He—is—asleep," he stammered. "Asleep!"

Barnes, who had taken the candle from the mantelpiece, stood peering at the sleepers in silence and dropping tallow over the floor.

"We must get out of this," said Meagle. "Quick!"

Barnes hesitated. "We can't leave them here—" he began.

"We must," said Meagle in strident tones. "If you go to sleep I shall go— Quick! Come."

He seized the other by the arm and strove to drag him to the door. Barnes shook him off, and putting the candle back on the mantelpiece, tried again to arouse the sleepers.

"It's no good," he said at last, and, turning from them, watched Meagle. "Don't you go to sleep," he said anxiously.

Meagle shook his head, and they stood for some time in uneasy silence. "May as well shut the door," said Barnes at last.

He crossed over and closed it gently. Then at a scuffling noise behind him he turned and saw Meagle in a heap on the hearthstone.

With a sharp catch in his breath he stood motionless. Inside the room the candle, fluttering in the draught, showed dimly the grotesque attitudes of the sleepers. Beyond the door there seemed to his overwrought imagination a strange and stealthy unrest. He tried to whistle, but his lips were parched, and in a mechanical fashion he stopped, and began to pick up the cards which littered the floor.

He stopped once or twice and stood with bent head listening. The unrest outside seemed to increase; a loud creaking sounded from the stairs.

"Who is there?" he cried loudly.

The creaking ceased. He crossed to the door and flinging it open, strode out into the corridor. As he walked his fears left him suddenly.

"Come on!" he cried with a low laugh. "All of you! All of you! Show your faces—your infernal ugly faces! Don't skulk!"

He laughed again and walked on; and the heap in the fireplace put out his head tortoise fashion and listened in horror to the retreating footsteps. Not until they had become inaudible in the distance did the listeners' features relax.

"Good Lord, Lester, we've driven him mad," he said in a frightened whisper. "We must go after him."

There was no reply. Meagle sprung to his feet.

"Do you hear?" he cried. "Stop your fooling now; this is serious. White! Lester! Do you hear?"

He bent and surveyed them in angry bewilderment. "All right," he said in a trembling voice. "You won't frighten me, you know."

He turned away and walked with exaggerated carelessness in the direction of the door. He even went outside and peeped through the crack, but the sleepers did not stir. He glanced into the blackness behind, and then came hastily into the room again.

He stood for a few seconds regarding them. The stillness in the house was horrible; he could not even hear them breathe. With a sudden resolution he snatched the candle from the mantelpiece and held the flame to White's finger. Then as he reeled back stupefied the footsteps again became audible.

He stood with the candle in his shaking hand listening. He heard them ascending the farther staircase, but they stopped suddenly as he went to the door. He walked a little way along the passage, and they went scurrying down the stairs and then at a jog-trot along the corridor below. He went back to the main staircase, and they ceased again.

For a time he hung over the balusters, listening and trying to pierce the blackness below; then slowly, step by step, he made his way downstairs, and, holding the candle above his head, peered about him.

"Barnes!" he called. "Where are you?"

Shaking with fright, he made his way along the passage, and summoning up all his courage pushed open doors and gazed fearfully into empty rooms. Then, quite suddenly, he heard the footsteps in front of him.

He followed slowly for fear of extinguishing the candle, until they led him at last into a vast bare kitchen with damp walls and a broken floor. In front of him a door leading into an inside room had just closed. He ran towards it and flung it open, and a cold air blew out the candle. He stood aghast.

"Barnes!" he cried again. "Don't be afraid! It is I—Meagle!"

There is no answer. He stood gazing into the darkness, and all the time the idea of something close at hand watching was upon him. Then suddenly the steps broke out overhead again.

He drew back hastily, and passing through the kitchen groped his way along the narrow passages. He could now see better in the darkness, and finding himself at last at the foot of the staircase began to ascend it noiselessly. He reached the landing just in time to see a figure disappear round the angle of a wall. Still careful to make no noise, he followed the sound of the steps until they led to the top floor, and he cornered the chase at the end of a short passage.

"Barnes!" he whispered. "Barnes!"

Something stirred in the darkness. A small circular window at the end of the passage just softened the blackness and revealed the dim outlines of a motionless figure. Meagle, in place of advancing, stood almost as still as a sudden horrible doubt took possession of him. With his eyes fixed on the shape in front he fell back slowly and, as it advanced upon him, burst into a terrible cry.

"Barnes! For God's sake! Is it *you?*"

The echoes of his voice left the air quivering, but the figure before him paid no heed. For a moment he tried to brace his courage up to endure its approach, then with a smothered cry he turned and fled.

The passages wound like a maze, and he threaded them blindly in a vain search for the stairs. If he could get down and open the hall door—

He caught his breath in a sob; the steps had begun again. At a lumbering trot they clattered up and down the bare passages, in and out, up and down, as though in search of him. He stood appalled, and then as they drew near entered a small room and stood behind the door as they rushed by. He came out and ran swiftly and noiselessly in the other direction, and in a moment the steps were after him. He found the long corridor and raced along it at top speed. The stairs he knew were at the end, and with the steps close behind he descended them in blind haste. The steps gained on him, and he shrank to the side to let them pass, still continuing his headlong flight. Then suddenly he seemed to slip off the earth into space.

Lester awoke in the morning to find the sunshine streaming into the room, and White sitting up and regarding with some perplexity a badly blistered finger.

"Where are the others?" inquired Lester.

"Gone, I suppose," said White. "We must have been asleep."

Lester arose, and stretching his stiffened limbs, dusted his clothes with his hands, and went out into the corridor. White followed. At the noise of their approach a figure which had been lying asleep at the other end sat up and revealed the face of Barnes. "Why, I've been asleep," he said in surprise. "I don't remember coming here. How did I get here?"

"Nice place to come for a nap," said Lester, severely, as he pointed to the gap in the balusters. "Look there! Another yard and where would you have been?"

He walked carelessly to the edge and looked over. In response to his startled cry the others drew near, and all three stood gazing at the dead man below.

THE INVASION OF THE CHURCH OF THE HOLY GHOST

by Russell Kirk

Some say no evil thing that walks by night
In fog, or fire, by lake, or moorish fen,
Blew meager Hag, or stubborn unlaid ghost,
No Goblin, or swart Faery of the mine,
Hath hurtful power o'er true virginity.

—COMUS

What occurred in my church last night must be committed to writing without delay. Having discovered my own feebleness, I do not know how long I might resist, should some other presence enter the church. Fork cast out the nightwalkers, and the girl too has gone, but there is no discharge in this war.

Perhaps the one devil who stared me in the face may gather seven other spirits more wicked than himself, so that my last state should be worse than my first. If such ruin comes to pass, at least I will have set down these happenings. Knowledge of them might preserve my successor at this Church of the Holy Ghost.

Successor? No likely prospect. Were I to depart, the bishop would lock the bronze doors—and soon demolish the hulking church, supposing him able to pay the wreckers' bills. Our bishop, saints forgive him, spends his days communicating the president of the United States and ordaining lesbians. The Right Reverend Soronson Hickey regards me as a disagreeable, if exotic, eccentric who fancies that he has a cure of souls—when every right-thinking cleric in this diocese has been instructed that the notion of souls is a fable. Had I been born white, the bishop would have thrust me out of the Church of the Holy Ghost months ago.

Whoever you are, reading these scribbled pages—why, I may be dead or vanished, and the dear bishop may be my reader—I must first set down my name and station. I am Raymond Thomas Montrose, doctor of divinity, rector of the Church of the Holy Ghost in the parish of Hawkhill. This parish and the neighboring districts make up the roughest quarter of what is called the "inner city." I am an Episcopalian priest, the only reasonably orthodox clergyman remaining in Hawkhill, which Satan claims for his own.

Thomas is my confirmation-name, and my patron is Saint Thomas of Canterbury. Like my patron, I stand six feet four in my armor. Yes, armor; but my mail is black leather, and I sleep with a pistol hanging from my bedhead.

A sergeant's son, I was born in Spanish Town, Jamaica, and I am shiny black: nobody excels me in negritude. The barmaids of Pentecost Road say I have a "cute British accent." I believe in the Father, the Son, and the Holy Ghost; the resurrection of the dead, and the life everlasting. I am celibate, not quite forty years of age, and since my ordination chaste of body. I have survived in Hawkhill a whole year.

My rectory is a safe-house, after a fashion. Occasionally I lodge behind its thick walls and barred windows—the builders of a century gone builded more wisely than they knew—girls off Pentecost Road, fugitive from their pimps. The bishop admonishes me that this unseemly hospitality may give rise to scandal. I have replied that I do not desire carnal knowledge of these young women. It is their souls I am after. At such superstitious discourse the bishop scowls. Were I a pathic, he would not reprove me.

My Church of the Holy Ghost is Richardsonian Romanesque in style, erected more than a century ago, when red sandstone and Hawkhill were fashionable. The bishop has exiled me to the furthest frontier of this diocese, no other clergyman applying for my present rectorship. I accepted cheerfully enough a cure of souls in what the humorists of our daily press call the Demilitarized Zone of our city. Would that it really had been demilitarized! I did not obtain a permit for a pistol out of mere bravado.

The Church of the Holy Ghost, Protestant Episcopal, looms handsomely though grimily over Merrymont Avenue, three blocks east of the junction with Pentecost Road. (In the believing early years of our city, those names were not thought absurd.) Some fine old houses still stand on Merrymont; many more have been burnt by arsonists (often hired arsonists) or have fallen into hopeless ruin. Where once our upper classes gloried and drank deep, the owl and bat their revel keep—or, more literally, the poorest of our poor get drunk and disorderly whenever they can.

I make no claim to have cured many souls near the junction of Pentecost and Merrymont. Occasionally my Sunday services are attended by perhaps seventy persons (in a building that might seat seven hundred), most of them immigrants (chiefly illegal) from the Caribbean like myself. There is a peppering of quiet little people from southeastern Asia, and a salting of old white folk stranded in Hawkhill by the pace of change in our city. One of the last group, Mrs. Simmons, still has some money, which enables me to keep the church doors open. The bishop doles me out next to nothing for any purpose.

The sheltered broad steps ascending to the magnificent doors of my church are carpeted wall to wall, on clement days, by the Old Soldiers, winos and other derelicts; some bums sleep on those steps all night in summer, although not at this season. (Were I to let them lodge inside, they'd have the church befouled, looted, and desecrated within an hour.) A brace of policemen clear the Old Soldiers off the steps for my Sunday morning service. Some few of these Ancient Pistols even join my congregation, to escape snow or wind. I have made Anglo-Catholics of two or three.

Although less poverty-racked than Merrymont Avenue, Pentecost Road is more dreadful. For Pentecost Road has become the heart of the domain of the pushers and the pimps. Young women and female children of several colors parade the Pentecost in hope of custom; so do a number of boys, also for general hire. "If you want it, we've got it," is the legend painted above the entrance to the best-patronized bar on Pentecost Road. At the devil's booth all things are sold.

Besides believing earnestly in the doctrine of the soul, I believe with all my heart in Satan, whose territories are daily enlarged. I know myself for a castellan of Castle Perilous—my Church of the Holy Ghost looking like a mighty fortress—beset every hour by Satan's minions.

Reader, whoever you are, you might call me an educated Salvation Nigger. I am called worse than that, frequently, on Pentecost Road. Few of Satan's minions on that street know me for a man of the cloth; they are not numbered among my communicants. In vestments, and with my hair brushed, I look quite unlike myself when in my Pentecost

Road armor. Touring the Pentecost bars. I wear a greasy broad-brimmed hat, and under my leather jacket a very loud suit. Somehow the word has been passed round that I am an unsuccessful chiropractor who likes his rum drinks.

I frequent Pentecost Road to snatch from the burning what brands I may. In this thankless labor I found an improbable coadjutor in the person of Fork Causland.

A source of the rumor that I am a chiropractor is Fork Causland's custom of addressing me as Doc. But I am in his debt for much more than that.

The first time I saw Fork, he was descending nimbly from a bus—nimbly for a blind man, that is. Under his left arm he gripped a sheaf of placards announcing a wrestling match; these he was posting in the windows of barber shops and other small businesses. This bill-posting was one of the several means by which Causland supported himself, accepting no welfare payments.

I watched him while he clanked his brass-shod stick upon the sidewalk and cried out to the world, in jovial defiance, "Northwest corner of Beryl and Clemens! Don't tell me I don't know where I am!"

Fork wore black goggles that fitted tight to his broad half-Indian face. Quite as invariably he wore, indoors and out, a black derby hat—what would have been called a bowler, down where I was born. Although not tall, Fork was formidably constructed and in prime condition. His face-mask was the hardest visage that ever I have looked upon: "tough as nails," they say. Also it was a face humorously stoical.

On that street corner I merely stared at Fork, who brushed past me to enter a cafeteria. It was a week later that I first conversed with him, in the Mustang Bar, Pentecost Road.

I was sipping a daiquiri—"pansy drink," a mugger type at the bar had growled, but I had stared him down—when somebody outside shouted. "The old Mustang! Wahoo!" Something rang upon concrete, and there bounced into view Fork Causland. I write "bounced": that is what he did. The burly blind man flung himself into the air, his left hand clutching the head of his stick; and he seemed to hold himself suspended in the air for half a minute, miraculously, his soles a foot or more above the pavement. Either Causland had a marvellously strong left wrist, or there was something preternatural about this blind man who could set at defiance the law of gravity.

Nobody else happened to be watching Fork's performance at that moment, but later I inquired among barflies about him. Some thought that Causland had been a circus performer in his youth, and had fallen from a high wire, destroying his eyes. Others said that he had been a sergeant of military police, blinded in line of duty. (If so, where was his pension?) Yet others suggested that acid had been thrown in his eyes when he was a strikebreaker, or perhaps a striker. Fork kept his own counsel. Surely that levitation-performance was odd, extremely odd; so were other feats of his, I was to learn.

"The old Mustang!" Fork announced again, very loudly, to an uncaring Pentecost Road. He passed through the open doorway of the Mustang to seat himself at the blond piano in the middle of the smoky room. (The Mustang reeks with marijuana.) "The regular, Ozzie," Fork called to the barman. A waitress fetched him a tumbler of cheap whiskey. Having tossed off half his drink, Fork began to play that battered piano.

I remember that he played "Redwing"—the taste of the elder spirits among the Mustang's patrons being oldfangled and sentimental; and he sang the lyrics in a melodious deep voice. "The breeze is sighing, the night birds crying . . ." He elevated the lyrics from bathos to pathos. He was not a piano-player merely, but a pianist, this blind chap.

I asked the waitress the man's name: "Homer Causland, but for the last two years they've called him Fork." She added, *sotto voce*, "Don't give him no cause to take offense."

I shifted to a table beside the piano. "Mr. Causland," I said to him, "have you ever played the organ?"

"You're from Jamaica?" he responded, without hesitation. His head turned in my direction, the hard taut face inscrutable.

"Not Long Island," I answered. "You've a good ear for speech, friend."

"That's part of my survival strategy. You a doctor, maybe?"

"Of divinity, Mr. Causland. I'm rector of Holy Ghost Church."

"If you need somebody to play the organ there, Doc, you could look further than me and do worse. What do you pay?"

We settled on five dollars a Sunday, all I could manage, but a substantial augmenting of Fork's income. I found that he could play Mendelssohn and Bach tolerably well from memory. Where Fork learned piano and organ, he never confided to me.

Pentecost Road took it for granted that Fork had "blown his lid" on some narcotic, so accepting his eccentricity. I found him neither mad nor half-mad, odd though he was. He was quick-witted, shrewd, and capable of serious reflection. From listening to records and tapes for the blind he had picked up a miscellany of literary and philosophical knowledge. The recurrent extreme oddity of his public conduct—his acrobatic tricks (if such they were) and his shouting—I judged to be part of a general pose or blind (not to pun). Yet for what purpose this concealment of his real nature?

In the course of a month, I extracted from Fork and from others the explanation of his soubriquet "Fork." That account, set down below, may seem a digression; but it is bound up with the unnerving things that occurred during the past week at my church.

Pentecost Road respects one thing chiefly: successful violence, better even than riches. From such an act Fork Causland had obtained his familiar name and his high repute on Pentecost Road.

Occasionally fragments of conversation of a sinister bent may be overheard by a sharp-eared man who for drinks and tips plays the piano in rough saloons. In the Mustang, Homer Causland happened to gather enough of one tipsy dialogue to recognize it as a conspiracy to murder. He informed the police.

It was a gruesome, interesting case, that conspiracy to murder: but I am trying to be succinct. Despite Causland's warning, the murder in question actually was perpetrated—while the police were trying to fit Causland's testimony into the jigsaw puzzle of the suspected conspiracy. It was the killing, the prolonged and hideous slaughter, of a disobedient young prostitute.

Although Causland's evidence did not prevent the crime, it did enable the police to identify the three principal criminals, leaders of a "vice ring." They had been often arrested, yet scarcely ever convicted. Now the charge was homicide in the first degree. With his accustomed stoic courage, Causland testified fully in open court; the police rarely had been able to produce so convincing a witness. Nevertheless, an intimidated jury and a judge who disgraced the bench found the three accused not guilty.

One of the accused was a Big Man on Pentecost Road: big in narcotics, big in prostitution. Generally he was called Sherm; sometimes Sherm the Screamer, from his accustomed mode of addressing young women under his control; also, perhaps, because of his talent for compelling other people to scream. He had been tried under the name (doubtless an alias, his original name being unknown in our city) of Sherman Stanton. He was a youngish man, lean, curlyhaired, even handsome except for the persistent sneer on his face. Nobody knew where Sherm had come from before he began to dominate Pentecost Road's traffic in drugs and flesh.

Such talented and aggressive criminals build up a following of young men and women, moved by the emulatory passion, in such districts as Hawkhill. Sherm, despite his nasty manners and ways, obtained a large and devoted band of disciples. What was less usual, he riveted his grip upon his dupes by posing as an occult prophet of sorts. Oh, he was clever!

We have a sufficient number of queer creeds in Jamaica, but Sherm's pseudoreligion was worse than any of those. In some ways his rubbish—cribbed from paperback novels, possibly—resembled the cult of Thuggee. How much of his own mystagogy about Kali and Ishtar did Sherm the Screamer actually believe? He was after domination of minds and bodies—especially bodies; but he seems to have subscribed to some of his own devilish dogmas. He claimed to be able to project his essence out of the body, and to travel as pure kinetic energy through space and time. Also he declared that he could not perish.

The pretense of exotic religiosity was of some utility to him. I am told that he tried to obtain exemption from property taxes for the storefront "church" that was his ring's headquarters; and he hired a lawyer to plead the first clause of the First Amendment when police asked for a warrant to search that "church." One detective remarked unguardedly to a reporter, "Hell, that 'Church of Ishtar and Kali' is just a kinky bawdy-house."

When I write that some of us are engaged in a holy war, I mean that literally. We are a scant rearguard, and we are losing, here below, in this fallen age. Like the Celts of the Twilight, we go forth often to battle, but rarely to victory.

Satan is come among us as a raging lion, having great wrath. Sherm was a limb of Satan: that too I mean literally. He corrupted and peddled young girls for the pleasure of seeing them destroyed. He laughed whenever he had persuaded some fool to burn out his own brains with hard drugs. In our day the Sherms multiply and prosper. You have only to spend a year in the neighborhood of Pentecost Road to understand that Satan is a person and a conscious force, no figure of myth merely. He takes possession of empty vessels.

On Pentecost Road I learned that the time is out of joint—and that though I could not see it right, still might I set my face against temptation, as did my patron Thomas à Becket. I digress: I must keep to the point, for the night cometh when no man shall work.

"But at my back in a cold blast I hear
The rattle of the bones, and chuckle spread from ear to ear."

Yes, Sherm and his friends were set at liberty. This enabled them to deal with Causland, whose testimony had come near to getting them life sentences. Sherm the Screamer did not tolerate informers on Pentecost Road. Blind Homer Causland knew what to expect.

Prosecutor and police conveniently forgot Causland when the trial had ended in acquittal; they had plenty of fish to fry. Had he gone to the prosecutor's office, perhaps some nominal protection might have been extended to him; but Causland, a one wolf, didn't bother. He hadn't the money, or perhaps the will, to leave the city altogether. Once upon a time Causland may have been good with a gun, possibly in line of duty; but a blind man has no use for such toys. All Causland could do was to wait upon the event, which might lie in the hand of God or in the hand of Satan.

On his way home from bill-posting one afternoon, Causland halted at a tumbledown secondhand shop. He had a speaking acquaintance with the proprietress, an alcoholic crone.

"What you rummagin' for today, Homer?"

"Garden tools, Mrs. Mattheson."

"Pardon me sayin' so, but I didn't never hear of no blind man growin' no garden." Mrs. Mattheson tittered at her own wit.

"Why, Mrs. Mattheson, a blind beggar can make a compost heap. Do you have in stock such a thing as a pitchfork?"

She did: an old rusty one, the upper part of its hickory shaft somewhat split. Causland fingered the crack, asked for a small saw, and skillfully sawed off the upper portion of the shaft, shortening the tool by a foot. He paid Mrs. Mattheson sixty-five cents for this purchase, and a quarter more for a little old greasy whetstone.

Causland lived in a tall brick house that had seen better days—much better. So had his ancient Christian Science landlady. A battered cast-iron fence still surrounded the yard. The several tenants, whatever their moral attributes, were tolerably clean and quiet. Three effeminate young men occupied most of the ground floor. Causland had one room on the top floor; a narrow staircase was the only normal means of access. But Causland's room was one of three in which the Christian Science landlady, Mrs. Bauer, took a peculiar pride. Those three had, or could have had, dumbwaiter service. The dumbwaiter was a forgotten token of genteel living on Merrymont Avenue. Though nothing much had gone up and down the dumbwaiter for years, its electric controls remained operable.

Causland's room had been furnished by the landlady. It was an old-fashioned widow's room, actually, with austere straight-backed chairs, cane-seated, bought cheaply about 1900; a vast heavy venerable wardrobe; an old chest; a pine table; a narrow iron bedstead. Everything was desiccated, and the lace curtains seemed ready to disintegrate. Yet the room was clean. Blind men, I suppose, are indifferent to furniture styles and the hues of wallpaper.

The one feature of that room to relieve the eye was the glossy-varnished oaken door to the dumbwaiter. It was a large dumbwaiter—possibly it had been used for carrying firewood and coals, before the house's fireplaces had been bricked up and papered over—so that a slim man might open the door and climb into the contraption, if he chose.

Causland's lodging-house stood on Merrymont, only three blocks east of my church. Here, in point of continuity, I digress again. By chance, one midnight I found myself strolling a few yards to Fork Causland's rear as he proceeded home. He was accompanied by boon companions, Old Soldiers, one on either side of him. It was a slippery winter night. The Old Soldiers reeled and staggered alarmingly, but Causland swaggered confidently between them, striking the sidewalk with his stick as he went, his derby roofed with snow.

"Where you livin' now, Fork?" one of those Old Soldiers ventured. "Same place where—where you give it to 'em?"

"Same place, my friend: old Mother Bauer's, top floor, hot as a fry-pan in summer and cold as James Bay these winter months."

"You don't have no bad feelin' about stayin' on there, Mr. Causland?" the other Old Soldier inquired. (This latter comrade was a white-bearded character known on Pentecost Road as The Ambassador from Poland.) "I don't mean a troubled conscience, like they say. I mean—well, like sumpthin' might jump out an' grab you?"

"Ambassador," Fork Causland said to his second henchman, "keep on that way, and you'll earn yourself a split lip. Wahoo! Take me to old Mother Bauer's, boys, or I'll jump out and grab *you*! Wahoo!"

Then Fork performed another of those astonishing tricks of his. He took his stick between his teeth; flung himself straight upward with a muscular jump; as he descended, he thrust his rigid forefingers upon the arms of his tipsy companions. Then he rode along as if those two were his native bearers, his feet well clear of the ground, he seemingly supported only by those strong forefingers of his resting on the Old Soldiers' forearms.

His companions did not seem oppressed by his weight, though they kept their forearms extended and parallel with the ground, as if they had done Fork like service before. On they reeled for another block, Fork riding between them, chanting some old tune I did not recognize. When they were about to cross Thistle Street, Fork dropped back to the sidewalk to swagger along as before.

I never have seen such a thing done by anybody else. I do not know if this may have been some sort of acrobatic play. Surely the two Old Soldiers were not acrobats. I don't know how to convey the wonder that I felt at that moment. Was I wandering in a world of *maya,* or illusion? Could any man make himself weightless when he chose?

At some distance I followed the three companions to the walk that led up to Mrs Bauer's house with the cast-iron railings. Causland slapped his comrades on the back, roared goodnight, and positively trotted all by himself up the steep steps of the porch, to vanish behind a handsome antique door. The Old Soldiers reeled onward, probably toward some doss-house or the Salvation Army hostel; I retreated to my citadel of a rectory.

But I am running ahead of my proper narrative. Of course the above nocturnal mystery occurred long after the battle at Mrs. Bauer's lodging-house, which converted Homer Causland into Fork Causland. I turn back to the dumb-waiter and the compost fork. Causland had whetted well the prongs' points. I surmise that there must have been a faint smile on his hard-as-nails sightless face as he fingered the tines.

No police patrol-cars rove Hawkhill at three of the morning. As Sergeant Shaugnessy said to me the other day, when I was imploring him for some effective help in rescuing girls, "What's all the world to a man when his wife's a widdy?" At that hour especially, Hawkhill belongs to Satan's limbs like Sherm the Screamer.

Sherm brought with him to Mrs. Bauer's house, at three of the morning, nine of his boys. As matters turned out, it would have been more prudent to have fetched fewer helpers; but *hubris* now afflicted Sherm the Screamer. Having special plans for the informing blind piano-player, he prepared to fend off any interference. Probably the original design was to snatch Causland, lock him into the trunk of one of the cars, and transport him elsewhere, to be tormented at leisure—perhaps in Sherm's "church." Sherm left the drivers in both of the cars, with the motors running quietly.

A merciful providence had sent Mrs. Bauer crosstown that weekend to visit a niece. Sherm's boys had successfully jimmied the front door when one of the three limp-wristed young men living on the ground floor happened to open the door of their apartment, intending to put out a milk bottle.

"What do you guys want?" he demanded. Eight men were filing into the corridor, all of them high on something costly. The tenant made out their faces. "O God! Billie, call the cops!" he screeched back to one of his friends.

They sapped him the next moment, and burst over his body into the ground-floor apartment. This taste of blood broke the invaders' fragile control over themselves. Roaring, they worked over the other two young men with blackjacks and bars. (One of those unfortunates was crippled lifelong, after that night.) The victims' screams roused the tenant at the top of the house. Causland always had been a light sleeper.

Instantly he understood what must be occurring below. In no way could he assist the ground-floor trio. The diversion downstairs gave him three or four minutes' grace, and for such an event he had made some preparation. Being a very strong man, he was able to thrust the huge wardrobe hard against his door. Back of the wardrobe he forced the iron bedstead. Thus he filled completely the space between the doorway and the outer wall of his room. His door opening inward, this defensive strategy made it impossible for the door to be opened by his enemies, no matter how numerous and frantic they were: they might have to chop their way through with axes, or else use explosives. Either method would require time and noise. He was well aware of the possibility that, so baffled, they might instead burn down the whole house with him inside.

There was no salvation for him through a window—not three flights up, with no fire-escape, and he blind. With admirable presence of mind, Causland took his whole cash reserve, seventy dollars, from his money-belt. The bills and some private papers he concealed under the carpet. Then he took up his pitchfork.

Now the gang came roaring up the stairs and burst against his barricaded door. He recognized some of the voices: they were careless in their howling, which signified that they did not mean him to come alive out of this, to bear witness against them. In particular he knew the torturer's voice of Sherm the Screamer.

"Come on, open up, Causland!" they were shouting, surprised at not being able to budge his door. "We're just going to ask you some questions." Causland said nothing in reply. He had no telephone in his room; and though he might shriek from a window, no one would rush to his assistance in this neighborhood, at this hour. No neighbor would venture so much involvement as to call the police, for that matter—not unless the tumult at Mrs. Bauer's house should threaten to spread to the adjacent houses.

Those smashing at his door were up to their eyes in cocaine, he guessed. Somebody out there was clearheaded enough to grunt, "Get the door off the hinges!" But their superfluity of numbers hampered the assailants in that narrow corridor. Then someone screamed—oh, he knew that voice—"There's another way!" Causland heard three or four men pounding back down the stairs. Meanwhile the savage smashing at the door continued.

Yes, there was another way: Sherm's men must have learned about Mrs. Bauer's dumbwaiter. That device was no escape-route for Homer Causland, for its mechanism could not be operated from within the dumbwaiter itself; and besides, what figure would a blind man make, emerging below, helpless before his enemies? Therefore Causland took his stand in a shadowy convenient corner, as he had planned awaiting the event.

The clanking of the dumbwaiter's chain and the growling of its motor, like Hallowe'en sound-effects, gave Causland plenty of notice of his enemy's approach. The car in the shaft halted opposite the aperture of Causland's room now; the man within knew what he was doing. It still might have been possible for Causland to press the "down" button by the dumbwaiter door, in hope of returning the car to the ground floor. But Causland preferred tactics more decisive.

"Hold it, Ralph!" the man in the car shouted to his helper below. "I'm getting out." It was the Screamer's dreadful voice.

Sherm had risen by audacity. And after all, how much resistance could be offered by a blind piano-player, twice Sherm's years?

Sherm banged open the dumbwaiter door and began to scramble through the narrow opening, into the total darkness of Causland's room. He cracked his head against the oaken door-frame, trying to emerge quickly, and cursed. Happily for Fork, as matters turned out, Sherm was carrying a sawed-off shotgun. "Homer Causland, you old stoolie," the Screamer screamed, "get down on your knees and start begging!"

"Hi!" said Causland softly, from the shadows. "I've something here for you, Screamer." As Sherm swung toward him raising the shotgun, Causland lunged. He contrived to drive the prongs of the fork straight through Sherm's lean belly. The force of Causland's rush bowled Sherm over, and Causland fell upon him. "Goodbye, Sherm," Causland panted.

Then Sherm the Screamer screamed his loudest ever. Causland heard the shotgun crash to the floor of his room. Groping about, he encountered the shaft of the fork; he tried to extract it from the belly of his enemy, whose heels were drumming on the floor. But this was an awkward undertaking, and Causland feared that meanwhile the door of his room might be taken off behind him.

So, panting, he managed in the darkness to thrust the dying Sherm, head first, back into the dumbwaiter. Blind Homer pressed the "down" button, sending the fatal car on its return journey to bear back to his disciples the Screamer, perforated, with the fork still in him. Like the beasts, the Prophet Sherm could perish, after all.

Disposing of Sherm had required about one minute. Yes, the door had been lifted off its hinges now; Causand's ears informed him that his adversaries were trying to kick their way through the second barrier, the sturdy back of the enormous wardrobe.

From the bottom of the stairs, a member of the gang shouted up, desperate, "*Christ, guys, he's gutted Sherm!* Get through that door and smash him!"

Causland had the shotgun in his hands: a double-barrelled repeater. His fingers checked its trigger and magazine. This gun would do very well.

Shifting his station to the foot of the iron bedstead, seven feet from the tottering wardrobe, he pointed the barrels carefully. There was mighty confusion beyond that blocked doorway, some men running upstairs and others downstairs. Sherm's screams from below seemed less vigorous; Causland had angled his fork somehat upward when he had made that dread thrust.

Now the carved doors of the wardrobe splintered into fragments, and a big body became entangled with the bedhead, struggling to enter the room. Causland gave this intruder one barrel.

In the little bedroom that reverberation was exquisitely painful to Causland's sensitive auditory nerves; but the result of his discharge was exquisitely gratfying. A body crashed backward. Later Causland learned that he had aimed a trifle high, so taking off the man's face.

Now Causland must carry the war into Africa. Risky strategy, that; yet not so risky as to wait for the gang to set the house afire. Gun at the ready, Causland clambered over some bloody bulky thing, through the demolished wardrobe. To clear the way, he fired the second barrel at a venture into the corridor beyond.

Someone else shrieked, fell, lay groaning hideously. Causland heard the whole crowd of them tumbling back down the stairs. Kneeling to thrust his weapon between the wooden balusters, the blind champion fired downward, both barrels. To judge by the anguished complaints, he had severely damaged one or two of the enemy.

Somebody fired back—a pistol, Causland thought—but missed him. Vexed, Causland gave them both barrels a second time: more screaming. It was like old times overseas.

At that moment, the horn of one car waiting at the curb began to honk furiously; then the horn of the second car. Later he was told that the drivers, on edge, had heard the siren of an ambulance on Pentecost Road and had taken that for a patrol car.

Causland struggled back into his room. A small window looked toward Merrymont Avenue. Flinging up the sash, Causland fired into the blackness toward the honking. He heard the cars begin to pull away; again Causland fired in their direction. To his pleased surprise, there came a loud resounding bang, but not a gunshot: he must have hit a tire. A moment later a crash followed, for the car with a blown front tire, in fact, had careened across the street and struck a tree.

The other car roared away. Causland heard the running feet of the members of the gang abandoned by the driver. Then the house fell silent except for the horrid moaning of the man whom Causland had shot in the third-floor corridor.

Having made his way down to Mrs. Bauer's telephone, Causland called the police. After five or six minutes, some of the bolder spirits in the neighborhood actually ventured out of their lairs and began to converse, in hushed tones, before Mrs. Bauer's house. But nobody dared ascend the steps until the police arrived.

Sergeant Shaugnessy and his men found one man dead, three dying, one shot in the legs and unable to walk, one stunned in a car that had rammed a tree, and gouts of blood on the sidewalk from one or two others who had escaped. Sherm the Screamer gave up the ghost in the ambulance bearing him to the hospital.

In Causland's phrase, "Sergeant Shaugnessy was flabbergasted but appreciative. They didn't indict me for anything."

After that he was "Fork" to boon companions and "Mr. Causland" to the less privileged. Nobody gave him trouble thereafter. He had attained the equivocal distinction of general recognition as Hawkhill's most accomplished resident. It is said in the Mustang that Fork sent a basket of poison ivy to Sherm's funeral; but that report I doubt. Wondrous to relate, all but two of the survivors of the attempt on Fork Causland were convicted on charges of attempted murder, criminal assault, unlicensed possession of a deadly weapon, or breaking and entering.

Fork Causland's fearsome reputation enabled him to walk the streets of Hawkhill at any hour, unmugged. There arose a popular belief that in reality he was not blind at all, but had especially keen sight behind those dark goggles. Some took him for an undercover detective. Who could have killed Sherm and his boys without seeing them? Or conceivably—this suggestion occurring particuarly among Hawkhill's West Indian element—Causland was a conjure-man, invulnerable and deadly.

Yes, he swaggered along the nocturnal streets. Yet the Screamer's band was not extinct; and those two who had survived the encoutner at Mrs. Bauer's, and had not been imprisoned, would not forget. Fearsomeness wears thin with time, and the disciples of Sherm might take heart again. But Fork said no word of that.

No one could enter my church without my knowledge. I must make that point wholly clear. Were it not so, there might be some quasi-rational explanation of last night's events.

What is rare in American churches of the Romanesque revival, the Church of the Holy Ghost has a narthex, or galilee. (I prefer the latter term.) Above the broad steps frequented by the Old Soldiers of Merrymont Avenue, the great doors open upon this galilee, which traditonally is less sacred than the body of the church.

Within this interior porch, or galilee, I conduct most of my business with comers to the church—particularly with the street girls. In a vaulted chamber off the galilee I maintain a desk, some chairs, and a typewriter; this chamber has a functioning fireplace. I frequent this sentry-post (so to speak) of the Holy Ghost because it is situated near the grand entrance to the church's west front. Only at this point may the whole church complex be entered nowadays.

For I have sealed the several other entrances, even that to the "service" regions of the complex, although closing the other doors has made it necessary for Lin, the Cambodian man whom I have appointed verger (janitor, in reality), to transport rubbish in a barrow to the west front. When I write "sealed," I mean bricked up. No doubt I have violated fire inspector's rules; but the public authorities, winking at worse offenses in Hawkhill, have not troubled me concerning my precautions.

The small roundheaded windows of the church, on the northern side, are set too high for burglars to operate without ladders; also they are narrow, with a stone pillar fixed in the middle of each window-arch. The rector who preceded me in this living (!) had a heavy wire screen attached to the outer side of every window, to protect the painted glass from boys' stones. The southern windows face upon the cloister, not upon a street, and in effect are protected by the tall rectory.

A benefaction from old Mrs. Simmons enabled me to secure the windows of the adjoining rectory with interior steel shutters. I have sealed the rectory's street doors, now reaching my rooms there by passing through the galilee and the cloister on the church's south side. Need I remark that no building is entirely secure against intruders who possess special tools for burglary? However that may be, on the nights to which I refer below these defenses of the Holy Ghost were undisturbed, and no alarm sounded on the electronic warning system purchased out of the Simmons benefaction. I am satisfied that no one could have entered the church except through the galilee.

In one of the massive bronze doors (opened only on great feast days) of the west front is set a kind of postern door, also of bronze, so narrow as to admit only one person at a time. It is this small door through which everybody and everything pass ordinarily. Only the verger and I possess keys to this door, which moreover is secured within, when I am there, by a police-lock and other devices. My small vaulted reception-chamber or office is situated close to this postern, so that when I am at my desk I may see who enters and leaves the church. I am as much porter as rector. Thus all my parishioners, and other callers, must pound the enormous bronze knocker or ring the electric bell, if they would see me.

The sacred vessels, the tapestries, and other furnishings of the Church of the Holy Ghost being highly valuable, efficient robbers might be attracted—were it not for the smoke-grimed exterior of the building, which suggests impoverishment and dereliction. I had provided as best I might against casual thieves, and for the safety of the complex's temporary or permanent inmates. Yet all these precautions seemed futile last night.

It should be understood that during daylight hours I make the nave accessible for private devotions (not that many take advantage of the opportunity) or for the rare visitor interested in the architecture of Holy Ghost Church. I do try to make sure that either the verger or his Cambodian wife (who does our mopping and the like) is present in nave or galilee during the hours when the postern door is unlocked. So it is barely conceivable that some person might have crept into the church and concealed himself until yesterday night, perhaps in the blindstory. Yet such an explanation is even more improbable than the supposition I will imply toward the close of this document.

When Fork Causland became our church organist, I offered him a key to the church, but he refused it, saying that he could ring for the verger or myself. From the first I was confident of his honesty. In corrupted Hawkhill, he appeared to have no corrupt habits. Though fond of whiskey, Fork never was drunken. He paid little or no attention to the girls hanging about the bars where he played the piano. The pushers feared him. His conversation was always decent and sometimes amusing. Considerably to my surprise, I found that he was familiar with our liturgy and that he prayed in church.

From asides in his talk, I gathered that he had been a wanderer, a beggar, a peddler, an acrobat, a carnival hand, a soldier—not in that order, presumably, but at one time or another. Was his proficiency at killing derived from military experience only? Two or three times I entered the church to hear the *Dies Irae* pouring from the organ: Fork at practice in his grim humorous fashion. "Doc," he would say, descending from his bench, "it will be with this city as with the cities of the plain." He was apt at biblical quotations and curious applications of them.

Yet I cannot say that we grew intimate. My situation is lonely; I have no Hawkhill friends; I would have been glad if Fork had accepted my offer of a room in the rectory, that echoing habitation not being less homelike than his room at Mrs. Bauer's. He thanked me, but said, "I'm not a comfortable neighbor, Doc."

I do not think that he held my color against me—not that he could discern it literally. And aside from chance drinking-companions, clearly he had no friends of his own. He seemed armored by a self-sufficient stoicism. I envied him that.

I inquired discreetly about Fork among my parishioners and among the denizens of Pentecost Road. Nobody seemed to know how long Causland had lived in Hawkhill. Some said, "Always, I guess"; others, "Three years, maybe"; yet others, "Never noticed him till this past winter." So far as I could ascertain, nobody ever had conversed seriously with Fork longer than I had. His oddity had tended to deter familiarities even before his bloody amazing victory at Mrs. Bauer's house. After Fork had killed Sherm and his chums, a certain deadliness seemed to hang about the piano-player. (I did not sense it myself; I refer to a discernible reverent uneasiness among the habitués of the Pentecost bars.) Despite Fork's isolation, somehow I fancied that of all the grotesques of Pentecost Road, he alone was permanent, the rest evanescent.

Occasionlly, after he had practiced at the creaky old vast organ, Causland and I talked in a parlor of the rectory, over tea brewed by the Cambodian woman. (Both of us took rum in our tea, in that damp stone building.) Fork could converse sensibly; also somewhat mystically. He knew all of Hawkhill's' secrets, and sometimes hinted at mysteries of the world beyond the world, as if he were Tiresias, or Homer, or some other blind seer. Now and again he deferred, during these talks, to my theological learning—or what he took for my erudition.

"Doc," he inquired at the session I best recollect, "what's possession? Being possessed by a spirit, I mean."

I endeavored to explain the church's doctrine concerning this, but that was not what he wished to know.

"I mean, Doc, how does it *feel*? Can something get inside you, and yet leave room enough for yourself? Can you be comfortable with it? Can you live with it as if it were your brother? Can it help you?"

Naturally, I was startled by this. "Are you talking about yourself, Fork?"

He nodded. "I think there's been somebody else with me for years now. Once, Doc, you said something about 'levitation' and that jumping I do—but then you beat around the bush. Well, it's not St. Vitus's dance, Doc. Something that's got into me does the jumping—not that I object much. And when I was in real need, it lent me its sight."

I drew a long breath. "You're talking about the time Sherm came for you?"

"That's it. I know the Old Soldiers say I can really see whenever I want to. But that's a lie." He tapped his goggles. "I could take these off to show you what's underneath my eyelids, Doc; but that would give you a turn. All the same, somebody or something lent me sight that rough time."

Fork's one indulgence, not counting the free whiskies, was Brazilian cigars. He unwrapped one now, and I lit it for him.

He puffed on the black wrinkled thing. "I've told this to nobody but you, Doc. Let me tell you, it came as a blessed shock to me. I'd made my preparations blinder than any bat, and I didn't expect miracles. But when it happened, everything was coming at me so quick that I just accepted the sight, no questions asked at the moment. It didn't come upon me until the last chance. You better believe me, Doc." He blew smoke from his nostrils.

"I kept this quiet because anybody that dared would have called me a damned liar. The moment Sherm pushed open that dumbwaiter door, sight came to me.

"Or maybe I shouldn't say 'sight': well, 'perception' —that's more the word. I seemed to see outlines. There was a twenty-watt bulb dangling in the dumbwaiter, and Sherm was outlined against it. That was no time for musing on miracles. I knew he couldn't make out hide nor hair of me. His outline, sort of like a paper doll, turned toward me, blindlike, when I spoke to him, and the outline of a shotgun went up to his shoulder. That cleared the way for me to dive under the gun and run him through the belly."

Deftly he relit his cigar.

"Mind you, Doc, I could make out only movement. So once I sent the elevator back down to the ground floor, I was blind as before. But when one of the gang broke through the wardrobe, I made out the shape of him plain, and blew the face off him. Then when I pushed into the corridor myself, I could—well, perceive, I guess—perceive the lot of Sherm's boys running back downstairs, and I fired into the midst of them. And when I gave both barrels to that car outside the house, I could see the thing moving away from the curb. After that, right after the last shot, whatever lent the perception to me took it back again. Is there a name for what happened to me, Doc?"

"'Not a medical term, Fork," I said to him. "There's a psychological term: extrasensory perception. Lord knows what that means."

"You half believe me, don't you, Doc? Nobody else would.

Well, what about the possession? Do you half believe that, too?"

Now the sun had sunk beneath the level of the barred windows of my rectory; we had no light but the glow from the coals in my fireplace. I shivered. "What could it be that's got into you? May it be a devil, do you think?"

"I'm asking you, Doc. How the hell should I know?" Fork sprang up and performed a little song-and-dance routine in my parlor, chanting—

"He's a devil, he's a devil,
He's a devil in his own hometown.
On the level, he's a devil . . ."

Then Fork sat down as abruptly as he had risen.

"Look out, Doc: that was it, the thing in me, just now. He hears you. But no, I don't think it's a demon. It's a killer, though, and not pretty."

The parlor door swung open; we both jumped at the sound and the draught of cold air. But it was only the verger's wife, my housekeeper, come to carry off the tea things. Evidently Fork thought that he had uttered too much already, for he clapped his derby on his large head and went out, back toward Pentecost Road.

We never had opportunity to resume that chilling conversation about the possessed and the possessor. I suspect that Fork may have been capable of elaborate hoaxes, for the fun of them—but not on that dark subject.

How often, my gun under my jacket, have I strolled almost the length of Pentecost Road, praying as I ambled! Desperate though the neighborhood is, some franchise eating-houses make a good profit there, at high nocturnal risk to their cashiers. Much of the road is brightly lit by neon. "Twenty Gorgeous Bottomless Dancers, Stark Naked or Your Money Back," one sign blinks on and off. I pass four or five massage parlors.

Shoddy little theaters for X-rated films (their marquees promising more than they can deliver, in competition with the living flesh next door or down the road); "adult" bookshops for retarded adolescents and middle-aged illiterates; scantly stocked tiny "notion" shops that are fronts for narcotics-peddling—these are the thriving enterprises of Pentecost Road, in this year of our Lord. The hideousness of it hurts as much as the depravity.

Now I have to write about Julie Tilton.

There is no coincidence: everything that occurs is part of a most intricate design.

The Mustang, where the daiquiris are good (though nothing else there has any admixture of good in it), is situated in the intersection of Pentecost and Merrymont. A great deal of money changes hands, more or less surreptitiously, at those corners. For that reason the sidewalk outside the Mustang is frequented by mendicants. I usually give something to the old man with no legs, selling pencils, who rides a board to which four roller-skates are fixed; he is there on the bitterest days. Another begging habitué is the idiot woman shaped like an interrogation point. Also "religious" freaks are to be seen, especially an Indian fakir in nothing but a loincloth.

The beggars and the madmen are outnumbered by the street girls, some promenading, some lounging against the wall, awaiting custom. Few are birds of paradise. I labor under no delusion about harlots. With very rare exceptions, the kindly prostitute is a creation of novelists and playwrights. As a class, such women are psychopathic, devouring, and treacherous. They have their uses, particularly to the police: in the hope of reward, or out of unblemished malice, they betray their bullies and lovers. I have discovered among them, on Pentecost Road, no heroic repentant Magdalene. All that I can accomplish among them, pastorally, is to persuade a few of the young ones, strutting down Pentecost under compulsion, to go back to their parents or to whoever in the hometown might receive them. I have facilitated a number of such escapes, after conversations at my office in the galilee. The first stage on my underground railway is a lodging for a night in that safe-house, my rectory. They do not tempt me. Ever since my ordination, I have kept myself under a most strict discipline; and even had I not vowed myself to celibacy and chastity, still I would be no fool—though sensual, more sensual than most, by nature.

On Monday evening, as I approached the Mustang, the girls were particularly numerous and importunate. I shouldered my way among them—black hat, black face, black leather jacket—in my role of hard-drinking impecunious chiropractor. Just outside the door of the Mustang someone gripped me by the arm—but not with the customary unimaginative "Want to have some fun, honey?" This person was saying, "Brother, have you been washed in the blood of the Lamb?"

I swung round. It was a young black man, fantastically dressed, a street preacher, wild-eyed. He had a companion.

This colleague, seated in a sort of primitive wheelchair, was paler than death. He did not move a muscle, not even of lips or eyes. At first I took him for a paralytic, trundled about for a holy show by his preacher-captor. Then the thought flashed through my mind that this white boy, bareheaded, neatly dressed, might be a corpse: things not much less shocking are seen from time to time at Pentecost and Merrymont.

"Brother, have you been saved?" the mad preacher was demanding of me. "Have you been washed in the blood of the Lamb?"

I unfixed his hand from my arm. "Nobody can answer that question with full knowledge, brother," I told him.

But already he had turned from me and was addressing the passing streams of tarts, procurers, pushers, drunkards, and males of varous ages "out for a little fun." "Brothers and sisters," he was crying, "where'll you spend eternity? Wine is a mocker, strong drink is raging, and whoever is deceived thereby is not wise."

He then plucked the white boy out of his chair and exhibited him at arms' length to the street-people. Praise be, the pallid thing was an inanimate manikin, marvellously realistic, after all. I wouldn't have to telephone Shaugnessy.

" 'Cept you take the Lord Jesus for your personal saviour, you're no better'n this here dummy!" the wild-eyed preacher was shouting. "Where are you goin' to spend eternity? You want to spend it with the Whore o' Babylon and the Beast, whose number is six six six? The wages of sin is death. You want to be like this here dummy, no brains in your head? You want to be cast into the fire eternal? Brothers and sisters, death is all around us. Old Mister Death, he comes here, he comes there. Old Mister Death, he grabs you when you're on a high, when you're drinkin' and fornicatin', and he takes the breath out o' your body, leavin' you no better than this here dummy! He takes you where the worm never dieth and the fire is not quenched. 'Cept you follow the Lord Jesus, Ol' Man Death put his bony hands on you, and you curl up like a worm. . . ."

Two mighty hands took me by the shoulders, from behind. Their clutch was terribly painful; a shock like electricity ran through me. "Gottcha, Doc!" said Fork. "You come along with me into this hell on earth they call the Mustang. Wahoo!"

His ears had singled me out in the crowd by my few words in retort to the street-preacher.

"In a minute, Fork, you Beast from the Abyss," I muttered.

With his stick tucked under his arm, the blind man stood beside me, listening to the crazy preacher. "It always was a scandal, that faith, eh, Doc?" He poked me in the ribs with the head of his stick. "That there raving and ranting fellow—sort of like a caricature of you, eh, Doc?"

"Go to hell, Fork," I told him.

"All in good time, Doc; all in God's own good time." He chuckled harshly.

" 'Cept you repent, brothers and sisters, you gonna die the body of this death," the crazy preacher was exhorting some tarts and three beggars. He brandished the manikin. "No brains, jes' like this here dummy; no heart, no guts, no nothin'. If you don't have no immortal soul washed in the blood of the Lamb, you got nothin'. Old Mister Death, he got your 'pointed day writ down on his calendar, you poor dummies. . . ."

"You've got some competition in the soul business, Doc," said Fork, half-needling me, half-serious. We were entering the Mustang. "You ever repent of taking up this line of work? Feel sorry about not marrying, and taking up the cross in Hawkhill?"

"It's a calling, Mr. Homer Causland; I wouldn't have it any other way. What's your calling? Speaking of Old Man Death, killing seems to be your talent."

"In the line of duty, Doc: add that qualification. You're welcome to call me a rat, Reverend Doc. On one of those records for no-eyes, once, I heard a poem by some Scotchman about a rat's prayer:

> " 'God grant me that
> I carrion find,
>   And may it stink;
> O Father, kind,
>   Permit me drink
> Of blood ensoured . . .
> There is no wate
>   Where rats are fed,
> And, for all haste,
>   Grace shall be said.' "

Fork had astounded me once again. "In what corner of hell did you hear that, you blind devil?"

"Devil? Not quite that, Doc; devil's cousin, maybe. Wahoo!"

He sat down at his piano, called for his whiskey, and began to play. I took a table near him. The Mustang was two-thirds full, that night, of the lost. The blind devil played for them like an angel. Even to acid rock he imparted a sombre pathos; or so it sounded to my priestly ears.

I was roused out of a reverie brought on by Fork's "not marrying" when a girl's voice, a sweet one, said, "Excuse me, sir." She withdrew a chair from my table, turned it in Fork's direction, and sat waiting for him to pause in his playing. I saw her in profile.

She was beautiful, but more than beautiful: lovely. She wore her blonde hair long, very long. Nose, lips, and chin all were delicate and perfect; so was her figure. She was six feet tall at least. Her blue eyes were impossibly innocent. I judged her to be sixteen or seventeen years old. This was nobody off Pentecost Road. Face aside, she was dressed too decently for that.

When Fork had stopped playing, she said to him, "Excuse me, sir. Maybe you can help me. Have you seen Alexander Tilton?"

Fork turned toward her his poker face with its black goggles, taking the cigar from his mouth. He removed his derby. "Why do you ask a blind man a question like that, lady?"

I watched her blush. Her fair skin was suffused with a soft delicious pink. "Oh, I'm sorry; I didn't know. I thought you looked like a man who might have met a good many people in this part of town."

"I do, lady, but I never met anybody by that name. Doc, could you check at the bar?"

I rose. Who wouldn't do anything for this young lady? Indeed, I bowed the first bow ever executed in the Mustang.

"Meet the Reverend Raymond Montrose, rector of Holy Ghost Church, lady, even if he doesn't look it."

"I don't want to disturb you, Reverend Montrose," the beauty said. She blushed again.

"It's a pleasure, young lady," I assured her, stuttering a little. "But not 'Reverend Montrose,' if you please. Father Montrose, or Dr. Montrose, or even Mr. Montrose; but never Reverend Montrose. I'm a stickler for forms, being an Anglo-Catholic."

"Oh, I'm a Methodist, I'm afraid, Father."

"Don't be afraid, not even in this bar. Excuse me, Miss . . ."

"I'm Julie Tilton, and Alexander Tilton is my brother, twelve years older. The last letter he sent us was on the stationery of the Tangiers Motel, Pentecost Road, and so I got a room there, half an hour ago, but they hadn't heard of him and said somebody at the Mustang Bar might know him. I took a taxi straight here." She was genuine!

"You better check out of the Tangiers Motel, lady; they got something worse than the veterans' disease there. Doc, stop your bowing and scraping, and ask after one Alexander Tilton at the bar. I'll keep an eye on this Miss Tilton, in a manner of speaking." Fork resumed his derby.

The bartender and the waitresses hadn't ever heard of an Alexander Tilton, they informed me. When I returned to the piano, I found three unpleasant young toughs standing by Fork and the girl, flies drawn to honey.

"How about a dance, baby?" said the biggest of them.

"Move on, brothers," I told them. They stared at me.

"You heard Doc," Fork growled. "Scoot, boys."

They went, swearing, but softly.

"Pay them no mind, lady," said Fork. "They'll get their come uppance before long, I promise you. Now this brother of yours—what did he look like?"

"My grandmother and I haven't seen him for nearly ten years, but he must still be very good-looking. He's about as tall as I am, and slim. The girls back home were wild about him. He got one—but that doesn't matter now." Another blush.

"He used to write about once a year," she went on; "then, better than two years ago, he stopped writing. I thought that everybody around here must know him, because he did so well in this city. He sent lots and lots of money for us to keep for him. 'Bury it in the cellar in tight cans,' he wrote to us. Some people don't trust banks, I guess, and he's one of them. He even sent the cash in little sealed boxes, by special messengers! Except for letting us know his money was on its way, Sherm never told us much in his letters."

"*Sherm?*" said Fork, drawling out the name.

"Here in Hawkhill, Miss Tilton," I put in, "a good many people get lost—and not found. I thought you said your brother's name was Alexander."

"Oh, it is, Father Montrose: Alexander Sherman Tilton.

But we've called him Sherm in the family ever since I can remember."

Fork, silent, relit his cigar.

"Possibly there are other ways you might identify your brother, Miss Tilton," I continued. "His voice, for instance: was it soft as yours?"

She smiled angelically. "Oh, no. Sherm always spoke very loudly—loud enough to hurt some people's ears. When he was angry, could he ever yell!"

"Ummm," from Fork. "Now this brother Sherm, lady: did he ever use other names?"

"Not that I know of. Why should he? But perhaps he used the 'Alexander' in this town, because he always signed his letters to us that way, as if he had gotten more formal. It was just 'Alexander,' not signing his last name. We mailed letters to Alexander Tilton, at the post-office box number he gave us; but he never answered until he decided to send more money home."

I presented to her my engraved card, in the hope of achieving in Miss Tilton's admirable eyes a respectability that my beard and my fancy boots would not convey to her. Or might she, untravelled, fancy that all doctors of divinity went about so attired? "Did you have some particular reason," I inquired, "for coming all this distance to look for your brother?"

"No, Father: it's just that he's my only brother, and I haven't any sisters, and Dad and Mom died five years ago. In his last letter, Sherm told me that I ought to come to the big city and live with him; that I'd really go places here. He practically ordered me to come. I wrote back that I would, whenever he wanted me to. He didn't answer me, though, so I waited until after graduation, and at last I decided that the thing for me to do was simply to come here and look him up. Here I am!"

Yes, here she was, Iphigenia in Aulis, come unwitting to the sacrifice. Here she was, a brand for me to snatch pastorally before she had been even singed!

"This gentleman at the piano is our church organist, Mr. Fork Causland," I informed her. I gave Fork a gentle stealthy dig in his ribs. "He and I will do what we can to help you."

"Sure, lady," Fork said. "I wouldn't go asking around this here bar, if I was you."

The three unpleasant young men had not scooted very far: I noticed them standing at the bar, scowling at us. I recollected, or thought I recollected, that two of them had been surreptitiously pointed out to me, months ago, as survivors of the Screamer's gang. It wouldn't do to linger. I put my hand on Fork's shoulder.

"The two of us had best take Miss Tilton back in a taxi to the Tangiers Motel, Fork, and get her bags now. I can put her up at the rectory, if she doesn't mind."

"Right, Doc—I guess. There's too many vermin at the Tangiers, lady. Just one more question, before we go." Fork swallowed the remnant of his whiskey. "Brother Sherm—in his last letter, better than two years ago, did he give you any idea of what he was going to have you doing in this town?"

"I'm quite a good typist, Mr. Fork, but Sherm didn't mention that. All he suggested was that he knew a lot of interesting boys to take me out." Here she colored more furiously than before.

We made our way to the door, I running interference. All the men in the Mustang were staring, and three or four whistled loudly. "Where you takin' that kid, Fork?" somebody called out. Somebody else muttered, "For Christsake, don't rile him."

A taxi was at the curb, letting out a drunken fare. Julie Tilton got in with us two strangers, ingenuously. Possibly my "cute British accent" was reassurance of sorts. With no other two men from the Mustang would she have been able to check out of the Tangiers uninsulted—or worse than that. Coincidence again? I think not.

"I fancy you come from a rather small town, Miss Tilton," I said on our way to the motel.

"How did you know, Father? Titus isn't much more than a church, a general store, and a dozen houses. Sherm used to call it Hicksville or Endsville."

"How you gonna keep 'em down on the farm, after they've seen Hawkhill?" Fork had been humming. He ceased, saying, "Julie, pardon my asking, but was this brother Sherm in more sorts of trouble than one, when he left Titus nearly ten years ago?"

"He got himself into a peck of troubles, Mr. Fork. But he must have straightened himself up, or he couldn't have earned all that money to send home."

At the flashy Tangiers, I thought it prudent to go with Julie to her room for her suitcase. I was pleased and somewhat surprised to find the bag still there; they had not given her a key for her room. While Julie and I were down the hall, the desk clerk tried to make trouble about this guest being taken away by two men, but Fork gave him the rough side of his tongue. Undoubtedly the desk clerk had plans for the lady guest. He asked her to come back any time; he meant it.

"How you goin' to keep 'em away from Pentecost, jazzin' around, paintin' the town?" Fork was humming as we drew up before the Church of the Holy Ghost.

The lovely big girl was overwhelmed by the scale of my church. "This must be a very religious town, Father Montrose! I hope I'm not causing your wife too much trouble."

"Once upon a time, it was. I'm celibate, Miss Tilton. Our housekeeper, the verger's wife, will get your room in order and bring your tea—and a sandwich, if you'd care for one." Providentially, no fugitive street-girl was lodged in the rectory that night. I unlocked the postern door, and we three entered.

The galilee of my church had taken the galilee of Durham Cathedral for its model, in part. The rows of pillars, and the roundheaded arches with their chevron moldings, took Julie's breath away. From my office, I rang a bell connected with the verger's rooms at the top of the rectory, summoning the little Cambodian woman, whose English was tolerable.

We had our ingénue safe out of the Mustang, safe out of the Tangiers Motel. What next?

"Will it be all right for me to stay here until I find my brother?" Julie asked, as the verger's wife waited to lead her across the cloister. "I don't know how to repay you, Father. I'm sure that Sherm's somewhere very close; I just simply feel it."

"We could have ridden on to Mrs. Simmons's, Doc. She'd have taken the girl in if you'd asked her. It wouldn't have been like imposing a streetwalker on the old lady."

"She's safer in the rectory, Fork."

We two sat in my office off the galilee. It was midnight, and Miss Tilton doubtless was sleeping the sleep of the guiltless—a few rods distant from me.

"Maybe," said Fork. "Probably they're looking for her right now."

"Who in particular?"

"Those three that wanted to dance with her at the Mustang. The guy that spoke to her and gave us some lip—I knew his voice. He was one of the two acquitted after my fracas at Mrs. Bauer's. His name's Franchetti. He was Sherm's number one enforcer. He's getting his nerve back, two years after the treatment I gave his pals. Sherm's sister would be worth plenty to him."

"Is she actually Sherm's sister?"

"Why not? It all fits together. I bet Franchetti saw they were two peas in a pod. Sherm must have told his boys she'd be along. What does the girl look like?"

"A rose in bloom." I had not been able to keep my eyes off young Miss Tilton; I supplied particulars, perhaps too enthusiastically.

"That's enough detail, Doc. Sherm was a good-looking goon, except for the smirk, they tell me. He was her height, her coloring, and 'Sherman Stanton' is close enough to 'Sherman Tilton.' "

"But her coming straight to the man who executed her brother? That's too much of a coincidence, Fork."

"There's wheels within wheels, Doc. She was sent, God knows why. It did give me a jolt when she said 'Sherm,' let me tell you."

We fell silent for a minute or two.

"We can't let Julie know what her brother was, nor how he ended," I said then.

Fork nodded. "She's got to go back to Titus, pronto."

"It won't be simple to persuade her of that, at least for a few days. She says her intuition tells her that Sherm's near at hand. Girls and their notions!"

"She may not be so far wrong, Doc. That's been my intuition, too."

"Don't be a fool, Fork."

"I never would have lasted this long if I'd been a fool, not with the life I've led. Now look: in this here Middle Ages church of yours, you've talked to me more than once about death and judgment. You're a Middle Ages parson, Doc, and I'm with you. What's the teaching about what you've called 'the interval'?"

He had cornered me with my own doctrine. "I know what you're thinking, Fork. Once upon a time, everybody believed it. When a man dies, that's not the end of his personality—not until the Last Judgment. There may be a kind of half-life, though the body has perished. After all, in the twentieth century we know that what we call 'matter' is a collection of electrical particles, held in an arrangement by a power we don't understand. That arrangement falls apart when a body disintegrates; but the particles, the energy . . . ah, there's the rub, Fork. Even a consciousness may survive, Fork, in a twilight realm of which we receive glimpses, sometimes, that startle us, the living. Until the Last Judgment, what we call ghosts . . ."

"All right, Doc: that's your teaching. You believe it?"

"Yes."

"And you believe in possession?"

"Yes."

"Sherm was possessed, Doc, if ever a man was. Maybe I am, though not in the same way. Something might possess you. Watch your step."

"What do you mean?"

"You ought to know, Doc."

I shrugged that off. Another interval of silence followed. Then I said, "Why did Sherm tell Julie to come to Hawkhill?"

"Unnatural affection, Doc. After he'd taken his pleasure with her, he'd have peddled her on Pentecost Road."

I crossed myself. "Lord! And this girl!"

"Sherm drove out any goodness that had been in him, leaving himself empty. A demon entered in. You better believe me, Doc."

I let my friend out of the church then, and he went his way into the darkness intrepidly; standing at the postern, I heard his stick striking the sidewalk occasionally as he made his way toward that desiccated room at Mrs. Bauer's.

Having secured the door, I passed through nave and choir to the apse. Tall archaic carvings of saints loomed above me. For half an hour I knelt in prayer. "Pray for us sinners now and at the hour of our death." I prayed even for Sherm, unlikely creature. As I passed back through the nave, my eye somehow was drawn upward to the blindstory along the north wall. But if there had been any slight movement, it must have been a rat's: the vermin plagued us; I had extirpated them from the rectory, but they continued, a few of them, to haunt the church itself.

In my rectory, I paused at Julie's door. The keys to the rectory's interior doors had been lost years ago. Should I knock? Should I simply look in upon her, silently, to make sure she was all right—and for a moment's glimpse of that perfect face in sleep? But restraining myself, I went on to my own whitewashed room (ascetic as any monk's cell), three doors farther on.

The rectory was so well built, and fitted with such heavy doors and draperies, that the Cambodians on the top floor could hear nothing of noise on this ground floor, I reflected.

On Tuesday morning, the housekeeper served a decent breakfast to Julie and me in the dining room, so seldom used, musty and sepulchral. I found the young lady surprisingly perceptive; and she could converse animatedly. She was interested in my Church of the Holy Ghost; I, in her charms. Her face helped me somewhat to drive out gross images from my thoughts: its purity was foreign to Hawkhill. The delicate flair of the tall beauty's nostrils! I thought of her dead brother, so like, so different.

She insisted upon combing the city for her brother. It would have been perilous to have taken her walking on the streets of Hawkhill, especially if the remnants of her brother's gang were looking for her. Having persuaded her to visit officialdom instead, I called a taxi and took the darling on a tour of police headquarters, city hall, the central post office, the county coroner's office. Nobody had heard of a youngish man called Alexander Tilton. Of course I did not inquire after a person called Sherman Stanton. Only four Tiltons were listed in the telephone directory, and from downtown we rang up all of those, unavailing.

Sergeant Shaugnessy, Vice and Homicide Squad, gave us half an hour of his time. That visit was risky; but though Shaugnessy stared at Julie fixedly, apparently he could not place the resemblance between this lovely innocent and the worst man in Hawkhill. He told us that if we would come back another day, he would try to go through his "morgue" of photographs with us. I did not mention that I intended to ship the girl back to Titus before that might occur. Happily Julie did not reveal to the sergeant that her brother's middle name was Sherman—though it is unlikely that he would have been quick-witted enough to make that improbable connection. Also she said nothing about the money he had sent home.

I took her to dinner at a cafeteria downtown, and then we returned to the rectory. Fork stopped by a few minutes after we had got back; we reported to him our failure.

"For all you know, Julie," said Fork, "your brother may have moved on east, or west. There's an Amtrak train tomorrow noon that could take you within ten miles of

Titus; I stopped by the station. Oh, you know about that? Take it, girl, take it."

It entered my mind that I did not wish to let her go so soon. She was protesting to Fork that she was ready to stay here a week, if there were any chance of finding brother Sherm.

"There'll be other trains, Fork," I said. "Or she could fly back, about the end of this week."

"And you'll comfort Julie spiritually until then?" Fork inquired, in his most sardonic way. But the girl appeared to catch no imputation. I could have struck Fork.

"Father Montrose already has given me such good advice!" she told the old blind devil. "He's taken me to see everybody who might know something about Sherm. I don't know what I can ever do to make it up to him for all his trouble."

I almost said at that point, "I do know."

"If you're going to hang on here, Julie," Fork was telling her, "don't go outdoors by yourself. Any girl's in danger on these streets, even in daylight—and you in particular, sweet girl graduate of Titus Rural High."

"Why especially?" Her eyes widened.

Fork ignored that question. "And if anything should happen to the reverend ecclesiastic here, call a taxi and go to Mrs. Simmons's house. Doc will write down the address for you."

She was startled and concerned. "Why, whatever could happen to Father Montrose?"

"Some of the boys at the Mustang Bar have it in for him now, and I'm told they've learned where he lives. That's one thing possible; there are other possibilities. Doc, take out your notepad and give her Mrs. Simmons's address right now."

I did that.

Julie was puzzled and shaken. "Ah, well," I told her, "that's merely for emergencies which don't happen. But I'll telephone Mrs. Simmons to tell her about you."

"I'll be off," Fork said, "and back tomorrow evening." Wednesday was his night for prolonged practice on the organ. "Keep her indoors, Doc. Tell her about Ol' Mister Death putting his bony hands on you here in Hawkhill. And, Doc, exert your will, as you're given to saying in your sermons: don't let anything occupy you."

He sauntered away down Merrymont, tapping past its

boarded-up storefronts, its derelict gasoline stations, its fire-gutted mansions, its wastelands of unprofitable parking-lots, a deadly kind man. At the moment I hated him: he surmised too much. Now I most bitterly repent that malign emotion.

It being nearly time for evensong, I must put on my vestments. I conscientiously perform my daily offices, although no one attends my services except on Sundays. Somehow I did not wish to have Julie at my vespers: I suppose now that I sensed, given my growing desire for her, how Julie for a congregation might have made evensong a mockery.

"What shall we do with you while I'm in the church, Julie?" (The phrase itself sounded erotic to me.) "Possibly you need to write a letter home? Do you play dominoes? Perhaps we'll have a match when I come back."

Or perhaps we'll have a match of something else, I added for my own delectation, silently. I had begun to lose control of my fancies about this Miss Julie Tilton, kid sister of the pillar of unrighteousness. Othello, Desdemona, and the beast with two backs were only the beginning.

That she was so innocent, and I under a vow, made these prospects yet more attractive. Abelard and Heloise! Or, from *Notre Dame,* the lascivious archdeacon and virginal Esmeralda. I would laugh, toying with her in the beginning, tugging at her long hair. . . .

Fork, the homicidal old devil, damn him, must have sensed my change of mood—my change of character, almost. What had he meant by his "don't let anything occupy you?" But Fork would not return until tomorrow evening. Meanwhile, Julie and I could have a very lively time. Perhaps. There were risks. . . .

While sinking into these amorous reveries, I had put on my vestments. I was about to enter the church, to celebrate evensong at the apsidal chapel of Saint Thomas of Canterbury, when the electric bell rang at the great doors. The Cambodian couple were out for the evening, at the cinema—a thoughtful suggestion of mine, that. Damn the bell: let it ring! But then, Julie might hear it and foolishly open the postern; Lord knows who might enter. No, I had best respond myself.

I endeavored, while passing through the galilee, to put Julie out of my mind. Her body had become an obsession, all six feet of her young inexperience. My amorous images were turning toward violent acts, in my mind's eye. It was as if the appetites of someone else...

Releasing the several locks, I swung open the postern door. A big man stood there. By the light of the small bulb that burns above the door, I made out his face. It was Franchetti, once Sherm's chief enforcer, the man who had accosted Julie in the Mustang the previous night.

Though not so massive as I am, Franchetti was tall and tough: that pleased me. Rather than slamming the door in his face, I said to him, "Good evening, Mr. Franchetti. You've come to evensong?"

He seemed taken aback at my knowing his name, and he did not understand my invitation. Also he may have been confused as to my identity: as I mentioned earlier, I look different in cassock and surplice.

"Hi, Doc—I mean, Rev," he began. "You're the chief honcho here, right? I got a deal to make with you."

"Do come in, Franchetti." I stood back to admit him.

The spectacle of the dimly lit galilee obviously bewildered my visitor. To him this splendid Romanesque porch, with its shadows and mysterious columns and many arches, must have seemed like the setting for a horror-movie—not that any mere film could be more horrid than Franchetti's own mode of existence. Locking automatically, the door closed behind him.

"You've come to divine worship, Franchetti?"

He snorted. "Some joker! Rev, we could do you a lot of damage."

"I'm aware of that, Brother Franchetti. You might even murder me—or try to. It could turn out like your attempt on Causland."

He stared at me; decided on a new tack. "Okay, Rev, let's drop that line. I come here to give you money, real money."

"How much?"

"A thousand bucks, right now, Rev."

"For the succor of the poor?"

He snorted again. "If that's the way you like to kid, Rev."

"Possibly you expect something in exchange?"

"We sure do. You're goin' to give us that young blonde you been amusin' yourself with. You got no claim on her."

"You have?"

"Sure. Sherm promised her to the boys two years ago,

and he took it in the guts, but now we're goin' to collect her."

"You take her to be Sherm's sister?"

"Sure, Rev. Sherm was goin' to have his kinky fun with her, and then turn her over to us to be eddicated for the street, understand? You didn't never meet Sherm? Well, her and Sherm coulda been identical twins, see, 'cept for differences in the right places. She's our stuff. You already had your pleasure, Rev, with what she's got."

I sucked in my breath: he had shot near the mark. My adrenalin could not be restrained much longer. Yet I contrived to prolong our conversation for a few moments.

"What makes you say that, dear Brother Franchetti?"

"Hell, Rev, we found out you took in four or five kids, two of 'em our property, for your private use in this here crazyhouse of yours. None of 'em ever showed up on Pentecost again. What'd you do with 'em, Rev? Got 'em chained in the cellar? Buried in the cellar? I hate to think of what you done with them girls, Rev— and one of 'em a goldmine. Why, you're a public menace. Somebody ought to turn you in to the pigs."

At this point in our dialogue I burst into laughter, hearty if hysterical. The sound echoed through the crepuscular galilee. Franchetti joined somewhat uneasily in the dismal mirth.

If we poor feeble sinners—of whom I am the chief—are engaged in a holy war against the forces of Satan, we ought to ensure that not all the casualties fall on our side.

"Franchetti," I said, "I have been unfair to you. Before you entered this place, I ought to have informed you that from the age of four upward, I was trained in the manly and martial arts by my sergeant-father, at Spanish Town. The door is locked. Do you think you can contrive to get out of this place alive?"

Being an old hand at such encounters, Franchetti reached very swiftly for what he carried within his jacket. Yet I, strung up for this contest, was swifter. I gave him a left in the belly, a right to the jaw, took him by the throat and pounded his head against the sandstone wall. He collapsed without being able to draw, and I disarmed him. He slumped down to the flags.

"You mistook me for a Creeping Jesus, perhaps," I remarked. I dragged him up and knocked him down again.

Then I proceeded to kick and trample my victim, with truly hellish fury.

I have been in many fights, principally before I was ordained, but never before had I treated a fallen adversary in that fashion. What was it Fork had said? "Watch out—something might get inside you, Doc?" I didn't care now.

Having unlocked the door, I took the broken man by his ankles and dragged him outside, face down. I pulled him some distance, round the corner to the lane that runs alongside the north wall of the church. A large trash-bin is chained there. In the chill rain, no witnesses passed. Having administered several more kicks to Franchetti, I heaved him into the bin, head down. The garbage truck would find him in the morning, if no one noticed the wreck before then. One more of the mugged would rouse no great sensation in Hawkhill. What Franchetti had done to others, now had been done to him.

On my way back to the postern, I noticed that Franchetti's billfold had fallen on the sidewalk. In it I found nearly two thousand dollars in hundred-dollar bills. The wallet and Franchetti's gun I flung down the opening of a convenient storm-sewer. The bills I stuffed into our poor-box within the galilee, so laying up treasure in heaven for Franchetti.

I felt like Hercules or Thomas à Becket. Should I swagger down to Pentecost Road, seeking out Franchetti's two particular chums, to give them a dose of the same medicine? But I was weary: it was as if abruptly the destructive energy were being drained out of me. Instead I went back into the church, forgetting evensong for the first time, and strode through the cloister to my rectory.

Libido dominandi, for the time being, had driven out a different lust. Besides, exhaustion and disgust had begun to set in. I passed Julie's door, reeled into my own room, and slept in my vestments.

Before breakfast, Sergeant Shaugnessy telephoned me to report that a man named Franchetti, who had a long criminal record, had been found badly damaged near my church, and now lay in critical condition in Receiving Hospital. He wondered if I had heard anything outside in the street, during the night. I informed him that no sounds penetrated through our great bronze doors. This seemed to satisfy the Sergeant, not solicitous for Franchetti's well-being. "Franchetti's got the d.t.'s," he informed me. "He keeps groaning that a nigger preacher who breaks bones took his money and beat his brains out."

I contrived to be urbane with Julie at breakfast. My ambition to conquer somehow was diminished in the morning; I felt affection more than appetite. We spent the day visiting, by taxi, the city office of the FBI, the state police headquarters, and the hospitals: no discoveries about any Tilton.

But as evening approached, images of concupiscence rose strong again in my head. I arranged for the verger and his wife, to their surprise, a second expedition to the flicks, in a suburb. They protested that the taxis would cost too much; I brushed that aside, handing them forty dollars. I would have Julie at my undisturbed disposal for at least three hours. Miss Tilton would be worth two twenties.

Yet there was Fork to be reckoned with: I had almost forgotten that he would arrive about nine or nine-thirty to practice on the organ. Well, he had no key to the church: let him ring in vain for admittance. I would not be diverted from what Julie had to offer.

I took the trouble to book a taxi, for precisely eight-thirty, to come to the church door and take the Cambodian couple to the suburban movie house. I would take Julie into the church itself, the moment they left: a piquant setting for what I intended. Tuesday night I had enjoyed battering Franchetti in the galilee; this night I would have the relish of sacrilege with Julie in the sanctuary.

I knew what I was doing and just how I would go about everything, rejoicing in outrage. Yet something else in me still protested against this wildness.

About seven o'clock, I went into the church, took some kneeler-cushions from pews, and laid them conveniently before the little altar in the apse-chapel of Thomas of Canterbury. Here I meant to celebrate my peculiar evensong with Julie Tilton.

An interesting architectural feature of my Church of the Holy Ghost is a large entrance, at the crossing, to the crypt. The stair downward, and the balustrades that guard it, are of splendid marble. I am told that this construction closely resembles the approach to the tombs at a church in Padua, which I have not visited.

As I returned from the apse toward the nave, I thought for a moment that I heard a voice down the sepulchral stair. Could it be the verger? My impression of a voice was so strong that I descended into the large low-vaulted crypt. I found everything in order, and no man or woman. My conflict of emotions must be affecting my perceptions. Julie would have to pay for that, in precisely an hour and a half.

The two of us ate a simple dinner in the rectory; I told the Cambodian housekeeper not to bother with the dishes until she came back from the cinema. Julie must have thought my manner odd: I talked confusedly of everything under the sun and the moon—theology, Jamaica, low life in Hawkhill, the bishop, Fork (but there I checked my tongue), Mrs. Simmons, the lonely existence of a celibate. I stared hard at her all the while. Though presumably a little disturbed by my eccentricity, Julie remained pleasant, now and again asking a sensible question, and occasionally a naive one. I must have her.

"I don't suppose you've ever been present at a liturgy of the sort we celebrate in this church, Julie."

"Oh, no, Father Montrose, I haven't; but I'd just love to."

"It happens that I have arranged a special evensong liturgy for you alone, Julie. You'll be my whole congregation, a few minutes from now, at our Chapel of Saint Thomas of Canterbury."

Her assent was delicious. What was to follow might be rather rough on Miss Tilton, but delicious for me. Let the consequences be damned.

I took my prize by the hand and led her to the galilee. My grasp did not startle her; quite possibly she thought it part of the liturgy.

It was nearly half-past eight. The old Cambodian verger was unlocking the postern door.

"Taxi honk, Father," he told me. "My wife, she come down in minute."

I had held open the carved wooden doors to the nave, but Julie hung back. "Just a minute, Father: I'll say 'Have a good time' to the housekeeper when she comes down."

Gripping her slender hand so that she winced a trifle, I tugged Julie through the entrance to the nave. "Come on, kid," I heard myself saying harshly, "we've got no time to waste."

"Oh!" she cried.

"What's wrong, Julie, you little fool?"

"It's funny: you sounded just like Sherm then. It could have been his own voice, Father Montrose."

We two stood at the foot of the central aisle. The Norman pillars of the nave interrupted the beams of dim religious light from such concealed fixtures as I had chosen to switch on. Far ahead of us, a huge ornate sanctuary-lamp shone upon the high altar; and smaller sanctuary-lamps glimmered from the side-chapels.

I squeezed her hand. "This is going to be a totally new experience for you, Julie. Perhaps you'll not enjoy all of it so much as I intend to."

"Father, I just know it's going to be marvellous!"

I had begun to lead her down the broad aisle.

Then for the second time I heard a harsh incoherent voice from the crypt-stair near the crossing.

I stopped dead. Julie almost tripped.

"What's wrong, Father?"

"I don't know. . . . What can have spoken?"

"Spoken, Father? I didn't hear anyone at all."

Then came the first scream, so terrible that I reeled against a bench-end. Ah, the ghastly echoes of it in nave, in aisles, in the choir, back from the blindstory!

"Oh, Father, are you all right? What's happening?"

"My God, Julie, didn't you hear that howl?" I could do no more than whisper the inquiry to her.

"I don't know what you mean. For just the littlest fraction of a second, though, I thought I heard my brother whispering in my ear."

At that moment, in the dim sanctuary light, a head emerged above the balustrade of the crypt-stair. Other heads followed it. They seemed like jelly, glistening.

In the horror of that moment, I broke free from the spirit that had entered into me. I knew of a sudden that I had been occupied and made an agent. Whether from shock or from grace, I was enabled to regain my will. Through me, these things from below had schemed to take Julie.

Swinging round, I snatched up Julie and ran with her, bursting through the doors into the galilee. The verger and his wife were going out the door to take the taxi. Upon them I thrust my Julie.

"Drive her to Mrs. Simmons, quick!" I ordered them. It seemed to me as if I were grunting like a hog. "Quick!"

And to Julie, "Goodbye, my darling. Don't ever come back here!"

Before I slammed the door behind them, I had one last glimpse of her astounded pallid lovely face, forbidden to me ever after.

Then I ran back into the nave, to impede the damned invaders.

Having emerged from the stair, the things were wavering slowly up the aisle toward me. In their insubstantiality, they seemed to shimmer. There came four of them, inexpressibly loathsome. I knew they must be the men who had died on Causland's fork or by his gun.

As they drew nearer, I could make out the face of the first only. Lips and nostrils were hideously contorted; yet the resemblance to Julie could not be denied. From four wounds, gouts of blood had run down the thing's middle.

In my extremity, I tried to stammer out the Third Collect:

Lighten our darkness, we beseech thee, O Lord, and by Thy great mercy defend us from all perils and dangers of this night, for the love of Thine only Son, our Saviour Jesus Christ.

Yet the words, inaudible, stuck in my craw. Then came the Screamer's second tremendous howl, surely from the Pit. This thing had told his disciples that his essence could transcend space and time.

I clutched a pillar. These "beasts with the souls of damned men" would overcome me, for too much of them had entered into me already. We were sib.

That second screech was followed by an unbearable silence. The Sherm-thing's tormented face drew nearer mine. He would enter. We would be one.

In that silence rang out the sound of brass upon stone. Fork thrust himself between me and the Screamer. "Wahoo!"

It seemed to my eyes that Fork leaped twenty feet into the air; lingered suspended there; then returned, laughing as a hyaena laughs.

The four dead things shrank from him. They seemed gelatinous, deliquescent; no words might express the ghastliness of them.

But Fork was all compact, glowing with energy, transfigured and yet in semblance himself, that hard taut face invincible.

"So must you ever be," said Fork, pointing at the four his blindman's stick. "This place and this man are too much for you. Into the fire, Sherm and all!"

They receded. Screaming, they were swept into nothingness. I fell.

If it was consciousness I regained, that was an awareness of the world beyond the world. Incapable of speech or movement, I seemed to be lying in some shadowy cold enclosed unknown place. Was it a sepulchre? The form of Fork Causland—derby, stick, cigar, and all—seemed to stand before me.

"In the hour of need, you were a man, Doc," he said to me, "a man in the mold of your friend Thomas à Becket. It was the old Adam in you that admitted those four spirits from below, but the better part in you withstood them. I take off my hat to you"—and so he did, sweepingly, in Fork's sardonic way.

"You'll not see the girl again, Doc, here below, nor Fork Causland. His time came; it would have come more terribly two years ago, had I not occupied him then and thereafter. The end arrived in a moment of grace while he was on his way to reinforce you; and it will be well with poor Fork."

Though I strove to speak, I failed; the semblance of Fork shook its head. "Listen. That you should see me without your blood freezing, I have come to you in the mask of your friend Fork. I shall come to you once more, Thomas Montrose—no, priest, I'll not specify the year, the day, the hour, humankind not being able to stand much reality—and then as a friend, civilly inviting you to enter upon eternity. Why, I'll stand then hat in hand before you, Doc, as I stand now. Shall I come in the semblance of Fork Causland, on that occasion too? I would please you."

Lying rigid with fright, I could not reply to this being. He smiled Fork's stoical humorous smile.

"Do you take me for a demon, Doc? No, I'm not what possessed Sherm, or what came close to possessing you. Through Fork's lips I told you that I was only cousin to devils. I'm a messenger, penetrating Time, taking such shapes as I am commanded: sometimes merciful, sometimes retributory.

"The old Greeks called me Thanatos. The Muslim call me

Azrael. You may as well call me—why, Fork will do as well as any other name. Fast and pray, Doc. You have been tried, but not found wanting. In the fullness of time, as our blind friend Fork would have put it, 'I'll be seeing you.' "

Then he was gone, taking everything with him.

The ringing telephone on my bedside table woke me. Somehow the returned Cambodian church-mice, taking me to be drunken merely, had contrived to drag me to my bed.

"Reverend Montrose?" the efficient voice of a woman inquired from the receiver. "Do you know somebody named Homer Causland? We found your name and number in one of his pockets."

"Yes. Something happened?"

"Mr. Causland was struck by a hit-and-run driver shortly after eight-thirty last night. His body was taken to Receiving Hospital, but there wasn't anything we could do for him here. He didn't suffer. The police have got the driver and booked him for murder. Can you make the arrangements— that is, was Mr. Causland a friend of yours?"

"My only one," I told her. "*Requiescat in pace.*"

I have sent Julie Tilton's bag by taxi to Mrs. Simmons's big house, and Mrs. Simmons will see that Julie flies home, however bewildered, this evening.

If an energumen from below may penetrate even to the fastness of the church, how shall we prevail? Yet I fast and pray as one should who has been in the company of the dead damned, and has heard the speech of the Death Angel.

In all of us sinners the flesh is weak; and the future, unknowable, has its many contrived corridors and issues. Lord, I am a miserable thing, and I am afraid.

Puffed up with pride of spirit, by which fault fell the angels, I came near to serving the Prince of the Air. From the ravenous powers of darkness, O Lord, let me be preserved; and I entreat thee, do cast the lurking unclean spirits, instead, into the swine of Gadara.

For hours I have sat here, meditating, now and again scribbling these pages at my table in the galilee. The coals having expired in the grate, I am cold now.

The race is not to the swift, nor the battle to the strong.

Winter coming on, this is a night of sleet. What is tapping

now, so faintly, at the great knocker on the bronze door? It never can be she. Has the order of release been sent? "Watch ye, stand fast in the faith, quit you like men, be strong." I'll unbar the little door. Pray for us sinners now and at the hour of our death.

A TERRIBLE VENGEANCE

By Mrs. J. H. Riddell

Chapter One

VERY STRANGE

Round Dockett Point and over Dumsey Deep the waterlilies were blooming as luxuriantly as though the silver Thames had been the blue Mummel Lake.

It was the time for them. The hawthorn had long ceased to scent the air; the wild roses had shed their delicate leaves; the buttercups and cardamoms and dog-daisies that had dotted the meadows were garnered into hay. The world in early August needed a fresh and special beauty, and here it was floating in its matchless green bark on the bosom of the waters.

If those fair flowers, like their German sisters, ever at nightfall, assumed mortal form, who was there to tell of such vagaries? Even when the moon is at her full there are few who care to cross Chertsey Mead, or face the lonely Stabbery.

Hard would it be, indeed, so near life, railways, civilization, and London, to find a more lonely stretch of country, when twilight visits the landscape and darkness comes brooding down over the Surrey and Middlesex shores, than the path which winds along the river from Shepperton Lock to Chertsey Bridge. At high noon for months together it is desolate beyond description—silent, save for the rippling and sobbing of the currents, the wash of the stream, the swaying of the osiers, the trembling of an aspen, the rustle of the withies, or the noise made by a bird, or rat, or stoat, startled by the sound of unwonted footsteps. In the warm summer nights also, when tired holiday-makers are sleeping soundly, when men stretched on the green sward outside their white tents are smoking, and talking, and planning excursions for the morrow; when in country houses young people are playing and singing, dancing or walking up and down terraces over-looking well-kept lawns, where the evening air is laden with delicious perfumes—there falls on that almost uninhabited mile or two of riverside a stillness which may be felt, which the belated traveller is loth to disturb even by the dip of his oars as he drifts down with the current past objects that seem to him unreal as fragments of a dream.

It had been a wet summer—a bad summer for the hotels. There had been some fine days, but not many together. The weather could not be depended upon. It was not a season in which young ladies were to be met about the reaches of the Upper Thames, disporting themselves in marvellous dresses, and more marvellous headgear, unfurling brilliant parasols, canoeing in appropriate attire, giving life and colour to the streets of old-world villages, and causing many of their inhabitants to consider what a very strange sort of town it must be in which such extraordinarily-robed persons habitually reside.

Nothing of the sort was to be seen that summer, even as high as Hampton. Excursions were limited to one day; there were few tents, few people camping-out, not many staying at the hotels; yet it was, perhaps for that reason, an enjoyable summer to those who were not afraid of a little, or rather a great deal, of rain, who liked a village inn all the better for not being crowded, and who were not heart-broken because their women-folk for once found it impossible to accompany them.

Unless a man boldly decides to outrage the proprieties and decencies of life, and go off by himself to take his pleasure selfishly alone, there is in a fine summer no door of escape open to him. There was a time—a happy time—when a husband was not expected to sign away his holidays in the marriage articles. But what boots it to talk of that remote past now? Everything is against the father of a family at present. Unless the weather help him, what friend has he? and the weather does not often in these latter days prove a friend.

In that summer, however, with which this story deals, the stars in their courses fought for many an oppressed paterfamilias. Any curious inquirer might then have walked ankle-deep in mud from Penton Hook to East Molesey, and not met a man, harnessed like a beast of burden, towing all his belongings up stream, or beheld him rowing against wind and tide as though he were a galley-slave chained to the oar, striving all the while to look as though enjoying the fun.

Materfamilias found it too wet to patronize the Thames. Her dear little children also were conspicuous by their absence. Charming young ladies were rarely to be seen—indeed, the skies were so treacherous that it would have been a mere tempting of Providence to risk a pretty dress on the water; for which sufficient reasons furnished houses remained unlet, and lodgings were left empty; taverns and hotels welcomed visitors instead of treating them scurvily; and the river, with its green banks and its leafy aits, its white swans, its water-lilies, its purple loosestrife, its reeds, its rushes, its weeping willows, its quiet backwaters, was delightful.

One evening two men stood just outside the door of the Ship, Lower Halliford, looking idly at the water, as it flowed by more rapidly than is usually the case in August. Both were dressed in suits of serviceable dark grey tweed; both wore round hats; both evidently belonged to that class which resembles flowers of the field but in the one respect that it toils not, neither does it spin; both looked intensely bored; both were of rather a good appearance.

The elder, who was about thirty, had dark hair, sleepy brown eyes, and a straight capable nose; a heavy moustache almost concealed his mouth, but his chin was firm and well cut. About him there was an indescribable something calculated to excite attention, but nothing in his expression to attract or repel. No one looking at him could have said offhand, "I think that is a pleasant fellow," or "I am sure that man could make himself confoundedly disagreeable."

His face revealed as little as the covers of a book. It might contain interesting matter, or there might be nothing underneath save the merest commonplace. So far as it conveyed an idea at all, it was that of indolence. Every movement of his body suggested laziness; but it would have been extremely hard to say how far that laziness went. Mental energy and physical inactivity walk oftener hand in hand than the world suspects, and mental energy can on occasion make an indolent man active, while more brute strength can never confer intellect on one who lacks brains.

In every respect the younger stranger was the opposite of his companion. Fair, blue-eyed, light-haired, with soft moustache and tenderly cared-for whiskers, he looked exactly what he was—a very shallow, kindly, good fellow, who did not trouble himself with searching into the depths of things, who took the world as it was, who did not go out to meet trouble, who loved his species, women included, in an honest way; who liked amusement, athletic sports of all sorts—dancing, riding, rowing, shooting; who had not one regret, save that hours in a Government office were so confoundedly long, "eating the best part out of a day, by Jove;" no cause for discontent save that he had very little money, and into whose mind it had on the afternoon in question been forcibly borne that his friend was a trifle heavy—"carries too many guns," he considered—and not exactly the man to enjoy a modest dinner at Lower Halliford.

For which cause, perhaps, he felt rather relieved when his friend refused to partake of any meal.

"I wish you could have stayed," said the younger, with the earnest and not quite insincere hospitality people always assume when they feel a departing guest is not to be overpersuaded to stay.

"So do I," replied the other. "I should have liked to stop with *you*, and I should have liked to stay here. There is a sleepy dullness about the place which exactly suits my present mood, but I must get back to town. I promised Travers to look in at his chambers this evening, and to-morrow as I told you, I am due in Norfolk."

"What will you do, then, till train-time? There is nothing up from here till nearly seven. Come on the river for an hour with me."

"Thank you, no. I think I will walk over to Staines."

"Staines! Why Staines in heaven's name?"

"Because I am in the humour for a walk—a long, lonely walk; because a demon has taken possession of me I wish to exorcise; because there are plenty of trains from Staines; because I am weary of the Thames Valley line, and any other reason you like. I can give you none better than I have done."

"At least let me row you part of the way."

"Again thank you, no. The eccentricities of the Thames are not new to me. With the best intentions, you would land me at Laleham when I should be on my (rail) way to London. My dear Dick, step into that boat your soul has been hankering after for the past half-hour, and leave me to return to town according to my own fancy."

"I don't half like this," said genial Dick. "Ah! here comes a pretty girl—look."

Thus entreated, the elder man turned his head and saw a young girl, accompanied by a young man, coming along the road, which leads from Walton Lane to Shepperton.

She was very pretty, of the sparkling order of beauty, with dark eyes, rather heavy eye-brows, dark thick hair, a ravishing fringe, a delicious hat, a coquettish dress, and shoes which by pretty gestures she seemed to be explaining to her companion were many—very many—sizes too large for her. Spite of her beauty, spite of her dress, spite of her shoes so much too large for her, it needed but a glance from one conversant with subtle social distinctions to tell that she was not quite her "young man's" equal.

For, in the parlance of Betsy Jane, as her "young man" she evidently regarded him, and as her young man he regarded himself. There could be no doubt about the matter. He was over head and ears in love with her; he was ready to quarrel—indeed, had quarrelled with father, mother, sister, brother on her account. He loved her unreasonably—he loved her miserably, distractedly; except at odd intervals, he was not in the least happy with her. She flouted, she tormented, she maddened him; but then, after having nearly driven him to the verge of distraction, she would repent sweetly, and make up for all previous shortcomings by a few brief minutes of tender affection. If quarrelling be really the renewal of love, theirs had been renewed once a day at all events, and frequently much oftener.

Yes, she was a pretty girl, a bewitching girl, and arrant flirt, a scarcely well-behaved coquette; for as she passed the two friends she threw a glance at them, one arch, piquant, inviting glance, of which many would instantly have availed themselves, venturing the consequences certain to be dealt out by her companion, who, catching the look, drew closer to her side, not too well pleased, apparently. Spite of a little opposition, he drew her hand through his arm, and walked on with an air of possession infinitely amusing to onlookers, and plainly distasteful to his lady-love.

"A clear case of spoons," remarked the younger of the two visitors, looking after the pair.

"Poor devil!" said the other compassionately.

His friend laughed, and observed mockingly paraphrasing a very different speech,—

"But for the grace of God, there goes Paul Murray."

"You may strike out the 'but,'" replied the person so addressed, "for that is the very road Paul Murray is going, and soon."

"You are not serious!" asked the other doubtfully.

"Am I not? I am though, though not with such a vixen as I dare swear that little baggage is. I told you I was due to-morrow in Norfolk. But see, they are turning back; let us go inside."

"All right," agreed the other, following his companion into the hall. "This is a great surprise to me, Murray: I never imagined you were engaged."

"I am not engaged yet, though no doubt I shall soon be," answered the reluctant lover. "My grandmother and the lady's father have arranged the match. The lady does not object, I believe, and who am I, Savill, that I should refuse good looks, a good fortune, and a good temper?"

"You do not speak as though you liked the proposed bride, nevertheless," said Savill dubiously.

"I do not dislike her, I only hate having to marry her. Can't you understand that a man wants to pick a wife for himself—that the one girl he fancies seems worth ten thousand of a girl anybody else fancies? But I am so situated—Hang it, Dick! what are you staring at that dark-eyed witch for?"

"Because it is so funny. She is making him take a boat at the steps, and he does not want to do it. Kindly observe his face."

"'What is his face to me?" retorted Mr. Murray savagely.

"Not much, I daresay, but it is a good deal to him. It is black as thunder, and hers is not much lighter. What a neat ankle, and how you like to show it, my dear. Well, there is no harm in a pretty ankle or a pretty foot either, and you have both. One would not wish one's wife to have a hoof like an elephant. What sort of feet has your destined maiden, Paul?"

"I never noticed."

"That looks deucedly bad," said the younger man, shaking his head. "I know, however, she has a pure, sweet face," observed Mr. Murray gloomily.

"No one could truthfully make the same statement about our young friend's little lady," remarked Mr. Savill, still gazing at the girl, who was seating herself in the stern. "A termagant, I'll be bound, if ever there was one. Wishes to go up stream, no doubt because he wishes to go down. Any caprice about the Norfolk 'fair'?"

"Not much, I think. She is good, Dick—too good for me," replied the other, sauntering out again.

"That is what we always say about the things we do not know. And so your grandmother has made up the match?"

"Yes: there is money, and the old lady loves money. She says she wants to see me settled—talks of buying me an estate. She will have to do something, because I am sure the stern parent on the other side would not allow his daughter to marry on expectations. The one drop of comfort in the arrangement is that my aged relative will have to come down, and pretty smartly too. I would wed Hecate, to end this state of bondage, which I have not courage to flee from myself. Dick, how I envy you who have no dead person's shoes to wait for!"

"You need not envy me," returned Dick, with conviction, "a poor unlucky devil chained to a desk. There is scarce a day of my life I fail to curse the service, the office, and Fate—"

"Curse no more, then," said the other; "rather go down on your knees and thank Heaven you have, without any merit of your own, a provision for life. I wish Fate or anybody had coached me into the Civil Service—apprenticed me to a trade—sent me to sea—made me enlist, instead of leaving me at the mercy of an old lady who knows neither justice nor reason—who won't let me do anything for myself, and won't do anything for me—who ought to have been dead long ago, but who never means to die—"

"And who often gives you in one cheque as much as the whole of my annual salary," added the other quietly.

"But you know you will have your yearly salary as long as you live. I never know whether I shall have another cheque."

"It won't do, my friend," answered Dick Savill; "you feel quite certain you can get money when you want it."

"I feel certain of no such thing," was the reply. "If I once offended her—" he stopped, and then went on: "And perhaps when I have spent twenty years in trying to humour such caprices as surely woman never had before, I shall wake one morning to find she has left every penny to the Asylum for Idiots."

"Why do you not pluck up courage, and strike out some line for yourself?"

"Too late, Dick, too late. Ten years ago I might have

tried to make a fortune for myself, but I can't do that now. As I have waited so long, I must wait a little longer. At thirty a man can't take pick in hand and try to clear a road to fortune."

"Then you had better marry the Norfolk young lady."

"I am steadily determined to do so. I am going down with the firm intention of asking her."

"And do you think she will have you?"

"I think so. I feel sure she will. And she is a nice girl—the sort I would like for a wife, if she had not been thrust upon me."

Mr. Savill stood silent for a moment, with his hands plunged deep in his pockets.

"Then when I see you next?" he said tentatively.

"I shall be engaged, most likely—possibly even married," finished the other, with as much hurry as his manner was capable of. "And now jump into your boat, and I will go on my way to—Staines—"

"I wish you would change your mind, and have some dinner."

"I can't; it is impossible. You see I have so many things to do and to think of. Good-bye, Dick. Don't upset yourself—go down stream, and don't get into mischief with those dark eyes you admired so much just now."

"Make your mind easy about that," returned the other, colouring, however, a little as he spoke. "Good-bye, Murray. I wish you well through the campaign." And so, after a hearty hand-shake, they parted, one to walk away from Halliford, past Shepperton Church, and across Shepperton Range, and the other, of course, to row up stream, through Shepperton Lock, and on past Dockett Point.

In the grey of the summer's dawn, Mr. Murray awoke next morning from a terrible dream. He had kept his appointment with Mr. Travers and a select party, played heavily, drank deeply, and reached home between one and two, not much the better for his trip to Lower Halliford, his walk, and his carouse.

Champagne, followed by neat brandy, is not perhaps the best thing to insure a quiet night's rest; but Mr. Murray had often enjoyed sound repose after similar libations; and it was, therefore, all the more unpleasant that in the grey dawn he should wake suddenly from a dream, in which he thought some one was trying to crush his head with a heavy weight.

A TERRIBLE VENGEANCE 221

Even when he had struggled from sleep, it seemed to him that a wet dead hand lay across his eyes, and pressed them so hard he could not move the lids. Under the weight he lay powerless, while a damp, ice-cold hand felt burning into his brain, if such a contradictory expression may be permitted.

The perspiration was pouring from him; he felt the drops falling on his throat, and trickling down his neck; he might have been lying in a bath, instead of on his own bed, and it was with a cry of horror he at last flung the hand aside, and, sitting up, looked around the room, into which the twilight of morning was mysteriously stealing.

Then, trembling in every limb, he lay down again, and fell into another sleep, from which he did not awake till aroused by broad daylight and his valet.

"You told me to call you in good time, sir," said the man.

"Ah, yes, so I did," yawned Mr. Murray. "What a bore! I will get up directly. You can go, Davis. I will ring if I want you."

Davis was standing, as his master spoke, looking down at the floor. "Yes, sir," he answered, after the fashion of a man who has something on his mind,—and went.

He had not, however, got to the bottom of the first flight when peal after peal summoned him back.

Mr. Murray was out of bed, and in the middle of the room, the ghastly pallor of his face brought into full prominence by the crimson dressing-gown he had thrown round him on rising.

"What is that?" he asked. "What in the world is that, Davis?" and he pointed to the carpet, which was covered, Mrs. Murray being an old-fashioned lady, with strips of white drugget.

"I am sure I do not know, sir," answered Davis. "I noticed it the moment I came into the room. Looks as if some one with wet feet had been walking round and round the bed."

It certainly did. Round and round, to and fro, backwards and forwards, the feet seemed to have gone and come, leaving a distinct mark wherever they pressed.

"The print is that of a rare small foot, too," observed Davis, who really seemed half stupefied with astonishment.

"But who would have dared—" began Mr. Murray.

"No one in this house," declared Davis stoutly. "It is not the mark of a boy or woman inside these doors;" and then the master and the man looked at each other for an instant with grave suspicion.

But for that second they kept their eyes thus occupied; then, as by common consent, they dropped their glances to the floor. "My God!" exclaimed Davis. "Where have the footprints gone?"

He might well ask. The drugget, but a moment before wet and stained by the passage and repassage of those small restless feet, was now smooth and white, as when first sent forth from the bleach-green. On its polished surface there could not be discerned a speck or mark.

Chapter Two

WHERE IS LUCY?

In the valley of the Thames early hours are the rule. There the days have an unaccountable way of lenghtening themselves out which makes it prudent, as well as pleasant, to utilize all the night in preparing for a longer morrow.

For this reason, when eleven o'clock p.m. strikes, it usually finds Church Street, Walton, as quiet as its adjacent graveyard, which lies still and solemn under the shadow of the old grey tower hard by that ancient vicarage which contains so beautiful a staircase.

About the time when Mr. Travers' friends were beginning their evening, when talk had abated and play was suggested, the silence of Church Street was broken and many a sleeper aroused by a continuous knocking at the door of a house as venerable as any in that part of Walton. Rap—rap—rap—rap awoke the echoes of the old-world village street, and at length brought to the window a young man, who, flinging up the sash, inquired,—

"Who is there?"

"Where is Lucy? What have you done with my girl?" answered a strained woman's voice from out the darkness of that summer night.

"Lucy?" repeated the young man; "is not she at home?"

"No; I have never set eyes on her since you went out together."

"Why, we parted hours ago. Wait a moment, Mrs. Heath; I will be down directly."

No need to tell the poor woman to "wait." She stood on

the step, crying softly and wringing her hands till the door opened, and the same young fellow who with the pretty girl had taken boat opposite the Ship Hotel bade her "Come in."

Awakened from some pleasant dream, spite of all the trouble and hurry of that unexpected summons, there still shone the light of a reflected sunshine in his eyes and the flush of happy sleep on his cheek. He scarcely understood yet what had happened, but when he saw Mrs. Heath's tear-stained face, comprehension came to him, and he said abruptly,—

"Do you mean that she has never returned home?"

"Never!"

They were in the parlour by this time, and looking at each other by the light of one poor candle which he had set down on the table.

"Why, I left her," he said, "I left her long before seven."

"Where?"

"Just beyond Dockett Point. She would not let me row her back. I do not know what was the matter with her, but nothing I did seemed right."

"Had you any quarrel?" asked Mrs. Heath anxiously.

"Yes, we had; we were quarrelling all the time—at least she was with me; and at last she made me put her ashore, which I did sorely against my will."

"What had you done to my girl, then?"

"I prayed of her to marry me—no great insult, surely, but she took it as one. I would rather not talk of what she answered. Where can he be? Do you think she can have gone to her aunt's?"

"If so, she will be back by the last train. Let us get home as fast as possible. I never thought of that. Poor child! she will go out of her mind if she finds nobody to let her in. You will come with me. O, if she is not there, what shall I do—what ever shall I do?"

The young man had taken his hat, and was holding the door open for Mrs. Heath to pass out.

"You must try not to fret yourself," he said gently, yet with a strange repression in his voice. "Very likely she may stay at her aunt's all night."

"And leave me in misery, not knowing where she is? Oh, Mr. Grantley, I could never believe that."

Mr. Grantley's heart was very hot within him; but he could not tell the poor mother he believed that when Lucy's temper was up she would think of no human being but herself.

"Won't you take my arm, Mrs. Heath?" he asked with tender pity. After all, though everything was over between him and Lucy, her mother could not be held accountable for their quarrel; and he had loved the girl with all the romantic fervour of love's young dream.

"I can walk faster without it, thank you," Mrs. Heath answered. "But Mr. Grantley, whatever you and Lucy fell out over, you'll forget it, won't you? It isn't in you to be hard on anybody, and she's only a spoiled child. I never had but the one, and I humoured her too much; and if she is wayward, it is all my own fault—all my own."

"In case she does not return by this train," said the young man, wisely ignoring Mrs. Heath's inquiry, "had I not better telegraph to her aunt directly the office opens?"

"I will be on my way to London long before that," was the reply. "But what makes you think she won't come? Surely you don't imagine she has done anything rash?"

"What do you mean by rash?" he asked evasively.

"Made away with herself."

"*That!*" he exclaimed. "No, I feel very sure she has done nothing of the sort."

"But she might have felt sorry when you left her—vexed for having angered you—heartbroken when she saw you leave her."

"Believe me, she was not vexed or sorry or heartbroken; she was only glad to know she had done with me," he answered bitterly.

"What has come to you, Mr. Grantley?" said Mrs. Heath, in wonder. "I never heard you speak the same before."

"Perhaps not; I never felt the same before. It is best to be plain with you," he went on. "All is at an end between us; and that is what your daughter has long been trying for."

"How can you say that, and she so fond of you?"

"She has not been fond of me for many a day. The man she wants to marry is not a poor fellow like myself, but one who can give her carriages and horses, and a fine house, and as much dress as she cares to buy."

"But where could she ever find a husband able to do that?"

"I do not know, Mrs. Heath. All I do know is that she considers I am no match for her; and now my eyes are opened, I see she was not a wife for me. We should never have known a day's happiness."

It was too dark to see his face, but his changed voice and words and manner told Lucy's mother the kindly lad, who a couple of years before came courting her pretty daughter, and offended all his friends for her sake, was gone away for ever. It was a man who walked by her side—who had eaten of the fruit of the tree, and had learned to be as a god, knowing good from evil.

"Well, well," she said brokenly, "you are the best judge, I suppose; but O, my child, my child!"

She was so blinded with tears she stumbled, and must have fallen had he not caught and prevented her. Then he drew her hand within his arm, and said,—

"I am so grieved for you. I never received anything but kindness from you."

"And indeed," she sobbed, "you never were anything except good to me. I always knew we couldn't be considered your equals, and I often had my doubts whether it was right to let you come backwards and forwards as I did, parting you from all belonging to you. But I thought, when your mother saw Lucy's pretty face—for it is pretty, Mr. Grantley—"

"There never was a prettier," assented the young man, though, now his eyes were opened, he knew Lucy's beauty would scarcely have recommended her to any sensible woman.

"I hoped she might take to her, and I'd never have intruded. And I was so proud and happy, and fond of you—I was indeed; and I used to consider how, when you came down, I could have some little thing you fancied. But that's all over now. And I don't blame you; only my heart is sore and troubled about my foolish girl."

They were on Walton Bridge by this time, and the night air blew cold and raw down the river, and made Mrs. Heath shiver.

"I wonder where Lucy is," she murmured, "and what she'd think if she knew her mother was walking through the night in an agony about her? Where was it you said you left her?"

"Between Dockett Point and Chertsey. I shouldn't have left her had she not insisted on my doing so."

"Isn't that the train?" asked Mrs. Heath, stopping suddenly short and listening intently.

"Yes; it is just leaving Sunbury Station. Do not hurry; we have plenty of time."

They had: they were at Lucy's home, one of the small houses situated between Battlecreese Hill and the Red Lion in Lower Halliford before a single passenger came along The Green, or out of Nannygoat Lane.

"My heart misgives me that she has not come down," said Mrs. Heath.

"Shall I go up to meet her?" asked the young man; and almost before the mother feverishly assented, he was striding through the summer night to Shepperton Station, where he found the lights extinguished and every door closed.

Chapter Three

POOR MRS. HEATH

By noon the next day every one in Shepperton and Lower Halliford knew Lucy Heath was "missing."

Her mother had been up to Putney, but Lucy was not with her aunt, who lived not very far from the Bridge on the Fulham side, and who, having married a fruiterer and worked up a very good business, was inclined to take such bustling and practical views of life and its concerns as rather dismayed her sister-in-law, who had spent so many years in the remote country, and then so many other years in quiet Shepperton, that Mrs. Pointer's talk flurried her almost as much as the noise of London, which often maddens middle-aged and elderly folk happily unaccustomed to its roar.

Girt about with a checked apron which lovingly enfolded a goodly portion of her comfortable figure, Mrs. Pointer received her early visitor with the sportive remark, "Why, it's never Martha Heath! Come along in; a sight of you is good for sore eyes."

But Mrs. Heath repelled all such humorous observations, and chilled those suggestions of hospitality the Pointers were never backward in making by asking in a low choked voice,—

"Is Lucy here?"

"Lor! whatever put such a funny notion into your head?"

"Ah! I see she is," trying to smile. "After all, she spent the night with you."

"Did what?" exclaimed Mrs. Pointer. "Spent the night—was that what you said? No, nor the day either, for this year nearly. Why, for the last four months she hasn't set foot across that doorstep, unless it might be to buy some cherries, or pears, or apples, or grapes, or suchlike, and then she came in with more air than any lady; and after paying her money and getting her goods went out again, just as if I hadn't been her father's sister and Pointer my husband. But there! for any sake, woman, don't look like that! Come into the parlour and tell me what is wrong. You never mean she has gone away and left you?"

Poor Mrs. Heath was perfectly incapable at that moment of saying what she did mean. Seated on a stool, and holding fast by the edge of the counter for fear of falling, the shop and its contents, the early busses, the people going along the pavement, the tradesmen's carts, the private carriages, were, as in some terrible nightmare, gyrating before her eyes. She could not speak, she could scarcely think, until that wild whirligig came to a stand. For a minute or two even Mrs. Pointer seemed multiplied by fifty; while her checked apron, the bananas suspended from hooks, the baskets of fruit, the pine-apples, the melons, the tomatoes, and the cob-nuts appeared and disappeared, only to reappear and disappear like the riders in a maddening giddy-go-round.

"Give me a drop of water," she said at last; and when the water was brought she drank a little and poured some on her handkerchief and dabbed her face, and finally suffered herself to be escorted into the parlour, where she told her tale, interrupted by many sobs. It would have been unchristian in Mrs. Pointer to exult; but it was only human to remember she had remarked to Pointer, in that terrible spirit of prophecy bestowed for some inscrutable reason on dear friends and close relations, she knew some such trouble must befall her sister-in-law.

"You made an idol of that girl, Martha," she went on, "and now it is coming home to you. I am sure it was only last August as ever was that Pointer—But here he is, and he will talk to you himself."

Which Mr. Pointer did, being very fond of the sound of his own foolish voice. He stated how bad a thing it was for people to be above their station or to bring children up above that rank of life in which it had pleased God to place them. He quoted many pleasing saws uttered by his father and grandfather; remarked that as folks sowed they were bound to reap; reminded Mrs. Heath they had the word of Scripture for the fact—than, which, parenthetically, no fact could be truer, as he knew—that a man might not gather grapes from thorns or even figs from thistles. Further he went on to observe generally—the observation having a particular reference to Lucy—that it did not do to judge things by their looks. Over and over again salesmen had tried to "shove off a lot of foreign fruit on him, but he wasn't a young bird to be taken in by that chaff." No; what he looked to was quality; it was what his customers expected from him, and what he could honestly declare his customers got. He was a plain man, and he thought honesty was the best policy. So as Mrs. Heath had seen fit to come to them in her trouble he would tell her what he thought, without beating about the bush. He believed Lucy had "gone off."

"But where?" asked poor Mrs. Heath.

"That I am not wise enough to say; but you'll find she's gone off. Girls in her station don't sport chains and bracelets and brooches for nothing—"

"But they did not cost many shillings," interposed the mother.

"She might tell you that," observed Mrs. Pointer, with a world of meaning.

"To say nothing," went on Mrs. Pointer, "of grey gloves she could not abear to be touched. One day she walked in when I was behind the counter, and, not knowing she had been raised to the peerage, I shook hands with her as a matter of course; but when I saw the young lady look at her glove as if I had dirtied it, I said, 'O, I beg your pardon, miss'—jocularly, you know. 'They soil so easily,' she lisped."

"I haven't patience with such ways!" interpolated Mrs. Pointer, without any lisp at all. "Yes, it's hard for you, Martha, but you may depend Pointer's right. Indeed, I expected how it would be long ago. Young women who are walking in the straight road don't dress as Lucy dressed, or dare their innocent little cousins to call them by their Christian names in the street. Since the Spring, and long before, Pointer and me has been sure Lucy was up to no good."

"And you held your tongues and never said a word to me!" retorted Mrs. Heath, goaded and driven to desperation.

"Much use it would have been saying any word to you," answered Mrs. Pointer. "When you told me about young Grantley, and I bid you be careful, how did you take my advice? Why, you blared out at me, went on as if I knew nothing and had never been anywhere. What I told you then, though, I tell you now: young Grantleys, the sons of rectors and the grandsons of colonels, don't come after farmer's daughters with any honest purpose."

"Yet young Grantley asked her last evening to fix a day for their marriage," said Mrs. Heath, with a little triumph.

"O, I daresay!" scoffed Mrs. Pointer.

"Talk is cheap," observed Mr. Pointer.

"Some folks have more of it than money," supplemented his wife.

"They have been, as I understand, keeping company for some time now," said the fruiterer, with what he deemed a telling and judicial calmness. "So if he asked her to name the day, why did she not name it?"

"I do not know. I have never seen her since."

"O, then you had only his word about the matter," summed up Mr. Pointer. "Just as I thought—just as I thought."

"What did you think?" inquired the poor troubled mother.

"Why, that she has gone off with this Mr. Grantley."

"Ah, you don't know Mr. Grantley, or you wouldn't say such a thing."

"It is true," observed Mr. Pointer, "that I do not know the gentleman, and, I may add, I do not want to know him; but speaking as a person acquainted with the world—"

"I'll be getting home," interrupted Mrs. Heath. "Most likely my girl is there waiting for me, and a fine laugh she will have against her poor old mother for being in such a taking. Yes, Lucy will have the breakfast ready. No, thank you; I'll not wait to take anything. There will be a train back presently; and besides, to tell you the truth, food would choke me till I sit down again with my girl, and then I won't be able to eat for joy."

Husband and wife looked at each other as Mrs. Heath spoke, and for the moment a deep pity pierced the hard crust of their worldly egotism.

"Wait a minute," cried Mrs. Pointer, "and I'll put on my bonnet and go with you."

"No," interrupted Mr. Pointer, instantly seizing his wife's idea, and appropriating it as his own. "I am the proper person to see this affair out. There is not much doing, and if there were, I would leave everything to obtain justice for your niece. After all, however wrong she may have gone, she is your niece, Maria."

With which exceedingly nasty remark, which held a whole volume of unpleasant meaning as to what Mrs. Pointer might expect from that relationship in the future, Mr. Pointer took Mrs. Heath by the arm, and piloted her out into the street, and finally to Lower Halliford, where the missing Lucy was not, and where no tidings of her had come.

Chapter Four

MR. GAGE ON PORTENTS

About the time when poor distraught Mrs. Heath, having managed to elude the vigilance of that cleverest of men, Maria Pointer's husband, had run out of her small house, and was enlisting the sympathies of gossip-loving Shepperton in Lucy's disappearance, Mr. Paul Murray arrived at Liverpool Street Station, where his luggage and his valet awaited him.

"Get tickets, Davis," he said; "I have run it rather close;" and he walked towards Smith's stall, while his man went into the booking-office.

As he was about to descend the stairs, Davis became aware of a very singular fact. Looking down the steps, he saw precisely the same marks that had amazed him so short a time previously, being printed hurriedly off by a pair of invisible feet, which ran to the bottom and then flew as if in the wildest haste to the spot where Mr. Murray stood.

"I am not dreaming, am I?" thought the man; and he shut his eyes and opened them again.

The footprints were all gone!

At that moment his master turned from the bookstall and proceeded towards the train. A porter opened the door of a smoking carriage, but Murray shook his head and passed on. Mr. Davis, once more looking to the ground, saw that those feet belonging to no mortal body were still following. There were not very many passengers, and it was quite plain to him that wherever his master went, the quick, wet prints went too. Even on the step of the compartment Mr. Murray eventually selected the man beheld a mark, as though some one had sprung in after him. He secured the door, and then walked away, to find a place for himself, marvelling in a dazed state of mind what it all meant; indeed, he felt so much dazed that, after he had found to seat to his mind, he did not immediately notice an old acquaintance in the opposite corner, who affably inquired,—

"And how is Mr. Davis?"

Thus addressed, Mr. Davis started from his reverie, and exclaimed, "Why, bless my soul, Gage, who'd have thought of seeing you here?" after which exchange of courtesies the pair shook hands gravely and settled down to converse.

Mr. Davis explained that he was going down with his governor to Norwich; and Mr. Gage stated that he and the old general had been staying at Thorpe, and were on their way to Lowestoft. Mr. Gage and his old general had also just returned from paying a round of visits in the West of England. "Pleasant enough, but slow," finished the gentleman's gentleman. "After all, in the season or out of it, there is no place like London."

With this opinion Mr. Davis quite agreed, and said he only wished he had never to leave it, adding,—

"We have not been away before for a long time; and we should not be going where we are now bound if we had not to humour some fancy of our grandmother's."

"Deuced rough on a man having to humour a grandmother's fancy," remarked Mr. Gage.

"No female ought to be left the control of money," said Mr. Davis with conviction. "See what the consequences have been in this case—Mrs. Murray outlived her son, who had to ask for every shilling he wanted, and she is so tough she may see the last of her grandson."

"That is very likely," agreed the other. "He looks awfully bad."

"You saw him just now, I suppose?"

"No; but I saw him last night at Chertsey Station, and I could but notice the change in his appearance."

For a minute Mr. Davis remained silent. "Chertsey Station!" What could his master have been doing at Chertsey? That was a question he would have to put to himself again, and answer for himself at some convenient time; meanwhile he only answered,—

"Yes, I observe an alteration in him myself. Anything fresh in the paper?"

"No," answered Mr. Gage, handing his friend over the *Daily News*—the print he affected: "everything is as dull as ditchwater."

For many a mile Davis read or affected to read; then he laid the paper aside, and after passing his case, well filled with a tithe levied on Mr. Murray's finest cigars, to Gage, began solemnly,—

"I am going to ask you a curious question, Robert, as from man to man."

"Ask on," said Mr. Gage, striking a match.

"Do you believe in warnings?"

The old General's gentleman burst out laughing. He was so tickled that he let his match drop from his fingers unapplied.

"I am afraid most of us have to believe in them, whether we like it or not," he answered, when he could speak. "Has there been some little difference between you and your governor, then?"

"You mistake," was the reply. "I did not mean warnings in the sense of notice, but warnings as warnings, you understand."

"Bother me if I do! Yes, now I take you. Do I believe in 'coming events casting shadows before,' as some one puts it? Has any shadow of a coming event been cast across you?"

"No, nor across anybody, so far as I know; but I've been thinking the matter over lately, and wondering if there can be any truth in such notions."

"What notions?"

"Why, that there are signs and suchlike sent when trouble is coming to any one."

"You may depend it is right enough that signs and tokens are sent. Almost every good family has its special warning: one has its mouse, another its black dog, a third its white bird, a fourth its drummer-boy, and so on. There is no getting over facts, even if you don't understand them."

"Well, it is very hard to believe."

"There wouldn't be much merit in believing if everything were as plain as a pikestaff. You know what the Scotch minister said to his boy: 'The very devils believe and tremble.' You wouldn't be worse than a devil, would you?"

"Has any sign ever appeared to you?" asked Davis.

"Not exactly; but lots of people have told me they have to them; for instance, old Seal, who drove the Dowager Countess of Ongar till the day of her death, used to make our hair stand on end talking about phantom carriages that drove away one after another from the door of Hainault House, and wakened every soul on the premises, night after night till the old Earl died. It took twelve clergymen to lay the spirit."

"I wonder one wasn't enough!" ejaculated Davis.

"There may have been twelve spirits, for all I know," returned Gage, rather puzzled by this view of the question; "but anyhow, there were twelve clergymen, with the bishop in his lawn sleeves chief among them. And I once lived with a young lady's-maid, who told me when she was a girl she made her home with her father's parents. On a winter's night, after everybody else had gone to bed, she sat up to make some girdle-bread—that is a sort of bread the people in Ireland, where she came from, bake over the fire on a round iron plate; with plenty of butter it is not bad eating. Well, as I was saying, she was quite alone; she had taken all the bread off, and was setting it up on edge to cool, supporting one piece against the other, two and two, when on the table where she was putting the cakes she saw one drop of blood fall, and then another, and then another, like the beginning of a shower.

"She looked to the ceiling, but could see nothing, and still the drops kept on falling slowly, slowly; and then she knew something had gone wrong with one dear to her; and she put a shawl over her head, and without saying a word to anybody, went through the loneliness and darkness of night all by herself to her father's."

"She must have been a courageous girl," remarked Mr. Davis.

"She was, and I liked her well. But to the point. When she reached her destination she found her youngest brother dead. Now what do you make of that?"

"It's strange, but I suppose he would have died all the same if she had not seen the blood-drops, and I can't see any good seeing them did her. If she had reached her father's in time to bid brother good-bye, there would have been some sense in such a sign. As it is, it seems to me a lot of trouble thrown away."

Mr. Gage shook his head.

"What a sceptic you are, Davis! But there! London makes sceptics of the best of us. If you had spent a winter, as I did once, in the Highlands of Scotland, or heard the Banshee wailing for the General's nephew in the county of Mayo, you wouldn't have asked what was the use of second sight or Banshees. You would just have stood and trembled as I did many and many a time."

"I might," said Davis doubtfully, wondering what his friend would have thought of those wet little footprints.

"Hillo, here's Peterborough! Hadn't we better stretch our legs? and a glass of something would be acceptable."

Of that glass, however, Mr. Davis was not destined to partake.

"If one of you is Murray's man," said the guard as they jumped out, "he wants you."

"I'll be back in a minute," observed Mr. Murray's man to his friend, and hastened off.

But he was not back in a minute; on the contrary, he never returned at all.

Chapter Five

KISS ME

The first glance in his master's face filled Davis with a vague alarm. Gage's talk had produced an effect quite out of proportion to its merit, and a cold terror struck to the valet's heart as he thought there might, spite of his lofty scepticism, be something after all in the mouse, and the bird, and the drummer-boy, in the black dog, and the phantom carriages, and the spirits it required the united exertions of twelve clergymen (with the bishop in lawn sleeves among them) to lay; in Highland second sight and Irish Banshees; and in little feet paddling round and about a man's bed and following wherever he went. What awful disaster could those footprints portend? Would the train be smashed up? Did any river lie before them? and if so, was the sign vouchsafed as a warning that they were likely to die by drowning? All these thoughts, and many more, passed through Davis' mind as he stood looking at his master's pallid face and waiting for him to speak.

"I wish you to come in here," said Mr. Murray after a pause, and with a manifest effort. "I am not quite well."

"Can I get you anything, sir?" asked the valet. "Will you not wait and go by another train?"

"No; I shall be better presently; only I do not like being alone."

Davis opened the door and entered the compartment. As he did so, he could not refrain from glancing at the floor, to see if those strange footsteps had been running races there.

"What are you looking for?" asked Mr. Murray irritably. "Have you dropped anything?"

"No, sir; O, no! I was only considering where I should be most out of the way."

"There," answered his master, indicating a seat next the window, and at the same time moving to one on the further side of the carriage. "Let no one get in; say I am ill—mad; that I have scarlet fever—the plague—what you please." And with this wide permission Mr. Murray laid his legs across the opposite cushion, wrapped one rug round his shoulders and another round his body, turned his head aside, and went to sleep or seemed to do so.

"If he is going to die, I hope it will be considered in my wages, but I am afraid it won't. Perhaps it is the old lady; but that would be too good fortune," reflected Davis; and then he fell "a-thinkynge, a-thinkynge," principally of Gage's many suggestions and those mysterious footprints, for which he kept at intervals furtively looking. But they did not appear; and at last the valet, worn out with vain conjections, dropped into a pleasant doze, from which he did not awake till they were nearing Norwich.

"We will go to an hotel till I find out what Mrs. Murray's plans are," said that lady's grandson when he found himself on the platform; and as if they had been only waiting this piece of information, two small invisible feet instantly skipped out of the compartment they had just vacated, and walked after Mr. Murray, leaving visible marks at every step.

"Great heavens! what is the meaning of this?" mentally asked Davis, surprised by fright after twenty prayerless and scheming years into an exclamation which almost did duty for a prayer. For a moment he felt sick with terror; then clutching his courage with the energy of desperation, he remembered that though wet footprints might mean death and destruction to the Murrays, his own ancestral annals held no record of such a portent.

Neither did the Murrays', so far as he was aware, but then he was aware of very little about that family. If the Irish girl Gage spoke of was informed by drops of blood that her brother lay dead, why should not Mr. Murray be made aware, through the token of these pattering footsteps, that he would very soon succeed to a large fortune?

Then any little extra attention Mr. Davis showed his master *now* would be remembered in his wages.

It was certainly unpleasant to know these damp feet had come down from London, and were going to the hotel with them; but "needs must" with a certain driver, and if portents and signs and warnings were made worth his while, Mr. Davis conceived there might be advantages connected with them.

Accordingly, when addressing Mr. Murray, his valet's voice assumed a more deferential tone than ever, and his manner became so respectfully tender, that onlookers rashly imagined the ideal master and the faithful servant of fiction had at last come in the flesh to Norwich. Davis' conduct was, indeed, perfect: devoted without being intrusive, he smoothed away all obstacles which could be smoothed, and even, by dint of a judicous two minutes alone with the doctor for whom he sent, managed the introduction of a useful sedative in some medicine, which the label stated was to be taken every four hours.

He saw to Mr. Murray's rooms and Mr. Murray's light repast, and then he waited on Mr. Murray's grandmother, and managed that lady so adroitly, she at length forgave the offender for having caught a chill.

"Your master is always doing foolish things," she said. "It would have been much better had he remained even for a day or two in London rather than risk being laid up. However, you must nurse him carefully, and try to get him well enough to dine at Losdale Court on Monday. Fortunately to-morrow is Sunday, and he can take complete rest. Now Davis, remember I trust to you."

"I will do my best, ma'am," Davis said humbly, and went back to tell his master the interview had gone off without any disaster.

Then, after partaking of some mild refreshment, he repaired to bed in a dressing-room opening off Mr. Murray's apartment, so that he might be within call and close at hand to administer those doses which were to be taken at intervals of four hours.

"I feel better to-night," said Mr. Murray last thing.

"It is this beautiful air, sir," answered Davis, who knew it was the sedative. "I hope you will be quite well in the morning."

But spite of the air, in the grey dawn Mr. Murray had again a dreadful dream—a worse dream than that which laid its heavy hand on him in London. He thought he was by the riverside beyond Dockett Point—beyond where the water-lilies grow. To his right was a little grove of old and twisted willows guarding a dell strewed in dry seasons with the leaves of many autumns, but, in his dream, wet and sodden by reason of heavy rain. There in June wild roses bloomed;

there in winter hips and haws shone ruddy against the snow. To his left flowed a turbid river—turbid with floods that had troubled its peace. On the other blank lay a stagnant length of Surrey, while close at hand the Middlesex portion of Chertsey Mead stretched in a hopeless flat on to the bridge, just visible in the early twilight of a summer's evening that had followed after a dull lowering day.

From out of the gathering gloom there advanced walking perilously near to Dumsey Deep, a solitary female figure, who, when they met, said, "So you've come at last;" after which night seemed to close around him, silence for a space to lay its hands upon him.

About the same time Davis was seeing visions also. He had lain long awake, trying to evolve order out of the day's chaos, but in vain. The stillness fretted him; the idea that even then those mysterious feet might in the darkness be printing their impress about his master's bed irritated his brain. Twice he got up to give that medicine ordered to be taken every four hours, but finding on each occasion Mr. Murray sleeping quietly, he forebore to arouse him.

He heard hour after hour chime, and it was not till the first hint of dawn that he fell into a deep slumber. Then he dreamt about the subject nearest his heart—a public house.

He thought he had saved or gained enough to buy a roadside inn on which he had long cast eyes of affectionate regard—not in London, but not too far out: a delightful inn, where holiday-makers always stopped for refreshment, and sometimes for the day; an inn with a pretty old-fashioned garden filled with fruit trees and vegetables, with a grass-plot around which were erected little arbours, where people could have tea or stronger stimulants; a skittle-ground, where men could soon make themselves very thirsty; and many other advantages tedious to mention. He had the purchase-money in his pocket, and, having paid a deposit, was proceeding to settle the affair, merely diverging from his way to call on a young widow he meant to make Mrs. Davis—a charming woman, who, having stood behind a bar before, seemed the very person to make the Wheatsheaf a triumphant success. He was talking to her sensibly, when suddenly she amazed him by saying, in a sharp, hurried voice, "Kiss me, kiss me, kiss me!" three times over.

The request seemed so strange that he stood astounded, and then awoke to hear the same words repeated.

"Kiss me, kiss me, kiss me!" some one said distinctly in

Mr. Murray's room, the door of which stood open, and then all was quiet.

Only half awake, Davis sprang from his bed and walked across the floor, conceiving, so far as his brain was in a state to conceive anything, that his senses were playing him some trick.

"You won't?" said the voice again, in a tone which rooted him to the spot where he stood; "and yet, as we are never to meet again, you might *Kiss me once,*" the voice added caressingly, "*only once more.*"

"Who the deuce has he got with him now?" thought Davis; but almost before the question was shaped in his mind there came a choked, gasping cry of "Unloose me, tigress, devil!" followed by a sound of desperate wrestling for life.

In a second, Davis was in the room. Through the white blinds light enough penetrated to show Mr. Murray in the grip apparently of some invisible antagonist, who seemed to be strangling him.

To an from from side to side the man and the unseen phantom went swaying in that awful struggle. Short and fast came Mr. Murray's breath, while making one supreme effort, he flung his opponent from him and sank back across the bed exhausted.

Wiping the moisture from his forehead, Davis, trembling in every limb, advanced to where his master lay, and found *he was fast asleep!*

Mr. Murray's eyes were wide open, and he did not stir hand or foot while the man covered him up as well as he was able, and then looked timidly around, dreading to see the second actor in the scene just ended.

"I can't stand much more of this," Davis exclaimed, and the sound of his own voice made him start.

There was brandy in the room which had been left overnight, and the man poured himself out and swallowed a glass of the liquor. He ventured to lift the blind and look at the floor, which was wet, as though buckets of water had been thrown over it, while the prints of little feet were everywhere.

Mr. Davis took another glass of brandy. *That* had not been watered.

"Well, this is a start!" he said in his own simple phraseology. "I wonder what the governor has been up to?"

For it was now borne in upon the valet's understanding that this warning was no shadow of any event to come, but the tell-tale ghost of some tragedy which could never be undone.

Chapter Six

FOUND DROWNED

After such a dreadful experience it might have been imagined that Mr. Murray would be very ill indeed; but what we expect rarely comes to pass, and though during the whole of Sunday and Monday Davis felt, as he expressed the matter, "awfully shaky," his master appeared well and in fair spirits.

He went to the Cathedral, and no attendant footsteps dogged him. On Monday he accompanied his grandmother to Losdale Court, where he behaved so admirably as to please even the lady on whose favour his income depended. He removed to a furnished house Mrs. Murray had taken, and prepared to carry out her wishes. Day succeeded day and night to night, but neither by day nor night did Davis hear the sound of any ghostly voices or trace the print of any phantom foot.

Could it be that nothing more was to come of it—that the mystery was never to be elucidated but fade away as the marks of dainty feet had vanished from floor, pavement, steps, and platform?

The valet did not believe it; behind those signs made by nothing human lay some secret well worth knowing, but it had never been possible to know much about Mr. Murray.

"He was so little of a gentleman" that he had no pleasant, careless ways. He did not leave his letters lying loose for all the world to read. He did not tear up papers, and toss them into a waste-paper basket. He had the nastiest practice of locking up and burning; and though it was Mr. Davis's commendable custom to collect and preserve unconsidered odds and ends as his master occasionally left in his pockets, these, after all, were trifles light as air.

Nevertheless, as a straw shows how the wind blows, so that chance remark anent Chertsey Station made by Gage promised to provide a string on which to thread various little beads in Davis' possession.

The man took them out and looked at them: a woman's

fall—white tulle, with black spots, smelling strongly of tobacco-smoke and musk; a receipt for a bracelet, purchased from an obscure jeweller; a Chertsey Lock ticket; and the return half of a first-class ticket from Shepperton to Waterloo, stamped with the date of the day before they left London.

At these treasures Davis looked long and earnestly.

"We shall see," he remarked as he put them up again; "there I think the scent lies hot."

It could not escape the notice of so astute a servant that his master was unduly anxious for a sight of the London papers, and that he glanced through them eagerly for something he apparently failed to find—more, that he always laid the print aside with a sigh of relief. Politics did not seem to trouble him, or any public burning question.

"He has some burning question of his own," thought the valet, though he mentally phrased his notion in different words.

Matters went on thus for a whole week. The doctor came and went and wrote prescriptions, for Mr. Murray either was still ailing or chose to appear so. Davis caught a word or two which had reference to the patient's heart, and some shock. Then he considered that awful night, and wondered how he, who "was in his sober senses, and wide awake, and staring," had lived through it.

"My heart, and a good many other things, will have to be considered," he said to himself. No wages could pay for what has been put upon me this week past. I wonder whether I ought to speak to Mr. Murray now?"

Undecided on this point, he was still considering it when he called his master on the following Sunday morning. The first glance at the stained and polished floor decided him. Literally it was interlaced with footprints. The man's hand shook as he drew up the blind, but he kept his eyes turned on Mr. Murray while he waited for orders, and walked out of the room when dismissed as though such marks had been matters of customary occurrence in a nineteenth century bedroom.

No bell summoned him back on this occasion. Instead of asking for information, Mr. Murray dropped into a chair and nerved himself to defy the inevitable.

Once again there came a pause. For three days nothing occurred; but on the fourth a newspaper and a letter arrived, both of which Davis inspected curiously. They were

A TERRIBLE VENGEANCE

addressed in Mr. Savill's handwriting, and they bore the postmark "SHEPPERTON."

The newspaper was enclosed in an ungummed wrapper, tied round with a piece of string. After a moment's reflection Davis cut that string, spread out the print, and beheld a column marked at top with three blue crosses, containing the account of an inquest held at the King's Head on a body found on the previous Sunday morning, close by the "Tumbling Bay."

It was that of a young lady who had been missing since the previous Friday week, and could only be identified by the clothes.

Her mother, who, in giving evidence, frequently broke down, told how her daughter on the evening in question went out for a walk and never returned. She did not wish to go, because her boots were being mended, and her shoes were too large. No doubt they had dropped off. She had very small feet, and it was not always possible to get shoes to fit them. She was engaged to be married to the gentleman with whom she went out. He told her they had quarrelled. She did not believe he could have anything to do with her child's death; but she did not know what to think. It had been said her girl was keeping company with somebody else, but that could not be true. Her girl was a good girl.

Yes; she had found a bracelet hidden away among her girl's clothes, and she could not say how she got the seven golden sovereigns that were in the purse, or the locket taken off the body; but her girl was a good girl, and she did not know whatever she would do without her, for Lucy was all she had.

Walter Grantley was next examined, after being warned that anything he said might be used against him.

Though evidently much affected, he gave his evidence in a clear and straightforward manner. He was a clerk in the War Office. He had, against the wishes of all his friends, engaged himself to the deceased, who, after having some time professed much affection, had latterly treated him with great coldness. On the evening in question she reluctantly came out with him for a walk; but after they passed the Ship she insisted he should take a boat. They turned and got into a boat. He wanted to go down the river, because there was no lock before Sunbury. She declared if he would not row her up the river, she would go home.

They went up the river, quarrelling all the way. There had

been so much of this sort of thing that after they passed through Shepperton Lock he tried to bring matters to a conclusion, and asked her to name a day for their marriage. She scoffed at him and asked if he thought she meant to marry a man on such a trumpery salary. Then she insisted he should land her; and after a good deal of argument he did land her; and rowed back alone to Halliford. He knew no more.

Richard Savill deposed he took a boat at Lower Halliford directly after the last witness, with whom he was not acquainted, and rowed up towards Chertsey, passing Mr. Grantley and Miss Heath, who were evidently quarrelling. He went as far as Dumsey Deep, where, finding the stream most heavily against him, he turned, and on his way back saw the young lady walking slowly along the bank. At Shepperton Lock he and Mr. Grantley exchanged a few words, and rowed down to Halliford almost side by side. They bade each other good-evening, and Mr. Grantley walked off in the direction of Walton where it was proved by other witnesses he arrived at eight o'clock, and did not go out again till ten, when he went to bed.

All efforts to trace what had become of the unfortunate girl proved unavailing, till a young man named Lemson discovered the body on the previous Sunday morning close by the Tumbling Bay. The coroner wished to adjourn the inquest, in hopes some further light might be thrown on such a mysterious occurrence; but the jury protested so strongly against any proceeding of the sort, that they were directed to return an open verdict.

No one could dispute that the girl had been "found drowned," or that there was "no evidence to explain how she came to be drowned."

At the close of the proceedings, said the local paper, an affecting incident occurred. The mother wished the seven pounds to be given to the man "who brought her child home," but the man refused to accept a penny. The mother said she would never touch it, when a relation stepped forward and offered to take charge of it for her.

The local paper contained also a leader on the tragedy, in the course of which it remarked how exceedingly fortunate it was that Mr. Savill chanced to be staying at the Ship Hotel, so well known to boating-men, and that he happened to go up the river and see the poor young lady after Mr. Grantley left her, as otherwise the latter gentleman might have found himself in a most unpleasant position. He was much to be pitied, and the leader-writer felt confident that every one who read the evidence would sympathize with him. It was evident the inquiry had failed to solve the mystery connected with Miss Heath's untimely fate, but it was still competent to pursue the matter if any fresh facts transpired.

"I must get to know more about all this," thought Davis as he refolded and tied up the paper.

Chapter Seven

DAVIS SPEAKS

If there be any truth in old saws, Mr. Murray's wooing was a very happy one. Certainly it was very speedy. By the end of October he and Miss Ketterick were engaged, and before Christmas the family lawyers had their hands full drawing settlements and preparing deeds. Mrs. Murray disliked letting any money slip out of her own control, but she had gone too far to recede, and Mr. Ketterick was not a man who would have tolerated any proceeding of the sort.

Perfectly straightforward himself, he compelled straightforwardness in others, and Mrs. Murray was obliged to adhere to the terms proposed when nothing seemed to her less probable than that the marriage she wished ever would take place. As for the bridegroom, he won golden opinions from Mr. Ketterick. Beyond the income to be insured to his wife and himself, he asked for nothing. Further he objected to nothing. Never before, surely, had man been so easily satisfied.

"All I have ever wanted," he said, "was some settled income, so that I might not feel completely dependent on my grandmother. That will not be secured, and I am quite satisfied."

He deferred to Mr. Ketterick's opinions and wishes. He made no stipulations.

"You are giving me a great prize," he told the delighted father, "of which I am not worthy, but I will try to make her happy."

And the gentle girl was happy: no tenderer or more devoted lover could the proudest beauty have desired. With truth he told her he "counted the days till she should be his." For he felt secure when by her side. The footsteps had never followed him to Losdale Court. Just in the place that of all others he would have expected them to come, he failed to see that tiny print. There were times when he even forgot it for a season; when he did remember it, he believed, with the faith born of hope, that he should never see it again.

"I wonder he has the conscience," muttered Mr. Davis one morning, as he looked after the engaged pair. The valet had the strictest ideas concerning the rule conscience should hold over the doings of other folks, and some pleasingly lax notions about the sacrifices conscience had a right to demand from himself. "I suppose he thinks he is safe now that those feet are snugly tucked up in holy ground," proceeded Davis, who, being superstitious, faithfully subscribed to all the old formulæ. "Ah! he doesn't know what I know—yet;" which last word, uttered with much gusto, indicated a most unpleasant quarter of an hour in store at some future period for Mr. Murray.

It came one evening a week before his marriage. He was in London, in his grandmother's house, writing to the girl he had grown to love with the great, entire, remorseful love of his life, when Davis, respectful as ever, appeared, and asked if he might speak a word. Mr. Murray involuntarily put his letter beneath some blotting-paper, and, folding his hands over both, answered, unconscious of what was to follow, "Certainly."

Davis had come up with his statement at full-cock, and fired at once.

"I have been a faithful servant to you, sir."

Mr. Murray lifted his eyes and looked at him. Then he knew what was coming. "I have never found fault with you, Davis," he said, after an almost imperceptible pause.

"No, sir, you have been a good master—a master I am sure no servant who knew his place could find a fault with."

If he had owned an easy mind and the smallest sense of humour—neither of which possessions then belonged to Mr. Murray—he might have felt enchanted with such a complete turning of the tables; but as matters stood, he could only answer, "Good master as I have been, I suppose you wish to leave my service. Am I right, Davis?"

"Well, sir, you are right and you are wrong. I do not want to leave your service just yet. It may not be quite convenient to you for me to go now; only I want to come to an understanding."

"About what?" Mr. Murray asked, quite calmly, though he could feel his heart thumping hard against his ribs, and that peculiar choking sensation which is the warning of what in such cases must come some day.

"Will you cast your mind back, sir, to a morning in last August, when you called my attention to some extraordinary footprints on the floor of your room?"

"I remember the morning," said Mr. Murray, that choking sensation seeming to suffocate him. "Pray go on."

If Davis had not been master of the position, this indifference would have daunted him; as it was, he again touched the trigger, and fired this: *"I know all!"*

Mr. Murray's answer did not come so quick this time. The waters had gone over his head, and for a minute he felt as a man might if suddenly flung into a raging sea, and battling for his life. He was battling for his life with a wildly leaping heart. The noise of a hundred billows seemed dashing on his brain. Then the tempest lulled, the roaring torrent was stayed, and then he said interrogatively, "Yes?"

The prints of those phantom feet had not amazed Davis more than did his master's coolness.

"You might ha' knocked me down with a feather," he stated, when subsequently relating this interview. "I always knew he was a queer customer, but I never knew how queer till then."

"Yes?" said Mr. Murray, which reply quite disconcerted his valet.

"I wouldn't have seen what I have seen, sir," he remarked, "not for a king's ransom."

"No?"

"No, sir, and that is the truth. What we both saw has been with me at bed and at board, as the saying is, ever since. When I shut my eyes I still feel those wet feet dabbling about the room; and in the bright sunshine I can't help shuddering, because there seems to be a cold mist creeping over me."

"Are you not a little imaginative, Davis?" asked his master, himself repressing a shudder.

"No, sir, I am not; no man can be that about which his own eyes have seen and his own ears have heard; and I have heard and seen what I can never forget, and what nothing could pay me for going through."

"Nevertheless?" suggested Mr. Murray.

"I don't know whether I am doing right in holding my tongue, in being so faithful, sir; but I can't help it. I took to you from the first, and I wouldn't bring harm on you if any act of mine could keep it from you. When one made the remark to me awhile ago it was a strange thing to see a gentleman attended by a pair of wet footprints, I said they were a sign in your family that some great event was about to happen."

"Did you say so?"

"I did, sir, Lord forgive me!" answered Davis, with unblushing mendacity. "I have gone through more than will ever be known over this affair, which has shook me, Mr. Murray. I am not the man I was before ghosts took to following me, and getting into trains without paying any fare, and waking me in the middle of the night, and rousing me out of my warm bed to see sights I would not have believed I could have seen if anybody had sworn it to me. I have aged twenty-five years since last August—my nerves are destroyed; and so, sir, before you got married, I thought I would make bold to ask what I am to do with a constitution broken in your service and hardly a penny put by;" and, almost out of breath with his pathetic statement, Davis stopped and waited for an answer.

With a curiously hunted expression in them, Mr. Murray raised his eyes and looked at Davis.

"You have thought over all this," he said. "How much do you assess them at?"

"I scarcely comprehend, sir—assess what at?"

"Your broken constitution and the five-and-twenty years you say you have aged."

His master's face was so gravely serious that Davis could take the question neither as a jest nor a sneer. It was a request to fix a price, and he did so.

"Well, sir," he answered, "I have thought it all over. In the night-watches, when I could get no rest, I lay and reflected what I ought to do. I want to act fair. I have no wish to drive a hard bargain with you, and, on the other hand, I don't think I would be doing justice by a man that has worked hard if I let myself be sold for nothing. So, sir, to cut a long story short, I am willing to take two thousand pounds."

"And where do you imagine I am to get two thousand pounds?"

A TERRIBLE VENGEANCE

Mr. Davis modestly intimated he knew his place better than to presume to have any notion, but no doubt Mr. Murray could raise that sum easily enough.

"If I could raise such a sum for you, do you not think I should have raised it for myself long ago?"

Davis answered that he did; but, if he might make free to say so, times were changed.

"They are, they are indeed," said Mr. Murray bitterly; and then there was silence.

Davis knocked the conversational ball the next time.

"I am in no particular hurry, sir," he said. "So, long as we understand one another I can wait till you come back from Italy, and have got the handling of some cash of your own. I daresay even then you won't be able to pay me off all at once; but if you would insure your life—"

"I can't insure my life: I have tried, and been refused."

Again there ensued a silence, which Davis broke once more.

"Well, sir," he began, "I'll chance that. If you will give me a line of writing about what you owe me, and make a sort of a will, saying I am to get two thousand, I'll hold my tongue about what's gone and past. And I would not be fretting, sir, if I was you: things are quiet now, and, please God, you might never have any more trouble."

Mr. Davis, in view of his two thousand pounds, his widow, and his wayside public, felt disposed to take an optimistic view of even his master's position; but Mr. Murray's thoughts were of a different hue. "If I do have any more," he considered, "I shall go mad;" a conclusion which seemed likely enough to follow upon even the memory of those phantom feet coming dabbling out of an unseen world to follow him with their accursed print in this.

Davis was not going abroad with the happy pair. For sufficient reason Mr. Murray had decided to leave him behind, and Mrs. Murray, ever alive to her own convenience, instantly engaged him to stay on with her as butler, her own being under notice to leave.

Thus, in a semi-official capacity, Davis witnessed the wedding, which people considered a splendid affair.

What Davis thought of it can never be known, because when he left Losdale Church his face was whiter than the bride's dress; and after the newly-wedded couple started on the first stage of their life-journey he went to his room, and stayed in it till his services were required.

"There is no money would pay me for what I've seen," he remarked to himself. "I went too cheap. But when once I handle the cash I'll try never to come anigh him or them again."

What was he referring to? Just this. As the bridal group moved to the vestry he saw, if no one else did, those wet, wet feet softly and swiftly threading their way round the bridesmaids and the groomsman, in front of the relations, before Mrs. Murray herself, and hurry on to keep step with the just wed pair.

For the last time the young wife signed her maiden name. Friends crowded around, uttering congratulations, and still through the throng those unnoticed feet kept walking in and out, round and round, backward and forward, as a dog threads its way through the people at a fair. Down the aisle, under the sweeping dresses of the ladies, past courtly gentlemen, Davis saw those awful feet running gleefully till they came up with bride and bridegroom.

"She is going abroad with them," thought the man; and then for a moment he felt as if he could endure the ghastly vision no longer, but must faint dead away. "It is a vile shame," he reflected, "to drag an innocent girl into such a whirlpool;" and all the time over the church step the feet were dancing merrily.

The clerk and the verger noticed them at last.

"I wonder who has been here with wet feet?" said the clerk; and the verger wonderingly answered he did not know.

Davis could have told him, had he been willing to speak or capable of speech.

Conclusion

HE'D HAVE SEEN ME RIGHTED

It was August once again—August, fine, warm, and sunshiny—just one year after that damp afternoon on which Paul Murray and his friend stood in front of the Ship at Lower Halliford. No lack of visitors that season. Hotels were full, and furnished houses at a premium. The hearts of lodging-house keepers were glad. Ladies arrayed in rainbow hues flashed about the quiet village streets; boatmen reaped a golden harvest; all sorts of crafts swarmed on the river. Men in flannels gallantly towed their feminine belongings up against a languidly flowing stream. Pater and materfamilias, and all the olive branches, big and little, were to be met on the Thames, and on the banks of Thames, from Richmond to Staines, and even higher still. The lilies growing around Dockett Point floated with their pure cups wide open to the sun; no close folding of the white wax-leaves around the golden centre that season. Beside the water purple loosestrife grew in great clumps of brilliant colour dazzling to the sight. It was, in fact, a glorious August, in which pleasure-seekers could idle and sun themselves and get tanned to an almost perfect brown without the slightest trouble.

During the past twelvemonth local tradition had tried hard to add another ghost at Dumsey Deep to that already established in the adjoining Stabbery; but the unshrinking brightness of that glorious summer checked belief in it for the time. No doubts when the dull autumn days came again, and the long winter nights, full of awful possibilities, folded water and land in fog and darkness, a figure dressed in grey silk and black velvet fichu, with a natty grey hat trimmed with black and white feathers on its phantom head, with small feet covered by the thinnest of openwork stockings, from which the shoes, so much too large, had dropped long ago, would reappear once more, to the terror of all who heard, but for the time being, snugly tucked up in holy ground the girl whose heart had rejoiced in her beauty, her youth, her admirers, and her finery, was lying quite still and quiet, with closed eyes and ears, that heard neither the church bells nor the splash of oars nor the murmur of human voices.

Others, too, were missing from—though not missed by—Shepperton (the Thames villages miss no human being so long as other human beings, with plenty of money, come down by rail, boat, or carriage to supply his place). Paul Murray, Dick Savill, and Walter Grantley were absent. Mrs. Heath, too, had gone, a tottering, heartbroken woman, to Mr. Pointer's, where she was most miserable, but where she and her small possessions were taken remarkably good care of.

"Only a year agone," she said one day, "my girl was with me. In the morning she wore her pretty cambric with pink spots; and in the afternoon, that grey silk in which she was buried—for we durst not change a thread, but just wrapped a winding-sheet round what was left. O! Lucy, Lucy, Lucy!

to think I bore you for that!" and then she wept softly, and nobody heeded or tried to console her, for "what," as Mrs. Pointer wisely said, "was the use of fretting over a daughter dead a twelvemonth, and never much of a comfort neither?"

Mr. Richard Savill was still "grinding away," to quote his expression. Walter Grantley had departed, so reported his friends, for the diamond-fields; his enemies improved on this by carelessly answering,—

"Grantley! O, he's gone to the devil;" which latter statement could not have been quite true, since he has been back in England for a long time, and is now quite well to do and reconciled to his family.

As for Paul Murray, there had been all sorts of rumours floating about concerning him.

The honeymoon had been unduly protracted; from place to place the married pair wandered—never resting, never staying; alas! for him there was no rest—there could be none here.

It mattered not where he went—east, west, south, or north—those noiseless wet feet followed; no train was swift enough to outstrip them; no boat could cut the water fast enough to leave them behind; they tracked him with dogged persistence; they were with him sleeping, walking, eating, drinking, praying—for Paul Murray in those days often prayed after a desperate heathenish fashion—and yet the plague was not stayed; the accursed thing still dogged him like a Fate.

After a while people began to be shy of him, because the footsteps were no more intermittent; they were always where he was. Did he enter a cathedral, they accompanied him; did he walk solitary through the woods or pace the lakeside, or wander by the sea, they were ever and always with the unhappy man.

They were worse than any evil conscience, because conscience often sleeps, and they from the day of his marriage never did. They had waited for that—waited till he should raise the cup of happiness to his lips, in order to fill it with gall—waited till his wife's dream of bliss was perfect, and then wake her to the knowledge of some horror more agonizing than death.

There were times when he left his young wife for days and days, and went, like those possessed of old, into the wilderness, seeking rest and finding none; for no legion of demons could have cursed a man's life more than those wet feet, which printed marks on Paul Murray's heart that might have been branded by red-hot irons.

All that had gone before was as nothing to the trouble of having involved another in the horrible mystery of his own life—and that other a gentle, innocent, loving creature he might just as well have killed as married.

He did not know what to do. His brain was on fire; he had lost all hold upon himself, all grip over his mind. On the sea of life he tossed like a ship without a rudder, one minute taking a resolve to shoot himself, the next turning his steps to seek some priest, and confess the whole matter fully and freely, and, before he had walked a dozen yards, determining to go away into some savage and desolate land, where those horrible feet might, if they pleased, follow him to his grave.

By degrees this was the plan which took firm root in his dazed brain; and accordingly one morning he started for England, leaving a note in which he asked his wife to follow him. He never meant to see her sweet face again, and he never did. He had determined to go to his father-in-law and confess to him; and accordingly, on the anniversary of Lucy's death, he found himself at Losdale Court, where vague rumours of some unaccountable trouble had preceded him.

Mr. Ketterick was brooding over these rumours in his library, when, as if in answer to his thoughts, the servant announced Mr. Murray.

"Good God!" exclaimed the older man, shocked by the white, haggard face before him, "what is wrong?"

"I have been ill," was the reply.

"Where is your wife?"

"She is following me. She will be here in a day or so."

"Why did you not travel together?"

"That is what I have come to tell you."

Then he suddenly stopped and put his hand to his heart. He had voluntarily come up for execution, and now his courage failed him. His manhood was gone, his nerves unstrung. He was but a poor, weak, wasted creature, worn out by the ceaseless torment of those haunting feet, which, however, since he turned his steps to England had never followed him. Why had he travelled to Losdale Court? Might he not have crossed the ocean and effaced himself in the Far West, without telling his story at all?

Just as he had laid down the revolver, just as he had

turned from the priest's door, so now he felt he could not say that which he had come determined to say.

"I have walked too far," he said, after a pause. "I cannot talk just yet. Will you leave me for half an hour? No; I don't want anything, thank you—except to be quiet." Quiet!—ah, heavens!

After a little he rose and passed out on to the terrace. Around there was beauty and peace and sunshine. He—he—was the only jarring element, and even on him there seemed falling a numbed sensation which for the time being simulated rest.

He left the terrace and crossed the lawn till he came to a great cedar tree, under which there was a seat, where he could sit a short time before leaving the Court.

Yes, he would go away and make no sign. Dreamily he thought of the wild lone lands beyond the sea, where there would be none to ask whence he came or marvel about the curse which followed him. Over the boundless prairie, up the mountain heights, let those feet pursue him if they would. Away from his fellows he could bear his burden. He would confess to no man—only to God, who knew his sin and sorrow; only to his Maker, who might have pity on the work of his hands, and some day bid that relentless avenger be still.

No, he would take no man into his confidence; and even as he so decided, the brightness of the day seemed to be clouded over, warmth was exchanged for a deadly chill, a horror of darkness seemed thrown like a pall over him, and a rushing sound as of many waters filled his ears.

An hour later, when Mr. Ketterick sought his son-in-law, he found him lying on the ground, which was wet and trampled, as though by hundreds of little feet.

His shouts brought help, and Paul Murray was carried into the house, where they laid him on a couch and piled rugs and blankets over his shivering body.

"Fetch a doctor at once," said Mr. Ketterick.

"And a clergyman," added the housekeeper.

"No, a magistrate," cried the sick man, in a loud voice.

They had thought him insensible, and, startled, looked at each other. After that he spoke no more, but turned his head away from them and lay quiet.

The doctor was the first to arrive. With quick alertness he stepped across the room, pulled aside the coverings, and took the patient's hand; then after gently moving the averted face, he said solemnly, like a man whose occupation has gone,—

"I can do nothing here; he is dead."

It was true. Whatever his secret, Paul Murray carried it with him to a country further distant than the lone land where he had thought to hide his misery.

"It is of no use talking to me," said Mr. Davis, when subsequently telling his story. "If Mr. Murray had been a gentleman as was a gentleman, he'd have seen me righted, dead or not. *She* was able to come back—at least, her feet were; and he could have done the same if he'd liked. It was as bad as swindling not making a fresh will after he was married. How was I to know that will would turn out so much waste paper? And then when I asked for my own, Mrs. Murray dismissed me without a character, and Mr. Ketterick's lawyers won't give me anything either; so a lot I've made by being a faithful servant, and I'd have all servants take warning by me."

Mr. Davis is his own servant now, and a very bad master he finds himself.

ELLE EST TROIS, (LA MORT)

by Tanith Lee

Across the river, the clock of Notre Dame aux Luminères was striking seven. How deep the river, and how dark, and how many bones lying under it that the strokes of the great gilded clock upon the Gothic tower, winged with its lacework, did not rouse. Down there, all those who had thrown themselves from the bridges, off the quays of the city: the starving, the sick and the drugged, the desperate and the insane.

Armand looked down in the water, black as the night, looked down and searched for them—and there, a pale hand waved from the flowing darkness, a drift of drowning hair, now passed under the parapet—a girl had flung herself into the river, and should he rescue her, was it morally right that he should save her from whatever horror had driven her to this?

The young man, a poet, rushed across the bridge and stared over from the other parapet. This time there was help. A lamp globe at the bridge's far end caught the suicide as she glided out again into view. The poet, Armand, sighed with relief and a curious disappointment. The thing in the water was only a string of rags and garbage woven together by the current.

Straightening, Armand pulled his threadbare coat about him. It was spring, but the city was cold in spring. There was no stirring in its stones, or in his blood. He glanced now, with familiar depression, at the cathedral towers on the far bank of the river, the tenements on the nearer bank, towards which, returning, he was bound. Above, the stars, and here and there below a greenish lamp. So little light in the darkness.

He had not eaten in two days, but there had come to be

enough money to buy cheap wine in the café on the Rue Mort. And for the other thing, purchased—was it yesterday?

He had been walking all afternoon until purpose ended in a leaden sunset. As flakes of the day sank in the river, Notre Dame aux Luminères towered up before him, as if out of the water itself, an edifice from a myth. Compelled as any knight, he had entered her vast drum of incense and shadow. Standing beyond the ghostly rainbow bubbles that were cast from the stained-glass windows to the ground, he lit one of her candles.

(My name is Armand Valier. I announce myself since I think you don't remember me, God. As why should you? Why am I lighting the candle? For a dead work, a dead poem. She died in my arms today. I burned her.)

When night had wiped away the coloured windows, Armand left and began to walk back across the bridge.

He walked slowly, lost not in thought but in some inner country that faintly resembled the bridge, the river, the dimming banks—one drawing away, one drawing nearer, both equally unreal—a country nourished by facts of surrounding and atmosphere, yet denying them. So that halfway across the bridge, the young man paused in the clinging chill, his dark head bowed. (Where am I, then, if not here? Is it some place I recall from a dream? Have I crossed some barrier in time and latitude? And is this some world so like the world I have just vacated I may be deceived for a while, as though I had moved through the surface of a mirror?)

The impression of change, or of strangeness, became then so sharp a galvanic sensation ran through his nerves. In that instant, seeing no apparent alteration, he looked over the bridge and beheld the dead girl in the water who, a moment later, from the other parapet, became a chain of flotsam. Which convinced Armand, the poet, that merely by crossing from one parapet of the bridge to the other, he had re-crossed the boundaries of normality.

But it was very cold. Shuddering in the inadequate coat, he began to stride briskly on, toward the pallid globe of the lamp that swam there against the uninviting homeward bank.

Mist was rising from the river, fraying out the poor light mysteriously, like a gauzy scarf. As Armand hurried closer, the impulse came to him that he should once more cross to the opposite parapet, and pass by the mysterious lamp in, as it were, that other partly-different world where rags became drowned girls.

Presently, he obeyed the impulse; it was easy enough to accommodate, merely the matter of a briefly diagonal path. He found, unaccountably, his heart—but perhaps only from lack of food, and tiredness—beating urgently now. He gazed into the misty ambience of the light as it approached nearer and nearer.

Until, suddenly, he saw a figure at the end of the bridge beneath the lamp.

Armand checked, continuing to move forward, yet much more slowly now. He heard his footsteps very keenly, over the counterpoint of the river, over the remote whisperings of the city. Louder than both, his own breathing. He could already see clearly the figure was that of a woman.

She was dressed in a wave of black velvet. It was a cloak such as those worn by the rich and the fashionable to the Opéra. But it wrapped her within itself as if it, too, were alive, some organic creature, folding her as if in the petals of a black orchid. Behind her head, one petal was raised, a hood like the hood of a striking cobra, framing a face smudged by the mist. He made out an impression of her features. They were aristocratic and quite fixed, perhaps incapable of expression. All but the eyes, which were overlined by long black sloping brows, and which had an indecipherable blueness about the upper lids that was neither paint nor shadow, but suggested the translucent wings of two iris-like insects, pasted there. . . . Her mouth was hardly generous, yet it was soft, and seemed disposed to smile. Yet this might have been, as so much else, a trick of the mist. But now there was a turn of the whole head. Against the cameo cheek a tendril of night-coloured hair, the twenty simultaneous struck sparks of jewel-drops fringing the hood. A gloved hand pierced the cloak like a knife. The material of the glove was a curious mauvish-blue, pearly and luminescent, insubstantial as a newborn gas flame. The gloved hand made the unmistakable mime of drawing closed a curtain.

Understanding, before understanding reached him, Armand quickened his pace again, to match his heartbeats, but already it was too late. The apparition had vanished.

Gaining the lamp, he quested about for her, vainly. He even called to her once, his voice echoing mournfully, mockingly: "Mademoiselle Fantôme—"

He did not search very long. The nausea of hunger was

coming over him, prompting him to seek, not food, but wine, warmth, the company of others.

Ten strides off the bridge, beyond the lamp, he swiftly glanced back—only the mist, the unravelling gauze of light, the darkness emptied on the water.

The Café Vule on the Rue Mort was crowded, a raucous cave, its walls springing with black-stockinged dancers, its tables scattered by cards, papers, dice, and red wine. The drinkers sprawled, talked, pounded woodwork and each other, all washed by a shrill gamboge illumination, or else in the terracotta twilight to be found under the barrel-vaulting to the rear.

In this twilight, Etiens Corbeau-Marc, half blinded by his fair hair and by the drizzle of one dull candle, sat sketching anything in the café. The strokes of the charcoal were spare and penetrating, with a slight distortion that tended to aid rather than dismiss reality.

(One day, such sketches will sell for hundreds of American dollars. But Corbeau-Marc will be safely shut in the earth by then.)

"I receive your shadow on my paper, Armand, without thanks. Please sit down or go away. Simply get out of my light."

"My shadow and the shadow of a wine bottle. An improvement?"

"Oh, we are rich tonight?"

"Oh, we are poor. But we can also be drunk. And here the bottle comes."

"But yes. Sit, generous friend. You see that woman? She has the face of a horse-fly. Do you think she would come and pose for me in my room?"

"Why not? All the other flies do." Armand poured wine in two murky glasses and drank from one thirstily, closing his eyes. He seemed to wait a moment, as if for some rush of sensation that did not arrive. His voice was melancholy and listless when he spoke again. "I saw a woman by the river tonight that you really should paint, Etiens."

"Give her my address, provided she doesn't want to be paid."

"I think"—Armand raised his lids, found the world, the glass, and drank again—"she would want to be paid in blood."

"A vampire. Excellent."

Etiens left his sketches and drank.

"Armand, you're very irritating. Are you going to elaborate or not? Or is this some dream you've been having? When did you last eat?"

"Yesterday, I think. Or the day before. A dream? I don't dream any more, asleep or awake." Armand put his arms on the table and laid his head on them. He said something inaudible.

"I can't hear you. You've stopped me working; at least you can entertain me."

"I said I burned my latest disaster this morning. A moment before noon. The clock struck just after, and then I went out and over the river. When I came back, it was dark. The lamp was alight at the end of the bridge, and there was a woman standing there in black velvet and gas-colour gloves, with the face of the virgin mother of Monsieur."

"What? Oh, you mean the Devil. Did you speak to her?"

"No."

"Afraid of disillusion? No doubt wise. She was probably some luckless little whore."

Armand refilled his yawning glass from habit. It seemed to him he might have been drinking water. Only a distant throbbing in his temples conveyed the idea that it might be wine.

"It's strange. At first she surprised me. But then—I think I saw her once before. Or twice. She vanished, Etiens. Like a blown-out flame."

"There was, perhaps, a mist."

"Not in the mist."

"Tonight," said Etiens, "I will buy some cheese and a loaf. I shall sit sternly over you while you eat."

"Food makes me ill," said Armand.

"Of course it does. Your stomach's forgotten what food is for. You eat every tenth day and your inside cries: Help! What is this alien substance? I am poisoned."

"The woman," said Armand. "I know who she must be."

Etiens Corbeau-Marc had produced another scrap of paper and begun to draw again. This, at last, was nothing in the Café Vule. Armand, turning to him abruptly, hesitated.

An urchin girl stood on the paper, slender as a pen, wafted by hair blond as the hair of Etiens, perhaps more blond. Her eyes became white streaks in the cinnamon paper as he delicately scratched it away with his fingernail, as if he would blind her, or uncover her true eyes.

ELLE EST TROISE, (LA MORT)

* * *

"And who is that?"

"Dear Armand, I can scarcely remember. A small wraith of my childhood. For some reason I just now recollected her—"

"One day, such sketches will be worth sheafs of francs, boxes full of American dollars. When you are safely dead, Etiens, in a pauper's grave."

Armand looked up, although Etiens did not, and found between them both, red-haired in the heavy reddish shadow, like the dusk of Mars, the occasional third member of this table in the Café Vule.

"Little bird," said Etiens, "sweet France, you are in my light. Move the candle, move yourself, move the earth—but do it quickly."

"The earth has been moved," said France, taking a seat around the table and pouring himself a glass of wine. He had already been drinking and the long upper lids of his eyes were partly lowered like fine white blinds. "Well, well, I'm here for refuge, not earthquakes. I have had earthquakes enough in my room."

"What trouble are you in now, beloved angel? Can it be Jeannette has at last come to her senses and abandoned you?"

"Jeannette has been gone a month. She was becoming like a wife, a mother. Eat this, sit here, be home by such. Everything mended, the place horribly clean and so showing every wretched item of its meanness. And ragoût. All she would cook for me—ragoût. And two glasses of wine, no more. And tears. Who were you with? Where have you been? Say that you love me. Why *don't* you love me? And my piano—Oh God, God, God. What did she do?"

"Well, what?" exclaimed Etiens.

"Armand, you are not listening to me."

"I am listening."

"My piano—she brought in a man to value it."

Etiens clapped one hand on the rickety table. Armand let out a stilted snarl of amusement.

"Well, it would fetch some money, I suppose."

"Her own words. You never play it, she said to me. Where are the concertos, the preludes. . . . You make music only in the beds of other women. While we starve." France drank wine, directly from the bottle now. He stared at them. "I threw her clothes from the window. And her damnable flowers in pots. I very nearly threw her after them, but she ran out shrieking."

"Poor little girl," said Etiens. "But then, she was a fool to live with you. You use your women like rags."

"There's another rag now."

Armand retrieved the bottle. The wine was gone. He shut his eyes again, the length of the lashes on his cheeks making him look like an exhausted child.

"This latest one," said France, "she seemed to understand, and she had a little money. Now she says to me: 'I'm not jealous of your women. I am jealous of the music in your head. I'm jealous of your Negro mistress, the piano. You sit and fondle her, but you're tired of me.' Which is true. She's dreary. I threw her out."

"From the window?" said Etiens. "I do hope not."

"No, no, in God's name. Who has money for more wine?"

"Wine and bread," said Etiens.

"You are rich now?" France demanded.

"Someone bought a painting. Oh, a very modest sale. A couple of francs."

France turned to Armand.

"Drink, food. Wake up. Be happy! Dance on the table."

"Be happy? When I can't write any more?"

"What rubbish."

"I can't, I tell you."

"Nor can I write a note," said France. "Jeannette's whining did that to me. And Clairisse, with her craziness. A melody comes—it's another man's melody. The development limps, falls down, expires. But do you see me? Look. I'll go on. It will come back."

"Wine used to help me," Armand muttered. "Before that—I can hardly believe it when I think back—just to be alone, and to walk somewhere—anywhere. The visions would rise and flow, like breathing. I could barely restrain the ideas, barely stop myself shouting aloud in the street with pure ecstasy. Now, nothing. A void. I need something more than drink, or solitude. I need something, some sort of searing acid, to release what's inside me. It's there. I can feel it, tapping on the inside of my mind like a bird in a cage. My God. What will become of me?"

"Be quiet," France grumbled. "You're annoying me now. You begin to sound like Jeannette."

The wine came, the bread and cheese.

Etiens moved his sketches. That of the strange urchin girl

slid to the floor under the table, where feet, unknowingly, scuffed it.

The group itself had become one of Etiens' paintings. Theatrically dashed by light and shade, highlighted by a gem of candle-fire in the wine bottle, the three young men ripping bread savagely in pieces.

How alike each of them was to the others, in some uncoordinated, extraordinary way. Not a likeness of the flesh, though in some respects they were alike, slender in their squalid clothing, which in France was also garish, like his hair; their faces hollowed and desperate, leaning inwards like three aspects of one whole. Poverty, anger, tenacity, despair, and possibly genius. But who, at this hour, could be sure of that? The Artist, the Composer, the Poet. Blond, auburn, dark—like chess pieces of some three-handed game.

"Where's your sketch?" France asked suddenly.

They looked for it, the white-eyed gamine.... Some boot had borne her away on the sole. France swore. Armand offered to search the packed and riotous café.

"No matter," Etiens waved them down. "I'm glad it has gone. It wasn't as I wanted it. Or else, too much as I wanted it."

"It put me in mind of that old rhyme," said France, drinking from the second bottle. "I've no notion why. But you recall the one I mean? A sort of game. A circle and three figures, and should you come against them at the end of the saw, you're out of the play. How is it? *Elle est trois—Soit! Soit! Soit!*"

Armand glanced at him:

"*Mais La Voleuse, La Séductrice—*"

"That's it!" France shouted, a pale flush on his white cheekbones. "*La Séductrice et Madame Tueuse—*"

"*Ne cherchez pas,*" Etiens finished.

France rose, graceful and barbaric, raising the bottle, now his alone. He bellowed through the café, sporadically cursed, while here and there a woman giggled, or a voice joined him.

"*Elle est trois.*"
"*Soit! Soit! Soit!*"
"*Mais La Voleuse,*"
"*La Séductrice*"
"*Et Madame Tueuse*"
"*Ne cherchez pas!*"
"*Ne cherchez pas!*"

France slid back into his seat. He pressed the empty wine bottle lovingly on Armand.

"What in hell does it mean?"

Etiens, who was not drunk, said sadly, "It means death."

Elle est trois. . . . *She is three.*
 Fine! (One.) *Fine!* (Two.) *Fine!* (Three.)
 But the Thief—
 The Thief.

The spring rain, cold as the city's glass-like blood, was falling viciously in splinters on the streets and Etiens walked towards his lodging. His fair hair, rat-coloured now, plastered itself to his eyes; his shoes were full of water. It was midnight, the clock of the cathedral was striking, a wolf's howl across the river. Our Lady of Lights, with the little candles fluttering out and dying in her stony womb.

It was a lie about the sale of the picture. But it had seemed necessary to make a contribution of food. What did it matter? Etiens considered the beautiful words jammed behind the dam of Armand's fear, the sonatas trapped by France's appetites and lack of human-feeling. But yet, Armand saw visions on the bridge, France touched the battered piano and notes leapt in the air.

(And I, I can build pictures on leaves of paper and canvas, pictures good or bad, but ceaseless, responsive, nourishing. Life. *Life.*)

Yes, but he could still remember La Voleuse.

How old had he been then? Perhaps six, or seven. Probably seven. And he had been ill; this was a vivid yet curiously disjointed memory. He recollected the onset of the illness—some childish fever—as a bizarre uninterest in everything about him and a bewildered lack of comprehension in himself as to why this should be. Then came a patchy area of monochromes, shadows limned by light, and light too bright to be borne, a murmur of voices, and his mother's harried irritability that, in the midst of penury, filth, and hopelessness, she must also nurse an ailing child. He recaptured the most, for some reason, definite incident of all: that of being given water in a little spoon because he was too weak to lift his head. He had not been afraid, of course. The self-absorption of childhood, its blind reliance, obviated any qualms. He had not been aware of mortality, though mortality in some form must surely have come hovering about the attic, with its odours of garlic and rotten wood. Mortality at this time, perhaps, in the shape of a huge brown moth, had visited him by night, peering over into his unconscious face with its glittering pins of eyes.

Beyond the narrow attic windows, at the back of the house, was an unusual feature, a balcony with balustrade of wrought iron, like a black spiderweb. Here a cracked pot or two with dead geraniums vied with blown washing tied across the rail. The dirty, uninspiring roofs and skylights clustered close, and five floors below stared a cobbled yard of an uncompromising hardness and lack of beauty.

His first awareness of the other child came, in some way, from this meagre balcony beyond the window.

Who is she? How did she get in? For here she sat in the pane of moonlight that sometimes evolved on the floor between the window and his bed. The stove was alight, but now it was out. Behind a screen across the room the mother and father snored and sighed.

The female child sat unblinkingly on in the flat container of moonlight, watching him.

He saw her only a moment. Then he slept again.

In the morning she was gone, and when he spoke of her he was told he had been dreaming.

The attic was often full also of the smell of cabbage soup, which Etiens recalled with slight loathing, aware that as a child of seven it had not offended him.

Adult head down against the rain, he crossed a square. He thought of La Voleuse, the Thief.

He saw her many times after that.

At first, she remained near to the window, and was expressionless. Then she came somewhat closer and she began to have an expression. Suddenly she smiled at him, and he became alert to her. Her skin was brownish, her hair a bleached rag. Her clothes, too, were bleached of colour, and ragged, but in a most formal way, as if holes had been carefully cut in them rather than torn or worn. In some respects she was like a tiny scandalised version of a Pierrette, and indeed now she was actually clowning. She scampered about the attic noiselessly, balanced on her hands, cartwheeled, turned a somersault, all with an astonished insouciance, so he had to stifle his laughter with an edge of the blanket. It was only when she was very close that he noticed her eyes were almost all white, except for the two small black dots of the pupils. Her eyes frightened him for a moment, making him think of those of a blind dog on the Rue Dantine. But, as she could obviously see perfectly well, his fear soon vanished.

After a long time of performing for him, she laughed soundlessly and ran away straight through the attic window and was gone. This did not seem peculiar. He would assume, if it were essential for him to assume anything, that she had a rope, and by means of this climbed down from the balcony. She was so agile that, even in adult recollection, it appeared partly feasible.

The convalescent child was disappointed. He had wanted to join in the play. Will she come back?

As if to tantalise him, she failed to return for a number of nights. He was by now at that stage of convalescence where he was horribly bored, still rather too weak to be about and occupy himself, but mentally fretful, anxious for diversion. And tonight his parents had left him alone, for he was thought well enough now to fend for himself. It was a wedding they had gone to. There would be gâteaux and wine. His mother had promised to bring him home a bag of pastries, but he had come to distrust her promises.

He had been dozing when she heard the clock strike from across the river: nine o'clock. The stove was unlit and it was cold as well as dark. The child Etiens prepared to huddle more deeply in the blankets, when he saw the other child, the pale Pierrette, step through the window. And for the first time he realized that now, as in all other instances, the window had been, was, closed.

He wanted to ask her what she meant by it, but she forestalled him, dancing towards him in her neatly punctured rags. He was so amused, so captivated, he said nothing. The reward was immediate. She capered. She performed incredible tricks. She bent backward in a white hoop, then elevated herself, balancing first on her hands, next only on her fingertips. Coming down she sprang—her spring was like a cat's—and landed on the table-top. She spun, whirled over the edge, arrived on the back of a chair and ran along it—sprang again, and came to rest, on the ball of one foot, standing on the stove like a statue on a pedestal, her arms outflung. And from this position, motionless and in total equilibrium, she offered him the second reward. She beckoned.

He could hardly believe it. He had been invited to join in

the fun. He knew she would teach him her tricks. They looked so easy that, although so far, practising alone and without strength in a corner, he had not mastered them, he was certain that with her guidance, her mere approval, he would learn them all.

As he emerged from the bed and stepped out on the floor of the attic, his friend smiled rapturously at him. Then, when he went to her, she flew from the stove and melted out again through the window.

He was dismayed. Was she deserting him, at the very moment when he looked for involvement, enlightenment?

Then he saw she was still there, on the balcony now, beyond the wing of the broken shutter and the grimy glass, her whiteness like a lamp against the dark winter sky and the army of darkly marching roofs. And again, urgently now, she beckoned to him.

He managed to open the window. Stepping out beside her, the cold struck him like a hand, the hand of his father in rage. Pierrette laughed, without a sound. She darted upward, and suddenly she was standing on the thin curving rail of the wrought-iron balustrade. Soundlessly laughing, she ran up and down it, up and down, and despite the cold, he was entranced. Behind her flying hair like clawed string, the stars shrieked with frosty light. They seemed to snag on her hair, become caught in it, and two white stars had become her eyes.

At the far end of the rail, where one piece of forgotten washing still hung, she poised. With her outflung hand she showed him what she wanted him to do.

Climb up, climb up, follow me along the balustrade. This was what her hand, her face—tensed and nodding—the spikes of her hair, the stick of her body, were prompting him to do. Even her rags leaned out towards him, beckoning, explaining how simple it was.

He hesitated. Not out of caution, exactly; out of a sort of wonderment. As in miraculous dreams, it never occurred to him before how facile such an act could be. Of course it was simple. straightforward.

As if to prove it to him, she ran back along the balustrade. The rail was perhaps an inch wide, and where it curved it had buckled slightly. Her feet skimmed over it, sure and prehensile, and he knew that whatever she did he would be able, presently, to do.

But he was careful as he climbed over the flowerpots and

up on to the balustrade, concerned, not of falling into the yard five floors below, but of tumbling back on to the balcony.

With the same care, he stood upright, his bare feet gripping the iron, which was icy and burned them, and pressed into them like a wire, but this did not bother him.

Pierrette was in ecstasy. She clapped her hands, she dazzled. Come, do as I do.

He heard, from a long way away, an agonised gasp from the room behind him. Initially it did not concern him, but then he understood, in some surprise, that he was already losing his balance.

He looked at Pierrette to see what he should do, but Pierrette was smiling, smiling at him. Could it be she had failed to note what was happening?

There ensued a long, long inexplicable second as he felt the rail of the balustrade turning under his foot, and the whole world tilting sideways. Automatically he was floundering now, his arms thrown wide, but this was a reflex. In fact he was bemused still as to what had taken place.

Even the stars were falling like rain away from him, and Pierrette going with them.

And then there was a fearsome crash, an awful concussion. Stunned, he found himself in the midst of a burst of pressure and shouting.

His father, too drunk to reason—for reason would have informed him he could not possibly reach the toppling child in time—had lunged towards the open window, half-fallen into space himself, and grabbed his son back out of it. Both had plunged thereafter to the floor of the balcony in a welter of pots.

The unique stink of wine on his father's breath and the sound of his mother's wailing, now released, demolished the child, who began to cry.

"We should never have left him—never, *never*. He was walking in his sleep—"

Etiens saw, through his tears, she had forgotten to bring the pastries. Venturing to glance at the balcony, he found the white child had gone.

Gone for good. He never saw her afterwards. But what, he might ask himself, and had done so from time to time, had she been, that apparition? Some dream of fever? Some ghostly thing inhabiting the attic, perhaps a child who had died there in similar circumstances, eager to see another fare as she had fared? Or a conjuration of the Devil, of Monsieur le Prince?

The rhyme had told him. The rhyme knew, apparently. Lady Death, in her three modes—*Elle est trois, Soit! Soit! Soit! Mais La Voleuse*—Yes, what had Pierrette been but a thief, dressed like one, too, or the stage-like presentation of one. A thief of life who would have stolen existence from him by means of a trick.

Etiens, turning a corner, caught himself saying the rhyme once more aloud, the rain entering his mouth with each sentence.

She was three. Fine! Fine! Fine! But the Thief, the Seductress, and Madame Slaughterer—*Ne cherchez pas*.

"Don't seek them out," he said again. Why had he never repeated his macabre story to Armand? "Once, when I was seven . . ." Armand, though probably discrediting the truth of it, might well have been able to use such an idea. Or he himself, the painter—why had he never attempted to depict that terrifying child with her eyes of snow? Nothing but a sketch, tonight, and that swept away.

Etiens checked, raising his head into the shattering tumult of the rain. He swore, but ritually. He had taken a wrong street and brought himself, not to his own lodging, but to that sprawling quarter of steps and crouching shops where France lived with his piano and whatever woman was foolish enough to indulge his parasitism. Looking about, Etiens beheld an alley, and along it the steep stair and the overhanging storey above, which housed the composer. There were lights burning.

(Why am I here? What am I doing here? I feel no amazement at having come here. Do I intend to visit him at this hour of the night? He may not even be there—true, he left the café before me, but most likely he's drinking elsewhere, or with a woman other than whichever woman is up there now, lamenting over his uninterest.)

From the core of the rain and the dark, coincidentally from the overhanging storey that shelled in France's room, a woman began frenziedly to scream.

Leaving the Café Vule before the others, France had not immediately returned to his room above the alley. He had loitered for a few free drinks with a woman he knew, the draper's widow, who lived behind the bourse. By keeping up a romantic fiction that he was almost inclined to go to bed with her—she was a plain, unappetizing woman—France had gained many things for nothing, including a selection of astonishing neckties.

Perhaps fifteen minutes before the gilded clock of Notre Dame aux Lumières struck midnight, however, he was toiling up the rickety stairs to the room Jeannette had struggled so thanklessly and ill-advisedly to maintain. He was very drunk, in a fog of drunkenness that frankly did not wish to see beyond itself. So, finding the door unlocked, he did not consider it very much. He himself, storming forth in an angry mood, had most probably left it so. What, after all, might it be anybody's fortune to steal from him? Save the piano, too large and cumbersome for a common thief to shift down the vile staircase.

The piano. His "Negro Mistress."

A drunken sneering laugh burst from him. Quite so. His mistress. His cold armour who would render him only the music of others.

He did not pause to light a lamp. Having slammed the door, he careened across the room and plunged his hands down on the keyboard in a blow. The discord jarred his ears, his very brain, and he let loose a string of oaths at her. (At *her*, why not? Why not?) This one female entity who did not court him or help him, and who he could not dismiss as he had dismissed legions of women, even the submissive Jeannette, clinging like a wretched creeper. Even that bitch Clairisse, who understood him so well and used her understanding to prey on him—she too had been shown the door, and run out of it, weeping and threatening him. And here alone stood his real devil, on her four legs, bestially grinning her discoloured teeth.

France sat down before her, a furious penitent in the darkness. There was only a glimmer, seeping in from a lighted window left unshuttered across the alley, whereby to find his way over the keys. Well then, a piece of bad-tempered Monsieur Beethoven would suit the occasion.

As the chords crashed forth, he thought of neighbours wakened alongside and below, and grinned with malice.

"Wake, wake, *mes enfants*! It is the crack of bloody doom."

Then, halfway through the Beethoven, he lost patience with it and left off.

He squinted down at the keys and his hands clenched on

them, and a trickle of notes went through his head. He started upright, listening, avid to follow the insistent impulse—and something distracted him, something at which he gazed, puzzled, mislaying the thread of melodic harmony, trying to detain it, trying also to make sense of what he saw, failing in both.

The inadequate second-hand illumination falling in his room from the window had been describing one panel of the piano, a dim flush of light, which he himself sporadically shut out through the movements of his body. But now the light on the panel, undisturbed by him, was curiously dividing itself in two portions about an area of darkness.

It was a singular, abstract darkness, a kind of hump, that slowly, incongruously—and quite formlessly—was rising upward, upward—

France turned and came to his feet clumsily, upsetting the chair as he did so.

There was really something there, across the room, a darkness darker than the darkness, and the open window behind it making it darker yet. It continued to rise up. He was peculiarly put in mind of dough rising in an oven.

"Who is it?" France demanded. Possibilities, laughable or unpleasant, suggested themselves. Instead of blundering forward to seize the intruder, he fumbled for a match. He considered perhaps Jeannette had come back to plead with him, or conceivably some creditor had lain in wait.

The shape had reached its required elevation and was now in stasis. What was that? There had been a muddy flash, an indoor lightning against the rainy window.

Then France had the match and struck it wildly.

The flame exploded like the detonation of a bomb, then fell through the air, a blazing leaf, and went out. France was speechless. He had seen something he did not believe in, and his terror could not cry out. Nevertheless he was stumbling backwards, attempting to reach the door.

He did not reach it.

The screaming had stopped almost as soon as it began, but people had flung open windows and were glaring out into the night. At the end of the alley loomed a vehicle, shrouded in rain. And at the foot of the stairs leading to France's room were two police, who refused to let Etiens by. A small crowd, others who inhabited the building, had gathered on the landing above, and eventually Etiens heard a ghastly moaning noise break out among these people overhead, and then the tramp of persons coming down.

As he stood there, nauseated by apprehension and distress, Etiens was soon able to watch a white-faced young woman, rigid with an unnatural, maniacal composure, escorted by police out into the rain. He would learn from the newspapers in the morning that this had been Clairisse Gabrol, the former mistress of an impoverished composer who had ceased to care for her despite her gifts of money, and whom she had subsequently murdered. Her choice of weapon would cause some comment. In the gloom by the stair-foot, Etiens had not seen how her dress and her coat were patterned, here and there. But shortly the body was brought down on the first stage of its journey to the morgue. Even through the covering, Etiens could not fail to remark the quantities of blood. In the doorway one of the policemen, who had been in the room above, doubled over and vomited helplessly into a puddle.

The scene in the room would later be described as resembling a butcher's shop. Etiens would read this sentence coldly. He would not paint for several months.

Et Madame Tueuse—

The neighbour whose cries had alerted Étiens as she entered for the first into France's room had summoned the police. The insane piano recital had woken her; she had been on the very landing outside the pianist's door, gathering herself to knock, and upbraid him—when a succession of unidentifiable yet strangely disturbing noises sent her instead to seek aid. She had not been able to explain her conviction that something evil had taken place. It was retentive though unconscious memory that had informed her. The analogy of the butcher's shop had not been random, and she, who had had cause to frequent such establishments often, recognised, unknowingly, the familiar, unmistakable sound that had no business in a human dwelling by night.

There was no other clue. France himself had not cried out, even when the meat cleaver, which Clairisse had cunningly stolen some hours before, severed his left hand at the wrist, his right hand midway between the wrist and the knuckles. Possibly he had peered after them, his pianist's hands, in the darkness, perturbed by such sudden and absolute loss. But then the cleaver passed through his neck, efficient as any guillotine, and the moment for all perturbation was done.

So it had been only Clairisse, one of so many abused and silly women who had loved or thought they loved, and suffered for it. One, nevertheless, who was different, who wished that France should suffer, too. Only Clairisse, then, who with the colossal strength of the maddened had hacked her lover into segments and strewn these about the floor. Only Clairisse who had been, for these minutes, Madame Tueuse—the Slaughterer.

But it had not, in the fractional ignition of his match, been Clairisse that France saw posed before him.

She was very tall, at least, one might assume, two metres in height. In the best tradition of her trade, a tradition adopted more by the military than the civilian branch of her fraternity, she was clothed in pulsing madder. Splashed by life-blood, after the merest moment, she would again appear immaculate. It would seem her long-sleeved gown was dyed in blood to begin with. Her head, naturally, was also fastidiously covered. The scarlet headdress called to mind the starched winged wimple of a nun of some unusual order. Held in this frame her face was shrivelled, blanched, and sightless. Genuinely sightless, for the eyelids were firmly sealed, sealed in a way that implied they could not, for whatever reason, be uplifted. The hands were also white, they would show the blood when it splashed. They were sensitive, the hands, long-fingered and slim, in fact quite beautiful: the hands of an artist. For one could tell from the implements hanging at her sash that her method was not always as brutish as on this occasion. There were many knives of varying scope; some daggers; an awl; even a solitary, though very elongated, needle; a cut-throat razor, scissors; a shard of mirror; a hat-pin—and much more, not all of it instantly to be named. Everything was finely honed and highly polished. Cared for. In perfect working order.

He saw her come towards him, but only as a shadow. There was not enough light in the room after the match had fallen to show how, at the first slicing stroke, the eyes of the woman opened wide after all. Each is a transparent void, shaped like a little bowl, and like a little bowl each one begins to fill with a pure and scintillant red.

And somehow, even without light, he did see, did see, did—

Until all seeing stopped.

* * *

As the clock of Our Lady of Lights struck one, beginning the new day in its blackness, Armand woke from a comfortless doze. The room, his own, was veiled over rather than revealed by its low-burning lamp. The bed, a stale shambles on which he had thrown himself, now repelled him, forcing him to sit, and next to stand up. On the table no manuscript lay to exalt or reproach him. There was, however, something.

Armand looked, his eyes enlarged, as if he had never before seen such an array, though he himself had bought and amalgamated these articles yesterday. Or the day before that.

It was stupid, then, to regard them with such misgiving. Indeed, the arrangement was rather attractive, something Etiens might have liked to paint. The utensils themselves were beautiful.

The preparation was not even very complex. To achieve what he wished would take a modicum of time.

Armand moved to the window and flung it wide on the black and rainy night. In the rain, the city itself might seem to lie beneath the river. (We are then, the drowned, already lost, yet measuring out our schemes, our prayers, as if they might be valid even now.)

Across the city, the bloody corpse that had been France was being trundled on its route to the morgue. Armand did not know this, nor that, some minutes before, bemused and soaking wet, Etiens had passed below, looking up at the poet's drearily-lighted window—and finding himself completely unable to proceed to Armand's door, had gone away again.

The poet stared into the external dark. Roofs and chimneys held back the sky. Here and there a ghost of light, like a flaw in vision, evidenced some other vigil, its purpose concealed.

Armand did not know the death of France, nor of Etiens's white child. Possessed of these things, coupling them with his own oppression, his own knowledge of where the night, like a phantom barge, was taking him, the poet would have presented this history quite differently. It would have been essential, for example, to provide some linking device, some cause, a romantic mathematic as to why such elements had fused within those hours sloughed from the great clock between the striking of seven and of three in the morning that was yet to come. What should it have been? A ring,

ELLE EST TROISE, (LA MORT) 273

possibly, with a curse upon it, given to Etiens in his infancy, inducing thereafter the first image of death: the white-eyed Pierrette; passed to France in disbelief or spite, summoning the second, the monstrous nun in her wimple of blood. While Armand, drawing the ring from the portioned body of France, would thereby unwittingly or in despair arouse the final aspect of the appalling triad.

But Armand, a character entangled by events, and not their reporter, had no say in the structure, apparently random—though immensely terrible—of what is taking place.

When then should one say? Merely perhaps that most children will, at some point, behave with dangerous foolishness, as if led on by imps, but it is only that they know no better. And that the Pierrette was an analogy for this which Etiens had fabricated for himself from a feverish dream and a patch of moonlight through a dirty window. And then, that France had suffered an hallucination invoked by drunken horror—if he had even seen the thing which was described. No proof of this is offered. Maybe he saw nothing but Clairisse, the stolen cleaver in her hand. There was a gruesome murder, a crime of cold passion. That was enough. And for Armand, the poet, he had perceived a shadow in the half-lit mist at the end of the bridge, a shadow of malnutrition and self-doubt and inner yearning. And in a moment he would have every reason to see her again, as he would see many things that thereafter would leave his work like a riot of jewels, inextinguishable, profound, terrifying, indisputable, cast in the wake of his own wreckage.

La Mort, Lady Death, La Voleuse, La Tueuse. The trick, the violent blade. And then the third means to destruction, the seductive death who visited poets in her irresistible caressing silence, with the petals of blue flowers or the blue wings of insects pasted on the lids of her eyes, and: See, your flesh, also, taken to mine, can never decay. And this will be true, for the flesh of Armand, becoming paper written over by words, will endure as long as men can read.

And so he left the window. He prepared, carefully, the opium that would melt away within him the iron barrier that no longer yielded to thought or solitude or wine. And when the drug began to live within its glass, for an instant he thought he saw a drowned girl floating there, her hair swirling in the smoke.... Far away, in another universe, the clock of Notre Dame aux Luminères struck twice.

After a little while, he opened the door, and looked out

at the landing beyond. There in the nothing of the dark he sensed her, and moved aside, welcoming her with an ironic courtesy into his room, his bones.

She was even more beautiful, now he saw her closely, than when he noted her at the end of the bridge.

Her skin was so pale he could gaze through it to a sort of tender, softly-blooming radiance. Her eyes were mysteriously sombre. As her cloak unfurled, he observed the ice-blue flowers on her breasts, and the corsetting of her bodice where La Danse Macabre was depicted in sable embroidery.

She seated herself with a smile before him, and he, his hand already moving of its own volition, as if possessed, began to write.

La Séductrice was his death. The drug would kill him in a year, having burned out his brain, nervous system, and marrow. But his spirit would be left behind him in the words he had now begun to find. We are not given life to cast it aside, but neither is life to be lived for life's sake only. What cries aloud within us must be allowed its voice. Or so it seemed to him, dimly, as the seascapes of the opium overwhelmed him, and the caverns of stars, and the towering crystal cities higher than heaven.

She is three: Thief, Butcher, Seducer. Do not seek her out. She is all around you, in the blowing leaves, the cloud across the moon, the sweet sigh behind your ear, the scent of earth, the whisper of a sleeve. If she is to be yours, she will come to you.

Across the river the clock sounded again.
Un, deux, trois.

A PASSION FOR HISTORY

by Stephen Minot

Picture: On the shore where the river joins the sea, a lobsterman's boathouse-home, gray-shingled and trim, morning dew drifting in vapor from the roof, a column of smoke rising from the chimney, flower boxes with petunias.

It's enough to turn the stomach.

He is not naive. He will not be trapped by sentimentality. He will not be seduced by those Currier and Ives virtues—thrift, honesty, piety, and hard work. These are slogans devised by the rich, by landholders and factory owners. There is no beauty in poverty.

Picture: On the ledge next to the lobsterman's home stands a couple. She wears a dress only a country girl would buy. Tall, long-boned, graceful, she would be beautiful if she had any notion of style. Beauty is there, hidden.

He has rumpled white pants and a blue polo shirt, the costume of a man consciously trying to be informal but not quite succeeding. He is older than she. But they are not father and daughter or brother and sister. As they look out on the glisten of the river which blends into the sea beyond, his right hand rests ever so gently on her right buttock.

They are mismatched, these two. It is more than her mail-order dress and his rumpled elegance, though that is a part of it. There is some deeper aberration here. Like a parent, he can sense something wrong without being able to describe it. But he is not the man's parent. He is the man himself.

It is Kraft himself who is standing there. The woman beside him is Thea. The cottage where she lives is to their left. He is conscious now where his right hand is and can, in fact, feel the warmth of her body.

This kind of thing has been happening to Kraft lately. He can't be sure whether some microcircuit in his brain is loose, blacking out certain periods of time, allowing him to stand on a bank *planning* to take a walk with someone and then skipping ahead to the actual event, or whether it works the other way around—being in the middle of an experience and suddenly viewing it from a distance, with historical perspective, as it were.

"Brooding?" she asks.

"Me? No. I don't brood. That's an indulgence. Thinking, maybe. Sorry. I was just thinking."

"Perhaps you miss teaching. Miss students and all that."

"No, not in the least. I'm not that kind of teacher, you know. A course here, a lecture series there. Not regular teaching. Not in my field."

He always underrates his academic work, he being a radical and teaching being a bourgeois profession and history departments generally being elitist and unenlightened. He prefers to think of himself as a political organizer, though he has done little of that since the 1960s. He hopes that, now in his forties, he is better known for his articles and his recent volume on the radical movement in America. But Thea, his lovely Thea, has read nothing, heard nothing. She has lived her life here in rural Nova Scotia, and as everyone knows, rural Nova Scotia is nowhere. She has never heard of him. He is for her just what he tells her about himself. No less and no more.

"I'd love to learn history," she says.

"Never mind that," he says. "You've got history in you. That's enough."

"No, I really would."

"Not the way *they* teach it you wouldn't. All dates and kings."

"And you?"

"Me? I teach about people. History is people. Little people. The way they live. Know how one person lives and you know a whole period. Not kings. People. Do you understand?"

"Of course," she says, taking half a step back and turning just slightly to the right as if to search the treetops, checking to see if an osprey nest had been built during the night, and incidentally, innocently, pressing ever so gently against the palm of his hand with the curve of her bottom.

Picture: On the smooth gray ledge which forms the bank of the Worwich River at the point where it flows into the sea, a man in white pants embraces a long limber girl, kissing her and now beginning to undo the first of one hundred and two tiny, cloth-covered buttons which run down the back of her dress, she laughing, the sound drifting up like a loon's call.

From this height one can see not only the little boathouse-home but the marshy estuaries formed by the meeting of river and sea and farther, on the sea side, a great gray rectangle of a house surrounded by tall grass, ledge outcroppings, and a scattering of overturned tombstones.

This large rectangle is the house Kraft has bought for himself and his family as a summer home—house and barn and outhouse and woodsheds and 953 acres of land. This is what he has bought with the royalties from his book on the radical movement in America.

Like a mistress it is an embarrassment and a pleasure. He makes a point of keeping it out of the press. His name *is* mentioned in the press from time to time since he is known to liberals as "the guru of radicals" and to hard radicals as "a running-dog revisionist." Thus he has no following whatever but he is read.

When interviewers press him, he refers to his property as his "rural retreat" or his "wilderness camp." Once a Maoist sheet—a sloppy mimeographed affair—reported scathingly that he had bought up a thousand acres of land in Nova Scotia. This, of course, he brands as a total fabrication. They have exaggerated by forty-seven acres.

His house up on the high land is in a permanent state of disrepair. He has not allowed one can of paint to be used inside or out. It is a weathered gray. There is no electricity and water must be lifted bucketful by bucketful from an open well. The plaster was half gone when he bought it, so they removed the other half, leaving the horizontal laths as semi-partitions between the rooms. It is, he reminds his family from time to time, their rural slum.

But this spring there is no family. He came up alone in mid-April, leaving his wife and three children in New Haven by mutual agreement. He was to have two and a half absolutely clear months to type the final draft of his most recent book, this one on the *liberal* tradition.

It was a perfect arrangement. No meetings to attend, no speeches to present, no teaching, no family to sap his energies. So of course he has done no writing.

There are times when he can't stand the clutter and filth of his own house—clutter, filth, and whispering deadlines.

Those are the times when he comes here to the neat little boathouse-home on the river, the little Currier-and-Ives home Thea shares with her father.

Right now he is walking beside Thea, walking back to that perfect little place, his arm around her and hers around him. Seven of the one hundred and two tiny cloth-covered buttons down her back are undone. Ninety-five to go.

Kraft is not entirely certain that this is right. His wife, a sure and competent and rational woman with a law degree and a practice of her own, would consider this a serious malady. Worse than the flu. Akin to income tax evasion. And of course she would be right.

With these thoughts passing through his mind he sees in the far distance, inland, just coming out of the woods and beginning to cross the rocky field, approaching the boathouse-home, old Mr. McKnight.

"Oh," Kraft says, noticing for the first time that the barrow which the old man pushes has a wooden wheel. Involuntarily Kraft's mind provides a parenthetical notation. (*Hand-fashioned oak wheels disappeared from each county at the point when mail-order houses reached that district.*)

"Oh," Thea says, not hearing his unspoken observation. "It's father."

Kraft likes the old man—his courtly, country way. But he has mixed feelings about delaying what he and Thea had been heading toward.

"Well," she says, "no matter. He'll stay for a while and we'll talk. But then it'll be time for his scavenging."

Every day at low tide the old man scours the beaches for usable items—timbers, orange crates, even nails which can be pried out and ground smooth on the whetstone. (*Recycling has been an economic necessity until the last half of the twentieth century.*) Clearly old McKnight lives in the previous century.

"I don't mind," Kraft says. Actually he does and he doesn't mind. Both. But that is too complicated to explain. Even to himself. "I don't mind," he says again. They are on the front stoop—a simple porch with no roof. She sits in the big rocker and he is perched on a nail keg old Mr. McKnight has salvaged from the sea. It would be a time before the old man put the wood in the shed and came around to suggest a cup of coffee. Nothing whatever moves rapidly in rural Nova Scotia. Especially time.

"I don't mind," Kraft says, thinking that the last time he

said it to himself in his own head. "It's good talking with the old man. Just this morning I wrote in my journal, 'I hope I see old Mr. McKnight today. He is my link with the region. I like hearing his voice. I learn a lot from him.' "

"Are you perhaps spending too much time with that journal of yours?" It is exactly the question his wife asked by letter the week before. Unsettling.

"I've kept that going ever since I was ten. I'm not going to stop now." He is, though, spending too much time writing in his journal and she knows it just as clearly as he does, so it is essential that he defend himself. "It's an act of survival, writing that journal."

"Survival?"

"Did you know that shipwrecked sailors rowing a lifeboat are taught to study their own wake? Otherwise they turn in great circles. Did you know that?" She shakes her head. "I wrote about that last week, as a matter of fact. 'Sheepherders,' I pointed out, 'talk to themselves and address their members with obscene endearments.' Well, I mean, here I am living in an ark of a house up there without electricity or running water miles from anywhere, adrift for two months with only a rough draft and a set of correction notes to work with and a publisher's deadline for navigation. Did you know that mermaids are an optical illusion caused by solitude and malnutrition?"

"I didn't know you believed in mermaids."

"I don't. You don't have to believe in them to know that they exist. I've got an entry about that too."

"Those entries," she says, shaking her head. He notices that she is shelling lima beans. Where did they come from? "You spend too much time with them," she says.

"It's just a trail of where my thoughts have been."

She shrugs. She is no lawyer and never argues. She makes commentary on his thoughts, but she never presses her point. "All that looking back," she says gently. "It'll turn you to salt." She smiles and a loon laughs. Either that or a loon smiles and she laughs. "Time to do up the dishes," she says. "He'll be coming in and he'll want a cup of coffee right soon. Come sit with me while I fix up."

Picture in sepia: A woman stands by the soapstone sink, her hand on the pump. There is little light in the room because the windows are small. (*Large windows were avoided not only because of expense but because of a strong sense of nocturnal dangers. Except in cities police protection was practically unknown.*) There is no view of the river or the sea.

The kitchen walls are made of the narrow tongue-in-groove boarding, a poor man's substitute for plaster. Open shelves rather than cupboards—the price of a hinge saved. Kitchen table bare pine, unvarnished, scrubbed with salt—to be replaced in the 1920s with white enamel. Kraft can glance at a photograph of an American kitchen and date it within a decade and can lecture without notes on its impact on the status of women, the institution of marriage, and the hierarchy within the family. Here in Worwich he has found a lost valley. Time has moved on like a great flock of geese, leaving a strange silence and sepia prints.

"He's been cutting wood," Thea says, pumping cold water into the dishpan and adding hot from the aluminum teakettle. Kraft's mind flashes a notation. (*The shift from the heavy cast-iron kettle to the aluminum was as significant for women as the replacement of the wood range by gas.*) "I imagine on your land."

"He's welcome to it. I've got enough problems without clearing my own woodlots." He has a quick vision of his study, the upper room in the big house on the bluff, his papers scattered about like leaves after a storm. His manuscript, the one on the American liberal movement, in cluttered piles; and in addition to his own journals there are his *father's* journals which he has foolishly brought. One more distraction. One more bit of clutter. So if old Mr. McKnight wants to poach, wants to clear land, he is welcome to it. Perhaps Kraft can persuade the old man to steal unfinished manuscripts as well.

Simplicity. Order. He looks at Thea there at the sink. She is both. Her cottage, her life is harmony. His own place is a shambles. How can a man, he wonders, pick a summer home so far from the complexities of contemporary society, so painstakingly distant, and work so hard to keep the place unimproved, simple, true to Thoreau, and still end up with such an enormous rubbish heap in his own study?

Thea has finished washing. She rinses the plates and mugs with one more spurt from the pump, dries each item, places each on open shelves, each in the correct place. He feels a great wave of envy for her life, a passionate and agonized longing which he mistakes for healthy sexual desire.

"It is madness to romanticize the nineteenth-century rural life," he has written in his journal only that morning. "Even a cursory examination of the McKnight family reveals a history of backbreaking work, sickness, and early death."

He silently recites his observation verbatim, cursed with total recall. No, blessed. Without some kind of historical sense of reality this recent affair with Thea will turn into a nightmare of complications.

There is nothing to envy in Thea's life, he tells himself, and the affair is only a passing sexual fancy, a mildly comic sample of male menopause.

The evidence of brutish living is all around him, after all. Abandoned houses, cellar holes where families were burned out in midwinter; private cemetery plots grown over the chokecherry, no one left to tend them. One such is right on the rocky scrub grass he calls his front lawn. McKnights. Half of them children. A family shattered by the brutality of what they had hoped would be their New Scotland.

They came from Scotland, looking for the good life, and they hung on for more than two hundred years. But now as a clan they are broken and scattered, beaten by isolation, by madness, by sudden death, the younger ones fleeing to Montreal, to Toronto, to the States, the survivors selling the last remaining house and most of the land to this American historian and his family who come north as summer residents, looking for the good life.

"Find it?" she asks.

"What?"

"Find it?" For an instant he thinks she has a witch's ability to read minds. (*Statements made about witches in the eighteenth century closely resemble fantasies of present-day patients described as paranoid; thus our diagnosis of mental illness depends from the outset on our current view of reality.*) But she has asked him for a pitcher of milk she has left on the window sill to keep cool.

He sees it, hands it to her. She smiles. "If you don't want him cutting your wood," she says, "you should tell him."

Kraft shakes his head. "I'll never get around to clearing up those woodlots," he says. "There was a time when all the fixing up around the place went well. We really got a lot done. The boys and me working outside clearing fields and cutting back chokecherry. Good, honest work. And Tammy and my daughter working inside, making the place livable. Like a bunch of colonists."

"But then . . ." His voice fades out. Why tell her all that? The second and the third summer, complaints from the children about the isolation; excuses to avoid the work; wry jokes about the lack of plumbing, the lack of electricity, the enforced intimacy, wisecracks growing sharper, less funny each summer. He finds this embarrassing. It is not the way he likes to think of his family. There is no need to share this with Thea.

She has finished the dishes and dries her hands on the roller towel, looking at him. Just the touch of a smile.

"They don't understand," she says. He wonders whether he has just voiced some of his disappointments or whether, again, she is reading his mind. "They don't understand, but I do."

"I don't know what I'd do without you," he says. Actually he does know. It is unutterable. Everything would fall to pieces without her around to listen, to be his lover. It is not just sexual; it is human contact. He depends on both her and her father. Their presence. Both of them.

And there, suddenly, is old Mr. McKnight. He is standing at the kitchen door. Gray-bearded but with no mustache—a tintype. No smile but not unfriendly. (*It is a significant comment on the impact of the industrial revolution that from the introduction of the camera in the mid-nineteenth century until after the first world war it was not customary to smile when having one's picture taken.*) Old Mr. McKnight gives just the ghost of a nod of recognition and extends his hand in an old-world handshake.

"I couldn't seem to get any work done this morning," Kraft says. He doesn't want to seem like a summer resident. He *isn't* a summer resident.

"All that work with your head," Mr. McKnight says. "It can't be good."

"Right."

"Come look at this," the old man says. Kraft follows him into the workroom where there is a skeleton of ribs fashioned to a backbone. It is the beginnings of a rowboat upside down, raised on two sawhorses. Mr. McKnight builds one a year, shaping the oak ribs in a crude boiler out back.

"Here," Mr. McKnight says, seizing Kraft's wrist. The old man's fingers are armored, rough plates joined. He takes Kraft's hand as if it were a plane and slides the palm along the oak keel. Kraft winces, expecting splinters from any unpainted surface. But of course it is perfectly sanded. Needlessly sanded.

"A filly's ass," the old man says.

"She's beautiful," Kraft says. "Like everything of yours."

"Ha!" Mr. McKnight smiles for the first time. The two men share their chauvinistic joke like a brotherhood—the younger one uneasily. "Time for a cup of coffee," the old one says just loud enough for it to become an order for Thea. "Tide's not about to wait for me or you."

Kraft nods, thinking: When the tide's out for you it will be high for Thea and me. He smiles to himself but Mr. McKnight casts a quick questioning look. Does the old man read thoughts too?

Thea has placed three mugs of coffee on the kitchen table and beside each a cloth napkin and a spoon. They sit down. (*Informal eating was considered bad taste well into the 1920s and still is frowned on in rural Ireland and Scotland. The eating of food even under picnic circumstances was invested with ritual significance and required sitting correctly at a table.*)

"That skiff," old Mr. McKnight says, "is as fine as you can find here to Boston." (Boston *became a Nova Scotian term for all of New England by the* 1780s.) "Not one bit of metal in her, you know. No nails. All pegged. Even the cleat is cedar heart. Hard as brass and it won't tarnish." He nods to himself in full agreement with himself. "Gives pleasure twice, it does—once in the building and again in the owning."

"In Halifax," Thea says, "they make them out of plywood."

They all three smile. "Imagine that," the old man says. Kraft does not mention fiberglass. For the McKnights it doesn't exist yet. "Halifax skiffs are nailed too. Full of nails. Rust out on you sooner or later. Ten, fifteen years they'll rust out on you. Drown you sooner or later. Like putting a metal wheel on a barrow. Takes me a winter to shape a wooden wheel. Eight pieces glued and pegged. It's work, but it'll last a lifetime. Two, with luck. Same for lobster traps. Pegged and laced. You can't find a better trap."

Kraft nods, letting the old man continue, though he knows that in the States they are using a plastic lobster trap which is in every way superior. Ugly and indestructible as the aluminum beer can. "I build the best traps around here," the old man says. "The very best." They all nod, a part of the ritual. "Well, can't sit here all day. Tide's calling me," he says and abruptly he is gone. Quick as that.

And now, oddly, when the two of them are free, Kraft is hesitant. The room seems small, airless. Enclosing. Warily he looks to the window, to the door. He hears again the old man's proclamation—"I build the best traps."

He looks at her sitting there opposite him. For an instant she is in sepia again, posed there, a tall woman, high cheekboned. She is an image which would startle young readers browsing through an old photo album. "Who was that?"—the patronizing surprise of moderns who cannot imagine passion cloaked in formality. A sepia print. Colorless. How does such a lovely person stand a colorless life? How does she exist?

"What's wrong?" she asks. "You're having dark thoughts again."

"You're the one who should be having dark thoughts," he says.

"Why?"

"Cooped up here, trapped."

"I'm not trapped."

"With nothing to read."

"I'm not much for reading."

"No profession."

"I keep the place neat. I mend. Grow things."

"The monotony—it must be suffocating. I should think the isolation would drive you crazy."

"I'm not alone now."

"Now." She has no conception of future time. *"Now."* He stands up. He needs motion. "You know, don't you, that Tammy is coming up in ten days. Tammy and the children. And the dog. The whole bit. Did you forget that?"

"That's in a week. Now is now."

She floats in an eternal present. He can't imagine how that would be. He feels rage and envy. For him the present is the peak of a slippery hummock; he is forever sliding down one side or the other—either counting the days to something out there ahead of him or slithering back into the past.

He is standing behind her, his hands on her shoulders. She reaches up and takes both his hands and draws them down and around to her breasts. There is only the cotton fabric between his palms and the softness of her flesh. He feels her nipples. He stops thinking for an instant about past and future. I am holding the present in my hands, he thinks.

He is undoing the buttons down the back of her dress. She has leaned her head back so that it is against him, rocking gently.

"You're right," he says softly in her ear. "I'm not even going to think about Tammy."

Mistake! Mistake! The very word *Tammy* jars the mood, breaks his hold on the present. What is he doing? Somehow the action goes on, but he has floated up. The overview, the damned overview.

Picture: A man embraces a woman in an old-fashioned kitchen, her dress is loosened at the back, is down over one shoulder. The man is not at ease; he is harried by his passion, planning the next move, thinking ahead. He leads her up the stairs and into a simple, unadorned room: walls of vertical boarding, varnished dark. An iron bed, a rocking chair, a bureau with a wavy mirror attached, and a commode on which stand a kerosene lamp and a wash basin. Two books, a Bible and a copy of *Pilgrim's Progress,* both old. Perfect neatness. Perfect order.

Ninety-five tiny buttons open in a ripple and she stands barebreasted in her petticoat. She shakes her hair down and it is long. Her petticoat slips to the floor at her feet. He has seen this image somewhere before, standing this way in the palm of an enormous seashell. But this is no time for art. She is with him on the bed. Her skin radiates warmth.

"Fast," he says. "Quickly." He is on an anxious schedule, racing to meet a sudden departure. The bed cries out like a flock of frantic gulls.

Then, silence. Perfect silence.

That, one might imagine, was the climax of the day for him. But it was only the first of two. The second came after leaving.

He headed up the path toward his own house, not looking forward to returning, and he made the terrible mistake of looking back. A part of him knew that he shouldn't. But he had been living in the present and was careless. "Don't," he said to himself just as he turned, but it was too late.

There was the McKnight boathouse, the one he had just left, chimney smokeless, cracked, and leaning; the roof rotted through, sagging beams exposed, skeletal; windows all broken, flower boxes gone, holes black as empty eye sockets. Even the porch was gone, wrenched off by the grinding ice of winter storms years ago. Dead. All dead and gone. All history.

DAEMON

by C. L. Moore

Padre, the words come slowly. It is a long time now since I have spoken in the Portuguese tongue. For more than a year, my companions here were those who do not speak with the tongues of men. And you must remember, *padre,* that in Rio, where I was born, I was named Luiz *o Bobo,* which is to say, Luiz the Simple. There was something wrong with my head, so that my hands were always clumsy and my feet stumbled over each other. I could not remember very much. But I could see things. Yes, *padre,* I could see things such as other men do not know.

I can see things now. Do you know who stands beside you, *padre,* listening while I talk? Never mind that. I am Luiz *o Bobo* still, though here on this island there were great powers of healing, and I can remember now the things that happened to me years ago. More easily than I remember what happened last week or the week before that. The year has been like a single day, for time on this island is not like time outside. When a man lives with *them,* there is no time.

The *ninfas,* I mean. And the others. . . .

I am not lying. Why should I? I am going to die, quite soon now. You were right to tell me that, *padre.* But I knew. I knew already. Your crucifix is very pretty, *padre.* I like the way it shines in the sun. But that is not for me. You see, I have always known the things that walk beside men—other men. Not me. Perhaps they are souls, and I have no soul, being simple. Or perhaps they are daemons such as only clever men have. Or perhaps they are both these things. I do not know. But I know that I am dying. After the *ninfas* go away, I would not care to live.

Since you ask how I came to this place, I will tell you if the time remains to me. You will not believe. This is the

286

one place on earth, I think, where they lingered still—those things you do not believe.

But before I speak of them, I must go back to an earlier day, when I was young beside the blue bay of Rio, under Sugar Loaf. I remember the docks of Rio, and the children who mocked me. I was big and strong, but I was *o Bobo* with a mind that knew no yesterday or tomorrow.

Minha avó, my grandmother, was kind to me. She was from Ceará, where the yearly droughts kill hope, and she was half blind, with pain in her back always. She worked so that we could eat, and she did not scold me too much. I know that she was good. It was something I could see; I have always had that power.

One morning my grandmother did not waken. She was cold when I touched her hand. That did not frighten me for the—good thing—about her lingered for a while. I closed her eyes and kissed her, and then I went away. I was hungry, and because I was *o Bobo,* I thought that someone might give me food, out of kindness....

In the end, I foraged from the rubbish-heaps.

I did not starve. But I was lost and alone. Have you ever felt that, *padre*? It is like a bitter wind from the mountains and no sheepskin cloak can shut it out. One night I wandered into a sailors' saloon, and I remember that there were many dark shapes with eyes that shone, hovering beside the men who drank there. The men had red, windburned faces and tarry hands. They made me drink *'guardiente* until the room whirled around and went dark.

I woke in a dirty bunk. I heard planks groaning and the floor rocked under me.

Yes, *padre,* I had been shanghaied. I stumbled on deck, half blind in the dazzling sunlight, and there I found a man who had a strange and shining daemon. He was the captain of the ship, though I did not know it then. I scarcely saw the man at all. I was looking at the daemon.

Now, most men have shapes that walk behind them, *padre*. Perhaps you know that, too. Some of them are dark, like the shapes I saw in the saloon. Some of them are bright, like that which followed my grandmother. Some of them are colored, pale colors like ashes or rainbows. But this man had a scarlet daemon. And it was a scarlet beside which blood itself is ashen. The color blinded me. And yet it drew me, too. I could not take my eyes away, nor could I look at it long without pain. I never saw a color more beautiful, nor more frightening. It made my heart shrink within me, and quiver like a dog that fears the whip. If I have a soul, perhaps it was my soul that quivered. And I feared the beauty of the color as much as I feared the terror it awoke in me. It is not good to see beauty in that which is evil.

Other men upon the deck had daemons too. Dark shapes and pale shapes that followed them like their shadows. But I saw all the daemons waver away from the red, beautiful thing that hung above the captain of the ship.

The other daemons watched out of burning eyes. The red daemon had no eyes. Its beautiful, blind face was turned always toward the captain, as if it saw only through his vision. I could see the lines of its closed lids. And my terror of its beauty, and my terror of its evil, were nothing to my terror of the moment when the red daemon might lift those lids and look out upon the world.

The captain's name was Jonah Stryker. He was a cruel man, dangerous to be near. The men hated him. They were at his mercy while we were at sea, and the captain was at the mercy of his daemon. That was why I could not hate him as the others did. Perhaps it was pity I felt for Jonah Stryker. And you, who know men better than I, will understand that the pity I had for him made the captain hate me more bitterly than even his crew hated him.

When I came on deck that first morning, because I was blinded by the sun and by the redness of the scarlet daemon, and because I was ignorant and bewildered, I broke a shipboard rule. What it was, I do not know. There were so many, and I never could remember very clearly in those days. Perhaps I walked between him and the wind. Would that be wrong on a clipper ship, *padre*? I never understood.

The captain shouted at me, in the Yankee tongue, evil words whose meaning I did not know, but the daemon glowed redder when he spoke them. And he struck me with his fist, so that I fell. There was a look of secret bliss on the blind crimson face hovering above his, because of the anger that rose in him. I thought that through the captain's eyes the closed eyes of the daemon were watching me.

I wept. In that moment, for the first time, I knew how truly alone a man like me must be. For I had no daemon. It was not the simple loneliness for my grandmother or for human companionship that brought the tears to my eyes. That I could endure. But I saw the look of joy upon the blind daemon-face because of the captain's evil, and I remembered the look of joy that a bright shape sometimes wears who follows a good man. And I knew that no deed of mine would ever bring joy or sorrow to that which moves behind a man with a soul.

I lay upon the bright, hot deck and wept, not because of the blow, but because I knew suddenly, for the first time, that I was alone. No daemon for good or evil would ever follow me. Perhaps because I have no soul. *That* loneliness, father, is something not even you could understand.

The captain seized my arm and pulled me roughly to my feet. I did not understand, then, the words he spoke in his Yankee tongue, though later I picked up enough of that speech to know what men were saying around me. You may think it strange that *o Bobo* could learn a foreign tongue. It was easy for me. Easier, perhaps, than for a wiser man. Much I read upon the faces of their daemons, and there were many words whose real sounds I did not know, but whose meaning I found in the hum of thoughts about a man's head.

The captain shouted for a man named Barton, and the first mate hurried up, looking frightened. The captain pushed me back against the rail so that I staggered, seeing him and the deck and the watching daemons through the rainbows that tears cast before one's eyes.

There was loud talk, and many gestures toward me and the other two men who had been shanghaied from the port of Rio. The first mate tapped his head when he pointed to me, and the captain cursed again in the tongue of the foreigners, so that his daemon smiled very sweetly at his shoulder.

I think that was the first time I let the captain see pity on my face when I looked at him.

That was the one thing he could not bear. He snatched a belaying pin from the rail and struck me in the face with it, so that I felt the teeth break in my mouth. The blood I spat upon the deck was a beautiful color, but it looked paler than water beside the color of the captain's daemon. I remember all the daemons but the red one leaned a little forward when they saw blood running, snuffing up the smell and the brightness of it like incense. The red one did not even turn his blind face.

The captain struck me again because I had soiled his

deck. My first task aboard the *Dancing Martha* was to scrub up my own blood from the planking.

Afterward they dragged me to the galley and threw me into the narrow alley at the cook's feet. I burned my hands on the stove. The captain laughed to see me jump back from it. It is a terrible thing that, though I heard his laughter many times a day, I never heard mirth in it. But there was mirth on his daemon's face.

Pain was with me for many days thereafter, because of the beating and the burns, but I was glad in a way. Pain kept my mind from the loneliness I had just discovered in myself. Those were bad days, *padre*. The worst days of my life. Afterward, when I was no longer lonely, I looked back upon them as a soul in paradise might look back on purgatory.

No, I am still alone. Nothing follows me as things follow other men. But here on the island I found the *ninfas*, and I was content.

I found them because of the Shaughnessy. I can understand him today in a way I could not do just then. He was a wise man and I am *o Bobo*, but I think I know some of his thoughts now, because today I, too, know I am going to die.

The Shaughnessy lived many days with death. I do not know how long. It was weeks and months in coming to him, though it lived in his lungs and his heart as a child lives within its mother, biding its time to be born. The Shaughnessy was a passenger. He had much money, so that he could do what he willed with his last days of living. Also he came of a great family in a foreign land called Ireland. The captain hated him for many reasons. He scorned him because of his weakness, and he feared him because he was ill. Perhaps he envied him too, because his people had once been kings and because the Shaughnessy was not afraid to die. The captain, I know, feared death. He feared it most terribly. He was right to fear it. He could not know that a daemon rode upon his shoulder, smiling its sweet, secret smile, but some instinct must have warned him that it was there, biding its time like the death in the Shaughnessy's lungs.

I saw the captain die. I know he was right to fear the hour of his daemon....

Those were bad days on the ship. They were worse because of the great beauty all around us. I had never been at sea before, and the motion of the ship was a wonder to me, the clouds of straining sail above us and the sea all about, streaked with the colors of the currents and dazzling where the sun-track lay. White gulls followed us with their yellow feet tucked up as they soared over the deck, and porpoises followed too, playing in great arcs about the ship and dripping diamonds in the sun.

I worked hard, for no more wages than freedom from blows when I did well, and the scraps that were left from the table after the cook had eaten his fill. The cook was not a bad man like the captain, but he was not a good man, either. He did not care. His daemon was smoky, asleep, indifferent to the cook and the world.

It was the Shaughnessy who made my life worth the trouble of living. If it had not been for him, I might have surrendered life and gone into the breathing sea some night when no one was looking. It would not have been a sin for me, as it would be for a man with a soul.

But because of the Shaughnessy I did not. He had a strange sort of daemon himself, mother-of-pearl in the light, with gleams of darker colors when the shadows of night came on. He may have been a bad man in his day. I do not know. The presence of death in him opened his eyes, perhaps. I know only that to me he was very kind. His daemon grew brighter as the man himself grew weak with the oncoming of death.

He told me many tales. I have never seen the foreign country of Ireland, but I walked there often in my dreams because of the tales he told. The foreign isles called Greece grew clear to me too, because the Shaughnessy had dwelt there and loved them.

And he told me of things which he said were not really true, but I thought he said that with only half his mind, because I saw them so clearly while he talked. Great Odysseus was a man of flesh and blood to me, with a shining daemon on his shoulder, and the voyage that took so many enchanted years was a voyage I almost remembered, as if I myself had toiled among the crew.

He told me of burning Sappho, and I knew why the poet used that word for her, and I think the Shaughnessy knew too, though we did not speak of it. I knew how dazzling the thing must have been that followed her through the white streets of Lesbos and leaned upon her shoulder while she sang.

He told me of the nereids and the oceanids, and once I think I saw, far away in the sun-track that blinded my eyes, a mighty head rise dripping from the water, and heard the music of a wreathed horn as Triton called to his fish-tailed girls.

The *Dancing Martha* stopped at Jamaica for a cargo of sugar and rum. Then we struck out across the blue water toward a country called England. But our luck was bad. Nothing was right about the ship on that voyage. Our water-casks had not been cleaned as they should be, and the drinking water became foul. A man can pick the maggots out of his salt pork if he must, but bad water is a thing he cannot mend.

So the captain ordered our course changed for a little island he knew in these waters. It was too tiny to be inhabited, a rock rising out of the great blue deeps with a fresh spring bubbling high up in a cup of the forested crags.

I saw it rising in the dawn like a green cloud on the horizon. Then it was a jewel of green as we drew nearer, floating on the blue water. And my heart was a bubble in my chest, shining with rainbow colors, lighter than the air around me. Part of my mind thought that the island was an isle in Rio Bay, and somehow I felt that I had come home again and would find my grandmother waiting on the shore. I forgot so much in those days. I forgot that she was dead. I thought we would circle the island and come in across the dancing Bay to the foot of the Rua d'Oporto, with the lovely city rising on its hills above the water.

I felt so sure of all this that I ran to tell the Shaughnessy of my delight in homecoming. And because I was hurrying, and blind to all on deck with the vision of Rio in my eyes, I blundered into the captain himself. He staggered and caught my arm to save his footing, and we were so close together that for a moment the crimson daemon swayed above my own head, its eyeless face turned down to mine.

I looked up at that beautiful, smiling face, so near that I could touch it and yet, I knew, farther away than the farthest star. I looked at it and screamed in terror. I had never been so near a daemon before, and I could feel its breath on my face, sweet-smelling, burning my skin with its scorching cold.

The captain was white with his anger and his—his envy? Perhaps it was envy he felt even of me, *o Bobo*, for a man with a daemon like that one hanging on his shoulder may well envy the man without a soul. He hated me bitterly, because he knew I pitied him, and to receive the pity of *o Bobo* must be a very humbling thing. Also he knew that I could not look at him for more than a moment or two, because of the blinding color of his daemon. I think he did not know why I blinked and looked away, shuddering inside, whenever he crossed my path. But he knew it was not the angry fear which other men felt for him which made me avert my eyes. I think he sensed that because he was damned I could not gaze upon him long, and that too made him hate and fear and envy the lowliest man in his crew.

All the color went out of his face as he looked at me, and the daemon above him flushed a deeper and lovelier scarlet, and the captain reached for a belaying pin with a hand that trembled. That which looked out of his eyes was not a man at all, but a daemon, and a daemon that quivered with joy as I was quivering with terror.

I heard the bone crack when the club came down upon my skull. I saw lightning dazzle across my eyes and my head was filled with brightness. I remember almost nothing more of that bad time. A little night closed around me and I saw through it only when the lightning of the captain's blows illumined the dark. I heard his daemon laughing.

When the day came back to me, I was lying on the deck with the Shaughnessy kneeling beside me bathing my face with something that stung. His daemon watched me over his shoulder, bright mother-of-pearl colors, its face compassionate. I did not look at it. The loneliness in me was sharper than the pain of my body, because no daemon of my own hung shining over my hurts, and no daemon ever would.

The Shaughnessy spoke in the soft, hushing Portuguese of Lisboa, that always sounded so strange to me.

"Lie still, Luiz," he was saying. "Don't cry. I'll see that he never touches you again."

I did not know until then that I was weeping. It was not for pain. It was for the look on his daemon's face, and for loneliness.

The Shaughnessy said, "When he comes back from the island, I'll have it out with him." He said more than that, but I was not listening. I was struggling with a thought, and thoughts came hard through the sleepiness that always clouded my brain.

The Shaughnessy meant kindly, but I knew the captain was master upon the ship. And it still seemed to me that we were anchored in the Bay of Rio and my grandmother awaited me on the shore.

I sat up. Beyond the rail the high green island was bright,

sunshine winking from the water all around it, and from the leaves that clothed its slopes. I knew what I was going to do.

When the Shaughnessy went away for more water, I got to my feet. There was much pain in my head, and all my body ached from the captain's blows, and the deck was reeling underfoot with a motion the waves could not give it. When I got to the rail, I fell across it before I could jump, and slid into the sea very quietly.

I remember only flashes after that. Salt water burning me, and great waves lifting and falling all around me, and the breath hot in my lungs when the water did not burn even hotter there. Then there was sand under my knees, and I crawled up a little beach and I think I fell asleep in the shelter of a clump of palms.

Then I dreamed that it was dark, with stars hanging overhead almost near enough to touch, and so bright they burned my eyes. I dreamed I heard men calling me through the trees, and I did not answer. I dreamed I heard voices quarreling, the captain's voice loud and angry, the Shaughnessy's tight and thin. I dreamed of oarlocks creaking and water splashing from dipping blades, and the sound of it receding into the warmth and darkness.

I put up a hand to touch a star cluster that hung above my head, and the cluster was bright and tingling to feel. Then I saw that it was the Shaughnessy's face.

I said, "Oh, *s'nhor*," in a whisper, because I remembered that the captain had spoken from very close by.

The Shaughnessy smiled at me in the starlight. "Don't whisper, Luiz. We're alone now."

I was happy on the island. The Shaughnessy was kind to me, and the days were long and bright, and the island itself was friendly. One knows that of a place. And I thought, in those days, that I would never see the captain again or his beautiful scarlet daemon smiling its blind, secret smile above his shoulder. He had left us to die upon the island, and one of us did die.

The Shaughnessy said that another man might have perished of the blows the captain gave me. But I think because my brain is such a simple thing it mended easily, and perhaps the blow that made my skull crack let in a little more of wit than I had owned before. Or perhaps happiness did it, plenty of food to eat, and the Shaughnessy's tales of the things that—that you do not believe, *meu padre*.

The Shaughnessy grew weak as I grew strong. He lay all day in the shade of a broad tree by the shore, and as his strength failed him, his daemon grew brighter and more remote, as if it were already halfway through the veil of another world.

When I was well again, the Shaughnessy showed me how to build a thatched lean-to that would withstand the rain.

"There may be hurricanes, Luiz," he said to me. "This *barraca* will be blown down. Will you remember how to build another?"

"*Sim,*" I said. "I shall remember. You will show me."

"No, Luiz. I shall not be here. You must remember."

He told me many things, over and over again, very patiently. How to find the shellfish on the rocks when the tide was out, how to trap fish in the stream, which fruit I might eat and what I must never touch. It was not easy for me. When I tried to remember too much it made my head hurt.

I explored the island, coming back to tell him all I had found. At first I was sure that when I had crossed the high hills and stood upon their peaks I would see the beautiful slopes of Rio shining across the water. My heart sank when I stood for the first time upon the heights and saw only more ocean, empty, heaving between me and the horizon.

But I soon forgot again, and Rio and the past faded from my mind. I found the pool cupped high in a hollow of the crags, where clear sweet water bubbled up in the shadow of the trees and the streamlet dropped away in a series of pools and falls toward the levels far below. I found groves of pale trees with leaves like streaming hair, rustling with the noise of the waterfall. I found no people here, and yet I felt always that there were watchers among the leaves, and it seemed to me that laughter sounded sometimes behind me, smothered when I turned my head.

When I told the Shaughnessy this he smiled at me.

"I've told you too many tales," he said. "But if anyone could see them, I think it would be you, Luiz."

"*Sim, s'nhor,*" I said. Tell me again of the forest-women. Could they be here, do you think, *s'nhor*?"

He let sand trickle through his fingers, watching it as if the fall of sand had some meaning to his mind that I could not fathom.

"Ah, well," he said, "they might be. They like the olive groves of Greece best, and the tall trees on Olympus. But every mountain has its oread. Here, too, perhaps. The

Little People left Ireland years ago and for all I know the oreads have fled from civilization too, and found such places as this to put them in mind of home. . . .

"There was one who turned into a fountain once, long ago. I saw that fountain in Greece. I drank from it. There must have been a sort of magic in the waters, for I always went back to Greece after that. I'd leave, but I couldn't stay away long." He smiled at me. "Maybe now, because I can't go back again, the oreads have come to me here."

I looked hard at him to see if he meant what he said, but he shook his head and smiled again. "I think they haven't come for me. Maybe for you, Luiz. Belief is what they want. If you believe, perhaps you'll really see them. I'd be the last man to deny a thing like that. You'll need something like them to keep you company, my friend—afterward." And he trickled sand through his fingers again, watching it fall with a look upon his face I did not understand.

The night came swiftly on that island. It was a lovely place. The Shaughnessy said islands have a magic all their own, for they are the place where earth and ocean meet. We used to lie on the shore watching the fire that burned upon the edges of the waves lap up the beach and breathe away again, and the Shaughnessy told me many tales. His voice was growing weaker, and he did not trouble so much any more to test my memory for the lessons he had taught. But he spoke of ancient magic, and more and more in these last days, his mind turned back to the wonders of the country called Ireland.

He told me of the little green people with their lanterns low down among the ferns. He told me of the *unicórnio*, swift as the swiftest bird, a magical stag with one horn upon its forehead as long as the shaft of a spear and as sharp as whatever is sharpest. And he told me of Pan, goat-footed, moving through the woodland with laughter running before him and panic behind, the same panic terror which my language and the Shaughnessy's get from his name. *Pânico*, we Brazilians call it.

One evening he called to me and held up a wooden cross. "Luiz, look at this," he said. I saw that upon the arms of the cross he had made deep carvings with his knife. "This is my name," he told me. "If anyone ever comes here asking for me, you must show them this cross."

I looked at it closely. I knew what he meant about the name—it is that sort of enchantment in which markings can speak with a voice too tiny for the ears to hear. I am *o Bobo* and I never learned to read, so that I do not understand how this may be done.

"Some day," the Shaughnessy went on, "I think someone will come. My people at home may not be satisfied with whatever story Captain Stryker invents for them. Or a drunken sailor may talk. If they do find this island, Luiz, I want this cross above my grave to tell them who I was. And for another reason," he said thoughtfully. "For another reason too. But that need not worry you, *meu amigo*."

He told me where to dig the bed for him. He did not tell me to put in the leaves and the flowers. I thought of that myself, three days later, when the time came. . . .

Because he had wished it, I put him in the earth. I did not like doing it. But in a way I feared not to carry out his commands, for the daemon of the Shaughnessy still hovered above him, very bright, very bright—so bright I could not look it in the face. I thought there was music coming from it, but I could not be sure.

I put the flowers over him and then the earth. There was more to go back in the grave than I had taken out, so I made a mound above him, as long as the Shaughnessy was long, and I drove in the stake of the wooden cross, above where his head was, as he had told me. Then for a moment I laid my ear to the markings to see if I could hear what they were saying, for it seemed to me that the sound of his name, whispered to me by the marks his hands had made, would lighten my loneliness a little. But I heard nothing.

When I looked up, I saw his daemon glow like the sun at noon, a light so bright I could not bear it upon my eyes. I put my hands before them. When I took them down again, there was no daemon.

You will not believe me when I tell you this, *padre*, but in that moment the—the feel of the island changed. All the leaves, I think, turned the other way on the trees, once, with a rustle like one vast syllable whispered for that time only, and never again.

I think I know what the syllable was. Perhaps I will tell you, later—if you let me.

And the island breathed. It was like a man who has held his breath for a long while, in fear or pain, and let it run out deeply when the fear or the pain departed.

I did not know, then, what it was. But I thought I would go up the steep rocks to the pool, because I wanted a place that would not remind me of the Shaughnessy. So I climbed the crags among the hanging trees. And it seemed to me that I heard laughter when the wind rustled among them. Once I saw what I thought must be a *ninfa*, brown and green in the forest. But she was too shy. I turned my head, and the brown and green stilled into the bark and foliage of the tree.

When I came to the pool, the unicorn was drinking. He was very beautiful, whiter than foam, whiter than a cloud, and his mane lay upon his great shoulders like spray upon the shoulder of a wave. The tip of his long, spiraled horn just touched the water as he drank, so that the ripples ran outward in circles all around it. He tossed his head when he scented me, and I saw the glittering diamonds of the water sparkling from his velvet muzzle. He had eyes as green as a pool with leaves reflecting in it, and a spot of bright gold in the center of each eye.

Very slowly, with the greatest stateliness, he turned from the water and moved away into the forest. I know I heard a singing where he disappeared.

I was still *o Bobo* then. I drank where he had drunk, thinking there was a strange, sweet taste to the water now, and then I went down to the *barraca* on the beach, for I had forgotten already and thought perhaps the Shaughnessy might be there. . . .

Night came, and I slept. Dawn came, and I woke again. I bathed in the ocean. I gathered shellfish and fruit, and drank of the little stream that fell from the mountain pool. And as I leaned to drink, two white dripping arms rose up to clasp my neck, and a mouth as wet and cold as the water pressed mine. It was the kiss of acceptance.

After that the *ninfas* of the island no longer hid their faces from me.

My hair and beard grew long. My garments tore upon the bushes and became the rags you see now. I did not care. It did not matter. It was not my face they saw. They saw my simpleness. And I was one with the *ninfas* and the others.

The oread of the mountain came out to me often, beside the pool where the unicorn came to drink. She was wise and strange, being immortal. The eyes slanted upward in her head, and her hair was a shower of green leaves blowing always backward in a wind that moved about her when no other breezes blew. She used to sit beside the pool in the hot, still afternoons, the unicorn lying beside her and her brown fingers combing out his silver mane. Her wise slanting eyes, the color of shadows in the forest, and his round green eyes the color of the pool, with the flecks of gold in each, used to watch me as we talked.

The oread told me many things. Many things I could never tell you, *padre*. But it was as the Shaughnessy had guessed. Because I believed, they were glad of my presence there. While the Shaughnessy lived, they could not come out into the plane of being, but they watched from the other side. . . . They had been afraid. But they were afraid no longer.

For many years they have been homeless now, blowing about the world in search of some spot of land where no disbelief dwells, and where one other thing has not taken footing. . . . They told me of the isles of Greece, with love and longing upon their tongues, and it seemed to me that I heard the Shaughnessy speak again in their words.

They told me of the One I had not yet seen, or more than glimpsed. That happened when I chanced to pass near the Shaughnessy's grave in the dimness of the evening, and I saw the cross that bore his name had fallen. I took it up and held it to my ear again, hoping the tiny voices of the markings would whisper. But that is a mystery which has never been given me.

I saw the—the One—loitering by that grave. But when I put up the cross, he went away, slowly, sauntering into the dark woods, and a thin piping floated back to me from the spot where he had vanished.

Perhaps the One did not care for my presence there. The others welcomed me. It was not often any more, they said, that men like me were free to move among them. Since the hour of their banishment, they told me, and wept when they spoke of that hour, there had been two few among mankind who really knew them.

I asked about the banishment, and they said that it had happened long ago, very long ago. A great star had stood still in the sky over a stable in a town whose name I do not know. Once I knew it. I do not remember now. It was a town with a beautiful name.

The skies opened and there was singing in the heavens, and after that the gods of Greece had to flee. They have been fleeing ever since.

They were glad I had come to join them. And I was doubly glad. For the first time since my grandmother died, I knew I was not alone. Even the Shaughnessy had not been as close to me as these *ninfas* were. For the Shaughnessy had a daemon. The *ninfas* are immortal, but they have no souls. That, I think, is why they welcomed me so warmly. We without souls are glad of companionship among others of our kind. There is a loneliness among our kind that can only be assuaged by huddling together. The *ninfas* knew it, who must live forever, and I shared it with them, who may die before this night is over.

Well, it was good to live upon the island. The days and months went by beautifully, full of clear colors and the smell of the sea and the stars at night as bright as lanterns just above us. I even grew less *Bobo*, because the *ninfas* spoke wisdom of a kind I never heard among men. They were good months.

And then, one day, Jonah Stryker came back to the island.

You know, *padre*, why he came. The Shaughnessy in his wisdom had guessed that in Ireland men of the Shaughnessy's family might ask questions of Captain Stryker—questions the captain could not answer. But it had not been guessed that the captain might return to the island, swiftly, before the Shaughnessy's people could discover the truth, with the thought in his evil mind of wiping out all traces of the two he had left to die.

I was sitting on the shore that day, listening to the songs of two *ninfas* of the nereid kind as they lay in the edge of the surf, with the waves breaking over them when the water lapped up the slopes of sand. They were swaying their beautiful rainbow-colored fish-bodies as they sang, and I heard the whisper of the surf in their voices, and the long rhythms of the undersea.

But suddenly there came a break in their song, and I saw upon one face before me, and then the other, a look of terror come. The green blood in their veins sank back with fear, and they looked at me, white with pallor and strangely transparent, as if they had halfway ceased to be. With one motion they turned their heads and stared out to sea.

I stared too. I think the first thing I saw was that flash of burning crimson, far out over the waves. And my heart quivered within me like a dog that fears the whip. I knew that beautiful, terrible color too well.

It was only then that I saw the *Dancing Martha*, lying at

anchor beyond a ridge of rock. Between the ship and the shore a small boat rocked upon the waves, light flashing from oar-blades as the one man in the boat bent and rose and bent to his work. Above him, hanging like a crimson cloud, the terrible scarlet glowed.

When I looked back, the *ninfas* had vanished. Whether they slid back into the sea, or whether they melted away into nothingness before me I shall never know now. I did not see them again.

I went back a little way into the forest, and watched from among the trees. No dryads spoke to me, but I could hear their quick breathing and the leaves trembled all about me. I could not look at the scarlet daemon coming nearer and nearer over the blue water, but I could not look away long, either. It was so beautiful and so evil.

The captain was alone in the boat. I was not quite so *Bobo* then and I understood why. He beached the boat and climbed up the slope of sand, the daemon swaying behind him like a crimson shadow. I could see its blind eyes and the beautiful, quiet face shut up with bliss because of the thing the captain had come to do. He was carrying in his hand a long shining pistol, and he walked carefully, looking to left and right. His face was anxious, and his mouth had grown more cruel in the months since I saw him last.

I was sorry for him, but I was very frightened, too. I knew he meant to kill whomever he found alive upon the island, so that no tongue could tell the Shaughnessy's people of his wicked deed.

He found my thatched *barraca* at the edge of the shore, and kicked it to pieces with his heavy boots. Then he went on until he saw the long mound above the Shaughnessy's bed, with the cross standing where his head lay. He bent over the cross, and the markings upon it spoke to him as they would never speak to me. I heard nothing, but he heard and knew. He put out his hand and pulled up the cross from the Shaughnessy's grave.

Then he went to the ruins of my *barraca* and to the embers of the fire I kept smouldering there. He broke the cross upon his knee and fed the pieces into the hot coals. The wood was dry. I saw it catch flame and burn. I saw, too, the faint stirring of wind that sprang up with the flames, and I heard the sighing that ran through the trees around me. Now there was nothing here to tell the searchers who might come afterward that the Shaughnessy lay in the island earth. Nothing—except myself.

He saw my footprints around the ruined *barraca*. He stopped to look. When he rose again and peered around the shore and forest, I could see his eyes shine, and it was the daemon who looked out of them, not the man.

Following my tracks, he began to move slowly toward the forest where I was hiding.

Then I was very frightened. I rose and fled through the trees, and I heard the dryads whimpering about me as I ran. They drew back their boughs to let me pass and swept them back after me to bar the way. I ran and ran, upward among the rocks, until I came to the pool of the unicorn, and the oread of the mountain stood there waiting for me, her arm across the unicorn's neck.

There was a rising wind upon the island. The leaves threshed and talked among themselves, and the oread's leafy hair blew backward from her face with its wise slanting eyes. The unicorn's silver mane tossed in that wind and the water ruffled in the pool.

"There is trouble coming, Luiz," the oread told me.

"The daemon. I know." I nodded to her, and then blinked, because it seemed to me that she and the unicorn, like the sea-*ninfas*, were growing so pale I could see the trees behind them through their bodies. But perhaps that was because the scarlet of the daemon had hurt my eyes.

"There is a man with a soul again upon our island," the oread said. "A man who does not believe. Perhaps we will have to go, Luiz."

"The Shaughnessy had a daemon too," I told her. "Yet you were here before his daemon left him to the earth. Why must you go now?"

"His was a good daemon. Even so, we were not fully here while he lived. You must remember, Luiz, that hour I told you of when a star stood above a stable where a child lay, and all our power went from us. Where the souls of men dwell, we cannot stay. This new man has brought a very evil soul with him. It frightens us. Yet since he had burned the cross, perhaps the Master can fight. . . ."

"The Master?" I asked.

"The One we serve. The One you serve, Luiz. The One I think the Shaughnessy served, though he did not know it. The Lord of the opened eyes and the far places. He could not come until the Sign was taken down. Once you had a glimpse of him, when the Sign fell by accident from the grave, but perhaps you have forgotten that."

"I have not forgotten. I am not so *Bobo* now."

She smiled at me, and I could see the tree behind her through the smile.

"Then perhaps you can help the Master when the time comes. We cannot help. We are too weak already, because of the presence of the unbeliever, the man with the daemon. See?" She touched my hand, and I felt not the firm, soft brush of fingers but only a coolness like mist blowing across my skin.

"Perhaps the Master can fight him," the oread said, and her voice was very faint, like a voice from far away, though she spoke from so near to me. "I do not know about that. We must go, Luiz. We may not meet again. Good-by, *caro bobo,* while I can still say good-by. . . ." The last of it was faint as the hushing of the leaves, and the oread and the unicorn together looked like smoke blowing from a campfire across the glade.

The knowledge of my loneliness came over me then more painfully than I had felt it since that hour when I first looked upon the captain's daemon and knew at last what my own sorrow was. But I had no time to grieve, for there was a sudden frightened whispering among the leaves behind me, and then the crackle of feet in boots, and then a flicker of terrible crimson among the trees.

I ran. I did not know where I ran. I heard the dryad crying, so it must have been among trees. But at last I came out upon the shore again and I saw the Shaughnessy's long grave without a cross above it. And I stopped short, and a thrill of terror went through me. For there was a Something that crouched upon the grave.

The fear in me then was a new thing. A monstrous, dim fear that moves like a cloud about the Master. I knew he meant me no harm, but the fear was heavy upon me, making my head spin with panic. *Pânico.* . . .

The Master rose upon the grave, and he stamped his goat-hoofed foot twice and set the pipes to his bearded lips. I heard a thin, strange wailing music that made the blood chill inside me. And at the first sound of it there came again what I had heard once before upon the island.

The leaves upon all the trees turned over once, with a great single whispering of one syllable. The syllable was the

Master's name. I fled from it in the *pânico* all men have felt who hear that name pronounced. I fled to the edge of the beach, and I could flee no farther. So I crouched behind a hillock of rock on the wet sand, and watched what came after me from the trees.

It was the captain, with his daemon swaying like smoke above his head. He carried the long pistol ready, and his eyes moved from left to right along the beach, seeking like a wild beast for his quarry.

He saw the Master, standing upon the Shaughnessy's grave.

I saw how he stopped, rigid, like a man of stone. The daemon swayed forward above his head, he stopped so suddenly. I saw how he stared. And such was his disbelief, that for an instant I thought even the outlines of the Master grew hazy. There is great power in the men with souls.

I stood up behind my rock. I cried above the noises of the surf, "Master—Great Pan—I believe!"

He heard me. He tossed his horned head and his bulk was solid again. He set the pipes to his lips.

Captain Stryker whirled when he heard me. The long pistol swung up and there was a flash and a roar, and something went by me with a whine of anger. It did not touch me.

Then the music of the pipes began. A terrible music, thin and high, like the ringing in the ears that has no source. It seized the captain as if with thin, strong fingers, making him turn back to the sound. He stood rigid again, staring, straining. The daemon above him turned uneasily from side to side, like a snake swaying.

Then Captain Stryker ran. I saw the sand fly up from under his boots as he fled southward along the shore. His daemon went after him, a red shadow with its eyes still closed, and after them both went Pan, moving delicately on the goathoofs, the pipes to his lips and his horns shining golden in the sun.

And that midday terror I think was greater than any terror that can stalk a man by dark.

I waited beside my rock. The sea was empty behind me except for the *Dancing Martha* waiting the captain's orders at its anchor. But no *ninfas* came in on the foam to keep me company; no heads rose wreathed with seaweed out of the water. The sea was empty and the island was empty too, except for a man and a daemon and the Piper who followed at their heels.

Myself I do not count. I have no soul.

It was nearly dark when they came back along the beach. I think the Piper had hunted them clear around the island, going slowly on his delicate hoofs, never hurrying, never faltering, and that dreadful thin music always in the captain's ears.

I saw the captain's face when he came back in the twilight. It was an old man's face, haggard, white, with deep lines in it and eyes as wild as Pan's. His clothing was torn to ribbons and his hands bled, but he still held the pistol and the red daemon still hung swaying above him.

I think the captain did not know that he had come back to his starting place. By that time, all places must have looked alike to him. He came wavering toward me blindly. I rose up behind my rock.

When he saw me he lifted the pistol again and gasped some Yankee words. He was a strong man, Captain Stryker. With all he had endured in that long chase, he still had the power to remember he must kill me. I did not think he had reloaded the pistol, and I stood up facing him across the sand.

Behind him Pan's pipes shrilled a warning, but the Master did not draw nearer to come between us. The red daemon swayed at the captain's back, and I knew why Pan did not come to my aid. Those who lost their power when the Child was born can never lay hands upon men who possess a soul. Even a soul as evil as the captain's stood like a rock between him and the touch of Pan. Only the pipes could reach a human's ears, but there was that in the sound of the pipes which did all Pan needed to do.

It could not save me. I heard the captain laugh, without breath, a strange, hoarse sound, and I saw the lightning dazzle from the pistol's mouth. The crash it made was like a blow that struck me here, in the chest. I almost fell. That blow was heavy, but I scarcely noticed it then. There was too much to do.

The captain was laughing, and I thought of the Shaughnessy, and I stumbled forward and took the pistol by its hot muzzle with my hand. I am strong. I tore it from the captain's fist and he stood there gaping at me, not believing anything he saw. He breathed in dreadful, deep gasps, and I found I was gasping too, but I did not know why just then.

The captain's eyes met mine, and I think he saw that even now I had no hate for him—only pity. For the man behind the eyes vanished and the crimson daemon of his rage looked out, because I dared to feel sorrow for him. I looked into the eyes that were not his, but the eyes behind the closed lids of the beautiful, blind face above him. It I hated, not him. And it was it I struck. I lifted the pistol and smashed it into the captain's face.

I was not very clear in my head just then. I struck the daemon with my blow, but it was the captain who reeled backward three steps and then fell. I am very strong. One blow was all I needed.

For a moment there was no sound in all the island. Even the waves kept their peace. The captain shuddered and gave one sigh, like that of a man who comes back to living reluctantly. He got his hands beneath him and rose upon them, peering at me through the hair that had fallen across his forehead. He was snarling like an animal.

I do not know what he intended then. I think he would have fought me until one of us was dead. But above him just then I saw the daemon stir. It was the first time I had ever seen it move except in answer to the captain's motion. All his life it had followed him, blind, silent, a shadow that echoed his gait and gestures. Now for the first time it did not obey him.

Now it rose up to a great, shining height above his head, and its color was suddenly very deep, very bright and deep, a blinding thing that hung above him too hot in color to look at. Over the beautiful blind face a look of triumph came. I saw ecstasy dawn over that face in all its glory and its evil.

I knew that this was the hour of the daemon.

Some knowledge deeper than any wisdom warned me to cover my eyes. For I saw its lids flicker, and I knew it would not be good to watch when that terrible gaze looked out at last upon a world it had never seen except through the captain's eyes.

I fell to my knees and covered my face. And the captain, seeing that, must have known at long last what it was I saw behind him. I think now that in the hour of a man's death, he knows. I think in that last moment he knows, and turns, and for the first time and the last, looks his daemon in the face.

I did not see him do it. I did not see anything. But I heard a great, resonant cry, like the mighty music that beats through paradise, a cry full of triumph and thanksgiving, and joy at the end of a long, long, weary road. There was mirth in it, and beauty, and all the evil the mind can compass.

Then fire glowed through my fingers and through my eyelids and into my brain. I could not shut it out. I did not even need to lift my head to see, for that sight would have blazed through my very bones.

I saw the daemon fall upon its master.

The captain sprang to his feet with a howl like a beast's howl, no mind or soul in it. He threw back his head and his arms went up to beat that swooping, beautiful, crimson thing away.

No flesh could oppose it. This was its hour. What sets that hour I do not know, but the daemon knew, and nothing could stop it now.

I saw the flaming thing descend upon the captain like a falling star. Through his defending arms it swept, and through his flesh and his bones and into the hollows where the soul dwells.

He stood for an instant transfixed, motionless, glowing with that bath of crimson light. Then I saw the crimson begin to shine *through* him, so that the shadows of his bones stood out upon the skin. And then fire shot up, wreathing from his eyes and mouth and nostrils. He was a lantern of flesh for that fire of the burning spirit. But he was a lantern that is consumed by the flame it carries. . . .

When the color became too bright for the eyes to bear it, I tried to turn away. I could not. The pain in my chest was too great. I thought of the Shaughnessy in that moment, who knew, too, what pain in the chest was like. I think that was the first moment when it came to me that, like the Shaughnessy, I too was going to die.

Before my eyes, the captain burned in the fire of his daemon, burned and burned, his living eyes looking out at me through the crimson glory, and the laughter of the daemon very sweet above the sound of the whining flame. I could not watch and I could not turn away.

But at last the whine began to die. Then the laughter roared out in one great peal of triumph, and the beautiful crimson color, so dreadfully more crimson than blood, flared in a great burst of light that turned to blackness against my eyeballs.

When I could see again, the captain's body lay flat upon the sand. I know death when I see it. He was not burned at all. He looked as any dead man looks, flat and silent. It was his soul I had watched burning, not his body.

The daemon had gone back again to its own place. I knew that, for I could feel my aloneness on the island.

The Others had gone too. The presence of that fiery daemon was more, in the end, than their power could endure. Perhaps they shun an evil soul more fearfully than a good one, knowing themselves nothing of good and evil, but fearing what they do not understand.

You know, *padre*, what came after. The men from the *Dancing Martha* took their captain away next morning. They were frightened of the island. They looked for that which had killed him, but they did not look far, and I hid in the empty forest until they went away.

I do not remember their going. There was a burning in my chest, and this blood I breathe out ran from time to time, as it does now. I do not like the sight of it. Blood is a beautiful color, but it reminds me of too much that was beautiful also, and much redder....

Then you came, *padre*. I do not know how long thereafter. I know the Shaughnessy's people brought you with their ship, to find him or his grave. You know now. And I am glad you came. It is good to have a man like you beside me at this time. I wish I had a daemon of my own, to grow very bright and vanish when I die, but that is not for *o Bobo* and I am used to that kind of loneliness.

I would not live, you see, now that the *ninfas* are gone. To be with them was good, and we comforted one another in our loneliness but, *padre*, I will tell you this much. It was a chilly comfort we gave each other, at the best. I am a man, though *bobo*, and I know. They are *ninfas*, and will never guess how warm and wonderful it must be to own a soul. I would not tell them if I could. I was sorry for the *ninfas*, *padre*. They are, you see, immortal.

As for me, I will forget loneliness in a little while. I will forget everything. I would not want to be a *ninfa* and live forever.

There is one behind you, *padre*. It is very bright. It watches me across your shoulder, and its eyes are wise and sad. No, daemon, this is no time for sadness. Be sorry for the *ninfas*, daemon, and for men like him who burned upon this beach. But not for me. I am well content.

I will go now.

THE LADY'S MAID'S BELL

by Edith Wharton

It was the autumn after I had the typhoid. I'd been three months in hospital, and when I came out I looked so weak and tottery that the two or three ladies I applied to were afraid to engage me. Most of my money was gone, and after I'd boarded for two months, hanging about the employment agencies, and answering any advertisement that looked any way respectable, I pretty nearly lost heart, for fretting hadn't made me fatter, and I didn't see why my luck should ever turn. It did though—or I thought so at the time. A Mrs. Railton, a friend of the lady that first brought me out to the States, met me one day and stopped to speak to me: she was one that had always a friendly way with her. She asked me what ailed me to look so white, and when I told her, "Why, Hartley," says she, "I believe I've got the very place for you. Come in tomorrow and we'll talk about it."

The next day, when I called, she told me the lady she'd in mind was a niece of hers, a Mrs. Brympton, a youngish lady, but something of an invalid, who lived all the year round at her country place on the Hudson, owing to not being able to stand the fatigue of town life.

"Now, Hartley," Mrs. Railton said, in that cheery way that always made me feel things must be going to take a turn for the better—"now understand me; it's not a cheerful place I'm sending you to. The house is big and gloomy; my niece is nervous, vaporish; her husband—well he's generally away; and the two children are dead. A year ago I would as soon have thought of shutting a rosy active girl like you into a vault; but you're not particularly brisk yourself just now, are you? and a quiet place, with country air and wholesome food and early hours, ought to be the very thing for you. Don't mistake me," she added, for I suppose I looked a trifle downcast; "you may find it dull but you won't be unhappy. My niece is an angel. Her former maid, who died last spring, had been with her twenty years and worshiped the ground she walked on. She's a kind mistress to all, and where the mistress is kind, as you know, the servants are generally good-humored, so you'll probably get on well enough with the rest of the household. And you're the very woman I want for my niece: quiet, well-mannered, and educated above your station. You read aloud well, I think? That's a good thing; my niece likes to be read to. She wants a maid that can be something of a companion: her last was, and I can't say how she misses her. It's a lonely life.... Well, have you decided?"

"Why, ma'am," I said, "I'm not afraid of solitude."

"Well, then, go; my niece will take you on my recommendation. I'll telegraph her at once and you can take the afternoon train. She has no one to wait on her at present, and I don't want you to lose any time."

I was ready enough to start, yet something in me hung back; and to gain time I asked, "And the gentleman, ma'am?"

"The gentleman's almost always away, I'll tell you," said Mrs. Railton, quicklike—"and when he's there," says she suddenly, "you've only to keep out of his way."

I took the afternoon train and got to the station at about four o'clock. A groom in a dogcart was waiting, and we drove off at a smart pace. It was a dull October day, with rain hanging close overhead, and by the time we turned into Brympton Place woods the daylight was almost gone. The drive wound through the woods for a mile or two, and came out on a gravel court shut in with thickets of tall black-looking shrubs. There were no lights in the windows, and the house *did* look a bit gloomy.

I had asked no questions of the groom, for I never was one to get my notion of new masters from their other servants: I prefer to wait and see for myself. But I could tell by the look of everything that I had got into the right kind of house, and that things were done handsomely. A pleasant-faced cook met me at the back door and called the housemaid to show me up to my room. "You'll see madam later," she said. "Mrs. Brympton has a visitor."

I hadn't fancied Mrs. Brympton was a lady to have many visitors, and somehow the words cheered me. I followed the housemaid upstairs, and saw, through a door on the upper landing, that the main part of the house seemed well furnished, with dark paneling and a number of old portraits.

Another flight of stairs led up to the servants' wing. It was almost dark now, and the housemaid excused herself for not having brought a light. "But there's matches in your room," she said, "and if you go carefully you'll be all right. Mind the step at the end of the passage. Your room is just beyond."

I looked ahead as she spoke, and halfway down the passage I saw a woman standing. She drew back into a doorway as we passed and the housemaid didn't appear to notice her. She was a thin woman with a white face, and a dark gown and apron. I took her for the housekeeper and thought it odd that she didn't speak, but just gave me a long look as she went by. My room opened into a square hall at the end of the passage. Facing my door was another which stood open: the housemaid exclaimed when she saw it:

"There—Mrs. Blinder's left that door open again!" said she, closing it.

"Is Mrs. Blinder the housekeeper?"

"There's no housekeeper: Mrs. Blinder's the cook."

"And is that her room?"

"Laws, no," said the housemaid, crosslike. "That's nobody's room. It's empty, I mean, and the door hadn't ought to be open. Mrs. Brympton wants it kept locked."

She opened my door and led me into a neat room, nicely furnished, with a picture or two on the walls; and having lit a candle she took leave, telling me that the servants' hall tea was at six, and that Mrs. Brympton would see me afterward.

I found them a pleasant-spoken set in the servants' hall, and by what they let fall I gathered that, as Mrs. Railton had said, Mrs. Brympton was the kindest of ladies; but I didn't take much notice of their talk, for I was watching to see the pale woman in the dark gown come in. She didn't show herself, however, and I wondered if she ate apart; but if she wasn't the housekeeper, why should she? Suddenly it struck me that she might be a trained nurse, and in that case her meals would of course be served in her room. If Mrs. Brympton was an invalid it was likely enough she had a nurse. The idea annoyed me, I own, for they're not always the easiest to get on with, and if I'd known I shouldn't have taken the place. But there I was and there was no use pulling a long face over it; and not being one to ask questions I waited to see what would turn up.

When tea was over the housemaid said to the footman:

"Has Mr. Ranford gone?" and when he said yes, she told me to come up with her to Mrs. Brympton.

Mrs. Brympton was lying down in her bedroom. Her lounge stood near the fire and beside it was a shaded lamp. She was a delicate-looking lady, but when she smiled I felt there was nothing I wouldn't do for her. She spoke very pleasantly, in a low voice, asking me my name and age and so on, and if I had everything I wanted, and if I wasn't afraid of feeling lonely in the country.

"Not with you I wouldn't be, madam," I said, and the words surprised me when I'd spoken them, for I'm not an impulsive person; but it was just as if I'd thought aloud.

She seemed pleased at that, and said she hoped I'd continue in the same mind; then she gave me a few directions about her toilet, and said Agnes the housemaid would show me next morning where things were kept.

"I'm tired tonight, and shall dine upstairs," she said. "Agnes will bring me my tray, so that you may have time to unpack and settle yourself; and later you may come and undress me."

"Very well, ma'am," I said. "You'll ring, I suppose?"

I thought she looked odd.

"No—Agnes will fetch you," says she quickly, and took up her book again.

Well—that was certainly strange: a lady's maid having to be fetched by the housemaid whenever her lady wanted her! I wondered if there were no bells in the house; but the next day I satisfied myself that there was one in every room, and a special one ringing from my mistress's room to mine; and after that it did strike me as queer that, whenever Mrs. Brympton wanted anything, she rang for Agnes, who had to walk the whole length of the servants' wing to call me.

But that wasn't the only queer thing in the house. The very next day I found out that Mrs. Brympton had no nurse; and then I asked Agnes about the woman I had seen in the passage the afternoon before. Agnes said she had seen no one, and I saw that she thought I was dreaming. To be sure, it was dusk when we went down the passage, and she had excused herself for not bringing a light; but I had seen the woman plain enough to know her again if we should meet. I decided that she must have been a friend of the cook's, or of one of the other women servants; perhaps she had come down from town for a night's visit, and the servants wanted it kept secret. Some ladies are very stiff about having their servants' friends in the house overnight. At any rate, I made up my mind to ask no more questions.

In a day or two another odd thing happened. I was chatting one afternoon with Mrs. Blinder, who was a friendly-disposed woman, and had been longer in the house than the other servants, and she asked me if I was quite comfortable and had everything I needed. I said I had no fault to find with my place or with my mistress, but I thought it odd that in so large a house there was no sewing room for the lady's maid.

"Why," says she, "there *is* one: the room you're in is the old sewing room."

"Oh," said I; "and where did the other lady's maid sleep?"

At that she grew confused, and said hurriedly that the servants' rooms had all been changed about last year, and she didn't rightly remember.

That struck me as peculiar, but I went on as if I hadn't noticed: "Well, there's a vacant room opposite mine, and I mean to ask Mrs. Brympton if I mayn't use that as a sewing room."

To my astonishment, Mrs. Blinder went white, and gave my hand a kind of squeeze. "Don't do that, my dear," said she, trembling-like. "To tell you the truth, that was Emma Saxon's room, and my mistress has kept it closed ever since her death."

"And who was Emma Saxon?"

"Mrs. Brympton's former maid."

"The one that was with her so many years?" said I, remembering what Mrs. Railton had told me.

Mrs. Blinder nodded.

"What sort of woman was she?"

"No better walked the earth," said Mrs. Blinder. "My mistress loved her like a sister."

"But I mean—what did she look like?"

Mrs. Blinder got up and gave me a kind of angry stare. "I'm no great hand at describing," she said; "and I believe my pastry's rising." And she walked off into the kitchen and shut the door after her.

II

I had been near a week at Brympton before I saw my master. Word came that he was arriving one afternoon, and a change passed over the whole household. It was plain that nobody loved him below stairs. Mrs. Blinder took uncommon care with the dinner that night, but she snapped at the kitchenmaid in a way quite unusual with her; and Mr. Wace, the butler, a serious, slow-spoken man, went about his duties as if he'd been getting ready for a funeral. He was a great Bible reader, Mr. Wace was, and had a beautiful assortment of texts at his command; but that day he used such dreadful language, that I was about to leave the table, when he assured me it was all out of Isaiah; and I noticed that whenever the master came Mr. Wace took to the prophets.

About seven, Agnes called me to my mistress' room; and there I found Mr. Brympton. He was standing on the hearth; a big fair bull-necked man, with a red face and little bad-tempered blue eyes: the kind of man a young simpleton might have thought handsome, and would have been like to pay dear for thinking it.

He swung about when I came in, and looked me over in a trice. I knew what the look meant, from having experienced it once or twice in my former places. Then he turned his back on me, and went on talking to his wife; and I knew what *that* meant, too. I was not the kind of morsel he was after. The typhoid had served me well enough in one way: it kept that kind of gentleman at arm's length.

"This is my new maid, Hartley," says Mrs. Brympton in her kind voice; and he nodded and went on with what he was saying.

In a minute or two he went off, and left my mistress to dress for dinner, and I noticed as I waited on her that she was white, and chill to the touch.

Mr. Brympton took himself off the next morning, and the whole house drew a long breath when he drove away. As for my mistress, she put on her hat and furs (for it was a fine winter morning) and went out for a walk in the gardens, coming back quite fresh and rosy, so that for a minute, before her color faded, I could guess what a pretty young lady she must have been, and not so long ago, either.

She had met Mr. Ranford in the grounds, and the two came back together, I remember, smiling and talking as they walked along the terrace under my window. That was the first time I saw Mr. Ranford, though I had often heard his name mentioned in the hall. He was a neighbor, it appeared, living a mile or two beyond Brympton, at the end of the village; and as he was in the habit of spending his winters in the country he was almost the only company my mistress had at that season. He was a slight tall gentleman of about thirty, and I thought him rather melancholy looking till I saw his smile, which had a kind of surprise in it, like the first warm day in spring. He was a great reader, I heard, like my mistress, and the two were forever borrowing books of one another, and sometimes (Mr. Wace told me) he would read aloud to Mrs. Brympton by the hour, in the big dark library where she sat in the winter afternoons. The servants all liked him, and perhaps that's more of a compliment than the masters suspect. He had a friendly word for every one of us, and we were all glad to think that Mrs. Brympton had a pleasant companionable gentleman like that to keep her company when the master was away. Mr. Ranford seemed on excellent terms with Mr. Brympton too; though I couldn't but wonder that two gentlemen so unlike each other should be so friendly. But then I knew how the real quality can keep their feelings to themselves.

As for Mr. Brympton, he came and went, never staying more than a day or two, cursing the dullness and the solitude, grumbling at everything, and (as I soon found out) drinking a deal more than was good for him. After Mrs. Brympton left the table he would sit half the night over the old Brympton port and madeira, and once, as I was leaving my mistress's room rather later than usual, I met him coming up the stairs in such a state that I turned sick to think of what some ladies have to endure and hold their tongues about.

The servants said very little about their master; but from what they let drop I could see it had been an unhappy match from the beginning. Mr. Brympton was coarse, loud and pleasure-loving; my mistress quiet, retiring, and perhaps a trifle cold. Not that she was not always pleasant-spoken to him: I thought her wonderfully forbearing; but to a gentleman as free as Mr. Brympton I dare say she seemed a little offish.

Well, things went on quietly for several weeks. My mistress was kind, my duties were light, and I got on well with the other servants. In short, I had nothing to complain of; yet there was always a weight on me. I can't say why it was so, but I know it was not the loneliness that I felt. I soon got used to that; and being still languid from the fever, I was thankful for the quiet and the good country air. Nevertheless, I was never quite easy in my mind. My mistress, knowing I had been ill, insisted that I should take my walk regularly, and often invented errands for me: a yard of ribbon to be fetched from the village, a letter posted, or a book returned to Mr. Ranford. As soon as I was out of doors my spirits rose, and I looked forward to my walks through the bare moist-smelling woods; but the moment I caught sight of the house again my heart dropped down like a stone in a well. It was not a gloomy house exactly, yet I never entered it but a feeling of gloom came over me.

Mrs. Brympton seldom went out in winter; only on the finest days did she walk an hour at noon on the south terrace. Excepting Mr. Ranford, we had no visitors but the doctor, who drove over from town about once a week. He sent for me once or twice to give me some trifling direction about my mistress, and though he never told me what her illness was, I thought, from a waxy look she had now and then of a morning, that it might be the heart that ailed her. The season was soft and unwholesome, and in January we had a long spell of rain. That was a sore trial to me, I own, for I couldn't go out, and sitting over my sewing all day, listening to the drip, drip of the eaves, I grew so nervous that the least sound made me jump. Somehow, the thought of that locked room across the passage began to weigh on me. Once or twice, in the long rainy nights, I fancied I heard noises there; but that was nonsense, of course, and the daylight drove such notions out of my head. Well, one morning Mrs. Brympton gave me quite a start of pleasure by telling me she wished me to go to town for some shopping. I hadn't known till then how low my spirits had fallen. I set off in high glee, and my first sight of the crowded streets and the cheerful-looking shops quite took me out of myself. Toward afternoon, however, the noise and confusion began to tire me, and I was actually looking forward to the quiet of Brympton, and thinking how I should enjoy the drive home through the dark woods, when I ran across an old acquaintance, a maid I had once been in service with. We had lost sight of each other for a number of years, and I had to stop and tell her what had happened to me in the interval. When I mentioned where I was living she rolled up her eyes and pulled a long face.

"What! The Mrs. Brympton that lives all the year at her place on the Hudson? My dear, you won't stay there three months."

"Oh, but I don't mind the country," says I, offended

somehow at her tone. "Since the fever I'm glad to be quiet."

She shook her head. "It's not the country I'm thinking of. All I know is she's had four maids in the last six months, and the last one, who was a friend of mine, told me nobody could stay in the house."

"Did she say why?" I asked.

"No—she wouldn't give me her reason. But she says to me, 'Mrs. Ansey,' she says, 'if ever a young woman as you know of thinks of going there, you tell her it's not worthwhile to unpack her boxes.'"

"Is she young and handsome?" said I, thinking of Mr. Brympton.

"Not her! She's the kind that mothers engage when they've gay young gentlemen at college."

Well, though I knew the woman was an idle gossip, the words stuck in my head, and my heart sank lower than ever as I drove up to Brympton in the dusk. There *was* something about the house—I was sure of it now....

When I went in to tea I heard that Mr. Brympton had arrived, and I saw at a glance that there had been a disturbance of some kind. Mrs. Blinder's hand shook so that she could hardly pour the tea, and Mr. Wace quoted the most dreadful texts full of brimstone. Nobody said a word to me then, but when I went up to my room Mrs. Blinder followed me.

"Oh, my dear," says she, taking my hand, "I'm so glad and thankful you've come back to us!"

That struck me, as you may imagine. "Why," said I, "did you think I was leaving for good?"

"No, no, to be sure," said she, a little confused, "but I can't a-bear to have madam left alone for a day even." She pressed my hand hard, and, "Oh, Miss Hartley," says she, "be good to your mistress, as you're a Christian woman." And with that she hurried away, and left me staring.

A moment later Agnes called me to Mrs. Brympton. Hearing Mr. Brympton's voice in her room, I went round by the dressing room, thinking I would lay out her dinner gown before going in. The dressing room is a large room with a window over the portico that looks toward the gardens. Mr. Brympton's apartments are beyond. When I went in, the door into the bedroom was ajar, and I heard Mr. Brympton saying angrily: "One would suppose he was the only person fit for you to talk to."

"I don't have many visitors in winter," Mrs. Brympton answered quietly.

"You have *me*!" he flung at her, sneeringly.

"You are here so seldom," said she.

"Well—whose fault is that? You make the place about as lively as the family vault."

With that I rattled the toilet things, to give my mistress warning, and she rose and called me in.

The two dined alone, as usual, and I knew by Mr. Wace's manner at supper that things must be going badly. He quoted the prophets something terrible, and worked on the kitchenmaid so that she declared she wouldn't go down alone to put the cold meat in the icebox. I felt nervous myself, and after I had put my mistress to bed I was half tempted to go down again and persuade Mrs. Blinder to sit up awhile over a game of cards. But I heard her door closing for the night and so I went on to my own room. The rain had begun again, and the drip, drip, drip seemed to be dropping into my brain. I lay awake listening to it, and turning over what my friend in town had said. What puzzled me was that it was always the maids who left. . . .

After a while I slept; but suddenly a loud noise wakened me. My bell had rung. I sat up, terrified by the unusual sound, which seemed to go on jangling through the darkness. My hands shook so that I couldn't find the matches. At length I struck a light and jumped out of bed. I began to think I must have been dreaming; but I looked at the bell against the wall, and there was the little hammer still quivering.

I was just beginning to huddle on my clothes when I heard another sound. This time it was the door of the locked room opposite mine softly opening and closing. I heard the sound distinctly, and it frightened me so that I stood stock still. Then I heard a footstep hurrying down the passage toward the main house. The floor being carpeted, the sound was very faint, but I was quite sure it was a woman's step. I turned cold with the thought of it, and for a minute or two I dursn't breathe or move. Then I came to my senses.

"Alice Hartley," says I to myself, "someone left that room just now and ran down the passage ahead of you. The idea isn't pleasant, but you may as well face it. Your mistress has rung for you, and to answer her bell you've got to go the way that other woman has gone."

Well—I did it. I never walked faster in my life, yet I thought I should never get to the end of the passage or reach Mrs. Brympton's room. On the way I heard nothing and saw nothing: all was dark and quiet as the grave. When I reached my mistress' door the silence was so deep that I began to think I must be dreaming, and was half minded to turn back. Then a panic seized me, and I knocked.

There was no answer, and I knocked again, loudly. To my astonishment the door was opened by Mr. Brympton. He started back when he saw me, and in the light of my candle his face looked red and savage.

"*You?*" he said, in a queer voice. "*How many of you are there, in God's name?*"

At that I felt the ground give under me; but I said to myself that he had been drinking, and answered as steadily as I could: "May I go in, sir? Mrs. Brympton has rung for me."

"You may all go in, for what I care," says he, and, pushing by me, walked down the hall to his own bedroom. I looked after him as he went, and to my surprise I saw that he walked as straight as a sober man.

I found my mistress lying very weak and still, but she forced a smile when she saw me, and signed to me to pour out some drops for her. After that she lay without speaking, her breath coming quick, and her eyes closed. Suddenly she groped out with her hand, and "*Emma,*" says she, faintly.

"It's Hartley, madam," I said. "Do you want anything?"

She opened her eyes wide and gave me a startled look.

"I was dreaming," she said. "You may go, now, Hartley, and thank you kindly. I'm quite well again, you see." And she turned her face away from me.

III

There was no more sleep for me that night, and I was thankful when daylight came.

Soon afterward, Agnes called me to Mrs. Brympton. I was afraid she was ill again, for she seldom sent for me before nine, but I found her sitting up in bed, pale and drawn-looking, but quite herself.

"Hartley," says she quickly, "will you put on your things at once and go down to the village for me? I want this prescription made up—" here she hesitated a minute and blushed "—and I should like you to be back again before Mr. Brympton is up."

"Certainly, madam," I said.

"And—stay a moment—" she called me back as if an idea had just struck her "—while you're waiting for the mixture, you'll have time to go on to Mr. Ranford's with this note."

It was a two mile walk to the village, and on my way I had time to turn things over in my mind. It struck me as peculiar that my mistress should wish the prescription made up without Mr. Brympton's knowledge; and, putting this together with the scene of the night before, and with much else that I had noticed and suspected, I began to wonder if the poor lady was weary of her life, and had come to the mad resolve of ending it. The idea took such hold on me that I reached the village on a run, and dropped breathless into a chair before the chemist's counter. The good man, who was just taking down his shutters, stared at me so hard that it brought me to myself.

"Mr. Limmel," I says, trying to speak indifferently, "will you run your eye over this, and tell me if it's quite right?"

He put on his spectacles and studied the prescription.

"Why, it's one of Dr. Walton's," says he. "What should be wrong with it?"

"Well—is it dangerous to take?"

"Dangerous—how do you mean?"

I could have shaken the man for his stupidity.

"I mean—if a person was to take too much of it—by mistake of course—" says I, my heart in my throat.

"Lord bless you, no. It's only lime water. You might feed it to a baby by the bottleful."

I gave a great sigh of relief and hurried on to Mr. Ranford's. But on the way another thought struck me. If there was nothing to conceal about my visit to the chemist's, was it my other errand that Mrs. Brympton wished me to keep private? Somehow, that thought frightened me worse than the other. Yet the two gentlemen seemed fast friends, and I would have staked my head on my mistress' goodness. I felt ashamed of my suspicions, and concluded that I was still disturbed by the strange events of the night. I left the note at Mr. Ranford's, and hurrying back to Brympton, slipped in by a side door without being seen, as I thought.

An hour later, however, as I was carrying in my mistress's breakfast, I was stopped in the hall by Mr Brympton.

"What were you doing out so early?" he says, looking hard at me.

"Early—me, sir?" I said, in a tremble.

"Come, come," he says, an angry red spot coming out on his forehead, "didn't I see you scuttling home through the shrubbery an hour or more ago?"

I'm a truthful woman by nature, but at that a lie popped out ready-made. "No, sir, you didn't," said I and looked straight back at him.

He shrugged his shoulders and gave a sullen laugh. "I suppose you think I was drunk last night?" he asked suddenly.

"No, sir, I don't," I answered, this time truthfully enough.

He turned away with another shrug. "A pretty notion my servants have of me!" I heard him mutter as he walked off.

Not till I had settled down to my afternoon's sewing did I realize how the events of the night had shaken me. I couldn't pass that locked door without a shiver. I knew I had heard someone come out of it, and walk down the passage ahead of me. I thought of speaking to Mrs. Blinder or to Mr. Wace, the only two in the house who appeared to have an inkling of what was going on, but I had a feeling that if I questioned them they would deny everything, and that I might learn more by holding my tongue and keeping my eyes open. The idea of spending another night opposite the locked room sickened me, and once I was seized with the notion of packing my trunk and taking the first train to town; but it wasn't in me to throw over a kind mistress in that manner, and I tried to go on with my sewing as if nothing had happened. I hadn't worked ten minutes before the sewing machine broke down. It was one I had found in the house, a good machine but a trifle out of order: Mrs. Blinder said it had never been used since Emma Saxon's death. I stopped to see what was wrong, and as I was working at the machine a drawer which I had never been able to open slid forward and a photograph fell out. I picked it up and sat looking at it in a maze. It was a woman's likeness, and I knew I had seen the face somewhere—the eyes had an asking look that I had felt on me before. And suddenly I remembered the pale woman in the passage.

I stood up, cold all over, and ran out of the room. My heart seemed to be thumping in the top of my head, and I felt as if I should never get away from the look in those eyes. I went straight to Mrs. Blinder. She was taking her afternoon nap, and sat up with a jump when I came in.

"Mrs. Blinder," said I, "who is that?" And I held out the photograph.

She rubbed her eyes and stared.

"Why, Emma Saxon," says she. "Where did you find it?"

I looked hard at her for a minute. "Mrs. Blinder," I said, "I've seen that face before."

Mrs. Blinder got up and walked over to the looking glass. "Dear me! I must have been asleep," she says. "My front is all over one ear. And now do run along, Miss Hartley, dear, for I hear the clock striking four, and I must go down this very minute and put on the Virginia ham for Mr. Brympton's dinner."

IV

To all appearances, things went on as usual for a week or two. The only difference was that Mr. Brympton stayed on, instead of going off as he usually did, and that Mr. Ranford never showed himself. I heard Mr. Brympton remark on this one afternoon when he was sitting in my mistress' room before dinner:

"Where's Ranford?" says he. "He hasn't been near the house for a week. Does he keep away because I'm here?"

Mrs. Brympton spoke so low that I couldn't catch her answer.

"Well," he went on, "two's company and three's trumpery; I'm sorry to be in Ranford's way, and I suppose I shall have to take myself off again in a day or two and give him a show." And he laughed at his own joke.

The very next day, as it happened, Mr. Ranford called. The footman said the three were very merry over their tea in the library, and Mr. Brympton strolled down to the gate with Mr. Ranford when he left.

I have said that things went on as usual; and so they did with the rest of the household; but as for myself, I had never been the same since the night my bell had rung. Night after night I used to lie awake, listening for it to ring again, and for the door of the locked room to open stealthily. But the bell never rang, and I heard no sound across the passage. At last the silence began to be more dreadful to me than the most mysterious sounds. I felt that *someone* was cowering there, behind the locked door, watching and listening as I watched and listened, and I could almost have cried out, "Whoever you are, come out and let me see you face to face, but don't lurk there and spy on me in the darkness!"

Feeling as I did, you may wonder I didn't give warning. Once I very nearly did so; but at the last moment something held me back. Whether it was compassion for my mistress, who had grown more and more dependent on me, or unwillingness to try a new place, or some other feeling that I couldn't put a name to, I lingered on as if spellbound, though every night was dreadful to me, and the days but little better.

For one thing, I didn't like Mrs. Brympton's looks. She had never been the same since that night, no more than I had. I thought she would brighten up after Mr. Brympton left, but though she seemed easier in her mind, her spirits didn't revive, nor her strength either. She had grown attached to me, and seemed to like to have me about; and Agnes told me one day that, since Emma Saxon's death, I was the only maid her mistress had taken to. This gave me a warm feeling for the poor lady, though after all there was little I could do to help her.

After Mr. Brympton's departure, Mr. Ranford took to coming again, though less often than formerly. I met him once or twice in the grounds, or in the village, and I couldn't but think there was a change in him too; but I set it down to my disordered fancy.

The weeks passed, and Mr. Brympton had now been a month absent. We heard he was cruising with a friend in the West Indies, and Mr. Wace said that was a long way off, but though you had the wings of a dove and went to the uttermost parts of the earth, you couldn't get away from the Almighty. Agnes said that as long as he stayed away from Brympton the Almighty might have him and welcome; and this raised a laugh, though Mrs. Blinder tried to look shocked, and Mr. Wace said the bears would eat us.

We were all glad to hear that the West Indies were a long way off, and I remember that, in spite of Mr. Wace's solemn looks, we had a very merry dinner that day in the hall. I don't know if it was because of my being in better spirits, but I fancied Mrs. Brympton looked better too, and seemed more cheerful in her manner. She had been for a walk in the morning, and after luncheon she lay down in her room, and I read aloud to her. When she dismissed me I went to my own room feeling quite bright and happy, and for the first time in weeks walked past the locked door without thinking of it. As I sat down to my work I looked out and saw a few snowflakes falling. The sight was pleasanter than the eternal rain, and I pictured to myself how pretty the bare gardens would look in their white mantle. It seemed to me as if the snow would cover up all the dreariness, indoors as well as out.

The fancy had hardly crossed my mind when I heard a step at my side. I looked up, thinking it was Agnes.

"Well, Agnes—" said I, and the words froze on my tongue; for there, in the door, stood *Emma Saxon*.

I don't know how long she stood there. I only know I couldn't stir or take my eyes from her. Afterward I was terribly frightened, but at the time it wasn't fear I felt, but something deeper and quieter. She looked at me long and hard, and her face was just one dumb prayer to me—but how in the world was I to help her? Suddenly she turned, and I heard her walk down the passage. This time I wasn't afraid to follow—I felt that I must know what she wanted. I sprang up and ran out. She was at the other end of the passage, and I expected her to take the turn toward my mistress' room; but instead of that she pushed open the door that led to the backstairs. I followed her down the stairs, and across the passageway to the back door. The kitchen and hall were empty at that hour, the servants being off duty, except for the footman, who was in the pantry. At the door she stood still a moment, with another look at me; then she turned the handle, and stepped out. For a minute I hesitated. Where was she leading me to? The door had closed softly after her, and I opened it and looked out, half-expecting to find that she had disappeared. But I saw her a few yards off hurrying across the courtyard to the path through the woods. Her figure looked black and lonely in the snow, and for a second my heart failed me and I thought of turning back. But all the while she was drawing me after her; and catching up an old shawl of Mrs. Blinder's I ran out into the open.

Emma Saxon was in the wood path now. She walked on steadily, and I followed at the same pace, till we passed out of the gates and reached the highroad. Then she struck across the open fields to the village. By this time the ground was white, and as she climbed the slope of a bare hill ahead of me I noticed that she left no footprints behind her. At sight of that my heart shriveled up within me, and my knees were water. Somehow, it was worse here than indoors. She made the whole countryside seem lonely as the grave, with none but us two in it, and no help in the wide world.

Once I tried to go back; but she turned and looked at me, and it was as if she had dragged me with ropes. After that I followed her like a dog. We came to the village and she led me through it, past the church and the blacksmith's shop, and down the lane to Mr. Randford's. Mr. Ranford's house stands close to the road: a plain old-fashioned building, with a flagged path leading to the door between box borders. The lane was deserted, and as I turned into it I saw Emma Saxon pause under the old elm by the gate. And now another fear came over me. I saw that we had reached the end of our journey, and that it was my turn to act. All the way from Brympton I had been asking myself what she wanted of me, but I had followed in a trance, as it were, and not till I saw her stop at Mr. Ranford's gate did my brain begin to clear itself. I stood a little way off in the snow, my heart beating fit to strangle me, and my feet frozen to the ground; and she stood under the elm and watched me.

I knew well enough that she hadn't led me there for nothing. I felt there was something I ought to say or do— but how was I to guess what it was? I had never thought harm of my mistress and Mr. Ranford, but I was sure now that, from one cause or another, some dreadful thing hung over them. *She* knew what it was; she would tell me if she could; perhaps she would answer if I questioned her.

It turned me faint to think of speaking to her; but I plucked up heart and dragged myself across the few yards between us. As I did so, I heard the house door open and saw Mr. Ranford approaching. He looked handsome and cheerful, as my mistress had looked that morning, and at sight of him the blood began to flow again in my veins.

"Why, Hartley," said he, "what's the matter? I saw you coming down the lane just now, and came out to see if you had taken root in the snow." He stopped and stared at me. "What are you looking at?" he says.

I turned toward the elm as he spoke and his eyes followed me; but there was no one there. The lane was empty as far as the eye could reach.

A sense of helplessness came over me. She was gone, and I had not been able to guess what she wanted. Her last look had pierced me to the marrow; and yet it had not told me! All at once, I felt more desolate than when she had stood there watching me. It seemed as if she had left me all alone to carry the weight of the secret I couldn't guess. The snow went round me in great circles, and the ground fell away from me....

A drop of brandy and the warmth of Mr. Ranford's fire soon brought me to, and I insisted on being driven back at once to Brympton. It was nearly dark, and I was afraid my mistress might be wanting me. I explained to Mr. Ranford that I had been out for a walk and had been taken with a fit of giddiness as I passed his gate. This was true enough; yet I never felt more like a liar than when I said it.

When I dressed Mrs. Brympton for dinner she remarked on my pale looks and asked what ailed me. I told her I had a headache, and she said she would not require me again that evening, and advised me to go to bed.

It was a fact that I could scarcely keep on my feet; yet I had no fancy to spend a solitary evening in my room. I sat downstairs in the hall as long as I could hold my head up; but by nine I crept upstairs, too weary to care what happened if I could but get my head on a pillow. The rest of the household went to bed soon afterward; they kept early hours when the master was away, and before ten I heard Mrs. Blinder's door close, and Mr. Wace's soon after.

It was a very still night, earth and air all muffled in snow. Once in bed I felt easier, and lay quiet, listening to the strange noises that come out in a house after dark. Once I thought I heard a door open and close again below: it might have been the glass door that led to the gardens. I got up and peered out of the window; but it was in the dark of the moon, and nothing visible outside but the streaking of snow against the panes.

I went back to bed and must have dozed, for I jumped awake to the furious ringing of my bell. Before my head was clear I had sprung out of bed, and was dragging on my clothes. *It is going to happen now*, I heard myself saying; but what I meant I had no notion. My hands seemed to be covered with glue—I thought I should never get into my clothes. At last I opened my door and peered down the passage. As far as my candle flame carried, I could see nothing unusual ahead of me. I hurried on, breathless; but as I pushed open the baize door leading to the main hall my heart stood still, for there at the head of the stairs was Emma Saxon, peering dreadfully down into the darkness.

For a second I couldn't stir; but my hand slipped from the

door, and as it swung shut the figure vanished. At the same instant there came another sound from below stairs—a stealthy mysterious sound, as of a latchkey turning in the house door. I ran to Mrs. Brympton's room and knocked.

There was no answer, and I knocked again. This time I heard someone moving in the room; the bolt slipped back and my mistress stood before me. To my surprise I saw that she had not undressed for the night. She gave me a startled look.

"What is this, Hartley?" she says in a whisper. "Are you ill? What are you doing here at this hour?"

"I am not ill, Madam; but my bell rang."

At that she turned pale, and seemed about to fall.

"You are mistaken," she said harshly; "I didn't ring. You must have been dreaming." I had never heard her speak in such a tone. "Go back to bed," she said, closing the door on me.

But as she spoke I heard sounds again in the hall below: a man's step this time; and the truth leaped out on me.

"Madam," I said, pushing past her, "there is someone in the house—"

"Someone—?"

"Mr. Brympton, I think—I hear his step below—"

A dreadful look came over her, and without a word, she dropped flat at my feet. I fell on my knees and tried to lift her: by the way she breathed I saw it was no common faint. But as I raised her head there came quick steps on the stairs and across the hall: the door was flung open, and there stood Mr. Brympton, in his traveling clothes, the snow dripping from him. He drew back with a start as he saw me kneeling by my mistress.

"What the devil is this?" he shouted. He was less high-colored than usual, and the red spot came out on his forehead.

"Mrs. Brympton has fainted, sir," said I.

He laughed unsteadily and pushed by me. "It's a pity she didn't choose a more convenient moment. I'm sorry to disturb her, but—"

I raised myself up aghast at the man's action.

"Sir," said I, "are you mad? What are you doing?"

"Going to meet a friend," said he, and seemed to make for the dressing room.

At that my heart turned over. I don't know what I thought or feared; but I sprang up and caught him by the sleeve.

"Sir, sir," said I, "for pity's sake look at your wife!"

He shook me off furiously.

"It seems that's done for me," says he, and caught hold of the dressing room.

At that moment I heard a slight noise inside. Slight as it was, he heard it too, and tore the door open; but as he did so he dropped back. On the threshold stood Emma Saxon. All was dark behind her, but I saw her plainly, and so did he. He threw up his hands as if to hide his face from her; and when I looked again she was gone.

He stood motionless, as if the strength had run out of him; and in the stillness my mistress suddenly raised herself, and opening her eyes fixed a look on him. Then she fell back, and I saw the death flutter pass over her face. . . .

We buried her on the third day, in a driving snowstorm. There were few people in the church, for it was bad weather to come from town, and I've a notion my mistress was one that hadn't many near friends. Mr. Ranford was among the last to come, just before they carried her up the aisle. He was in black, of course, being so pale. As he passed me, I noticed that he leaned a trifle on a stick he carried; and I fancy Mr. Brympton noticed it too, for the red spot came out sharp on his forehead, and all through the service he kept staring across the church at Mr. Ranford, instead of following the prayers as a mourner should.

When it was over and we went out to the graveyard, Mr. Ranford had disappeared, and as soon as my poor mistress's body was underground, Mr. Brympton jumped into the carriage nearest the gate and drove off without a word to any of us. I heard him call out, "To the station," and we servants went back alone to the house.

THE KING OF THIEVES

by Jack Vance

In all the many-colored worlds of the universe no single ethical code shows a universal force. The good citizen on Almanatz would be executed on Judith IV. Commonplace conduct of Medellin excites the wildest revulsion on Earth and on Moritaba a deft thief commands the highest respect. I am convinced that virtue is but a reflection of good intent.

—*Magnus Ridolph*

"There's much wealth to be found here on Moritaba," said the purser wistfully. "There's wonderful leathers, there's rare hardwoods—and have you seen the coral? It's purple-red and it glows with the fires of the damned! But"—he jerked his head toward the port—"it's too tough. Nobody cares for anything but telex—and that's what they never find. Old Kanditter, the King of Thieves, is too smart for 'em."

Magnus Ridolph was reading about Moritaba in *Guide to the Planets:*

> The climate is damp and unhealthy, the terrain is best described as the Amazon Basin superimposed on the Lunar Alps . . .

He glanced down a list of native diseases, turned the page.

> In the early days Moritaba served as a base and haven for Louie Joe, the freebooter. When at last the police ships closed in Louie Joe and his surviving followers fled into the jungles and there mingled with the natives, producing a hybrid race, the Men-men—this despite the

protests of orthodox biologists that such a union is impossible.

In the course of years the Men-men have become a powerful tribe occupying the section of Moritaba known as Arcady Major, the rumored site of a large lode of telex crystals . . .

Magnus Ridolph yawned, tucked the book in his pocket. He rose to his feet, sauntered to the port, looked out across Moritaba.

Gollabolla, chief city of the planet, huddled between a mountain and a swamp. There were a Commonwealth Control office, a Uni-Culture Mission, a general store, a school, a number of dwellings, all built of corrugated metal on piles of native wood and connected by rickety catwalks.

Magnus Ridolph found the view picturesque in the abstract, oppressive in the immediate.

A voice at his elbow said, "Quarantine's lifted, sir. You may go ashore."

"Thank you," said Magnus Ridolph and turned toward the door. Ahead of him stood a short barrel-chested man of pugnacious aspect. He darted Magnus Ridolph a bright suspicious glance, then hunched a step closer to the door. The heavy jaw, the small fire-black eyes, the ruff of black hair were suggestive of the simian.

"If I were you, Mr. Mellish," said Magnus Ridolph affably, "I would not take any luggage ashore until I found adequate thief-proof lodgings."

Ellis B. Mellish gave his briefcase a quick jerk. "No thief will get anything from me, I'll guarantee you."

Magnus Ridolph pursed his lips reflectively. "I suppose your familiarity with the tricks is an advantage."

Mellish turned his back. There was a coolness between the two, stemming from the fact that Magnus Ridolph had sold Mellish half of a telex lode on the planet Ophir, whereupon Mellish had mined not only his own property but Magnus Ridolph's as well.

A bitter scene had ensued in Mellish's office, with an exchange of threats and recriminations—the whole situation aggravated by the fact that the field was exhausted. Coincidentally both found themselves on the first packet for Moritaba, the only other known source of telex crystal.

rolled into their faces—a smell of dank soil, exultant plantlife,
Now the port opened and the pungent odor of Moritaba organic decay. They descended the ladder, blinking in the hot yellow light of Pi Aquarii.

Four natives squatted on the ground nearby—slender wiry creatures, brownish-purple, more manlike than not. These were the Men-men—the hybrid race ruled by Kanditter, the King of Thieves. The ship's purser, standing at the foot of the gangplank, turned on them a sharp glance.

"Be careful of those boys," he told Magnus Ridolph and Mellish. "They'll take your eyeteeth if you open your mouth in front of them."

The four rose to their feet, came closer with long sliding steps.

"If I had my way," said the purser, "I'd run 'em off with a club. But—orders say 'treat 'em nice.' " He noticed Mellish's camera. "I wouldn't take that camera with me, sir. They'll make off with it sure as blazes."

Mellish thrust his chin forward. "If they get this camera, they'll deserve it."

"They'll get it," said the purser.

Mellish turned his head, gave the purser a challenging look. "If anyone or anything gets this camera away from me I'll give you another just like it."

The purser shrugged. A buzzing came from the sky. "Look," he said. "There's the copter from Challa."

It was the oddest contraption Magnus Ridolph had ever seen. An enormous hemisphere of wire mesh made a dome over the whole vehicle, an umbrella of close-mesh wire under which the supporting blades swung.

"That's just how fast these johnnies are," said the purser in grudging admiration. "That net is charged—high voltage—as soon as the copter lands. If it wasn't for that there wouldn't be a piece left of it an hour after it touched ground."

Mellish laughed shortly. "This is quite a place. I'd like to be in charge here for a couple of months." He glanced to where Magnus Ridolph stood, quietly watching the copter.

"How about you, Ridolph? Think you're going to leave with your shirt?" He laughed.

"I am usually able to adapt myself to circumstances," said Magnus Ridolph, observing Mellish with detached curiosity. "I hope your camera was not expensive?"

"What do you mean?" Mellish reached for the case. The lid hung loosely; the case was empty. He glanced at the purser, who had tactfully turned his back, then around the field. The four natives sat in a line about thirty feet distant, watching the three with alert amber eyes.

"Which one of them got it?" demanded Mellish, now suffused with a red flush.

"Easy, Mr. Mellish," said the purser, "if you hope to do business with the king."

Mellish whirled on Magnus Ridolph. "Did *you* see it? Which one—"

Magnus Ridolph permitted a faint smile to pull at his beard. He stepped forward, handed Mellish his camera. "I was merely testing your vigilance, Mr. Mellish. I'm afraid you are poorly equipped for conditions on Moritaba."

Mellish glared a moment, then grinned wolfishly. "Are you a gambling man, Ridolph?"

Magnus Ridolph shook his head. "I occasionally take calculated risks—but gamble? No, never."

Mellish said slowly, "I'll put you this proposition. Now—you're going to Challa?"

Magnus Ridolph nodded. "As you know. I have business with the king."

Mellish grinned his wide yellow-toothed smile. "Let us each take a number of small articles—watch, camera, micromac, pocket screen, energizer, shaver, cigarette case, cleanorator, a micro library. Then we shall see who is the more vigilant, the more alert." He raised his bushy black eyebrows.

"And the stakes?" inquired Magnus Ridolph coolly.

"Oh"—Mellish made an impatient gesture.

"You owe me a hundred thousand munits for the telex you filched from my property," said Magnus Ridolph. "I'll take double or nothing."

Mellish blinked. "In effect," he said, "I'd be placing two hundred thousand munits against nothing—since I don't recognize the debt as collectable. But I'll bet you fifty thousand munits cash to cash. If you have that much."

Magnus Ridolph did not actually sneer but the angle of his fine white eyebrows, the tilt of his thin distinguished nose, conveyed an equivalent impression. "I believe I can meet the figure you mention."

"Write me a check," said Mellish. "I'll write you one. The purser will hold the stakes."

"As you wish," said Magnus Ridolph.

The copter took Mellish and Magnus Ridolph to Challa, the seat of Kanditter, the King of Thieves. First they crossed an arm of the old sea-bottom, an unimaginable tangle of orange, purple and green foliage, netted by stagnant pools and occasional pad-covered sloughs.

Then they rose over an army of white cliffs, flew low over a smooth plateau where herds of buffalo-like creatures on six splayed legs cropped mustard-colored shrubs. Down into a valley dark with jungle, toward a grove of tall trees looming above them like plumes of smoke. A clearing opened below, the copter sat down and they were in Challa.

Magnus Ridolph and Mellish stepped out of the copter, looked out through the cage of charged wire. A group of dark, big-eyed natives stood at a respectful distance, shuffling their feet in loose leather sandals with pointed toes.

On all sides houses sat off the ground on stilts, houses built of a blue white-veined wood, thatched with slabs of gray pith. At the end of a wide avenue stood a larger taller building with wings extending under the trees.

Three Earthmen stood watching the arrival of the copter with listless curiosity. One of these, a sallow thin man with a large beak of a nose and bulging brown eyes, suddenly stiffened in unbelief. He darted forward.

"Mr. Mellish! What on earth? I'm glad to see you!"

"I'm sure, Tomko, I'm sure," said Mellish. "How's everything going?"

Tomko glanced at Magnus Ridolph, then back to Mellish. "Well—nothing definite yet, sir. Old Kanditter—that's the king—won't make any concessions whatever."

"We'll see about that," said Mellish. He turned, raised his voice to the copter pilot. "Let us out of this cage."

The pilot said, "When I give you the word, sir, you can open that door—right there." He walked around the copter. "Now."

Mellish and Magnus Ridolph passed outside, each carrying a pair of magnesium cases.

"Can you tell me," inquired Magnus Ridolph, "where lodging may be found?"

Tomko said doubtfully, "There's usually a few empty houses around. We've been living in one of the wings of the king's palace. If you introduce yourself he'll probably invite you to do likewise."

"Thank you," said Magnus Ridolph. "I'll go pay my respects immediately."

A whistle came to his ears. Turning, he saw the copter pilot beckoning to him through the wire. He went as close to the charged mesh as he dared.

"I just want to warn you," said the pilot. "Watch out for the king. He's the worst of the lot. That's why he's king. Talk about stealing—*whoo*!" Solemnly shaking his head, he turned back to his copter.

"Thank you," said Magnus Ridolph. He felt a vibration through his wrist. He turned, said to the nearby native, "Your knife makes no impression in the alloy of the case, my friend. You would do better with a heat-needle."

The native slid quietly away. Magnus Ridolph set out for the king's palace. It was a pleasant scene, he thought, reminiscent of ancient Polynesia. The village seemed clean and orderly. Small shops appeared at intervals along the avenue—booths displaying yellow fruit, shiny green tubes, rows of dead shrimp-like insects, jars of rust-colored powder. The proprietors sat in front of the booths, not behind them.

A pavilion extended forward from the front of the palace, and here Magnus Ridolph found Kanditter, the King of Thieves, sitting sleepily in a low deep chair. He was to Magnus Ridolph's eye distinguishable from the other natives only by his headdress—a coronet-like affair woven of a shiny red-gold metal and set with telex crystals.

Unaware of the exact formalities expected of him, Magnus Ridolph merely approached the king, bowed his head.

"Greetings," said the king in a thick voice. "Your name and business?"

"I am Magnus Ridolph, resident of Tran, on Lake Sahara, Earth. I have come—to state the matter briefly—to—"

"To get telex?"

"I would be foolish to deny it."

"Ho!" The king rocked back and forth, pulled back his sharp dark features in a fish-like grin. "No luck. Telex crystal stay on Moritaba."

Magnus Ridolph nodded. He had expected refusal. "In the meantime may I trespass on the royal hospitality?"

The king's grin slowly faded. "Eh? Eh? What you say?"

"Where do you suggest that I stay?"

The king made a sweep of his arm toward the end of his palace. "Much room there. Go around, go in."

"Thank you," said Magnus Ridolph.

To the rear of the palace Magnus Ridolph found suitable quarters—one of a row of rooms facing out on the path like stalls in a stable. The resemblance was heightened by the stable-type door.

It was a pleasant lodging with the trees swaying far overhead, the carpet of red-gold leaves in front. The interior was comfortable though Spartan. Magnus Ridolph found a couch, a pottery ewer filled with cool water, a carved chest built into the wall, a table.

Humming softly to himself, Magnus Ridolph opened the chest, peered within. A soft smile disturbed his beard as he noted the back panel of the chest. It looked solid, felt solid, but Magnus Ridolph knew it could be opened from the outside.

The walls seemed sound—poles of the blue wood were caulked with a putty-like resin and there was no window.

Magnus Ridolph opened his suitcases, laid the goods out on the couch. From without he heard voices, and, looking forth, he saw Mellish rocking on his short legs down the center of the path, bulldog jaw thrust out, hands clenched, elbows swinging wide as he walked. Tomko came to the rear, carrying Mellish's luggage.

Magnus Ridolph nodded courteously, withdrew into his room. He saw Mellish grin broadly to Tomko, heard his comment: "They've got the old goat penned up for sure. Damned if he doesn't look natural with that beard hanging over the door."

Tomko snickered dutifully. Magnus Ridolph frowned. Old goat? He turned back to his couch—in time to catch a dark flicker, a glint of metal.

Magnus Ridolph compressed his lips. His micromac and power pack had disappeared. Peering under the couch, Magnus Ridolph saw a patch of slightly darker fiber in the matting. He straightened his back, just in time to see his pocket screen swinging up through the air into a hole high in the wall.

Magnus Ridolph started to run outside and into the adjoining room, then thought better of it. No telling how many natives would be pillaging his room if he left for an instant. He piled everything back into his suitcases, locked them, placed them in the middle of the floor, sat on the couch, lit a cigarette.

Fifteen minutes he sat in reflection. A muffled bellow made him look up.

"Thieving little blackguards!" he heard Mellish cry. Magnus Ridolph grinned ruefully, rose to his feet and, taking his suitcases, he stepped out into the street.

He found the copter pilot reading a newspaper inside his thief-proof cage. Magnus Ridolph looked through the mesh.

"May I come in?"

The pilot arose, cast the switch. Magnus Ridolph entered, set his suitcases on the ground.

"I just been reading about you," said the pilot.

"Is that right?" asked Magnus Ridolph.

"Yeah—in one of these old newspapers. See—" he pointed out the article with a greasy forefinger. It read:

GHOST-ROBBER APPREHENDED

STARPORT BANK LAUDS
EARTH CRIME-DOCTOR

A million munits looted from the Starport Bank were recovered by Magnus Ridolph, noted savant and freelance troubleshooter, who this morning delivered the criminal, Arnold McGurk, 35, unemployed space-man, to Starport police.

After baffling Starport authorities two weeks, Arnold McGurk refused to divulge how he robbed the supposedly thief-proof bank, other than to hint at the aid of 'ghosts.' Magnus Ridolph was similarly uncommunicative and the police admit ignorance of the criminal's *modus operandi* . . .

"Wouldn't ever have knowed you was a detective," said the pilot, eyeing Magnus Ridolph reverently. "You don't look the type."

"Thank you," said Magnus Ridolph. "I'm glad to hear it."

The pilot appraised him. "You look more like a professor or a dentist."

Magnus Ridolph winced.

"Just what was them 'ghosts' the article speaks of, Mr. Ridolph?" the pilot inquired.

"Nothing whatever," Magnus Ridolph assured him. "An optical illusion."

"Oh," said the pilot.

"There's something I'd like you to do for me," said Magnus Ridolph.

"Sure—glad to be of help."

Magnus Ridolph scribbled on a page in his notebook. "Take this to the ship right away before it leaves. Give it to the radio operator, ask him to send it ulrad special."

The pilot took the message. "That all?"

"No," said Magnus Ridolph. "There's another ship leaving Starport for Moritaba in—let's see—in four days. Six days passage makes ten days. I should have a parcel on that next ship.

"I want you to meet that ship, take that parcel aboard your copter, deliver it to me here immediately. When I get that parcel I'll pay you two hundred munits. Does that satisfy you?"

"Yes," said the pilot. "I'm off right now."

"Also," said Magnus Ridolph, "there is need for secrecy. Can you keep a close tongue in your head?"

"Haven't heard me say much yet, have you?" The pilot stretched his arms. "I'll see you in about ten days."

"Er—do you have any extra wire and a spare powerpack?" inquired Magnus Ridolph. "I think I'll need some sort of protection."

Magnus Ridolph returned to his room with his suitcases and what electrical equipment the pilot was able to spare. A half hour later he stood back. Now, he thought, next move to the Men-men.

A face appeared at the door—narrow, purple-brown, big-eyed, with a long thin nose, slit mouth, long sharp chin.

"King he want you come eat." The face peered cautiously around the room, brushed the wires Magnus Ridolph had strung up. *Crackle—spat.* The native yelped, bounded away.

"Ho, ho!" said Magnus Ridolph. "What's the trouble?"

The native uttered a volley of angry syllables, gesticulating, showing his pointed white teeth. Magnus Ridolph at last understood him to say, "Why you burn me, eh?"

"To teach you not to steal from me," Magnus Ridolph explained.

The native hissed scornfully. "I steal everything you got. I great thief. I steal from king. Sometimes I steal everything he got. Then I be king. I best stealer in Challa, you bet. I steal king's crown pretty soon."

Magnus Ridolph blinked his mild blue eyes. "And then?"

"And then—"

"Yes—and then?" came a third voice, harsh, angry. King Kanditter sprang close to the native, struck furiously with a length of cane. The native howled and leapt into the bushes. Magnus Ridolph hastily disconnected the powerpack lest the king receive a shock and inflict a like punishment on himself.

Kanditter threw the cane stalk to the ground, gestured to Magnus Ridolph. "Come, we eat."

"I'll be with you right away," said Magnus Ridolph. He picked up his suitcases, disconnected the powerpack, slung it under his arm and presented himself to the king. "Your invitation comes as a pleasant surprise, your Majesty. I find that carrying my possessions everywhere gives me quite an appetite."

"You careful, eh?" said Kanditter with a wide thin-lipped grin.

Magnus Ridolph nodded solemnly. "A careless man would find himself destitute in a matter of minutes." He looked sidewise at the king. "How do you guard your own property? You must own a great deal—micromacs, powerpacks and the like."

"Woman, she watch now. Woman, she very careful. She lose—*ugh!*" He flailed his long dark arms significantly.

"Woman indeed are very useful," agreed Magnus Ridolph.

They marched in silence for a few yards.

"What you like telex for?" the king asked.

"The telex crystal," said Magnus Ridolph, "vibrates—shakes—very fast. Very, very, very, very fast. We use it to send voices to other stars. Voices go very far, very fast, when given shake with telex."

"Too much noise," was the king's observation.

"Where are your fields?" asked Magnus Ridolph ingenuously. "I've heard a great deal about them."

Kanditter merely turned him a side-glance, grinned his narrow grin.

Days passed, during which Magnus Ridolph sat quietly in his lodgings, reviewing recent progress in mathematics, developing some work of his own in the new field of contiguous-opposing programs.

He saw little of Mellish, who spent as much time as

possible with the king—arguing, pleading, bluffly flattering, while Tomko was relegated to guarding the luggage.

Magnus Ridolph's barricade proved effective to the extent that his goods were safe so long as he sat within his room. When circumstances compelled him to walk abroad he packed everything into his suitcases, carried them with him. His behavior by no means set him apart or made him conspicuous.

Everywhere could be seen natives carrying their possessions in bags made from the thoraxes of large tree-dwelling insects. Mellish had fitted Tomko with a sack strapped to his chest and locked, in which reposed the objects named in the wager with Magnus Ridolph—or rather, those which still remained to him.

With disturbance Magnus Ridolph noted a growing ease and familiarity between Mellish and King Kanditter. They talked by the hour, Mellish plying the king with cigars, the king in his turn supplying wine. Observing this camaraderie, Magnus Ridolph shook his head, muttered. If Kanditter signed away any rights now, before Magnus Ridolph was ready to apply persuasion—what a fiasco!

His worst fears were realized when Kanditter strolled up to where he sat in the shade before his room.

"Good day, your Majesty," said Magnus Ridolph with urbane courtesy. Kanditter flipped a long black hand. "You come tonight. Big eat, big drink—everybody come."

"A banquet?" inquired Magnus Ridolph, debating within himself how best to avoid participation.

"Tonight we make everybody know big new thing for Men-men. Mellish, he good man—fine man. He need telex, not hurt land. No noise, no bad man, lots of money."

Magnus Ridolph raised his eyebrows. "Have you decided then to award the franchise to Mellish?"

"Mellish good man," said the king, watching Magnus Ridolph interestedly.

"What will you derive personally from the agreement?" inquired Magnus Ridolph.

"How you say?"

"What will you get?"

"Oh—Mellish he make me machine that go round-round in circles. Sit in, music-noise come. Good for king. Name merry-go-round. Mellish he build five-dime store here in Challa. Mellish good man. Good for Men-men, good for king."

"I see," said Magnus Ridolph.

"You come tonight," said Kanditter, and before Magnus Ridolph could state his excuses he passed on.

The banquet commenced shortly after sundown on the pavilion before the palace. Torches, hanging high in the trees, provided a flaring red light, glanced on the purple-brown natives, glinted on King Kanditter's crown and Magnus Ridolph's suitcases, these latter gripped firmly between their owner's knees.

There was little ceremony connected with the eating. Women passed around the loose circle of men, carrying wooden trays full of fruit, young birds, the shrimp-like insects. Magnus Ridolph ate sparingly of the fruit, tasted the birds, dismissed the dish of insects.

A tray came by with cups of native wine. Magnus Ridolph sipped, watching Mellish, as he talked and made jocose gesticulations near the king. Now the king arose and passed out into the darkness and Mellish occupied himself with his wine.

A great flare like a meteor—down from the darkness hurtled a great cloud of flame, past Magnus Ridolph's head, smashing into the ground at his feet in a great crush of sparks.

Magnus Ridolph relaxed—only a torch had fallen. But how close to his head! Negligence, reprehensible negligence! Or—and he looked around for his suitcases—*was* it negligence? The suitcases were gone. Perhaps the element of chance was lacking from the episode.

Magnus Ridolph sat back. Gone not only were the articles of the wager but also all his fresh clothes, his papers, his careful work on the contiguous-opposed programs.

King Kanditter presently stepped forward into the light, vented a short shrill scream. The banqueters immediately became quiet.

Kanditter pointed to Mellish. "This man is friend. He give good things to Kanditter, to all Men-men. He give merry-go-round, he give five-dime store, he build big water that shoot into the air—right here in Challa. Mellish is good. Tomorrow Kanditter, king of Men-men, give telex to Mellish."

Kanditter sat down, and the normal chitter and clatter was resumed. Mellish sidled on his short legs around behind the stiffly formal Magnus Ridolph.

"You see, my friend," said Mellish hoarsely, "that's how I do things. I get what I go after."

"Remarkable, remarkable."

"By the way," and Mellish pretended to be searching around Magnus Ridolph's feet. "Where are your suitcases? Don't tell me they're gone! Stolen? What a pity! But then—a mere fifty thousand munits—what's that, eh, Ridolph?"

Magnus Ridolph turned Mellish a deceptively mild glance. "You have a negligent attitude toward money."

Mellish swung his long arms vigorously, looked across the pavilion at Kanditter. "Money means very little to me, Ridolph. With the telex concession—or without it for that matter—I can arrange that things happen the way I want them to happen."

"Let us hope," said Magnus Ridolph, "that events continue to respond so facilely to your wishes. Excuse me, I think I hear the copter."

He hurried to the clearing. The pilot was climbing out of the cabin. He waved to Magnus Ridolph. "Got your package."

"Excellent." He reached in his pocket. "Ho! The blackguards have even picked my pocket!" He turned a rueful look to the pilot. "I'll pay you your fee in the morning— with a bonus. Now—would you assist me with this parcel to my room?"

"Sure thing." The pilot lifted one end of the long package, Magnus Ridolph the other, and they set off along the avenue.

Halfway they met King Kanditter, who eyed the bundle with a great deal of interest. "What that?"

"Ah," said Magnus Ridolph, "it's a wonderful new machine—very fine."

"Ch-ch-ch," said the king, gazing after them.

At his room Magnus Ridolph paused, mused a moment. "Now lastly," he said, "may I borrow your flash-lamp till tomorrow?"

The pilot handed him the article. "Just don't let those little devils snitch it."

Magnus Ridolph made a noncommittal remark, bade the pilot goodnight. Alone, he snapped loose the tapes, tore aside the fabric, pulled a can from out the case, then a large alumin box with a transparent window.

Magnus Ridolph peered within, chuckled. The box seemed full of moving flitting shapes—gauzy things only half visible.

In a corner of the box lay a rough black pitted sphere, three inches in diameter.

Magnus Ridolph opened the can which had come with the parcel, poured a few drops of its contents over the flash-lamp, set the lamp on his bed. Then, carrying the box outside, he sat and waited. Five—ten minutes passed.

He looked inside, nodded in satisfaction. The flash-lamp had disappeared. He returned within, rubbed his beard. Best to make sure, he thought. Looking outside, he saw the pilot lounging in front of Mellish's room, talking to Tomko. Magnus Ridolph called him over.

"Would you be kind enough to watch my box till I get back? I'll be gone only a moment."

"Take your time," said the pilot. "No hurry."

"I won't be long," said Magnus Ridolph. He poured some of the oil from the can upon his handkerchief, while the pilot watched curiously, then set off back down the street to the king's quarters.

He found Kanditter in the pavilion, quaffing the last of the wine. Magnus Ridolph made him a courteous greeting.

"How is your machine?" inquired Kanditter.

"In good condition," said Magnus Ridolph. "Already it has produced a cloth which makes all metal shine like the sun. As a sign of my friendship, I want you to have it."

Kanditter took the handkerchief gingerly. "Make shine, you say."

"Like gold," said Magnus Ridolph. "Like telex crystal."

"Ah." Kanditter turned away.

"Good night," said Magnus Ridolph, and returned to his quarters. The pilot departed and Magnus Ridolph, with a brisk rub of his hands, opened the alumin box, reached within, took the pitted black ball out, laid it on his bed. Flipping, running, flowing out of the box came two—four—six a dozen filmy creatures, walking, gliding, flitting on gossamer legs, merging into shadows, sometimes glimpsed, for the most part barely sensed.

"Be off with you," said Magnus Ridolph. "Be off and about, my nimble little friends. You have much work to do."

Twenty minutes later a ghostly flickering shape scuttled in through the door, up upon the bed, laid a powerpack tenderly beside the rough black sphere.

"Good," said Magnus Ridolph. "Now off again—be off!"

Ellis B. Mellish was wakened the next day by an unusual

hubbub from the pavilion. He raised his head from the pillow, peered out through puffed red eyes.

"Shut off that racket," he grunted.

Tomko, who slept spread-eagled across Mellish's luggage, sat up with a jerk, rose to his feet, stumbled to the door, squinted up the street.

"There's a big crowd up by the pavilion. They're yelling something or other—can't make it out."

A slender purple-brown face looked in the door. "King say come now." He waited expectantly.

Mellish made a rasping noise in his throat, turned over in his bed. "Oh—all right. I'll come." The native left. "Officious barbarians," muttered Mellish.

He rose, dressed, rinsed his face in cold water. "Confounded glad to be leaving," he told Tomko. "Just as soon live back in the Middle Ages."

Tomko expressed his sympathy, handed Mellish a fresh towel.

At last Mellish stepped out in the street, ambled up toward the palace. The crowd in the pavilion had not dwindled. Rather it seemed thicker—rows of Men-men, squatting, rocking, chattering.

Mellish paused, looked across the narrow purple-brown backs. His mouth dropped as if a weight had jerked his chin down.

"Good morning, Mellish," said Magnus Ridolph.

"What are you doing there?" barked Mellish. "Where's the king?"

Magnus Ridolph puffed at his cigarette, flicked the ashes, crossed his legs. "I'm the king now—the King of Thieves."

"Are you crazy?"

"In no respect," was the reply. "I wear the coronet—*ergo*, I am king." He nudged with his foot a native squatting beside him. "Tell him, Kanditter."

The ex-monarch turned his head. "Magnus now king. He steal crown—he king. That is law of the Men-men. Magnus he great thief."

"Ridiculous!" stormed Mellish, taking three steps forward. "Kanditter, what about our deal?"

"You'll have to dicker with me," came Magnus Ridolph's pleasant voice. "Kanditter has been removed from the situation."

"I'll do no such thing," declared Mellish, black eyes glittering. "I made a bargain with Kanditter—"

"It's no good," said Magnus Ridolph. "The new king has annulled it. Also—before we get too far astray—in the matter of that fifty-thousand munit bet I find that I have all my own gear except my watch and, I believe, a large proportion of yours also. Stolen honestly, you understand—not confiscated by royal decree."

Mellish chewed his lip. He looked up suddenly. "Do you know where the telex lode is?"

"Exactly."

"Well," said Mellish bluffly, coming forward, "I'm a reasonable man."

Magnus Ridolph bent his head, became interested in the heatgun he had extricated from his pocket. "Another one of Kanditter's treasures—you were saying?"

"I'm a reasonable man," stuttered Mellish, halting.

"Then you will agree that five hundred thousand munits is a fair value to set on the telex concession. And I'd like a small royalty also—one percent of the gross yield is not exorbitant. Do you agree?"

Mellish swayed. He rubbed his hand across his face.

"In addition," said Magnus Ridolph, "you owe me a hundred thousand for looting my property on Ophir and fifty thousand on our wager."

"I won't let you get away with this!" cried Mellish.

"You have two minutes to make up your mind," said Magnus Ridolph. "After that time I will send an ulrad message filing the concession in my own name and ordering equipment."

Mellish sagged. "King of thieves—king of bloodsuckers—extortioners—that's a better name for you! Very well, I'll meet your terms."

"Write me a check," suggested Magnus Ridolph. "Also a contract stipulating the terms of the agreement. As soon as the check is deposited and a satisfactory entry made in my credit book the required information will be divulged."

Mellish began to protest against the unexpected harshness of Magnus Ridolph's tactics—but, meeting the mild blue eyes, he halted in mid-sentence. He looked over his shoulder.

"Tomko! Where are you, Tomko?"

"Right here, sir."

"My checkbook."

Tomko hesitated.

"Well?"

"It has been stolen, sir."

THE KING OF THIEVES

Magnus Ridolph held up a hand. "Hush, Mr. Mellish, if you please. Don't rail at your subaltern. If I'm not mistaken I believe I have that particular checkbook among my effects."

Night had fallen in Challa and the village was quiet. A few fires still smouldered and cast red flickers along the network of stilts supporting the huts.

A pair of shadows moved along the leaf-carpeted lane. The bulkiest of these stepped to the side, silently swung open a door.

Crackle! Snap! "Ouch!" brayed Mellish. *"Hoo!"*

His lunges and thrashing broke the circuit. The current died and Mellish stood gasping hoarsely.

"Yes?" came a mild voice. "What is it?"

Mellish took a quick step forward, turned his hand-lamp on the blinking Magnus Ridolph.

"Be so good as to turn the light elsewhere," protested the latter. "After all, I am King of Thieves, and entitled to some small courtesy."

"Sure," said Mellish, with sardonic emphasis. "Certainly, Your Majesty. Tomko—fix the light."

Tomko set the light on the table, diffused the beam so as to illuminate the entire room.

"This is a late hour for a visit," observed Magnus Ridolph. He reached under his pillow.

"No you don't," barked Mellish, producing a nuclear pistol. "You move and I'll plug you."

Magnus Ridolph shrugged. "What do you wish?"

Mellish settled himself comfortably in a chair. "First I want that check and the contract. Second I want the location of that lode. Third I want that crown. Seems like the only way to get what you want around here is to be king. So I intend to be it." He jerked his head. *"Tomko!"*

"Yes, sir?"

"Take this gun. Shoot him if he moves."

Tomko gingerly took the gun.

Mellish leaned back, lit a cigar. "Just how did you get to be king, Ridolph? What's all this talk about ghosts?"

"I'd prefer to keep that information to myself."

"You *talk*!" said Mellish grimly. "I'd just as soon shoot you as not."

Magnus Ridolph eyed Tomko steadying the nuclear gun with both hands. "As you wish. Are you familiar with the planet Archaemandryx?"

"I've heard of it—somewhere in Argo."

"I have never visited Archaemandryx myself," said Magnus Ridolph. "However, a friend describes it as peculiar in many respects. It is a world of metals—mountain ranges of metallic silicon—"

"Cut the guff," snapped Mellish. "Get on with it!"

Magnus Ridolph sighed reproachfully. "Among the types of life native to this planet are the near-gaseous creatures which you call ghosts. They live in colonies, each centered on a nucleus. The nucleus serves as the energizer for the colony. The ghosts bring it fuel, it broadcasts energy on a convenient wavelength. The fuel is uranium and any uranium compound is eagerly conveyed to the nucleus.

"My friend thought to see commercial possibilities in this property—namely the looting of the Starport Bank. He accordingly brought a colony to New Acquitain, where he daubed a number of hundred-Munit notes with an aromatic uranium compound, deposited them at the bank. Then he opened the box and merely waited till the ghosts returned with millions in uranium-permeated banknotes.

"I chanced to be nearby when he was apprehended. In fact"—and Magnus Ridolph smoothed the front of his blue and white nightshirt—"I played a small part in the event. However, when the authorities thought to ask how he had perpetrated the theft the entire colony had disappeared."

Mellish nodded appreciatively. "I see. You just got the king to daub everything he owned with uranium and then let the things loose."

"Correct."

Mellish blew out a plume of smoke. "Now I want directions to get to the lode."

Magnus Ridolph shook his head. "That information will be given to you only when I have deposited your check."

Mellish grinned wolfishly. "You'll tell me alive—or I'll find out from Kanditter tomorrow with you dead. You have ten seconds to make up your mind."

Magnus Ridolph raised his eyebrows. "Murder?" He glanced at Tomko, who stood with beaded forehead holding the nuclear pistol.

"Call it that," said Mellish. "Eight—nine—*ten*! Are you going to talk?"

"I can hardly see my way clear to—"

Mellish looked at Tomko. "Shoot him."

Tomko's teeth chattered; his hand shook like a twig in a strong wind.

"*Shoot* him!" barked Mellish.

Tomko squeezed shut his eyes, pulled the trigger. *Click!*

"Perhaps I should have mentioned," said Magnus Ridolph, "that among the first of the loot my ghosts brought me was the ammunition of your pistol which as you know is uranium." He produced his own heat-gun. "Now, goodnight, gentlemen. It is late and tomorrow will be more convenient for levying the fifty-thousand munit fine your offenses call for."

"What offenses?" blustered Mellish. "You can't prove a thing."

"Disturbing the rest of the King of Thieves is a serious crime," Magnus Ridolph assured him. "However, if you wish to escape, the trail overland back to Gollabolla begins at the end of this land. You would not be pursued."

"You're crazy. Why, we'd die in the jungle."

"Suit yourself," was Magnus Ridolph's equable reply. "In any event, good night."

ORDER FORM

If you cannot find these titles in your bookshop, they can be obtained directly from the publisher. Please indicate the number of copies required and fill in the form overleaf in block letters.

The Mammoth Book of Short Science Fiction Novels
___ Presented by Isaac Asimov £4.95

The Mammoth Book of Short Fantasy Novels
___ Presented by Isaac Asimov £4.95

The Mammoth Book of Short Crime Novels
___ Edited by Bill Pronzini and Martin H. Greenberg £4.99

The Mammoth Book of Spy Thrillers
___ Edited by John Winwood £4.99

The Mammoth Book of Modern Crime Stories
___ Edited by George Hardinge £4.95

The Mammoth Book of Golden Age Science Fiction
___ Presented by Isaac Asimov £4.99

Best New Science Fiction 2
___ Edited by Gardner Dozois £5.95

Mythic Beasts
___ Edited by Isaac Asimov, C. Waugh and M. Greenberg £3.50

Spells
___ Edited by Isaac Asimov, C. Waugh and M. Greenberg £3.50

Intergalactic Empires
___ Edited by Isaac Asimov, C. Waugh and M. Greenberg
£2.95

Please fill in the form below in block letters:

NAME_____

ADDRESS_____

_____

_____

_____

Send to Robinson Publishing Cash Sales,
P.O. Box 11, Falmouth, Cornwall TR10 9EN

Please enclose cheque or postal order to the value of the cover price plus:

In UK only – 60p for the first book, 25p for the second book, and 15p for each additional book to a maximum £1.90.

BFPO – 60p for the first book, 25p for the second book, and 15p for the next seven books and 9p for each book thereafter.

Overseas – £1.25 for the first book, 75p per copy for the second, and 28p for each book thereafter.

Whilst every effort is made to keep prices low, it is sometimes necessary to increase prices at short notice. Robinson Publishing reserve the right to show on covers, and charge, new retail prices which may differ from those advertised in text or elsewhere.